Inlanda Reflections

AHRYZE SEES

ISBN:979-8-9867842-2-9 (Print)
979-8-9867842-1-2 (ePub)
979-8-9867842-0-5 (Amazon Epub)

JAH Pharm Publishing
ahryzesees@gmail.com

Interior design by Booknook.biz

This crafting of fiction contains conventional constructs, along with immutable truth. All names were created anew or changed (to protect the innocent), except those of the guilty; they change their appearance so often that we know them only by their deeds. Place changes: time, however, exists only through the entropic reasoning of consciousness. The sequence of this concoction did not take place in an actual coherent person, place, or time (except in my mind, of course). However, finite parts did have breath for an ephemeron: still, for the whole - who knows, it's an expansive universe and life but a dream.

Codices

Middle Way

At the beginning... unknown.
In the mid-portion... conjecture.
Definitely not the end.
Forget it; it's all relative!

At time's being, innate biology enabled an echo of the present to slip into continuance, forming the warp of remembrance, adding context to existence. This undivided essence subsequently affixed the weft of futurity onto the expanding fabric of space-time, subtly weaving expectation through the tapestry of life. This arising sensory faculty came to believe it subsisted as a distinct, lasting entity in a dualistic geometric complexity. Thus ignorance obscured absolute truth by clinging to the fiction of an enduring separate intrinsic existence.

The immutable wisdom of mutuality instead leads to understanding and compassion. Unfortunately, we have come to accept the deception of an abundant world manufacturing scarcity. In such a reality, gaining from another's loss achieves a greedy, empty imbalance. We can dismantle these fabrications by realizing that striving for permanence gains nothing in an ever-changing world and clinging to the illusion of separateness brings suffering.

This evolving universe increased the probability for life and the development of consciousness. A dualistic state of mind allows the self to create synthetic realities, believing them valid. But this convention only explains the mirage of existence.

The absolute runs deeper, involving a labyrinth of discovery, as does this story.

❧

The Great Grassland rolled on to the extent of vision, the distances impossible to judge. At this juncture in the Warming, the blades of grass appear a dark green on one face and a paler wash on the reverse. Waves of these differing hues give evidence of the wind moving slowly across this sea of thigh-high growth. Expansive, billowing clouds dot the sky - grey and flat below, extending like mountainous sails to brilliant white topgallants. The bold blue spaces between provide the palette for these ever-changing skyships plying the sea of green below.

The breezes blew warm, and the Solaura on Jahtara's face conveyed more heat. Traveling since the cool of the Rising, she had let her hood fall back earlier; now, she opened the cloak, letting it slip off her shoulders to lie astride her steed's flanks. Lifted by this act, Jahtara's spirit warmed to the dei. She felt joined to the moment, content with herself and the place - the only sounds were the gentle rustle of the grasses and the dun-colored steed's leisurely plod. A current wafted a curled strand of copper hair across her angled face. Jahtara breathed in the sweet, earthy scent of the grassland through her nose, letting it flow out her lips. She exhaled the tension of the last few deis like she had shed her cloak, letting it fall away. Jahtara moved effortlessly with the mount, at ease with herself – a feeling not encountered previously in her young life.

This sense of ease came from being alone yet arose effortlessly. Jahtara held no fear of herself, feeling comfortably self-contained. She grew up blessed with an education, loved to read, and used it to escape life's drudgery. The irony of riding through empty grasslands feeling so alive and replete contrasted with the dearth of association between herself, her people, and her culture. Jahtara marveled at having postponed and suffered for so long. Her emerald eyes filled with tears of release and joy. Jahtara spread her arms and turned her face to the sky, letting the tears cleanse in this moment of becoming.

In this state of openness, she perceived a new subtle scent: different from her mount's animal odor or the ripe, humic smell of the grasslands. An intermittent cooling breeze reminded her of water in the warming dei or was it her parched mouth dragging her back into a thirsting body. Her mount picked up the trace turning towards it. She heard gurgling and plashing, soon coming upon a bubbling spring making a shallow pool before winding away in the distance. The animal went to where the water condensed into a stream, lowering its head to drink, taking no heed of the rider on its back.

Jahtara considered the sparkling spring. She had ridden hard for five deis, eaten little, slept less, and always with an eye on the road behind. Yesterdei, she entered the Great Grassland and traveled for almost a full dei with no sign to the horizon of pursuit. She gave a mental shrug, content she evaded any hunt, confident her deception sent any who looked in another direction.

She slipped the mount with a bounce walking round to the spring's edge, lifted her full skirt, then squatted on the pond's bank plunging her hands into the cold, clear water. She pulled the liquid up her wrists and forearms, cleansing the dust from the ride. Reaching down for more, Jahtara brought it to her face and neck, delighting in the rivulets running drown her back and breasts. The cool water revived, and she filled her cupped hands, drinking deeply, marveling at the simple act. The tangible water in the hollow of her hands could quench thirst, float an imperial yacht, and erode solid rock. Yet appear sufficiently ethereal to see through, discern its sensualness, or slip through her grasp like time, an idea, or life.

As that thought slipped through Jahtara's mind, she heard a sound downwind like an animal giving chase but lacking the proper cadence. Time instantly slowed, the water solidified, and a delicate flying insect moved across her vision so slowly she could have reached out to pinch its wings between two fingers. The mount's head came up, water dripping from its muzzle in slow-moving clarity, hind quarter rippling a lento meter just before a blur leaped from behind onto its back. Time racing, the mount lowered its head, bucked, and turned. The offending would-be attacker blurred again, disappearing into the tall grass but immediately stood drawing a compact knife.

The womon assailant, shorter than Jahtara, though not stocky or petite but muscular and well proportioned, wiped a lock of short brown hair from her eyes, brown eyes open wide with thick brows adding contrast to the whites. A short scar ran through one brow, and her cheeks flushed on brown skin. She bared her teeth, thinning her lips, and produced a deep growl, a reaction to being thrown.

The newcomer thought to have made off with Jahtara's steed by now. Jahtara, with no weapon other than her body, would use another sort of disarming defense.

Sensing no immediate threat from Jahtara, the shorter womon straightened, staying in a wide-rooted stance. She wore a heavy earth tone shirt, squaring off at the mid-thigh. The sleeves rolled up to her elbows, and the neck opened to the mid-chest exposing a shiny pale green undergarment. Thick grey leggings covered down to the ankles, and she wore sandals. Her clothes looked worn yet clean, except for the new grass stain on the back of her shirt. The womon furrowed her brows, dropping the knifepoint slightly and grunting in an unrecognized accent, "You mock my attempt with your smile?"

"I smile not at the attempt but the consequence."

"I startled the animal with my surprise."

"I think you a bit more startled than the steed. The grooms trained the animal to accept only specific persons to lead or ride."

"Yet you mock me with your countenance. You consider me, with a knife, no threat that you smirk still."

"You would have attacked me first if wished to harm; instead, you desired the mount."

"Truly spoken," putting the free hand on her hip, she continued with a wry smile. "As I spied you, I thought you too silly in dress to bother with."

Jahtara considered her. Her speech and mannerisms indicated some education, yet her garments suggested a womon of lower bearing. But indeed, Jahtara's dress — bright blue bodice with lace ruffles at the top, full red skirt embroidered with gold flowers on the skirt and bodice, and black boots - spoke loudly of her origins. "The dress, in part, contains a deceit that brought me here."

"I think this deception fits you well. So comfortably, you appear out of place here."

"I detect pretense in your manner also."

Each considered the other, eyes meeting silently across the stream until the smaller womon unexpectedly bowed, saying, "Pardon my boldness in introducing myself. Heddha Jlussi. I have some wild rice and herbs; would you join in a shared supper?"

"I think your brazenness began when you designed to steal my mount. Therefore, I do not consider your introduction bold." Bowing her head, she continued, "And in return, I present myself, Jahtara Hakika Davuda. Perhaps we might share this spring and some company."

Collecting her knapsack, asymmetrical longbow, and quiver from their hiding place, Heddha considered the out-of-place Jahtara. She looks of high bearing, possibly a peer by birth, judging from her dress and specially trained mount. She certainly wasn't dressed for a lengthy journey on these plains. When Heddha first regarded her, she moved leisurely, certainly not like she was pursued. Quite frankly, she acted strangely, arms outstretched and face to the sky. Jahtara's copper hair and sand coloring with fine raised freckles, grey turning reddish higher on her cheeks, were typical of the lowland refined, making her appear even more out of place. Mayhap if returned, this unbalanced, lost refined womon would bring a reward. But she seemed well when they conversed. No, Heddha thought, the womon runs from some person or agency. Jahtara didn't appear to fear her after the failed thievery. Likely, a man or agency of the palatial household sought Jahtara, and she believed her deception successful. Heddha reflected that her past circumstances sounded much like Jahtara's.

Heddha sent Jahtara to gather the undercoat of dry grass while producing a small pot and rice from the bottom of her rucksack. She located some black fungus and loaded a tiny pea of it into the end of her fire piston. When Jahtara returned with an armful of grass, Heddha showed her how to twist the grass into tuber-shaped lengths.

It amused Jahtara how easily she had become Heddha's assistant; maybe Heddha just assumed her helpless. She watched Heddha slip the cylinder over the head of the piston, striking it sharply with her hand, quickly removing the piston with the glowing ember, and when applied to some dry grass and blown breath, it promptly burst into flame. Jahtara filled the pot from the spring while Heddha tented the grass rolls over the growing fire. Then Heddha placed the pot in the fire after adding rice and a yellow dried herb.

Heddha sat back on her heels, finding Jahtara's eyes, a grin baring her teeth. She abruptly stood striding to the spring shedding her sandals, leggings, a shirt she kept in hand, and finally, the delicately made undergarment. She squatted down in the chilly water divesting her shirt of the grass stain.

Jahtara wasn't helpless. Admittedly, servants cared for and pampered her, although she avoided the coddling. She strove to study even though she could have immersed herself in the gossip and backbiting of the refined household. Her parents, mostly her mother, even encouraged her to learn, if only to discourage her tomboyish tendencies. Jahtara romped with boys her age. She wanted to participate when they began training in combat skills and riding. Jahtara smiled, remembering how they thought she flirted at first but were surprised when she bested most with inexperienced yet furtive attacks. All the instructors shunned her but one, a kindly, widowed man. His seven sons matured into brutish braggarts. He saw in Jahtara someone studious and serious about learning the spirit of the old warrior ways.

Under the pretense of riding lessons, agreed to by her parents, and accompanied by a duenna, Jahtara practiced the warrior arts from the old armorer. But indeed, Jahtara's attendants started fires and cooked for her. Heddha's simple act of starting the fire and preparing the rice intrigued her and stimulated her to learn to do for herself, to be self-sufficient.

Feeling watched, Heddha turned her head towards Jahtara and, seeing her smiling at some thought, went back to finish scrubbing her garment. Her warm brown skin tinged blue, where it creased from squatting. Working the stain from her shirt, Heddha considered her life spent fleeing. A gut feeling invariably compelled her to anger; she couldn't stop and consider beforehand. Always, in the end, feeling out of control. Heddha remained aware of her actions, like watching herself in a marionette show, but her awareness didn't affect the rage coursing through her. Not that she couldn't justify the anger - Heddha wouldn't accept her position in life. Others seemed to bear their existence, but not her, especially when expected to yield to others. Heddha resisted her status, which often resulted in her running: lunas alone, hungry, foraging for wild rice, and always with an eye to her back.

When she finished cleaning her shirt, Heddha cupped handfuls of water over her head. The wetness sparkled in the Solaura, running off her short hair, across her back, narrow waist, broadening hips, and muscular buttocks to return to the flowing spring. She looked so solid in the yielding, moving water, comfortable with the sensual naturalness of standing naked in the great expanse of the plain.

Jahtara yearned for Heddha's openness, her directness, her friendship. She stood, striding to the steed, and removed a small food packet from the side saddle. Returning to the fire, she broke up a tuber, adding it to the cooking rice. She would add the dried fish to the finishing rice. She was able to fend for herself. She wanted the freedom to go wherever her thoughts and the prairie winds took her. She stood, slowly turning through the points of the horizon, seeing no barriers, only openness and a possible companion in her travels.

Heddha stood cleansed, water running from her naked body. Smelling the cooking rice, she turned towards Jahtara, who added something to the vessel. She watched Jahtara stand and turn in a tight circle, the Solaura radiating off her coppery hair and gold embroidery, floating, full skirt just touching the ground. Jahtara hadn't attacked during the attempted thievery; instead, she stood smiling, considering her, emanating a peace that sapped her rage. The water having evaporated from her body, Heddha warmed, realizing she would like a person that added to her life instead of lessening it. She desired a friend to walk with on her journey.

The stain removed, Heddha laid the garment out to dry. She quickly slipped on the pale green undergarment and leggings. Picking a handful of purple clover blossoms, she strode to the mount running her hand along its neck. She embraced its head and offered the blossoms, allowing the animal to get her scent. She turned to Jahtara, inquiring, "What does he answer to?"

"Trusted Companion, and he has been that over the last few deis."

At the sound of the name, the steed turned regarding Jahtara, then back to Heddha, nudging her hand for more clover blossoms. She caressed his muzzle instead while whispering in his ear. She turned to Jahtara, asking, "And how did you and Trusted Companion come to find yourselves at such an enchanted oasis?"

"A tale deserving a full stomach for the telling. Perhaps a cup of tea for divulging how a farm geyrle came to possess such a refined undergarment."

"Mayhap another mug for the telling of your deceptive garment," said Heddha, a wry smile spreading across her lips.

So, Heddha and Jahtara ate in silence, the first good supper enjoyed in deis, wondering about the other, contemplating their tale and how to tell it. In the end, they spoke honestly, trusting each other in the moment.

After eating, Heddha refilled the vessel with water, adding clover blossoms and mint found above the spring. Letting the tea steep, she sat tailor-style. Jahtara returned from washing her hands and sat with her folded legs to one side. Heddha gazed down at the delicate silk undergarment, placing a hand over her heart, sensing the soft, silky material against the beating of her chest. Tears welling up, Heddha cleared her throat of emotion to say, "To live in such unhappiness, suffering awake or in sleep, wears on the heart, even to hope provokes pain." Tears rolled down her cheeks like heavy raindrops across broad leaves at the start of a storm, singly at first, then joining together, falling off the edge in a torrent to the earth. Heddha made no attempt to wipe them away but let them fall, staining the pale green silk.

Her own eyes beginning to fill, Jahtara sat silently, giving Heddha time to continue.

"My father passed before my recollection. My first rememberings center on my uncle's anger. He detested us living with him, giving my mum the most menial work. I recall only dust and dirt, working until my hands were cracked, callused, and caked with grime. I would watch my cousins laughing and playing. They seemed so happy getting dirty."

Jahtara rose and poured tea into mismatched cups handing one to Heddha.

Heddha wiped the drying tears from her face, took the tea, and sipped the hot fluid. She sighed, regarding Jahtara's mount, "I did enjoy the stock, often spending time with my darlings even when it got me a beating." She paused, smiling at Jahtara, "I am taking the long way around the barn to get to the garment in question. I never told anyone my tale."

Jahtara smiled, leaning forward, and gently removed a remnant of clover blossom from Heddha's lip. "I have longed for intimacy. Yet, the palace's household gossiped like baying sheep about the silliest of occurrences: new shoes, which killed what animal at a hunt, or the latest lace obtained for their dress."

Heddha's gaze fell to the lace at the top of Jahtara's bodice, brows inquiringly arching.

Jahtara quickly moved to cover the lace. "I repeat, the gown acted the part of a deceit, albeit a costly and quite rare one from Burano," she grinned back. "And you shall hear its tale, yet I do not wish any distraction now." She leaned forward again, taking Heddha's hand. "Truly, I wish to hear the remainder of your tale."

Heddha continued, "As I grew older, he wished me around even less. Fate intervened when the palatial seat favored a distant cousin, and the kin's daughter became a laud in waiting for a minor patrician. My uncle, through some kindness, installed me as her trailer. The situation seemed quite laughable. Us country girls knew nothing of the refined high and mighty. No offense, milaud." Heddha made a half curtsy.

"None taken, bumpkin," Jahtara laughed. "Which household seat did you attend?"

"One travels towards the Solaura's rising. There emerge vast mountains and a pass. A difficult route, I vouch, with a high plateau beyond. By a mighty river stands the palatial city. I lived in the foot-hills on the other side."

"I recall such a place from the old maps. Keep on, please," Jahtara prompted.

"I felt out of place in these new surroundings. (What do they say? Feeding a Cawjia bird jewels will not make its feathers beautiful). Yet, I no longer suffered my uncle's thrashings. So, by fate, I found myself serving the refined at age ten. My distant relation, older at fourteen jahrs, grew altered by her elevated though lowly position, mistreating me. If I did not bow low enough or address her 'milaud,' I would get whacked with a hairbrush." Heddha lifted her eyes to gaze at Jahtara, her face solemn.

"I would not countenance such behavior if I knew of it, yet others did and worse. I'm sorry, Heddha."

Heddha shrugged, saying, "Not your doing. Even worse, she made me sleep on the cold stone at the foot of her bed."

"Did she give you the undergarment, or did you take it," Jahtara suggested.

Heddha snorted, "I would have accepted naught from her. Finish your tea. I am close to the garment's tale, though the story does not end there. I did get some learning though my 'mistress' did not condone it, mostly cause I bettered her. So, I soon learned to play dumb. I also received practice with a knife in the instance a creature threatened her when we walked unaccompanied, though I vowed not to place myself in danger for her life.

"Now to the garment," she said, clutching the cloth at her midsection. "While taking instruction in the knife with one of the armorers, I spied a squireling at archery practice. While womyn of the household commonly pursued standing archery for leisure, for me to do so seemed impossible, especially kneeling or with mounts. I contrived my presence when this squire, four jahrs older than I, took practice. I was at the palatial seat five jahrs by this time, and when my mistress partook in palace duties, I snuck away. T'was not long fore he took notice. Indeed, I intended to learn to handle the bow, yet in time, Amor's arrow pierced us.

"You know how unsuitable such a romance must be. Here in this vast isolation," Heddha gestured to the surrounding plain, "we from varied rank mayhap can talk womon to womon yet a son of one of the keyn's ministrants and a lowly fatherless geyrle, it cannot be. If he lied, saying the geyrle a playful diversion perhaps, yet the wonderful fool professed his love when caught, sealing my fate. The Privy Council stripped me to the waist, flogged, and pronounced me a whore. The tribunal that individually partakes yet together condemns. Then the keyn banished me back to my uncle, disgraced. At my leaving, the squire's tender presented this fine silk token to me with a note from the squire saying he would never forget."

Heddha loosened her grip on the garment, trying to straighten the cloth, "I cannot afford to remember." She rubbed her dry eyes, sighing deeply, "By fate, my mum took up with a man in possession of a small portion of land, and I need not return to my uncle. Alas, he likewise proved a brute, determined to have his way with me. Though he beat my mum, she could go nowhere else, so she turned her head at the fact. One dei, crazy with lust, he pinned me with his bulk. He cared naught who heard my resists and screams. He lowered his britches, pulling at my leggings when I kicked him in the jaw, sprawling him on his backside, his swollen pride pointing to the sky; seeing him like that enraged me. Not seeing clearly, I drew my knife and pared off one of his ballocks. The sight of blood made me realize my position, and I ran, throwing the bloody acorn to the pigs.

"He deserved retribution. Yet, it alarmed me to act in such a manner. Restraint leaves me when faced with anger." With a sigh, Heddha lay back in the grass.

"You intended to defend yourself. I have little understanding of what chains men to such acts." Jahtara sank back, and they lay silently watching the clouds pushed to their fate by the winds. Suddenly a shiver climbed Jahtara's back causing her to sit and scan the horizon.

Heddha alerted stood, saying, "What do you sense? I see nothing."

"Perhaps, yet I judge we should move."

They quickly cleaned and packed without further words, hanging Hedda's quiver and bow off the saddle. Heddha donned her overshirt and stomped the remains of the fire. Jahtara led the mount away from the spring, with Heddha catching up.

"Are you using this pretense to get out of telling of the deceitfully expensive and rare gown?" Heddha said, half accusingly.

"Not at all. I sometimes get a sense I cannot explain and heed it when I can. And after completing your chore with the hogs, how did you come here?"

"Being wanted or shunned in most of the keyndom, I kept on the move. I worked where I could and 'borrowed' when I could not. I often met unwanted attention from menfolk necessitating I defend myself." Heddha hung her head. "I cannot hold my rage, often necessitating a quick leaving. I heard talk of a distant land with new opportunities to the Solauraward, and in the three jahrs since my education with the refined household, I slowly work my way there. Although I get distracted often, and some of the tales bewilder, I cling to the goal. Movement through the Great Grassland appeared endless, and todei, I saw an opportunity to speed my way on the back of your mount. And thus, we come to you, su alteza."

"Quite right, of course. I am the only daughter to lineage Davuda, and my father reigns in the lands towards the Setting. I experienced a quite comfortable, although frustrating, life. I am ashamed to think it hard after hearing your tale. Yet, I longed for some meaning or purpose. Then recently, the ministrants held a judicature announcing I would wed some older, widowed, overstuffed, halfwit heir to the thronos of a backward keyndom called the Cold Waste." Jahtara involuntarily shivered at the thought before continuing, "I constitute the dowry to a treaty, a broodmare bearing offspring to shore up our borders. When I objected, my patrician parents admonished me for not doing my duty."

They walked in silence, Jahtara glancing sideways at Heddha, finally saying, "You must think me spoiled to complain so."

Reaching to hold Jahtara's hand on the rein, Heddha said, "What the ministrants dictated for you equals what the brute standing over me, britches around his ankles, wanted of me, except the refined household would hold you down with legs spread."

"I could not abide it. I wanted what you so unexpectedly found. Love truly." Jahtara snorted, "I secretly spied the widower out when he presented himself to the palatial seat. He repulsed me, and I retched at the sight of him. My only thought was to escape. I attended a formal afternoon social at one of my aunts, wearing this dress. I brought no other clothes, not wanting to alert my parents or brother. At the end of the social, I told my retainers I would stay, returning later with a mounted escort. My entourage went back to the palace without me. My deceived aunt thought I returned with them in the confusion of the coaches leaving.

"I needed help, of course. My sword tutor left Trusted Companion in a stand of trees with some provisions. I managed to slip unseen to the spot, riding away in the darkness. I rode mostly at noite to not be recognized or seen in my elegant attire until I rode openly onto this plain."

Both remained silent until Heddha observed, "It was by resolve you gained your intent. By the fates, I arrived."

The fugitives plowed a furrow through the thigh-high grass, lost in private thoughts. Arriving at a knoll, Jahtara halted and came around the mount's muzzle stopping in front of Heddha. She began, "We embark on our strange lives with no expectation of altering our lot. Most spend their lives in a rut, never seeing over the edge, ever content to dig it deeper. Some stumble out quite by accident. Some receive help from others. You chose when you did not allow the brute to have his way, your surgical husbandry speeding your exit! My exit appeared more calculating, yet I too faced a dire choice. We want to learn, see life differently, and get a glimpse over the edge of our rut. Now consider what we face," she said, spreading her arms. "A new life where we can go in any direction." She bowed to Heddha, placing her palm lightly on Heddha's chest, "And it would be my honor to share an adventure with you, oh brave of heart."

"You make this declaration hoping I will protect you in this adventure while you wear that exquisitely refined gown," Heddha pronounced with her hands on her hips and a broad grin.

"I appreciate the compliment, yet I can protect myself, thank you."

"A sight to see, especially in that deceitful dress!"

"Then you shall know its full deceit," Jahtara grinned distractedly, grabbing Heddha by the wrist, kicking her legs out from under her, and flipping her onto her back. Heddha quickly reversed the hold, rolling to her side, sending them tumbling down the hillock, laughing with dizzy delight. They came to a halt askew bosom to bosom, Heddha on top, pinning Jahtara's arm and Heddha's other arm held behind her back by Jahtara. Breathing heavily, they lay eye to eye until finally, Heddha said, "Draw," with Jahtara responding, "Draw."

Heddha admitted, "The deceit a good one, yet we need to find you some proper garments to continue our adventuring."

A sneering voice called from atop the knoll, "Are you needing assistance, sister?"

Mounted riders thundered down the slope bringing Heddha and Jahtara to their feet, the riders forming a semicircle around the two.

With her heart pounding, Jahtara calmly said, "Brother, what an unpleasant surprise. And no, I have the situation well in hand."

"I believe the farm cur held the upper hand," Prinus Baeddan insulted, dismounting.

Three warrior cnihts and close confidants of the prinus, a young tender, and the heir (Jahtara's presumed future husband) and his tender – dismounted quickly. Except for the future husband, he waited for assistance with dismounting. The younger tender collected the reins, tying them together, and led the mounts a short distance away.

Jahtara noticed the heir glistened uncomfortably in the warmth of the dei, wiping sweat from his forehead with a lace kerchief. A tingling at the back of Jahtara's neck drew her attention to a beautiful dagger with a silver sheath and handle, both inlaid with gold. The scabbard hung from a leather belt, holding up his britches. A plan formed in her mind, but Jahtara saw Heddha already in motion.

Heddha moved towards Trusted Companion, who had come down the hill. Heddha possessed no plan in truth, just a rising need for action and the hope she could find an escape in the ensuing rage and confusion. These were trained warriors, though, and her hopes remained humble.

Laud Kodo, dressed in black and grey, stepped between Heddha and the Trusted Companion. Heddha planted her feet and moved to draw her dagger when Jahtara said, "I place Heddha, a friend, under my protection." Raising her voice, she continued, "I would not want my family and friends mortally wounded. Equally, I should not like her harmed. Young Mahdi, how does your kindly mother fair?" Jahtara asked the young tender holding the reins.

The prinus, his eyes narrowed, asked, "Sister, what are you about?"

"Why no deceit, brother. I wish only to calm the waters. I recognize now how rash and silly I was. I only wish my friend kept safe."

"We have no mount for the stray. Laud Kodo will ensure her," Prinus Baeddan smiled, "safety."

Heddha, unsure of the plan, knew her situation turned dire. Jahtara desired her to keep calm and wait. That, she considered, might be difficult.

Jahtara distracted, "I behaved like a frightened child. Brother, please cause the introduction to my betrothed."

Still wary yet not divining her purpose, Prinus Baeddan was cautious. "Sister, may I present the heir to the Cold Waste and your future husband," he intoned, smirking.

The heir stumbled in eagerness, then picked up velocity extending his hand intending to kiss Jahtara's. "Prinus Alyeska. Understandable, you find yourself so aflutter at the approach of our marriage noite, my dear."

Giggling, Jahtara, in a slow-motion dance, took his hand, lifted it, and stepped under, neatly pirouetting the heir. Then switching hands, she withdrew the silver dagger from its scabbard. Prinus Alyeska ended up with one arm pinned behind his back and a knife at his throat.

Alarmed by the sudden movement, Laud Kodo drew his sword, turning towards Jahtara. Heddha used the distraction to join the dance. Drawing her dagger, she ducked under his sword arm, raking her blade across the exposed tendons at his wrist. Laud Kodo cried out in pain, his sword clattering to the ground. Catching his slashed wrist, Kodo turned to confront her, but Heddha vanished. Moving faster than a wolf at sheep, she leaped on Traveling Companion's back. A second cniht moved forward, drawing his sword. Trusted Companion reared at her urging, striking the cniht hard on the shoulder and chest. With a kick to the flanks, the mount sped to the top of the knoll and vanished.

Time resumed its pace as Jahtara watched Heddha speed out of sight. Considering Heddha rode her mount, Jahtara hoped she would not keep running. Concentrating on holding her hand steady, Jahtara turned awareness to her position.

Jahtara's brother turned back. "The farm bitch left you with no means of escape, dear sister."

"Step no closer, or I will harm your alliance."

"I doubt you capable. Besides, you just ended the alliance, and I intend to see you harmed for it." Prinus Baeddan shrilled, drawing his sword and moving towards Jahtara. Her brother raised his arm to strike, and the weak-kneed heir fell to the ground. Prinus Baeddan heard a dull thud and a spray of crimson. He wiped the red mist from his face using his non-sword hand and studied the blood with a confused expression. Dropping his gaze to a sword lying on the ground, Baeddan saw blood flowing from his empty sword hand. He could not fathom what had happened. Following the flowing blood, he discovered a blood-soaked tunic with a swallowtail-tipped shaft protruding from his shoulder joint. Unable to hold a sword or move his arm, his face paled.

Jahtara, hunting for the source of the arrow, saw Heddha emerging from a gulch. She had ridden around the hill, flanking the party, and now notched another arrow, letting it fly, striking the third cniht's thigh. Prinus Alyeska's tender ran screaming up the knoll leaving young Mahdi standing his ground, knife drawn.

Heddha hoped Mahdi would also run. She considered what to do and marveled at the process. Her mind continued clear, not clouded in anger. She envisioned Mahdi's mother standing beside him, weighing her actions. Heddha bore down on him, intent on separating him from the mounts. At the last moment, she veered using Trusted Companion to wrench the reins from the youngling's hand. Seeing him raise his knife, she feinted with her blade, catching his ear as he ducked out of the way. She turned Trusted Companion quickly, leaning out of the saddle to pick up the other animals' reins keeping Trusted Companion between her and Mahdi. The cniht battered earlier by the mount lay still on the ground. The other cnihts worked their wounded way to the prinuses. Heddha pulled Trusted Companion to a stop next to Jahtara and jumped to the back of one of the tied animals. She roused the steed as Prinus Baeddan reached a blooded hand for the mount's hindquarters. She galloped free, leaving a bloody smear on the animal's flank.

Jahtara bent to the cowering heir cutting his belt and releasing the sheath. "A betrothal gift to remember you by, milaud," she said, mounting Trusted Companion and spurred him after Heddha. Before rounding the next hillock, she turned back to see the cnihts tending to her brother and each other while the forsaken groom stood watching after her, holding his bitches up with both hands.

Catching up to Heddha, Jahtara heard laughing, almost screaming. "Are you wounded?" Jahtara asked.

"Not in the least, and you?"

"No, thanks to you! I heard screaming."

"Letting out the demons. I am running again, yet not in anger. I knew naught of what was in your mind and decided to wait for a sign. I understood not to kill any of them, especially the young tender. With some clarity, I decided to trust my new friend. The anger did not master me in the fray. And I saved your rump."

"With some help from me!"

"You helped more than you shall ever know!"

"How did you get Trusted Companion to obey you?"

"I have a way with animals: fed him some treats, paid him some heed, and let him get to know me. Much like I did with you!"

"I see you picked up a pack animal too."

Heddha spotted the neddy among the steeds. "An added surprise!"

They road hard till just before dark, slowing to rest the animals. Jahtara withdrew the silver-handled dagger from its fine sheath, a skilled piece of work. Metal crafting beyond anything metalsmiths of her keyndom could master, and the Cold Waste crafts exhibited inferior style and quality. The gold inlay demonstrated exquisite work with forms and designs unknown to Jahtara. Possibly arcane symbols or foreign script. The grip curved slightly for the fingers with a smooth indentation on top, a good fit for her thumb, and the rear bolster flared to a spherical knob. The heavy scabbard likewise incorporated strange designs, and the blade appeared unmarked by usage. The knife balanced beautifully. She handed it to Heddha to inspect, who did not recognize the designs or script. Jahtara slipped the blade back into its sheath and laid it away in her saddle pack. They continued in silence through the clear noite, the Axis star immobile behind them. The Maiden constellation, suspended above the distant mountains, poured a confluence of sparkling stars from her jug, filling the sky in an arc from the Arising to the Setting.

The noite sky lightened towards the Arising, expanding sight in grey tones, the coming dei balanced between light and darkness. They halted, allowing the animals to drink, and feed after their flight. Heddha and Jahtara stretched weary backs and limbs. They took stock of provisions after quenching their thirst upstream of the mounts, quickly moving foodstuffs to the encampment stores on the roan-colored pack animal. Between them, they gathered angora leggings, brown leather britches, and a blousy white shirt closing with a leather cord to the mid-chest. Finally, they found a fine leather sleeveless jerkin secured at the waist with antler buttons. These would kit out Jahtara, except for a too-small pair of boots, fitting Heddha, who recovered a sleeveless leather pullover.

"It's time to shed your deceit and don suitable riding attire," Heddha proposed.

"Yet what to do with the dress? Perhaps we can trade it for coin. We must release the mounts. They will return to the barn and perchance aid the wounded party along the way. Surely they shall not pursue us with so many injured."

"Perhaps. Methinks you too kind. The mounts will sell or trade easier than the dress. Such a fine garment will bring unwanted attention and suspicion." After considering, a grin spread across Heddha's face. "We will return the bride to her groom. Disrobe, and I will show you."

While Jahtara molted the refined dress and donned the seized clothes, Heddha spotted a low branch fitting her design among the riparian trees. She snapped the dead bough from the tree and trimmed it with her dagger. Besides the limb, Heddha gathered strips of stinging nettle stems from along the stream.

"Now braid these into cords," she said, handing Jahtara the nettle strips, "while I change to a shirt and draw on these boots."

Heddha pulled the long shirt over her head, cinching a belt around her middle. She drew on the boots and observed, "These must have belonged to Mahdi. I hope I did not harm him badly."

"My thanks for sparing them. Wounds will mend. The youngling will now have a mark of battle to brag about." Eyeing the bough, Jahtara said, "I try to divine your plan for the dress."

A straight spine ran the length of the branch, splitting into a Y at one end and midway to the other two offshoots to act as shoulders. Heddha placed it over the saddle of the professed groom's mount. Catching onto the plan, Jahtara helped Heddha lash the crouch of the bough over the saddle. Heddha lifted the gown onto the stick body, tying the bodice to the branches, and they arranged the dress to drape over the saddle. Stepping away, they inspected the form.

"Seems lacking," Jahtara stated. Then spotting the need, she dashed to the trees and tore down a tangle of rust-colored moss. Heddha affixed it to the top of the spine protruding from the bodice. A breeze stirred the wig convincingly.

"A far better deceit," laughed Heddha.

"I think not deceitful yet a more desirable bride to the groom: a beautiful, empty-headed spray to bow to his every need. Let us send the prinus off and embark on our daring adventure."

They kept a mount for Heddha, a filly she named Fate's Choice, the pack animal they called Stolen Pleasure, and of course, Trusted Companion. The cnihts' steeds moved off slowly back along the way they came. The groom's mount lingered to regard the two of them. Simultaneously they waved to the prinus it carried. The steed turned, following the herd.

Heddha and Jahtara mounted and rode leisurely up an incline, reaching the crest as the full Solaura cleared the distant mountains. Dew on the grasses sparkled in the new dei. Behind, the mounts disappeared around a hillock. Before the womyn, the Solaura illuminated a dirt path winding in and out of shadow through the hills ahead.

"A clear way awaits, sister," pronounced Heddha.

"Crystal clear," Jahtara declared. "The dei arises young, and time endures ageless." They rode down the slope towards their new path.

Possibilities

If the quantum universe consists of field potentialities interacting probabilistically, God indeed plays dice. Can we know the intent of a god? Maybe she doesn't play the odds. Or do we exist on faith alone, mass consensus smoothing out quantum probabilities onto the macro properties of matter in bulk? Well then, thank Goddess for the outliers; to choose a lesser-used path expands the possibilities. Under observation, these probabilities collapse into perceived reality, and odds are Schroder's cat would rather have a definite answer instead of superposition limbo. Perhaps we jump from one collapsing probability to another like leaping rock to rock across a stream? Skipping the light fandango of possibilities with a joy of the unknown.

Biological information resists entropy locally, producing consciousness, and extending the possibilities. So what's the probability it took several million years and a few billion primates to complete this story?

The Solaura hung suspended above its setting. As Heddha and Jahtara traveled Solauraward, its sultry heat blazed to their front all dei, an increasingly warm dei. The low rays added shadows and depth to the sensual rolling hillocks spotted with farms. In the distance, a small village emerged from a widening valley, white-walled edifices turning orange in the lengthening rays reminding Jahtara of a painting. Jahtara's freckles became stronger on her embrowning skin. Her copper hair, much like her discarded bodice, displayed golden highlights. Words drifted from her dry mouth in cadence with the plodding hooves on the dusty road, "Let us discover if this berg possesses a traveler's inn. I grow tired of the road and animal-scented barns accommodating us over the last half-luna."

Heddha's brown and weathered complexion contrasted even further with her bright eyes. She replied, "Those scents remember me of my farm home when young, yet the dust and grime could do with a change and the gullet with a good washing of fermented barley and hops."

Catching her grin, Jahtara mused, "My tastes tend toward the fermented offspring of a fine grape."

The two womyn and three animals continued in silence. The womyn had grown into one another, comfortable mute, or conversing, like a river separating around an island rejoins, sharing what it picked up during the separation. One would carry the force of the flow, and then the sister channel would provide direction and effort. Their bearing, high or low, often added to their connection, for each recognized their spirits' essential sameness no matter what adorned the shore. Though the riverbanks did grow steeply higher at times, the river narrower and the current swifter, encountering rough stretches of unfamiliar rapids when the two womyn entered territory appearing different from their parallax views.

One time especially, Jahtara spoke of the noble life these farm families led, working the land with care and cooperation. Heddha, of course, pointed out her own experience with the hardships involved in the 'noble' work of serfs cultivating land most didn't own: the toll from famine, grueling work, childbirth, and with most of what they produced going towards levies or liege lauds. They barely survived in deference to a laud that maintained themself through the hard toil of serfs. Jahtara knew little of work, wages, or the value of things. She never needed such knowledge.

Jahtara and Heddha initially camped along the trail but of late accepted the charity of straw-covered barn floors as farms became more frequent. When arriving at a farm, Heddha would pitch in with the evening chores while Jahtara would watch or distract the children. Heddha asked the prinus to help work for their lodging, which she did with spirit, pledging to mend her ways through hard labor, most of which she needed to be taught how to do. One morgn, Heddha woke to find Jahtara milking the goats. Jahtara eagerly attempted this work until, over the back end of a goat, she admitted, "I find a self-centered mentality difficult to vacate, especially with my life of privilege. Yet the sense of shared work and community have set my feet on the path." Licking milk off her fingers, she corrected, "set my hands on the teats."

Some folks accepted unaccompanied womyn on the road; most did not. Heddha concocted a story (at which she seemed particularly good) detailing how they traveled Solauraward searching for Jahtara's husband, having received no word from him after leaving to engage in remote work. People's ease at accepting this fabrication caused Heddha and Jahtara to believe many traveled Solauraward for work, making the rumors Heddha heard believable.

Under the circumstances, folks treated them fairly. This treatment suited Heddha, whose past wanderings were not so inconsequential. Jahtara observed a softening in Heddha: maybe not softening, yet a relaxing around her eyes and a broadening smile.

Upon arriving at the hamlet, the crier directed them to an inn called Way's Respite. After some discussion and show of coin, the dubious keeper allotted them a small room over the stable. The better bedchambers viewed the river, yet they were satisfied to be off the saddle and in a room with a large bed. For a trifle more, they obtained a warm bath filled by a young attendant.

Feeling refreshed, they proceeded downstairs in search of food. The dimly lit tavern, filled with smoky blue haze, sounded loud. Out the back in the still warm air, a flat rock expanse sprouted tables lit by candles, with a splendid view of the river. Only a few patrons were present in the dimming light. Heddha selected a table with a broad view of a masonry bridge traversing the slow-moving river and the incline beyond dotted with cottages, windows aglow. The other citizenry became quiet, turning to stare at the womyn moving to their table, then returned to low whispers with sidelong glances.

"I am utterly amazed you traveled far and long by yourself, Heddha. We seem to garner the interest of a three-legged helhest."

"Some might turn such a sight to their advantage. Might I suggest you not meet their gazes? Give them no excuse to advance. If you must, see without looking, much like the two in the darkened table towards the back who took little notice of these two-legged mares or mayhap wished to draw no attention to themselves."

"Truly," exclaimed Jahtara examining the dim nook in more detail.

"Jahtara!" Shrilled Heddha then more quietly, "Please, what are you doing? If someone wishes no attention, then afford them such and likewise draw none yourself."

"Perhaps. Yet, I want to explore the world to the fullest! I bow to your experience, although you seem to have drawn your share of trouble by your own account."

"I wished it not so, yet it found me out. Let it lie quietly here. I desire only a good and comfortable noite's rest."

Jahtara lay her hand on Heddha's arm. "And you shall have it. The only attention I wish is that of the serving attendant."

Heddha's beer tasted a little yeasty yet with a bold oak flavor to cover it. The wine grew more passable as Jahtara drank, considering the wonderful ambiance of companionship, warm noite air, and pleasing vista. They quietly conversed while sharing a tasty squash with wild rice in the hollow and roasted beets and carrots on the side. The bread turned out fabulous, warm with a hard-tangy crust. The scent alone had them reaching for a chunk.

Bathed, bellies full, and basking in the glow of the fermented spirits, they sat enjoying the noite air till most patrons moved away. Heddha excused herself to use the privy, leaving Jahtara to finish her wine. Glancing around the terrace, Jahtara spied the glow of a pipe toked among the recesses at the back. Before realizing it, she found herself squinting to see into the depths of the niche then the glowing moved. She looked away quickly, seeing two shadows detach from the darkness. Both wore hooded jerkins. The taller one slid his hood off as the two wove through the obstacles from two directions in the manner that pinned their prey in place.

Controlling her breath, Jahtara moved the schooner of wine to her lips, heart pounding. The smaller hooded one strode with a bit of a swagger. He halted at the table opposite, straddling a chair facing Jahtara. She could only see part of his face under the hood, which seemed fine-featured with thin lips and a hairless chin. They were taller than most in these parts. The hoodless one took Heddha's stool placing his arms on the table. He clasped a clay pipe, its bowl glowing, sending a thin waft of sweet-smelling vapor in her direction. The odor, or possibly the wine at the end of a weary dei, made her momentary swoon. She drew her head back, concentrating on the man across from her. He had a rough sort of face with a stubble-covered jaw. Wavy brown hair covered his ears and collar, and she could see some form of adornment in the left ear. He smiled broadly, hazel eyes dancing in the flickering candlelight. The unusual eyes startled her; the dark centers were round, something she had not seen before. Yet his smile was so disarming that Jahtara smiled back.

The stranger looked at his companion to confirm a prior discussion, then, returning to Jahtara, spoke in a deep stilted voice. "My companion and I wondered if you traveled the road from … I am unsure of the local name. The great expanse to the Nord?"

Jahtara grew guarded, regretting her momentary lapse. She took a closer look at them both. Upon closer inspection, their clothes appeared unusual, with an odd weave and sheen. Yet, she sensed no danger. Could she have been so fooled by a becoming countenance?

His speech sounded unfamiliar with a limited sense of the territorial dominions.

"The Nord?"

"A direction. My pardon, I am new to your dialect." He turned his head as if listening, then continued, "The Great Grassland and the dominions beyond."

"We arrive from my husband's small farming estate of ten deis ride. I know nothing of what you speak."

"So, you know nothing of any trouble in the dominions I speak?"

"The farm lies remotely. I have no tidings beneficial or malign."

"Your husband travels with you?"

"Who would query and speak to my mistress so?" Heddha spoke with authority startling them all. Striding with equal assertiveness, she came to stand between Jahtara and the shorter stranger who stood.

The intruder still seated smiled broadly once more. "Quite right, of course. Pardon our lapse. We have been on the road for many risings and have forgotten the correct protocols. I am called Jorma," he said. Then used the pipe to indicate his companion, "My traveling companion, Kasumi. You might call us explorers."

Kasumi met Heddha's gaze, nodded, and lowered himself to the chair.

"Explorers?" Heddha queried.

Jahtara caught Kasumi slightly shaking his head.

Watching Jahtara, Jorma continued, "Kasumi and I disagreed about conversing with you. We like to gather information from fellow travelers about conditions on the road. You could call us scholars; we travel to learn of others, hence explorers. The villagers persist in not sharing information. They consider us strange."

"Well, we agree there," Heddha smirked.

Jorma's grin didn't diminish. Looking at Heddha, he said, "Two womyn traveling alone seems strange, and I contend you may want to share common insights with fellow strangers."

"And what might we have in common with two men?"

Kasumi looked up, removing his hood revealing short spiked white hair and the fine smooth features of a woman. One of her ears also contained the unusual adornment. Her brows were light-colored, lashes long, and the unique pupils round. At Heddha and Jahtara's astonished look, her thin lips spread into a broadening smile. "Mayhap more than initially deemed likely," Kasumi said in a lilting voice.

Recovering first, Jahtara stammered to Jorma, "You travel with your spouse?"

Jorma smiled. Kasumi answered, "Our relationship does not constitute a marriage." Seeing Jahtara's reaction, she added quickly, "I mean to say, I have a partner, and Jorma is… perhaps, a bachelor?"

Heddha and Jahtara looked at each other confused. Heddha asked, "He attained the lowest level of a cniht?"

Now Kasumi looked confused, turning to Jorma for help.

"In our lands, a bachelor connotes an unmarried man. Kasumi's union amounts to an extended bonding, what you would call married. Her partner lives where we are from and does not travel with us. We travel in the manner of colleagues or friends." Jorma endeavored to explain. Seeing their blank stares, he concluded, "Our speech and customs make this awkward. Pardon our intrusion into your evening. Kasumi believed you would hesitate to share insights." Looking at Kasumi, he inclined his head towards the Inn. They stood, replaced their hoods, turning to walk away.

Jahtara looked to Heddha, who shook her head vigorously. Jahtara sighed deeply, gazing out at the bridge alight with lanterns. She saw a barge tied up to the dock, the push polers stacking their long staffs. Jahtara heard their laughter in anticipation of food and drink. She watched two people moving into darkness across the bridge. Beyond them, the noite became too deep to penetrate. She gave Heddha an apologetic smile and called after the strange pair, "We hesitate out of caution. I find your speech difficult to fathom, and a spoken-for womon traveling without a duenna appears a bit unusual."

"Might two womyn traveling without a male escort seem strange,"

Kasumi retorted.

"Breathing water may be perceived as strange yet quite comfortable for fish," said Heddha.

"Perhaps we are all fish out of water," Kasumi returned.

Jorma again removed his hood, turning to Kasumi to say, "Let us share to extend our perception of the circumstances. Thus fulfilling our purpose." He took her by the elbow, turning her back towards the two womyn, one scowling while the other smiled broadly. Kasumi abruptly pivoted, disappearing into the inn.

While watching the inn door close, Jorma continued, "My friend understands more of your situation than I. She sensed you would not confide in us."

"And what understanding of our 'situation' will you confide to us?" Heddha questioned.

"Only that you are two womyn traveling Solauraward, and we travel the contrary way."

"You mentioned some trouble in the dominions along this course?" Jahtara asked while sitting and motioning Heddha to do likewise.

Looking back at the inn, Jorma answered, "Aye, some hearsay of troubles concerning a broken alliance, missing prinus, and wounded cnihts." He said casually.

Jahtara laid her hand on Heddha's arm to keep her from rising while asking further, "You seem rather well informed traveling from Solauraward to hear such tidings from the reverse bearing."

"In our scholarly pursuit, we collect information and also artifacts."

On hearing this, Heddha stood, removing the room key from a pocket, and hastened to the inn. When she opened the door, Kasumi appeared, carrying a tray of mugs. Upon seeing Heddha, she said, "Quiet kind, I'm sure," and crossed the threshold. Heddha stood there, holding the door open, unsure whether to proceed to their room or return to the terrace. Meeting Jahtara's questioning eyes, she decided not to leave her alone with these peculiar fellow transients.

Kasumi distributed the steaming mugs explaining, "The noite starts to chill. I thought the tea would warm against the cool air and mayhap tender the heart."

Jahtara, Jorma, and Kasumi raised their mugs in friendly salute. Heddha stared deeply into her mug. She sampled the steaming brew tasting its bitter bite and returned it to the tray.

Jahtara blew across the top of the piping hot tea, holding the mug with both hands, feeling the warmth, and thought the flavor intriguing. She considered what Jorma said. His statements alarmed, yet she sensed no fear in herself. They approached her, knew she and Heddha came from the Great Grassland, and possibly knew of her flight and origins! Jorma was ruggedly handsome. His eyes, though strange, seemed kind, and his smile invited. Even more intriguing, Kasumi's assertive visage equaled her manner. She used her directness like a shield protecting what she kept secluded, yet the woman's independence matched Heddha's.

Heddha also bore a shield, one bashed and distorted by experience, taking the form of suspicion. The steaming concoction Jahtara now brewed needed a pinch of Heddha's skepticism. Yet the main ingredients constituted questioning trust simmered with negotiation, for the interaction reminded her of ministerial intrigue and negotiation for position, status, and power. She felt sure these strangers conveyed an invite for a parley. But they seemed constrained by some influence, especially Kasumi. Jorma spoke almost with abandon yet ceded restraint to his companion. Jahtara would proceed, with her friend in mind, taking solace in the feeling that Heddha would keep her shielded if needed.

"You spoke of alliances and prinuses," began Jahtara noticing a slight widening of Kusumi's eyes. "It seems strange you would hear such musings coming from Solauraward?"

"These events could have happened long ago and reached us on our journey," parried Kasumi.

"Or transpired more recently and reached us by other means,"

Jorma interjected.

"Such as," Heddha thrust back.

"(Unintelligible)," suggested Jorma. Then turning to Kasumi, they exchanged words in an unknown language. Turning back, Jorma said, "A form of bird."

Kasumi responded with a smile, confirming Heddha's growing suspicions. What started with prospects of a relaxing evening became a familiar noitemare, not of Heddha's doing. Jahtara, with naivety and reliance on feelings, engaged in a risky dialogue. They should leave the Way's Respite now! Danger emanated from these…. What? Strange-eyed foreign scholars radiating deceit. Yet, in deference to Jahtara, Heddha would work out the circumstances before reacting. Heddha knew Jahtara sought to gather information and hoped she would not give more than gained. Heddha admitted the two fascinated her. They dressed in common enough clothes, yet the garment's construction looked unusual and though traveled in, appeared spotless. The man's open, friendly countenance hinted a willingness to say more. A larger mystery fell to the womon, a strutting bird in full plumage with unknowable intentions. So be it. Heddha would see what Jahtara cooked up and extract them from the stew if it came to a boil.

"A bird," questioned Heddha.

"We have messenger birds at the rookery," Jahtara quickly added.

Heddha rolled her eyes. Jorma asked, "Rookery? You said you lived on a farm."

"I…mmm… when younger, I was an attendant at a laud's keep."

"And you work on the farm also…" Jorma gestured to Heddha?

"Heddha," interjected Jahtara quickly, "and I am called Jahtara."

Heddha buried her face in her hands. Then peeked at Jahtara, who looked at her with a knitted brow, wondering what she had said. She doesn't realize she gave the name of the missing prinus who ran away from a marriage, ruining an important alliance!

As it slowly dawned on Jahtara, her face turned the colors of the setting Solaura. She said casually, trying to cover her lapse, "A common enough name." Yet it came out pitched higher than intended.

Jahtara's blatant evasion failed when Heddha and Kasumi's eyes met. The folly and emotion of the past few moments burst forth from both, starting with a nervous giggle followed by uncontainable laughter breaking through the weakened dike. Even Jahtara laughed at her silliness while Jorma smiled broadly, observing all three.

"We truly mean you no harm," started Jorma. "We do travel towards the lands you have just left and seek some knowledge of what transpires there. Two of our colleges went into the Cold Waste, and we have no knowledge of them since."

Kasumi seemed to cast off her reluctance with this admission, "As with your desire for a measure of discretion, we also wish to keep what we reveal among us."

Heddha looked questioningly at Jahtara, then said, "If you mean we not expose each other, then aye, yet you seem to have the advantage. You have some knowledge of us ere our meeting this noite."

"A fortunate occurrence only, I assure you. We are interested in the Cold Waste and Keyn Alyeska due to a concern for our colleges."

"Keyn Alyeska?"

"Aye, Prinus Alyeska's father died of unknown causes while Alyeska traveled to meet his future bride in the realm of Davuda," Kasumi lowered her voice, addressing Jahtara, "prinus. We travel to gather information about our colleagues. What came of them? Were they harmed? If so, we wish to recover their belongings."

"You judge they might have come to harm," asked Jahtara.

"Aye, we believe so. We expected our companions to contact us some time ago. We hoped you knew something of these matters?"

"None," Jahtara attested. "I signify, prinus, now Keyn Alyeska presented himself to the privy council for a betrothment sealing an alliance between the two keyndoms. I could not abide the thought and fled the realm. Heddha and I met on the Great Grassland, and she aided in eluding my brother, Prinus Baeddan. I have no other knowledge of the keyn of the Cold Waste except by that unfortunate predicament."

"A tidy sum of knowledge. And may I say you have earned my respect by your actions, yet you know nothing of our companions or their belongings?"

Jahtara offered, "A fainthearted attendant accompanied the prinus, now keyn."

Jorma, sitting with his chair tipped back, legs stretched out, leaned forward, taping the pipe against the table leg to empty it, asking, "And no other man traveled with him?"

"I am sure a considerable party of retainers, counselors, and cooks traveled with him. I have no perception of them."

"A man? I thought you sought two," asked Heddha.

"The two were seeking a third. A meddlesome sort," explained Jorma.

"Meddlesome? Your tale expands in fits and starts," complained Heddha. "Please enlighten us as to how this fellow meddled."

"As scholars, we have a sort of code. We want to expand our understanding of people and places. We do not interfere with the lands we study. Our colleague seems to have done just that."

"In what way exactly did he interfere," Jahtara leaned forward, becoming concerned.

"I am uncomfortable discussing his transgression." Jorma squirmed in his seat, admitting this, and looked to Kasumi for help, who offered none. Sitting upright, he sighed, letting the following flow forth, "Apparently, he deeply inserted himself into local matters. We do not know with certainty how this happened, mayhap by bribing with goods or certain knowledge."

"The telling of this tale reminds one of ridding a planted field of its weeds, always more to come," chastened Heddha.

A tingling sensation trickled down Jahtara's spine with the uncomfortable turn of Jorma's explanation. In a low whisper, she intoned, "In what way does the interfering involve me?"

"Not exactly sure."

"What do you suppose then," she said forcefully.

"Well, the obvious: the alliance and betrothal."

Jahtara stood, knocking her stool over. She put her hands on the table, leaning close to Jorma, saying with determination, "The reason I am here flows from the alliance and betrothal. To be sure, I struggled in my position, yet the forced marriage accounted for my departure. Now you say one of your compatriots proved to be the causal agent!" She turned and strode to the edge of the terrace. Indeed, the privy council wished her to serve as equity for an alliance and the even baser aspect of a broodmare, which even now gave her weak knees. In truth, she had left for many reasons: the silliness of the elite, lack of intimacy, scarcity of faithful friends, and the dearth of fulfilling prospects for a woman.

Since fleeing, her life unfolded; all constraints lifted. She could take a deep breath. Now she was involved in... what exactly - intrigue, alliances, missing companions, and mayhap killings! The bridge lighting having been extinguished; the river fell into darkness. Most of the cottages on the slope opposite were dark, with only occasional lowing or baying heard in the distance. She felt the chill and dampness of the deepening noite. Jahtara turned and came to the table.

To Kasumi and Jorma, she asked, "Someone killed the former keyn, your companions, and involved me?"

"We have no direct knowledge." When Jahtara started to object, Kasumi quickly added, "Yet it seems possible, aye."

"You have released this tale in miserly scraps. I feel yoked by my lack of the whole; divulge the sum now without delay."

Kasumi answered, "I am ill at ease in telling this scheme." She looked toward Jorma before continuing, "Yet we take a risk in passing on these scraps. I feel a kinship with your difficulties, and it pains me to withhold any of the tale. Like your former situation, we have constraints on our actions. Truly I would prefer different circumstances."

"We believe you only innocently involved in this affair, which our talk affirmed." Kasumi nodded her confirmation, and Jorma continued, "I know it does not suffice, yet I beg your pardon for the distress we cause."

"You beg, yet provide no basis for a pardon, and you, sister, I gladly include among my kin who sell me like a broodmare or attempt to kill me for foiling their plans."

In the following silence, Kasumi nodded to Heddha and motioned to Jorma, who rose. He asked, "Did either of you notice any peculiarities concerning Alyeska?"

Heddha answered. "No, he seemed a normal man: vain, overly concerned with copulation, and surprised a woman bested him."

Jorma turned to Jahtara and, with eyes kinder than she expected, asked, "You would agree?"

With a satiric smile, Jahtara added, "Aye, he seemed unable to keep his britches up around me."

Jorma nodded, replaced his hood, and followed Kasumi into the inn.

Heddha blew out the candle on their table, "Let us discuss in our room."

They noticed only a few patrons in the quiet tavern: Kasumi and Jorma, not among them. Heddha set the latch in their room and wedged a piece of wood under the door.

Jahtara, in surprise, asked, "Do we linger? I thought you would want to leave."

"Earlier, aye. Yet now I consider this the safer place rather than a noite in the open. The room includes one door and a high window with no easy entrance. Ensure the knife's security. We will leave at the Rising. Do you reckon they have a room in the inn?"

"I know naught. Aye, the knife remains safely hidden. So, you considered Jorma seeks the knife?"

"It seemed so. At one time, I thought to leave the terrace to ensure Kasumi did not prowl here searching."

Removing her boots, Jahtara said in a palliative tone, "I feel like a fool. I trusted too much in my feelings and did not consider your warnings or experience. Forgive me."

"No need. You told these strangers naught they did not already know, and we, in return, know more of our situation. We possess only a small portion of the tale, I am sure. Though they withheld much, I grasp no malice." Then sitting on the bed with a broad smile, she said, "Yet it adds to my common good to have a prinus ask me for forgiveness!"

Jahtara came over solemnly, lifting one of Heddha's legs to remove her boot. With Heddha watching, mouth agape, Jahtara repeated the gesture with the other boot laying it neatly at the foot of the bed next to its partner.

Jahtara stood, crossed to the washstand, musing, "For so long, I existed as only a thin stock of myself, rarely expressed. I have branched and flourished over the past luna, producing a flowering I do not wish to lose. This noite, I saw that flowering threatened." She dipped her hands in the water, splashing her face, the cold quenching the fire in her cheeks. "I am not angry at Jorma or Kasumi; I like them. Their intrigue piques my interest. They seemed pained in their constraint, though I would like to know more of that hindrance. No, I threatened myself by conceiving I had no choice. And a little pruning here and there will make me sounder. I learned much from the encounter."

"Mmmmmm… and I could get used to such treatment from a prinus," said Heddha pulling the covers up, then suddenly sat up. "Wait… If you had married Alyeska, you would occupy the position of a queyn!"

"Truly dread such a notion," moaned Jahtara extinguishing the candle and slipping in beside Heddha. "No, a queyn I shall never be."

They lay there in silence, listening to the noises of the inn closing for the noite. The building creaked and groaned, commenting on the dei's comings and goings. To Heddha, the bed represented such a luxury it set her to consider what brought her here.

"Jahtara?"

"Aye."

"Do you consider choice or fate brought us here?"

"From here, looking back, choices brought me here. And looking forward, I see more choices in the morgn, bringing me to a new and divergent here."

"When I look back, I see no choice. Fate gave me my mum and pa in the first place. Fate made me a peasant and a womon, and fate dictated who I can love. Not many choices there. What choice caused your birth as a prinus, our meeting on the Great Grassland, or stopping here and meeting strangers connected to your past?"

"Perhaps...yet we both made choices putting us on the path of meeting at the spring. What happened next arose from choices. Mayhap a deeper root intention brought my continuance as a prinus, a womon, and meeting you. A thought affording new weight to the choices we make now."

"I did not choose the form of my creation!"

"The choice lies in how we perceive our existence. How did we come to regard one other in the role of refined or peasant? Why does it seem strange that I help you with your boots or bow to your insightful experience?"

"Where then lies the first choice?"

"An answer beyond my contemplation, we need to consult an immortal for such insights."

The sky glowed towards the Rising when Heddha and Jahtara led the animals out the stable gate. A mist welled up from the river, obscuring the bridge's center. Two steeds with their riders walking alongside emerged from the vapers. The riders wore hoods, but Heddha held little doubt who the cowls concealed.

"Well met. I feared we would not see you before our departure, yet I see you want an early start also," Heddha stated, attaching a sardonic smile at the end.

"Well met indeed. We were up early to see you off," responded

Kasumi.

Jahtara added, "Then I am glad we did not sleep late and add to your long journey towards the Cold Waste.

"You seem in improved spirits this morgn," greeted Jorma. "Do you go across the bridge and Solauraward or stay on the lesser road towards the Setting Sea?"

Heddha kept walking onto the bridge, joining Kasumi in the mist. Jahtara spying a loose cinch on Jorma's mount, walked it to the middle of the road to tighten the strap.

"Which would you advise?"

"Both roads eventually come to the same end. It matters naught to me; Kasumi suggested the journey might be more important than the destination from your perspective. With time to spare, she would advise the lesser road here. The way along the Setting Sea keeps cooler. Also, it seems less traveled, serving you better."

"Strange, we met here where the road divides," Jahtara said, securing the latigo strap.

"I would say convenient. We wish only fulfillment for you and Heddha, truly."

"Perhaps, when next we meet, you will have the results of your narrative from last evening."

"I would hope so and look forward to such a time." Taking the reins from her, he added, "Jahtara, you have something of immense value. I know you probably do not comprehend it fully now, yet you will eventually understand its importance."

Heddha and Kasumi appeared out of the mist walking side by side with their mounts behind. Drawing abreast, Jorma continued with Kasumi up past the inn. At one point, Jorma turned and smiled.

"A handsome looking man," Heddha observed.

"You think so?"

"I do, aye. Why do we tarry?"

"For them to ride out of sight."

"Ah, you begin to think like me."

When Kasumi and Jorma reached the road's crest, they mounted, and Kasumi turned in the saddle waving. Heddha waved back.

"And what did the two of you talk about?"

"Clothing."

"Truly!"

"She took notice of my green undergarment. She called it a name I could not understand, yet she liked it. I followed with difficulty what they said last noite, by the way."

"I also."

"I conveyed to her somewhat of its origin. She confided that she wore a keepsake, a wideband around her wrist. Beautiful! It bore similar markings to the knife." Heddha paused then nonchalantly added, "She wore one."

"What? A knife!"

"Aye, it could have been a matched pair. I caught a glimpse of it beneath her overshirt."

"Is the knife what he meant? He remarked I possess something of immense value and did not realize it. I find it hard to grasp their meaning since they do not speak our language well."

"Did he wear one?"

"I could not tell. Jorma said nothing about me having such a knife. Mayhap they do not know."

"Aye, perhaps. They move out of sight; shall we take our leave across the bridge?"

"What say you to taking the road on this side of the bridge? It does seem less traveled, which may suit us."

"You feel we should take this road?"

"I am asking you to choose the coastal pass road with me."

"Then I choose to travel with you, whatever the road."

Jahtara, Heddha, Trusted Companion, Fate's Choice, and Stolen Pleasure turned onto the Setting Sea road. The mist dissipated behind them, and the way forward brightened with the rising Solaura.

The Journey's many Paths

You know this.

Everyone advances along their path, understanding little of fellow trippers, hauling justification baggage, investing every step with ideology, burdening progress, following well-worn ruts, entrenching ever deeper impressions. We consciously or stupidly entangle companion travelers with our rationalizations, creating further impediments. Some allow themselves to be herded along increasingly constricted paths, wearing blinders and stuffing fears into hidden pockets. Even great faith can lead the self-confident down blind alleys too narrow to reverse course.

Enjoy life in the labyrinth; fill this intricate wandering with discovery and contemplation. Each juncture holds an opportunity to divest ourselves of baggage, empty the pockets, lighten the load, and seek wisdom. The path, with scenes of our own making, represents the distance traveled and the experience gained. The journey's purposeful intention embodies opening the heart! The tour never arrives at a final destination, and it's never too late to alter course. We follow different paths yet live the same adventure.

And so, our journey unfolds, written in invisible ink that appears at our presence.

Climbing up through the pass, the dei warmed. Tall, straight conifers, their bark reminding Heddha of fish scales, rose on the steepening canyon at acute angles. Sparse undergrowth grew under the trees and along the path covered with long brown needles that crackled when stepped on. They dismounted on the arduous slopes, walking up the pitch with the slippery needles adding to their toil. In contrast, a small river coursed down through the cleft, dancing and tumbling over and around rocks, obedient to the same gravity the small group labored to overcome. The trees provided shade, and the cool breeze off the water attenuated the heat.

Halfway up, Heddha waded into a pool, attempting to catch fish. Jahtara, never seeing someone fish without the aid of a hook or net, laughed until tears ran down her cheeks. Heddha lunged to and fro, stalking a fish only to see it slip away. Once, Heddha, with a fish trapped between her legs, attempted to grab it from the front, plunging headfirst into the pool. Through perseverance more than skill, she did manage to toss a large trout onto the rocks. Soaked from head to foot, she proudly displayed the fish, her broad grin shining. Jahtara felt her heart swell with pride in her friend.

As the Solaura sank before them, they stopped at the crest of a pass. Ridges continued to their front, part of a small range running to the sea. This path would take them several deis to transverse.

They camped on the edge of a meadow, allowing the animals to graze. While the catch cooked over coals on a latticework grille formed from woven green branches, Heddha and Jahtara put their backs to a log and gazed over the glowing embers towards the grazing animals in the meadow. The sky darkened, with deep reds visible towards the Setting and faint pink streaks in the high clouds chased by the noite.

Leaning forward to add wood chips to the embers, Heddha ventured, "Perhaps Jorma's statement at your departure involved a value you did not understand or needed to refine. I mean to say, a value in you rather than meaning the knife."

Jahtara put her head back against the log and watched the stars twinkle into existence, trying to divine some meaning there. "Me having a value formed my initial feeling, yet when you told me of Kasumi's knife, I turned to the knife. And if Jorma carries one, then mayhap his compatriots held similar knives. Otherwise, how would Alyeska come by such an object?"

"By these men, either directly or through the third."

"Aye. Alyeska could be involved in their disappearance or received the knife from the third."

"Too much remains unknown," said Heddha turning their supper over the heat.

Jahtara reached into her pack removing the knife. The metals sparkled in the firelight. "What could he mean?" She held it up to examine closely. "For it appears solely a knife. Unusual metal, fine artistry, expensive gold inlay," she continued drawing the knife from the exquisite sheath, "acute edge yet unusual blunt tip. Certainly, not made for thrusting. A fine, beautifully made blade yet still a knife."

"Perhaps he meant you have an edge that needs honing to realize your value."

"Saying I am dull then."

"Sharp, very sharp."

"Aye, I sleep in the knife box."

And after a pause, Heddha mused, "Could it involve your position as prinus or mayhap the alliance somehow?"

"Do you mean the dowry or my value as a broodmare?" Jahtara shrugged, saying, "I wish I knew. Now, all I know is my mouth waters from the smells of the evening meal."

Sitting by the warmth of the fire's glowing residue, they savored the hard-won trout under a sky filled with the effervescent brilliance of a starry noite.

Five deis later at middei, Heddha and Jahtara stood on the last low ridge descending to the sea. Through the trees, they glimpsed deep blue patches and, on the breeze, a hint of a salten sea.

Their journey through the forest passed uneventfully yet quite enjoyable. The flora thickened and diversified after the first ridge, including various evergreens, with delightfully pungent smells. Broad-leafed riparian trees cast dappled light on the rippling waters along the streams. The undergrowth consisted of shrubs with marvelous flowers, giant ferns, berry bushes taller than your head, and herbs, including some new ones unknown to Heddha. She dallied to harvest some and ran to catch up, explaining their signatures and uses to Jahtara. The streams teemed with fish and shelled creatures providing tasty suppers along the road. Though they often heard the hoots and calls of birds, they seldom saw them in flight. The woodlands were overflowing with ungulates and small carnivores, although they rarely caught sight of the more concerning predators. Even so, at noite, they kept the fire built up.

They occasionally passed folks heading to their homesteads or into the valley for trade. Riding past a stone lodge in a beautiful dell, they decided not to spend the noite as excellent camping was available. A short fall of water cascaded into an idyllic meandering brook at the edge of the dell's meadow. The valleys and windward ridges were shrouded in mists most morgn, making the ground and foliage damp, but by middei, everything dried in the warm breezes, including their traveling party.

Finally, they came within short walking distance of the Setting Sea. Heddha ran ahead; the slower-moving Jahtara and animals would not constrain her impatient curiosity. Where the road turned Solauraward, a broad beach ran the contrary way. Reaching the shore, Jahtara saw Heddha's discarded boots and leggings wet to the knees. She sat digging her hands into the warm sand, letting it spill through her fingers, exclaiming, "Is it not amazing? The water's warm and salty, stretching as far as I can see, possibly farther. Let us spend the noite. I want to listen to the waves and wake to them in the morgn."

They rode up the shore, leading the animals to shade in a hollow. Returning to the sand, Jahtara saw Heddha's clothing piled in a heap. Gazing up, she saw Heddha skipping through the waves, kicking and splashing slews of water above her head, again astonishing Jahtara with her natural ease unclothed. In broad deilight! The only times Jahtara occupied a naked state beside her birth occurred in the bath draped with towels when she stood. She grew up conditioned to cover her body. Heddha's nakedness seemed so innate. Heddha jumped high out of the water, waved for Jahtara to follow, and fell with arms and legs outstretched, crashing into a wave rolling to the shore, lost from sight. The water looked irresistible! Jahtara left her garments trailing along the beach, running and high stepping into the water until she fell laughing into the sea.

Jahtara and Heddha spent the rest of the afternoon playing in the combers, jumping over and diving under the constantly advancing waves. Laughing and clinging to each other, the rollers pushed them up the shore and pulled them down again. They lay on the hot sand baking while talking of their past, then moved to a shaded, shallow pool to continue their cozy chat.

The Solaura sank lower, and they found themselves lying on the sand again, Jahtara on her side facing Heddha, who lay prone, head cradled on her arms. Jahtara grasped a hand full of warm sand, letting it stream from her fist along Heddha's backbone, following the curves from shoulders to the small of her back.

"Heddha, how did you first know you loved the squire?"

"I cannot say precisely. When a sprout first appears, one cannot say what flower it will grow into or how bountiful it will become." She turned her head towards Jahtara to continue, "It grew from small things: a curl falling across his forehead, a smile when not expected, and small kindnesses. Touch, aye, touch, like the Luna's reflection on a lake, created by both possessed by neither. A reflection commemorated and grown in the heart."

Jahtara leaned closer, wiping the sand off Heddha's back, then

kissed her shoulder, tasting the salty aftermath of the afternoon, saying, "I desire to create such a love."

They sat up facing the Solaura, watching it sink into the Setting
Sea, lost in their thoughts and glowing after the new pleasures of this
dei.

The next dei, the sea rose with a wind: the waves crashing onto the
shore, creating a fine spray, delighting Heddha. They walked back
towards the road while the wind, picking up sand, stung their ankles.
Sitting on rocks by the road to slip on their boots, they watched a
two-wheel cart coming up the dirt track from Solauraward. A womon
walked to one side of the hackney, a shawl over her head, with a man
holding his hat tight and walking with the steed. Jahtara approached
them for information while Heddha spied three younglings with just
their eyes peering above the sideboards.

In response to Jahtara's inquiry, the man told of two small villages
to Solauraward with a three dei journey between them. Continuing
a couple of luna quarterns further, a larger town, Concupia, sat on
a bay, and for a small ferriage, one could proceed on Solauraward
or head inland. He continued in some detail to describe the road,
villages, and their inhabitants, seemingly unconcerned about carrying
on with his journey.

Heddha picked a few round leaves growing at the roadside and
offered them to the younglings. All three pairs of eyes darted to their
mother, coming up alongside the cart, who nodded to Heddha. While
the three enjoyed the sweet peppery taste of the treat, Heddha talked
quietly to their mother. Afterward, the younglings sat on supplies
piled in the hackney cart, waving goodbye to Heddha and Jahtara,
who turned Solauraward.

"What did you learn from the womon," Jahtara asked before journeying too far.

"She suggested bypassing the smaller villages, traveling on to Concupia. Less chance we will attract attention in the larger town."

"Then the port of Concupia awaits us!" pronounced Jahtara.

After a luna mediety of alternating sandy beaches, rocky shores, and deep forest, they crested a hill to view a wide bay, narrowed to the sea by a dune-covered spit. A town sat on their side of the estuary, which widened in its final bend, tapering to enter the Setting Sea. Concupia started with docks extending into the bay, continued up a mild slope, and finally dotted the steeper pitches beyond. Boats and ships of all kinds populated the inlet and docks. Concupia constituted a township of the traveled. Commerce drew merchants and tradespeople of all ilks from inland and seaward: raw and produced goods traveled every direction. Transitory teamsters riding the coastal range from inland and seafarers from the saltwater basin's maritime perimeter contrasted with the town's peered administrators, townsfolk, stevedores, and piscators. Travelers from and to various destinations added to the transient population. Those closest to the bottom rungs feed off them all: thieves, pickpockets, grifters, and beggars. Finally came those some would place in this last group while others would elevate to loftier heights; in truth, a continuum exists between those genuinely committed to spiritual enlightenment and those who use the facade to advance themselves. Knowing what lies in another's heart remains difficult to divine, and those who seek the sacred, at times, can get drawn into the flame.

To Heddha and Jahtara, the sights and sounds of Concupia excited and bewildered. The thoroughfares and stalls crowded with people were a fluctuating maze of wide throughways to dank alleys, often changing just by crossing a street. After getting rebuffed by several people, they came upon a market square and spied a youngling who seemed to pester everyone entering. He approached them, offering to hold their mounts for a small fee. They declined the offer but asked for suggestions on lodgings.

"Well now, that might depend on your purpose," he said, looking them and the animals over. "Methinks you not like the seafarer's hostels, though they ought to like you. Hoity-toity inn neither, lest you lookin' for a noite's work. Methinks no, not that kind anyways. You thinkin' of stayin' here ways a good portion?"

"Fair," Heddha replied, taking a liking to the boy.

He smiled broadly, "Methinks I know of a berth for you ma'ams; a boardin' house of my auntie's. It be clean, eats fillin', and there be a stable. Auntie likes them who stay a fair portion."

"You being the stable boy," Jahtara ventured.

"You be right."

"You could direct us, of course."

"For a small coin, I be takin' you."

"Lead away, youngling."

Whether by fate or choice, they ended up with a pleasant corner room providing a refreshing breeze and salient views of the river and bay. They sat on a rock wall overlooking the bay in the cooling evening breeze, drinking steaming black tea with milk. The proprietor turned out so delightful they ended up calling her Auntie. Most seemed to call her Auntie, and now they weren't sure if the stable boy was kin. Heddha and Jahtara watched two ships preparing to weigh anchor on the ebbing tide and could hear shouted orders riding the breezes.

"What becomes our intention in this place," Heddha said, stifling a yawn.

"Besides sleeping in a bed for a noite?"

Heddha nodded, her stifling having failed.

"Do we need a plan," Jahtara replied halfheartedly.

"For the short piece, mayhap not, yet the expectation for the whole would call for one."

"And your design?"

"Before crossing paths with you, I aimed to make my way Solau-raward to find work."

"Crossing paths! You attempted to steal my mount," this said with a grin and wink. "Why Solauraward then?"

"A place no one knew me, and the great distance seemed advantageous. The tales of this place Solauraward told of much work and, although vague, involved mining. I am uncertain if I could work the mines, yet incidental work might exist.

"And presently, what changed?"

"Well, now I have a traveling confidant and a steed you helped me steal, I might add! This seems for the good. My traveling companion stands hunted in two realms and remains the interest of some strange (what word did they use)... explorers. Probably not to the good."

"Let us not forget you wounded a prinus and three cnihts."

"Oh aye, thank you, I forgot," followed by one of Heddha's wry smiles. "Overall, the best approach follows not committing to one locality for overly long."

A black cat with yellow eyes came along the wall and proceeded to rub its head and neck against the two, purring loudly. When Jahtara scratched along its jaw and behind the ears, it rolled onto its back, exposing a swollen pregnant belly that Heddha could not resist stroking.

As their eyes met over the feline, Jahtara asked, "You wish to continue with me then, Heddha?"

"Without doubt. Adventure with a true companion furnishes life with shared enjoyment. My anger flowed from fear. Now my eyes take in all directions instead of narrowly focusing over my shoulder. I know that whatever our journey presents, one or both will find a solution. I still have misgivings, yet it does not bind me with rage."

"Airy words for someone with feet planted firmly on the ground. Heddha, I am not sure I could have survived my wanderings without you anchoring me to the practicalities of life. I easily get lost in how things should be instead of how they are. In my heart, I treasure your effort to keep me from floating away on my thoughts."

The cat kneaded Jahtara's thigh enjoying Heddha caressing her underbelly, and Heddha, in turn, felt the soothing vibration of the cat purring. Both womyn watched the two ships as the Solaura sank toward the silvery line separating sky from sea. One ship tacked with modest sail to gain the channel following the tide while the other unfurled sail to trail after.

Jahtara spoke again, "Let us halt awhile here. On the morrow, I will find a coin changer. I have mostly gold coins left, and it will be difficult or suspicious to use those to make purchases. I saw a dealer in blades when passing through town. Mayhap others exist. See if any have wares resembling the strangers' blade or any knowledge of such a blade. We can keep our ears open for any news from Solauraward or the lands towards the rising."

"Do you think asking after the knife will arouse suspicion?"

"Mayhap, you must take care. Just observe and generally inquire about fine artisanship or perhaps gold inlay. Take the youngling with you; he may help allay any misgivings of the locals and know of other merchants to visit."

"Good," Heddha answered, watching the vessels depart. They cleared the headland with all sails unfurled, the first tacking Solauraward, and the trailing ship headed straight out, silhouetted against the Solaura as it slowly sank into the Setting Sea.

Heddha rose with the Solaura and joined Auntie in the kitchen preparing breakfast. She enjoyed a scone with currant jelly and tolerated the local morgn drink with goat milk to cover the bitterness. She arranged with Pug (the youngling's name) to meet at the market after finishing his chores. She did discover he and Auntie were kin. Heddha didn't know his name's origin; however, she suspected it related to his pugnacious nature.

Heddha first went to the docks and found a woman selling bread and drink off a cart. After befriending the woman by asking about work, she lingered, listening to the dock workers. She then helped the woman move her cart to the corrals where the teamsters kept their animals. Once the teamsters hitched their teams and drove off, she bid farewell to the woman, having gleaned many particulars of interest.

Midmorgn, she met Pug at the market. After he finished loading purchases into a carriage for a wealthy merchant's spouse, Heddha, quite hungry, asked Pug for suggestions. Even though Pug ate a large meal at Auntie's, he led the way to a stall, and Heddha allowed Pug to order for them. After paying, Heddha sat on a low wall surrounding a fountain with figurines. Water spouted from the mouths of fish onto a womon with gills, a fan-like fin down her back, and webbed hands. Her iridescent eyes and blue-green fins created a mesmerizing effect, particularly her alluring eyes.

Pug brought the food over, handing Heddha hers. It consisted of chopped veggies with crumbled soy cake cooked and wrapped in a flatbread. The sweet, tangy sauce proved quite tasty.

Heddha asked Pug about the fountain. Plainly he became uncomfortable looking at the naked figure with Heddha sitting right there and, when pressed, said it represented a sea goddess, nymph, or seductress. Heddha nodded, remarking it seemed strange people could walk by naked statues without a second thought, yet if the figure came to life, they would put it in the stocks. The image brought a grin to Pug's face and a playful cuff to the side of his head from Heddha.

Pug knew of some blade sharpeners in the market. He suggested a blade dealer might serve better. They began with a dealer Pug said made the blades himself. Upon arriving, Heddha did indeed see a diverse selection with a smelting and blacksmith area behind the storefront. The proud principal smelter mistook the pair for emissaries of some important, an impression Heddha did little to dispel. He showed them the ores, charcoal, limestone, and tailings bins. After watching men breaking up the ore with massive mauls, the smelter explained the bloomer for roasting and how he added fluxes in the oven. The proud blacksmith extolled his lamination method. He employed engravers and artisans to do the refined work on the haft, blade, and scabbard. Although Heddha's experience was limited, the results accounted for the best pieces she'd seen, yet didn't come close to the quality needed to produce Jahtara's knife and sheath. None of the artisanship matched the heavy though balanced heft of the Jahtara's knife. After visiting two more dealers and seeing a variety of blades, nothing displayed appeared akin to Jahtara's knife.

Leaving the last shop, Heddha asked if Pug wanted an interest in a proposition benefiting them both. After a brief explanation and seeing an advantage in it for himself, he agreed if it didn't take away from his duties at Aunties. With Pug's assent, they made for the docks.

Perhaps due to his inclusion in Heddha's scheme, Pug said, "Heddha mighty fussy on a knife."

"Why say you so?"

"You be talkin' all dei pretendin' not to look."

"Was I that obvious?"

"Cause I be with ya all dei, Pug got sharp eyes. At the smelter's shop, one man says another look also."

"One of the crafters?"

"Aye, he say a man ask after such a knife, showin' his as an example."

"Pug, did he say he knew this man or where to find him?"

"No, cept this man wore a blue robe with a hood."

"Have you ever seen such a man?"

"At Quest Alley, men and womyn wear such robes."

"Good, excellent! You earned an extra coin this dei, Pug."

Arriving at the docks, Heddha told Pug she looked for a shipping firm named Morgn Star Carriers. Pug led the way to a two-story building and warehouse occupying a block just off the docks. Pug explained they were one of the biggest shippers, owned by a patrician house under a keyn's charter. When Heddha asked about the company's administrator, Pug knew precious little except his reputation as a stern man. They entered through double doors going upstairs to an area with several doorways and a counter across one side. Two men were conferring behind the counter: a short, thin man with an overbite and a sizable well-dressed man with his hair tied back with a black ribbon. When the large one noticed Heddha and Pug, he inclined his head toward them, and the thin one came over.

"Best of the dei to you. How may I serve?" he said upon reaching the counter.

"Thank you. We were wondering if we could interest you in our services."

"And what services would that be," he asked, looking at them closely.

The well-dressed man glanced up also to inspect the two: a young womon in riding clothes and a street urchin. He went back to examining the papers in his hand.

"Cleaning and making presentable the berths aboard your ships. We would clean them when passengers left after the voyage and...."

"Disembarked," interjected Pug.

With a double take on Pug, she corrected, "Quite right, disembarked. Then make them ready for the next voyage."

The clerk turned to catch the other's eye, who frowned and added a slight shake of his head. He turned to go into the office in the back.

"I am sure our crews aboard ship supply those services," the clerk said, dismissing them.

"Apparently not, at least from the passengers' complaints," said Heddha louder, making no effort to leave.

The large man's voice was heard from the other room, "Bring them to my office, Magar."

Magar opened the half-door, letting them through the counter, and showed them into the administrator's office. The office occupied the building's corner, with the docks and quays visible outside the second-story windows. Heddha noticed the immaculately organized office appeared well-appointed with a large table and leather chairs befitting the man's size.

The administrator sat behind the table, his back to the corner, with bright windows on either side, making it challenging to see his expression. He left Heddha and Pug standing in the light facing him. He motioned for Magar to stay, introducing himself as, "Chief Administrator and Director of Morgn Star Carriers - Atfi Dunnyn. Who, then would you be?"

"Heddha and Pug, sir."

When she didn't elaborate, the director sternly said, "Why do you malign the Morgn Star Carriers, an enterprise of a doux of the realm and under the patronage of the keyn?"

Pug took a step back, keeping his eyes to the floor. Expressionless, Heddha said, "My intention, I assure you, did not infer any disrespect, honorable sir. Only to repeat what I heard from those working the docks and local establishments with the intent of offering our services to remedy such grievances."

"What would an urchin and a conveyer of street gossip know of cleaning my staterooms?"

"Why, my experience derives not from the street, sir. While I have experienced refined gossip, serving as a retainer to a laud. Chief among my duties included cleaning my laud's quarters. Pug here, a stable groom has experience cleaning the manure of his charges."

In the following silence, Heddha glanced back to see Pug trying to pull his head into his shoulders. She placed a hand on his arm and guided him forward a step.

The director leaned forward into the light, exposing a slight upturning at the corners of his mouth. "Magar, what ships have we in port at present?"

"The Wave's Crest, sir. Arrived this middei."

"Captain Ikbar, if I am not mistaken."

"I believe in the warehouse at this moment."

"Have the good Captain meet us at Wave's Crest."

Atfi Dunnyn put on a light coat and led them down the stairs and into the street. At the quay, they turned upriver and then onto the next dock extending into the bay. The pier teemed with men carrying containers down planking to load into wagons. Large nets swung on and off ships tied alongside the moorage. The dockmaster warned them to keep clear in a loud voice until he saw the director and quickly tipped his hat with a slight bow.

Warf side at Wave's Crest waiting for the Captain, Heddha stood in awe of the vast ship with its tall triple masts and sweeping lines. The magnitude of the vessel dwarfed her. When the captain arrived, introductions proceeded without explanation, only that the director wished to inspect the staterooms.

The captain seemed amiable and immediately grasped that Pug and Heddha were unfamiliar with sailing ships. Once up the plank onto the main deck, he pointed out the quarter deck at the stern and the poop deck situated over the captain's quarters. The two staterooms were to the main deck's stern, each with large windows. Before or fore of these on either side of the vessel were privies without doors. They were boards with holes, creating a shelf over the ship's side with a wall at the back. They put a curtain across one side when womyn were on board. Forward to this came moderate single rooms with windows port or starboard. Then four small rooms, two on each side with portholes and one or two bunks, depending on whether passengers wished to share berths.

When Heddha asked about womyn traveling, the captain thought it quite common, especially with the larger staterooms. Emissaries or merchants sometimes traveled with wives, families, or escorts.

The rooms themselves were a mess. The beds were made and straightened, but no one aired the bedding. The sheets, if washed, were cleaned in salt water, making them stiff and course. The shelving, tables, and chairs were swept clean onto the floor and left. Heddha suggested opening a window to air the rooms, and the director seconded. Fortunately, the privies were dark because Heddha didn't want to see what caused the foul odor.

A stairway amidship went up to the captain's area, including a small galley for the officers and passengers who ate at the captain's mess. The party retired to the captain's quarters while an officer summoned the sailors responsible for cleaning the rooms. The captain and director sat at the mess table while Heddha and Pug stood to one side.

The Director started by mitigating his earlier statement to Heddha. "Your street gossip seems neither maligning nor untrue. Yet I am unsure I need to pay for services that sailors should do with proper direction."

"Perhaps, sir," Heddha responded. "If I may talk to those cleaning the rooms."

"I appreciate you pointing out the deficiency, yet these sailors work for the Morgn Star Carriers and answer only to the firm."

An old, stooped sailor accompanied by a youngling stepped into the cabin, and they both touched their caps with their hand. The old sailor grinned and blurted out on spotting Pug, "Aye, Pug, what ye do onboard ship." Then catching himself, said, "Begging thy pardon, Cap, Third's in the warehouse."

"You know this lad," questioned the director.

"Aye, sir. He be kin to Auntie."

Turning to Pug, the director asked, "The Auntie with the boarding house off High Street."

"Aye, sir," he affirmed, wondering what trouble he had stumbled into now.

"Ha! By the fates. Auntie's husband sold fish to my father's storefront in the fish market. When your uncle washed overboard, I brokered the sale of his three fishing boats in exchange for the boarding house and stable." He slapped Pug on the back, saying, "Ha! Well, Heddha, I believe you have some questions for old salty here."

"Grateful, sir. Sailor, you consider the cleaning of the staterooms done well?"

"Well," he started, eyes darting between the director and captain. "Aye, ma'am. Me and the youngling did clean em better than our bunks. And the third officer checks us."

"How did you clean the privies?"

"Splashed a pail o' bay water on them, we did."

"Captain Ikbar, this man a good sailor?"

"One of the best."

"Director, womyn pay a fare equal to men?"

"If they take up the same space, we charge them equal fare."

"Sir, I put forth, your paying passengers expect a different measure than the sailors cleaning the staterooms. I am suggesting accommodating such measures for both the men and womyn."

"And what specifically would you suggest?"

"Giving each berth a thorough cleaning when in port and airing the bedding and cabin. Also, washing the sheets with soap and freshwater followed by drying in a good breeze. Finally, scrubbing the privies with soda ash, prepared from burned seaweed."

"Anything else?"

Heddha considered pushing further. She decided a seed unplanted became a meal lost. "A door on one of the privies would do to make the womyn more comfortable on a ship filled with men. In the refined household I served, the privy seat were rings made of pottery, easier to clean than the wood. Truly, sir, I believe your voyagers will be pleased and mayhap your berths booked to the fullest."

Atfi Dunnyn, Chief Administrator and Director of the Morgn Star Carriers, sat tapping his chin, then said to the captain, "Captain Ikbar, if you will have the ship's carpenter build a door with a latch." Turning to Heddha, he continued, "I will supply the materials needed. If you could say where to obtain the potash and pottery rings."

Heddha turned to Pug, who nodded.

"Good. Have Pug come by on the morrow to get a tentative schedule, and Captain Ikbar can inform you of his schedule for starting on this ship. I am certain we can come to terms on remuneration. Pug, my best to your aunt." He strode out the cabin door ducking his head to miss the lintel.

Captain Ikbar walked them to the gangway and negotiated with Heddha to clean his quarters for a favorable sum. On returning to Auntie's boarding house, Heddha bought Pug a sweet roll. By the fates, he brought luck this dei. Heddha couldn't wait to share her dei with Jahtara.

Jahtara awoke with the Solaura full on her face. She rolled, opening her eyes to the view of the harbor out the opposite window. Heddha wasn't beside her, her clothes gone; she must have arisen early.

The luxurious, warming Solaura's rays filled the room. A cooling breeze conveyed gulls' squawking, seals' barking, and busy harbor sounds through the room. Jahtara stretched, arching her back before sinking back into the pillows. It seemed like a lifetime ago since experiencing extravagance like this. Each dei filled with lavishness, brimming with the pleasures of privilege, yet she viewed it as a prison and ran at the first sign of her royal charge. Jahtara knew what lay in store for a prinus of the realm. Yet, she lived in a fantasy believing her intended would be charming and understanding. She filled her mind with deceptions, then escaped responsibility when the spell shattered. At least she shared this new life with a familiar spirit better than any imagined prinus.

Downstairs she enjoyed a cup of Auntie's morgn beverage and found the rich black drink stimulating. She met Pug on his way to meet Heddha but decided to head out alone.

She began with a contented smile and exuberant heart. Turning down High Street towards town, she could see the harbor and lower Concupia laid out before her. Auntie advised her of an honest coin changer's whereabouts, and Jahtara looked forward to exploring.

When she turned onto the lower road, a shoeless womon dressed in rags pleaded for coin. Jahtara, distracted by the gaps in her teeth, jarred against a sour-smelling man. She absently pardoned herself before realizing he groped her. Remembering Auntie's warning, she checked for the coin purse hanging on a leather strap around her neck, relieved at finding the coins still there. Turning back, she saw the cackling crone, the man nowhere to be seen. Kneading her arm where the libertine jolted her, she discovered a small bleeding scratch.

She determined not to let the incident ruin her day and to appear less vulnerable, tied her hair back, and closed her jerkin. She pictured Heddha in her mind, feeling her body begin to stride with determination and purpose, not making eye contact with those she passed on the street. The guise worked like a glimmer; she appeared invisible to most of those she passed.

Jahtara discovered the coin changer in a small storefront just off the main quay. It consists of a tiny anteroom bound with a low worktop on one side. At the entrance sat a man, a knife visible at his belt and leaning in the corner, a large stone club with an ornately carved wooden handle. Jahtara nodded to the man and sat when the proprietor gestured towards a chair.

"How may I be of service this fine morgn, fair one?" He said through a neatly trimmed grey beard.

"I desire to change a coin."

"Ah, you have come to the right place then. May I observe the piece?" When Jahtara brought it out, he remarked, "Ah, a fine mint, surly. I have met this coinage before, from the treasury of lineage Davuda if I be not mistaken." He examined the coin with a glass making his eye appear prominent. He lowered the glass a trifle, exaggerating his next question, "Do you travel from there?"

After a slight pause, Jahtara lied, "No."

The changer stared at her with brows raised, waiting for elaboration. When none followed, he said, "I see. In any case, an excellent purity." He placed the coin on a balance scale, adding small counterweights until the mechanism reached equilibrium. He laid the gold piece on a cloth between them and counted out silver and copper pieces of the local coinage. "Does this seem fair, lass?"

"More than, expert changer."

"As I said, a fine piece of excellent purity, and if you obtain more, I would be honored to change them."

Jahtara's eyes drifted to the man in the corner.

"Ah, deaf as a bell ringer and responds only to signs from me."

"I might require your services again, sir. Thank you for your hospitality," she said, placing her coins in the pouch.

"May our dealings always be such a reciprocal pleasure," responded the changer lifting the gold coin.

Back in the street, Jahtara felt unsure of her purpose. She wished to see the city but didn't want to do so wearing the blinders of dispassion that delivered her to the coin changer. She stood at the head of the avenue running up through town and veering across the pitch to the hill's crest. There Jahtara could make out a stone structure. Her legs were begging for exertion, so she gave them the hilltop.

She proceeded up through town until she saw the market square down one of the cross streets. She ate a small plate of steamed beets, kale, and red beans drizzled with butter from a food stall. She also found water to drink at a public washing fount and learned the stone structure contained a cistern with an exceptional vista of the area. Before leaving the fount, she moistened a scarf and tied it around her neck; the dei would certainly warm during her excursion. Jahtara enjoyed the unusual treat of a ramble abroad without escorts where no one knew of her refined bearing.

She climbed the hill observing the architecture changing from individual storefronts to homes with shops beneath, then larger houses. Starting across the pitch, the abodes became larger estates on tiered parcels of land. One plaque near the crest piqued her interest. It read:

Official Agency and Residence
Thane Adron Esryn Kirrydon, Administrator of Concupia
A mesne laud to Doux d'Oilly,
In freehold tenure by serjeanty and in homage to Su Liege
Laud Sovereign Keyn Tergon II,
Serene Laud of the Middle Realms.

The thane's name brought back memories of her parents' palatial seat. Thane Kirrydon served as emissary to the lineage Davuda from Keyn Tergon II. They seemed a kind person with common roots who received their peerage in service to Keyn Tergon II. The thane possessed a wonderful smile, which they readily shared with the refined household. They married a younger womon, an arrangement advocated by the keyn. His liege laud claimed the right of marriage when this womon became widowed from her first husband, then married her to the future thane to control the land's descent, as no other heirs existed. Against many odds, the marriage grew into, if not love, respect, yielding two lovely daughters. After a couple of jahrs, the keyn recalled them to the Middle Realm, making them the administrator of Concupia. Jahtara doubted they would recognize her now, almost ten jahrs later and nearly six hands taller. She wished them well, continuing up the track to the cistern.

The vigor of the climb tested her stamina, and the welcome breeze over the crest refreshed her. Surrounding the cistern was a wide promenade from which she could look beyond the ridge to the road she and Heddha rode along into Concupia with its long stretch of white surf parading shoreward like the ranks of an advancing army. On the inlet side, she enjoyed a panoramic vista upriver of the bay narrowing among the hills. Seals hauled themselves onto the warm sands of the spit at the outlet to the sea. Across the bay, the land flattened into cleared pastures and farms. Below her, the township of Concupia flowed down the slope, spilling onto the docks and into the bay; a scattering of vessels floating at anchor making it appear pieces of the town broke loose to drift in the bay.

Jahtara discovered aqueducts gathered water from several jahr-round streams depositing it above the city. When back at the end of the promenade overlooking the town, she could make out a stone-covered effluent coursing out of the city to be covered by the dunes of the spit. She saw a swirl of gulls where discharge emptied into the sea.

Rested from the climb, Jahtara started to cool in the breeze and thought it best to start back. The journey back seemed shorter; her

steps quickened by the slope and a desire to share her dei with Heddha.

Heddha returned to the boarding house to discover Auntie and her
youngest daughter serving a supper of firm white fish in a dill sauce
and pickled Flinders Rose over wide egg noodles with garlic butter
and sprinkled roasted poppy seeds. After washing some of the dei
from her face and hands, Heddha joined Jahtara at the large dining table. They shared a most enjoyable meal with several boarders, including a middle-aged man and womon. The womon looked
perpetually flushed; whether from a reaction to her spouse's often
bawdy tales, exposure to the elements, or over-application of rouge
powder was difficult to determine. The man had married late, asking
for the hand of the youngest daughter of one of the firm's owners.
At twenty-five jahrs, her father feared she would forever be a spinster
and consented. Thusly the man advanced himself with the firm and
gained a permanent traveling companion. When younger, he traveled
extensively, gathering up his indelicate tales. They both seemed very
free with their particulars.

His current story occupied an awkward and humorous tale concerning travels with a companion through forested land and their
stop at an inn for the noite. His companion acquired a tick on his
rump and, unable to remove the mite himself, asked the storyteller for
assistance. The attempted removal commenced with his companion
bent over the bed, pants at his ankles, moaning from anguish when
the innkeeper entered the room with bed warmers and spied our nar-
rator on his knees, peering up the other's arse. The ensuing confusion
nearly resulted in a fire from the dropped warmers. Auntie asked him
to curtail the story due to the entrance of her youngest daughter, even
though tears rolled down her cheeks from the folly.

After the meal, Jahtara and Heddha went out to the fire pit to sip
their tea. Two gentlemen boarders, smoking pipes, were seated across
the crackling fire on another bench facing the bay. Auntie joined

them, plopping herself down in an oversized wooden chair, stretching her legs, crossing them at the ankles. She carried a large beer mug and soon produced a long-stemmed pipe, filling it with herb before lighting it with a taper from the fire. Puffing on the tavern pipe, she released, "Ahhhh, that feels right. I let the geyrles finish with the cleaning. My legs ache me something terrible this noite. I added the Flinders Rose to the fish, thinkin it would help me rheumatism."

"It certainly contributed to my appreciation of the meal, Auntie," Jahtara praised, with Heddha nodding her agreement.

"Pug tellin' me you and him gotta deal with Atfi Dunnyn," Auntie said, indicating Heddha with the pipe stem. "He gotta repute of being a hard man, yet me know he gotta soft spot at his marrow."

"Aye, ma'am, I agree. Besides, we do him some good and make us a bit of coin."

"No harm there. You all just be full of care on them docks. Lots of folks from strange places, and them dock workers not much better." Then Auntie seemed to drift off, pipe in her lap with a wisp of smoke wafting into the noite.

"So, you have become a deal maker on the docks now," Jahtara inquired.

"Pug and I have work cleaning cabins on ships upon their arrival," Heddha started, going through her dei, excitingly telling Jahtara of the blue-robed man inquiring about the knife and her afternoon on the docks.

The other two borders returned inside, and Auntie's chest rose and fell rhythmically. The two womyn conversed quietly in the light of the fire.

"It seems you have outdone me this dei. Very productive indeed." Jahtara proceeded with her account, including the tale of the Concupia administrator and their estate.

When Jahtara told of being groped in the street, Auntie, without opening her eyes, raised a finger saying, "Told ya, did I not." The finger then slowly returned to its mates, and her breath reverted to its slow rhythmic cycle.

Heddha gave Jahtara a wink, resuming their natter. "Jahtara, you pay for much of this journey. I wish to contribute by covering some of the expense."

"We each contribute in many ways, besides the money does not rightly belong to me, I suppose, since I fled the keyndom," Jahtara whispered.

"What of the morrow then?"

"Pug goes to Morgn Star Carriers in the morgn, right? You and he will clean the…?"

"Wave's Crest."

"Aye, Wave's Crest in the middei. In the morgn, we will search for the blue robes at… was it, Quest Alley?"

"Aye. Good, I rose early. Now I am off to bed hoping for another dei well spent on the morrow."

"My legs, after their climb, deserve an early repose also."

On their way in, Jahtara asked Auntie's oldest daughter to bring her inside before her joints stiffened in the noite air.

Realms of Desire

Desire seems such a funny thing, doesn't it? Funny meaning, strange and comical, but also delusional and obscuring. If you find a piece of chocolate in your hand, eat, enjoying it. Delight in the smooth, bittersweet taste, but know the delectation exists in you, not in the chocolate. Don't get attached to the illusion the mind creates, for such a perception proves empty.

Desire assumes many faces: want, take, need, wish, fancy, greed, envy, lust, hunger, grasping, seeking. Every one of these attachments sprouts hands for clinging. After obtaining a desire, the luster fades, and it's off after the next shiny abstraction, accolade, or power, the wanting more alluring than the having. Whole worlds subsist on fostering and feeding off these yearnings by fetishizing objects, emotions, and status. Can you imagine? All to get you to believe delight exists outside of yourself. Embracing this deceit allows others to profit from your self-doubt and ignorance.

Can someone make you love them? Of course, not! Yet, we believe others cause anger to arise in us or make us hate them. Dissatisfied desire or aversion can grow into doubt, anger, depression, or arrogance. These hungry ghosts of desire, with their needle-thin throats and balloted stomachs, can never be satisfied. A river has a source, as does desire. When the attachments of a clinging mind cease like a bird's flight leaves no trace, happiness spontaneously arises. Pure joy in the beauty of the world resides within you.

And yet desire and aversion continue, as does this story.

❦

The morgn dawned with an obscuring fog shrouding the lower bay, prompting a bell on the breakwater to toll its warning. Auntie opined the heat inland drew moisture off the sea.

Jahtara and Heddha sat in the kitchen, sharing a bowl of cooked rhubarb with honey. Auntie warned them to eat only a modest portion unless they desired a purging. They then went to the stables to borrow a cap from Pug. Heddha thought it best if Jahtara hid her distinctive copper locks. After arranging to meet Pug in the afternoon, they headed to the upriver area of town where most dock workers lived, searching for Quest Alley. Here the houses were haphazardly placed and made of more varied materials. Roofs took on a patchwork appearance from all the mendings. More dogs and children ran in the streets. Inhabitants decorated their porches with giant whale bones, knotted nets, and chimes made of thrasher teeth. They discovered a large marketplace containing a fountain used for potable water and washing. The buildings and stalls around the plaza sold or traded locally made, caught, or grown goods. Everyone seemed to know everyone else, judging by the chatter among adjacent booths and those passing by.

A person wearing a blue robe and carrying a basket of vegetables passed, and they simply followed. When the blue robe turned from the square onto a side street, the signage identified Quest Alley. The first buildings were taverns and a stable, followed by a small storefront with a sign touting the reading of tea leaves or the casting of stones. Next came signs proclaiming services for blessing new ventures, boats, or the recently birthed. One spiritual house offered varying levels of redemption for the appropriate fee.

Further up the alley, they encountered endorsed spiritual establishments providing arcane, esoteric, and spiritual study. Jahtara and

Heddha need not worry about losing the soul in the robe, for at the end of the alley, under a bluff, stood a high wood plank wall painted the blue of the robes. A circular gate with a stained wood arch halved the fence's run. Engravings on the archway symbolized the cycle of life, starting with birth and ending with death. The gate stood open, and they stepped over the raised threshold into a courtyard.

Single-story habitations bounded two sides of the yard. One side consisted of a kitchen, quite busy at the moment. The other side's purpose appeared less clear, possibly sleeping quarters. Against the escarpment was a twin-story lodge with a central gable overhanging the courtyard. A wooden walkway surrounded the main gathering area, covered by a cloth awning over the yard. Under the gable sat a small dais covered with a cushion.

As Jahtara and Heddha stood taking in the compound, a womon in the prescribed blue hooded garment approached, saying, "Greetings seekers, how may I serve?"

Heddha answered sincerely, "The beauty of your entrance drew us in. What takes place here?"

"We study our condition, seeking understanding and wisdom on our journey through life."

"Do not we all," Jahtara intoned with a smile.

The womon lifted her head to look Jahtara in the eye with a radiant smile. "Some more than others, sister. We seek truth with love and compassion in our hearts."

"And which truth do you seek?"

"The ultimate truth, beyond words. Our teacher will discourse with us soon. Why not tarry, hear the words, and meditate on them with us? We welcome you to join us for nourishment afterward."

This welcome fit Jahtara and Heddha's purpose, and they accepted an invitation to explore the compound. The low structure opposite the kitchen housed a dormitory with mats on the floor or tiered bunks: womyn in one portion and men in another, connected by a communal area. The lodge, extending two stories, opened to the meeting yard, and at its back rose the rock face of the escarpment with numerous ledges protruding from the rock holding candles. A spring bubbled from the back wall forming a pool at its base. The depth of the water was littered with pebbles just visible through the light reflecting on the surface. The womon seeker accompanying them explained each stone preserved a word engraved on it, placed there by seekers applying unique intention on the phrase. The muted, soaring space echoed the spring's babbling, adding weight to the lingering aspirations submerged below the surface.

Stairs on both sides led to a second floor above each wing. According to the accompanying seeker, the teacher's chamber occupied one lateral, and the other held an administrative workplace and an assistant's living quarters. A solitary meditator sat at the base of the stairs to the teacher's chamber.

Unexpectedly a clear oscillating note with harmonic resonances and increasing intensity filled the space. Their bodies absorbed the sound's slow oscillation, and the cliff face reverberated the sound to the surrounding city. The three emerged, observing that additional people had entered, and more stepped through the gate. Jahtara looked up to see a balcony protruding from the arched gable end with a long bell hanging from the ridge beam. She could still hear the campanular echoes returning from the surrounding hills, summoning those who wished to listen to the sage's wisdom or, barring that, a free meal.

Jahtara and Heddha decided to separate and obtain varied views of the compound and its inhabitants. Jahtara picked a spot on the steps leading down to the meeting yard from the sleeping dormitory. She could see the dais and across the yard to the food preparation area. The stairs raised her enough to see those sitting in the yard, although she saw only the backs of those in front. Jahtara observed a person in a blue robe enter to stand next to the small platform. She guessed a man from his stature, and when he lifted his head, pulling back the hood, she confirmed it. Smiling, he contemplated the gathered, starting on the side across from Jahtara, regarding everyone in turn and ending on Jahtara. She defocused her eyes, not engaging him, but he didn't linger; instead, he kneeled, sitting back on his heels.

Heddha worked her way along the front wall on the kitchen side of the gate. A couple of pushcarts, crates, and goats in a hay-filled pen filled the space. She leaned against one of the carts, turning her attention to the delectable smells from the kitchen. A robed man appeared under the gable, viewing those congregated. Seeing his gaze end on Jahtara, Heddha was relieved they covered her hair. The man then sat with his hands in his lap, and the aged teacher appeared, assisted onto the podium by another blue robe. The teacher's kind, ageless eyes moved with certainty, nodding to those he recognized sitting before him. He wore loose-fitting garments and, stepping out of his sandals, seated himself with a grace and ease belying his advanced age. Looking up again, he appeared pleased and almost surprised by the gathered crowd.

When the oratory commenced, Heddha concentrated on those wearing robes. Most were in the kitchen area, with more scattered around the compound. Two were by the front gate; one appeared a youngling, and the other an older man. The seeker, who greeted them earlier, stood on the wooden walkway behind Jahtara. Several seekers in blue sat throughout the listeners, but Heddha could only see their backs. That left those preparing food or listening at the wide pass-throughs of the eating area.

Heddha moved towards the walkway in front of the kitchen and up the two steps to get a better vantage point. Most of those in the food preparation room cut vegetables or stirred pots, while others set stacks of bowels on a serving table. Pug said a man inquired after the knife, yet Heddha couldn't think how to identify him, except for the blue robe. Then the thought struck her. If he were akin to Kasumi and Jorma, she could look for the round dark of his eyes, peculiar clothes, or the unusual closure of the boots. Maybe she could even spy the ornament worn in their ears. But, the problem persisted; all the seekers wore robes and hoods. It seemed impossible to get a closer look at each one individually. Then she recalled how the womon seeker greeted them. It seemed important to her to make eye contact with a radiate smile.

Heddha stepped closer to the low barrier separating the walkway and kitchen. The closest person looked up and, seeing Heddha's smile, made eye contact smiling back. Simple. She worked her way down the walkway smiling and making eye contact. When a view of someone's feet presented itself, she would bow her head, nod acknowledgment, and look at their footwear. This ploy didn't always work because the robes were longer on some, and others wore sandals or no shoes. After Heddha had covered the eating area, she saw most but not all of the men's eyes. She thought of retracing her steps to get the others' attention when she realized her movement garnered the assistant's scrutiny. She focused back on the lecturer, moving slowly to the railing. After a few heartbeats, during which she held her breath, the man returned his attention to the teacher.

Heddha's belly clenched; what caused this sudden apprehension? They didn't know if the man looked for the same knife or remained at Quest Alley. The strangers at Way's Respite seemed to recognize them, but the blue robe inquired about the blade before they arrived in Concupia. How long since she and Jahtara met? Heddha found it easy to lose track of time traveling with Jahtara. Was their meeting at the spring in the luna just past? No, it was longer. The man on the platform had stirred something up in Heddha. She turned slightly to catch sight of Jahtara, who smiled at her with a shrug of her shoulders.

Jahtara started casually observing those listening, but slowly her attention swung to the teacher. Resonance seemed to flow from him, and like the vibration from the bell, it affected her equilibrium, echoing through her. The feeling came not precisely from what he said. He seemed to strike a harmonious chord, bringing to the surface appreciation of 'a penetrating truth.' An upwelling of interconnectivity, not rational, but an emotional experience. She lost the sense of why 'Jahtara' came here and let the feeling wash over her.

Maybe this heightened sense of connectivity allowed her to see the assistant, seated next to the lecturer, turn his head toward the food area. She followed his line of sight, landing on Heddha. When Heddha returned her focus to the teacher, the deputy resumed looking to the front. Jahtara could sense Heddha's anxiety and gave her a weak smile and shrug, unsure of the source of Heddha's uneasiness.

At the finish of the teacher's talk, the assistant stood, asking for any questions for the teacher. A few in the gathering inquired about points in the discourse, and the teacher clarified an item or restated the question allowing the inquirer to comprehend the significance. The deputy thanked everyone for their presence, inviting them to share the middei meal.

Heddha waited for Jahtara in front of the dining room. On a small table sat a box for coin offerings, two bowls, one containing pebbles with a different word inscribed on each, and in the second, rocks with implements to mark your tailored intention. Jahtara dropped a coin in the box and looked through the pebbles with inscriptions. She found one with a word symbolizing her desire. Palming the rock, she strode off to the lodge until Heddha could only glimpse a wisp of movement in front of the candles.

Heddha stood watching after Jahtara, then sensing a presence turned, the teacher's assistant stood at her side. She felt the urge to draw her knife before seeing the man's smile.

"Thought you would lead the rush for food."

"Pardon?"

"I noticed a certain eagerness on your part to get near the vittles while the teacher spoke."

"Oh, the food. Aye, confronted with tempting aromas, the stomach quelled the ears. I ate little this morgn. Take no offense."

"Difficult to hear over the rumblings of the stomach, friend. Please enjoy, and find the teacher's message in action."

The seeker moved off, and only then did Heddha recognize the tense knot growing in her midsection.

Jahtara returned to the crowd of people shuffling into the dining area and saw Heddha talking to one of the seekers, who pivoted and walked into the kitchen. Heddha still gazed at his back when Jahtara laid a hand on her arm. Heddha jerked, turning to see who touched her.

"Oh, it's you. A little spooked just now. Can we leave?"

"You do not wish to eat?"

"Not here, please. Do you mind?"

After a slight hesitation, Jahtara said, "Of course not. Where to?"

"I feel the need to walk, create some distance. Pug showed me a place with delightful food, and I will introduce you to a water nymph."

They didn't speak on the brisk walk to the market square, but Jahtara noticed Heddha took a long look over her shoulder, leaving Quest Alley.

Jahtara sat on a stone bench under the shade of a tree. During the rattling walk from Quest Alley, she became overheated, resulting in a sheen of moisture covering her skin. Now sitting in the shade, an involuntary shiver overtook her. How could she have gone from feeling expansive to so abridged emotionally? Heddha showed her the fountain figurine and spoke of its textures, iridescence colors, the sensuous beauty of the water slipping across its surface, carrying on about the eyes following her, and the smooth, sensual surface calling to be touched and stroked.

Distracted, Jahtara had jabbered about the iridescent effect caused by flaked mica changing color depending on the light striking its surface, which the palace artisan explained to her once. Jahtara then started to ponder out loud about the image of the enticer luring men from their duty when Heddha cut her off by storming away, saying she would bring back food.

Jahtara missed something. She sensed the effect on Heddha but not the source. Jahtara would have liked to linger at the compound, prolonging her experience but felt Heddha's duress and agreed to leave.

When a youngling, Jahtara traveled to the sea and discovered a bizarre tide pool creature with multicolored tentacles waving with the motion of the rocky pool. She touched the swaying tentacles, which retracted so fast that she snapped her hand away. A slimy green blob remained, clinging to the rock. Jahtara felt like that creature now: contracted into a tight space, having withdrawn her tentacles from the world. Maybe this happened to Heddha! Heddha externalized her feelings about beauty, intimacy, and touching, being touched? And Jahtara babbled on about nonsense and temptresses.

Looking up, Jahtara considered the fountain from this new perspective. She focused on the coherent stream of water flowing from the mouths of the fish. She followed the interplay of force and gravity on the arc of water until it fell upon the womon's body. Small portions, stretched by the collision, attempted to break free but were pulled back by the liquid's attractive forces. Dynamic thin sheets of water washed over the form, clinging to even the dependent surfaces. Jahtara envisaged the water moving across her skin and breasts, feeling the kinetic force against her erecting nipples.

Heddha abruptly plopped down next to her with a sigh and set the food between them. Jahtara instinctively brought her hands up to cover her breasts and slowly lowered them, embarrassed by the abrupt motion. She continued to consider the nude figure in the fountain even as the passing townsfolk afforded it no attention. She reflected on the first time she met Heddha, standing naked in the spring, covered with sparkling droplets, then shifted to the vision of Heddha frolicking in the undulating waves. She sat up straighter, feeling the blouse pull against her taut nipples.

Heddha stared straight ahead as Jahtara turned towards her saying, "Has anyone caressed you like you talked about stroking the figurine?"

Staring ahead, Heddha sighed. "Because I appreciate the nymph's beauty does not signify I wish to be beguiled by her."

"I spoke of myself." Heddha turned to her. Jahtara continued, "I have never experienced love or felt the touch of a man."

Heddha's head dropped, staring at her open hand lying in her lap. Finally, she responded, "The two need not go together, Jahtara. Mind, being raised on a farm, I found copulation common, a farmer's way of increasing their fortunes."

"I know. I never imagined being touched in the way you spoke. I know I sound naive, Heddha. The squirelings thought I flirted when I wanted to join them in weapons training. One of my attendants had to explain the word to me. I never considered using my body to entice men. You seem so comfortable with your body, making me feel more confident in mine, like whiling away that dei on the beach."

"A delightful time." Heddha leaned closer. "The ministrant's son, Absan, and I spend part of a noite together, aye." Jahtara now leaned in. "Touch pulls you out of your head, two merging into one sharing a caress." Heddha put her hand over Jahtara's. "Like the gift of closeness on the beach."

A pair of legs appeared in front of the bench, and they quickly sat back. "Wacha all whisperin' bout?" Pug asked, eyeing the food.

"Pug, have mine. I am too overheated to eat." Heddha said, standing to let Pug sit. "Jahtara, desire water?"

"I am parched and need quenching. What will you carry it in?"

"A womon by the public fountain sells clay flasks in a leather case. She says if you get the outside wet, it keeps the water cool." And off she went, not looking back.

Jahtara pulled her jerkin together, saying to Pug, "Heddha says this food tastes delightful."

"Ish eee erry oood," his mouthful of reply.

The weather worsened the following morgn, and the whole bay lay covered by a somber gloom, thickening with distance, obscuring the inlet and town. The bell clanged its warning, the direction challenging to pinpoint in the sound-dampening fog.

Yesterdei Heddha and Pug had not returned by dinner, and Jahtara retired early. She heard Heddha slip in later, but they didn't talk. Heddha now slept peacefully, breathing deeply. Jahtara quietly left the room, heading for the kitchen, discovering Pug sitting at a kitchen table, eyes closed, his head held erect by an arm propped on the table. A bowl of porridge sat before him, gruel dripping down the up-right spoon onto his hand.

Pug didn't appear awake, so she said softly, "Pug dear." With no response, she removed the spoon, startling him awake with a confused expression.

Pug told Jahtara yesterdei's work took longer than expected. They first went to a pottery merchant and, after describing the commode bench, were assured such a piece would not be challenging to produce. They then set off for Wave's Crest, first cleaning the captain's quarters and mess, followed by the staterooms' more consuming task. They toiled away till the evening, dusting, scraping, and brooming away the grime, leaving the bedding and the washed coverings airing on deck. They thoroughly scrubbed the heads, one with a new door and latch. The Wave's Crest would sail later this dei, so they planned to return this morgn to remake the beds. Pug learned female guests would occupy two rooms and aimed to fetch fresh flowers for the staterooms on his way to the docks.

Although tired, Pug sounded excited about completing the task and getting coin from Captain Ikbar and the Morgn Star Carriers. Jahtara warned Pug about the fog, thinking the bedding would not dry in time, but he seemed unconcerned, saying the fog would burn off by midmorgn.

With Pug and Heddha's dei set, Jahtara would have to fend for herself. She walked out the back of the boarding house towards the stone wall, stepping over it, intending to sit. The thick fog diffused the light and dulled noise except for the nebulous ringing of the bell.

The wall behind her softened and sharpened in the dreamy mist. Jahtara cautiously approached the edge, the vegetation wet and slick where it dropped away to the bay. Except, this dei it merged with the murky dull grayness surrounding her. A sense of isolation sprang up to overwhelm her. The adventure of her flight from home faltered, and for the first time, she grew unsure of her course, what direction moved her forward. Heddha quickly integrated herself into life here, found work, and became independent of Jahtara with speed. What had Jahtara done: changed a stolen coin and taken a stroll to the water reservoir? The unknown obscured her vision; how could she move forward not knowing which direction she faced?

The knelling of the bell brought her around to the temple's bell. She wondered if she could bring back the feelings embodied in the teacher's message. She desired the closeness and intimacy the community offered. If not directly with the teacher, then perhaps with other devotees or the assistant. This direction appealed to her, and with the decision made, the orbed light of the Solaura appeared brighter through the fog.

The mist dissipated from upper Concupia as Jahtara stepped through the gate. Most of the followers were preparing a meal or cleaning the meeting yard. The devotee who showed her and Heddha around the preceding dei greeted Jahtara. The womon embraced her, and when Jahtara expressed a hope to be in the presence of the venerable teacher again, the womon smiled, telling her the teacher guided a session with a few advanced seekers but would speak just before the middei meal. Jahtara asked to help and soon assisted in straightening the dais and sweeping the walkways.

Jahtara sat in the same place as yesterdei for the daily dissertation, receiving nods of recognition from devotees she helped with cleaning. Like the previous talk, the assistant started by surveying those gathered, but this dei, his gaze lingered on Jahtara before he smiled and sat. Jahtara realized she'd forgotten to wear a cap covering her hair. Too late now. Besides, everyone appeared friendly and concerned here.

Scarce few beings comprise the right combination of elements to become influential guiding lights: a confluence of physical or mental uniqueness combined with a creative drive to move beyond previous achievements. They accomplish notable feats of heroic bravery, visionary diplomacy, sage insights, spiritual illumination, corporeal prowess, or expressive creativity. They reach such heights with an elegance that appears effortless yet belies their depth of diligence. Listening to the mentor's philosophical discourse Jahtara felt this mastery. He spoke to the emotional and the rational, his awareness touching her heart until it glowed with the light of love. A love that burned away the fog of doubt and fear, reflecting off every spirit present.

Afterward, while the teacher answered questions, Jahtara sat in revery, trying to fathom dream from reality. When a tear fell from her cheek onto the back of her wrist, Jahtara realized she wept with joy at the experience. The seeker who greeted her earlier came down the steps touching her shoulder, making eye contact, and exchanging smiles. Hugging for a long moment, the devotee introduced herself as Satilla, and they crossed to the dining hall to help serve the middei meal.

The teacher's deputy came through the kitchen, thanking each server for their service. Upon seeing Jahtara, his smile broadened. "I see you have returned to us," he stated.

"A wonder you recognize me."

"We all seek acknowledgment in the truth. I sincerely hope you find your heart's desire. Have you added a stone to the spring's water?"

"I have. Thank you for your thoughts, master."

He held up his hand, "I am an explorer of this world, a seeker, no master am I. If you wish to discuss your stone's intention, seek me out." He turned and joined others at a table.

Satilla nudged Jahtara with her elbow, bringing her back to the moment, "Apparently, some seekers receive more acknowledgment than others."

Jahtara spent the afternoon assisting with preparation for the early evening repast. She marveled at the turn the dei took. Her heart began the dei in solitude, without direction, and now she contributed to a community. She, the prinus, the privileged, the served one, shared a communion, swept floors, and attended others. It lightened her heart and provided direction for her desire to share herself for the common good.

After cleaning up, the approaching darkness quieted the compound, and activity slowed. Small areas of light showed devotees talking or moving to the dormitories. Jahtara stood by the dormitory, unsure what to do, unwilling to leave. Satilla's wave of goodbye set her in motion. Jahtara hadn't brought Heddha to mind since this morgn when she left her sleeping. It seemed strange not talking in over a dei after depending on each other's constant company.

Crossing towards the gate, she noticed movement in the common room. The teacher's assistant prepared to leave with two other seekers. They separated at the door, and the deputy moved towards the lodge.

Jahtara had come to the compound with Heddha, seeking knowledge of the knife and its connection to the strangers. They found no link, no strangers with unusual eyes or beautifully crafted artifacts. Jahtara, though, fortuitously found a sense of belonging, a connection to a community, a family. Without conscious thought, she turned to catch the deputy entering the lodge.

The deputy crossed to the stairs ascending to his chamber. The lodge's subdued light revealed a solitary meditator sitting among the shifting shadows and faint burbled sounds of the spring. The assistant's foot reached the first riser when Jahtara touched his arm. When he turned, Jahtara caught a glimpse of his darkened face under the hood, brows knotted, and bottom lip chewed in contemplation of some deep problem. She stepped back at his sideward glance. Then the deputy's head came up, his countenance relaxed, and a warm smile of recognition appeared, erasing all sense of his prior state.

"Pardon my intrusion, deputy," she said, intending to leave.

"Nonsense, you have rescued me from what I did not wish to ponder." Then casting an eye to the meditator, he indicated up the stairs, taking her hand and leading. She hesitated, unsure of her first step but then trod lighter, remembering the dei and the place.

At the top, he pulled a curtain aside and entered an ample anteroom with a table, two chairs, and some books on a shelf. Toward the lodge's center hung an open curtain revealing a bed against a walled railing with the dancing light of candles dimly seen on the ceiling beyond.

"Simpler to talk here and not disturb the other seekers," he said in a muted voice, closing the curtain to the stairs. "I have some cold tea and can add a refresher to soothe the spirit. I find it quite restorative at the end of the dei."

Jahtara nodded, not trusting her voice. She didn't expect to find herself in the deputy's chambers. She wasn't sure what possessed her intention.

"I attend to the duties of my office here." He continued, bringing down two mugs. "Well, most of the non-spiritual ones; the worldly duties the mentor deems not in his realm." Taking an unusual flask down from the shelf, he poured a dark liquid into the bottom of a mug, filling the cups from the teapot. "Truly, it's the spiritual duties fulfilling my desire. What brings you to me this noite, child?"

As he brought the tea to the table, she considered what did bring her here. She enjoyed the community, working together for a common cause. The teacher articulated a palpable love, and Jahtara wanted to share the experience. Covering her thoughts, she tasted the cool liquid, the initial flavor bitter, tingling in her throat. "Mmmm, an unusual taste." She continued, "I encountered a sense of belonging here, elusive in my past." Her lips feeling dry, she drank more of the tea before going on, "I wish to find a community or family since I seem, at the moment, to be lacking in one. I desire to belong, become part of something, and my time here allowed me to experience a possible fulfillment of this desire. I sense an..." Her words came tumbling out, her mind racing, and then Jahtara couldn't articulate; her thinning thoughts receded at an alarming rate. Her cheeks flushed. She slipped into that young girl discovering sword fighting wasn't what the squirelings expected of her. Her lips and tongue seemed puffed up. The room changed focus: the background fading with the foreground emphasis sharpening. Jahtara looked into the deputy's face; his sparkling eyes danced over her face in the candlelight.

He smiled tenderly, reaching up to tuck a curling lock behind her ear, then caressed her burning cheek, suggesting the word she lost, "intimacy?"

At the word's sound, Jahtara's mind filled with the image of Heddha on the beach. She felt close to Heddha, touching and talking intimately. She sensed the individual grains of sand slip through her hand, each grain crossing the space to Heddha, attracted by some force to fill the contours of Heddha's back. Compelled by the same attraction, she leaned forward to kiss Heddha's velvety brown shoulder.

But now, there existed no warm salty body, no interface, only a void, a chasm pulling her deeper. She felt her shirt drag across her sensitive skin with each ragged inhalation. Jahtara's back straightened as if a cord drew her forward. She struggled against the pull, then in the gaping abyss, a door swung open, and she fell across the threshold. She plunged through the darkness, her flailing arms reached out, attempting to hold Heddha's image only to clutch at the deputy's robe, the only solid object within reach.

Muddle-head filled the gap where her mind once resided, dragging one heavy foot after the other through the thick slurry of her thoughts. Was she outside? A gurgling brook, perhaps, and splashing. A bird's song? No. Someone singing or chanting? She snuggled with a warm comforter. No, not outside. In a bed. She pulled the cover up tighter, pulling her legs up, stiff and uncomfortable to move. Her stomach suddenly tightened; she lay at the edge of the abyss, threatening to drag her under again. Only by opening her eyes could she rescue herself. In the half-darkness, silhouetted by candlelight, stood the teacher's deputy. Jahtara restrained from squeezing her eyes shut again. Once opened, the door couldn't be closed. Slowly the plodding of her mind gained two desirable characteristics of sharing an intimacy: trust and discretion. Intimacy engendered these attributes. And it came to her all too forcefully neither existed in the dark silhouette before her.

The deputy engaged in his morgn ablutions. They included an eye ritual: he bent over bowls filled with perhaps sacred water, straightening and tipping his head back, then repeating the pattern. Finished, the deputy packed some of the articles used in the ceremony into a knapsack and removed his blue robe throwing it on the floor. He donned a hooded jerkin and fastened a belt with a pouch around his waist. Jahtara saw him checking the bag's contents and glancing about, missing an item in the dim predawn light. Spying it on the table, he slipped a small cylinder into the pouch, securing it with a tie. Grabbing the knapsack, he set off with not the barest of looks back.

Relief washed over Jahtara. He departed on some business for the teacher, no doubt, but she would have to face him at some point. Why the hesitancy? Was it shyness or shame she felt? She blushed at the vague remembering of last noite. Focusing on the memory, it dissipated with the effort like a mist under the Solaura's strengthening light, gone except for a feeling. A shred of what she tried to remember escaped down the stairs without the slightest acknowledgment, diminishing her.

She gingerly rolled to a sitting position. Yesterdei, she lingered, hesitant to leave, and now felt pressed to depart. She smelled the liquid in the bowls on the small altar, then a quick taste – slight salinity. Jahtara, needing to clean herself, used the sacred water, causing a momentary stinging on some parts. After dressing quickly, she stole down the stairs into the lodge, seeing the teacher before attaining half the mark.

A rhythmic chanting echoed off the cliff face. The sage stood in the spring-fed pool, naked except for a loincloth, splashing water from a bowl over his head and emaciated body unaffected by the chilly water. No other seeker occupied the lodge at this hour. Laying the bowl aside, the mentor rang the water from his long, grey hair, wrapping it deftly into a knot at the back of his head. His chanting stopped, and his head lifted to see Jahtara standing at the foot of the stairs, mouth agape.

This scene embodied more intimacy than she ever sought. The withered spiritual sage bathing in a sacred pool filled with disciples' pebbled aspirations reminded her of the old courtesans, their heavily painted faces concealing long-gone resplendency.

A smile crept onto the teacher's face, reading the emotions etched on Jahtara's. "You look shocked to see me bathing in the hopes of my followers. The pool, after all, remains just water." Moving to the edge, he extended his hand, saying, "Help an old man out, child." Taking Jahtara's hand, he mused, "I have made this journey before and have the wisdom to leave this existence. I remain to assist other seekers with their journey, mayhap their aspirations give me merit, aiding in my task this lifetime." Wrapping himself in a blanket, he turned to the pool, asking, "You placed a pebble?"

Jahtara nodded.

"Many inquire outside of themselves for answers. Do not endeavor for the superficial. What you seek, you already possess. We often try to find love and acceptance in someone else. What you seek cannot be written in stone yet simply in your heart." Looking up to the assistant's chamber, he continued, "Those closest to the master often contain the most need. The deputy seeks power, which he saw in you. He offered you false sympathy intending to steal your power: the power of kindness, love, creation. All things he strives to control. You possess worthiness others cannot dominate."

"What do I have of any value?"

"That you must determine." He paused before continuing, seeing that seekers started to stir, "You seemed happy the prior dei, working with others to a common purpose."

"A joyful dei, aye. I have long sought to belong yet feel separate."

"My child, have you ever watched a puppet show? The puppets act out distinct characters interacting to tell a story. Yet if a wind blows away the screen, we see the truth: the seemingly separate roles joined by the hands of the puppeteer. Separateness proves an illusion when we realize our interconnectedness. We should choose intentions wisely, not grasping at false desires or governed by the ignorant intent of others."

Tears rolled down Jahtara's cheeks, and a smile graced her lips. "I have, on many occasions, let outside proceedings impel my happiness. I now see in a different light. A curtain lifted. Seeing you in the bathing pool, pouring water over yourself, took me to another spring where I shared the initiation of friendship and intimacy. Feelings arose at that watering pool, and you have reminded me of my true passion. I seek what my heart already found."

"You weep tears of joy, I perceive. Perhaps you should find this friend, for I believe you have a truth to unveil."

Jahtara exited the compound through the circular gate. The Solaura climbed into the sky, dissipating the morgn chill. The streets expressed a bare token of the bustle they would convey as the dei progressed. The structures' crispness in the early light brought out each building's splendid individuality. Jahtara marveled at the effort shaping these edifices into a town.

Jahtara's lack of direction yesterdei withered away in the light of this new dei. Her heart filled with the need to express her naive missteps to Heddha. Had she lost her mind, disregarding Heddha so effortlessly? Jahtara longed to reestablish their entwining closeness. These thoughts urged her feet to tread with speed, the pulsing of her heart deepening the certainty of her feelings, each beat bringing her closer to Heddha.

Heddha woke to the Solaura on her face as it topped the hills up the bay. At least, no fog blanketed the bay this morgn; the state room's bedcoverings hadn't dried till late yesterdei. Heddha returned to Aunties at supper, going straight to bed, exhausted. Pug said he'd seen Jahtara early yesterdei yet didn't know where she went. Rolling to her side, she saw Jahtara's pillow fluffed and bedding cold. They hadn't talked for nearly two deis, and their discussion at the fountain occupied Heddha's mind last noite.

Danger lurked at the blue robes' compound. Heddha's distress at talking with the teacher's assistant pushed her to flee to the fountain. Yet something else lurked deeper, and she resisted its surfacing at first. Then the nymph's textures and colors, with its smooth marble and alluring moving water, exposed submerged novel emotions. Heddha let those feelings crest, discovering an unfamiliar prospect, yet it felt comfortable. Heddha felt confidence in her body but never in the sense of appearing pleasing to someone else. Expressing these feelings to another womon, especially a prinus bathed, pampered, and dressed in the light of beauty, felt awkward. Jahtara didn't understand a life of physical labor where a body represents a tool. When Heddha returned with food that dei, Jahtara revealed new feelings, alluding to the dei on the beach. Heddha remembered the unique joy of that dei too. She recalled the kiss of Jahtara's cool lips on hot skin.

Jahtara's beauty, combined with her trusting nature, worried Heddha, and she was concerned about her whereabouts. She heard Auntie moving downstairs, in fact, making quite a ruckus. Heddha decided to undertake a search for Jahtara. The thought of possibly returning to Quest Alley renewed the knot in her stomach; nevertheless, she threw back the covers and dressed hastily, moving to the stairs to search for her friend.

Jahtara opened the boarding house entrance to see Heddha coming down the stairs. The sight of her in leggings, shirttails out, sleeves rolled up, and her joyous smile sapped the strength from Jahtara's legs.

Heddha jumped the three remaining stairs and, in two strides, threw her arms around Jahtara, lifting her from the ground and turning in a circle before exclaiming, "You would not leave my thoughts, and thus, I was of a mind to find you!"

"Ha, I found you in my thoughts this morgn and have come to you!"

"Yet from where have you come? Fear overtook me that you met with danger."

"A sort of danger aye, which I need to discuss with you, yet, I have also discovered a promise of joy this morgn. Oh, Heddha, I have so much to tell you. I am naïve in the ways of the world I know, yet my eyes opened to something I wish to share with you!"

"Come then, let us get some of Aunties' morgn drink. I have missed our talks." Heddha took Jahtara by the hand, leading her to the kitchen.

Auntie, early to sleep and early to rise, let her daughters clean up at noite, leaving her alone in the kitchen in the morgn, so Heddha and Jahtara were surprised at seeing pots scattered on the flagstone floor. They staggered, realizing Auntie lay in a pool of dark blood flowing in a rivulet toward the open back door. The shocked womyn stood clutching hands until a breeze off the bay moved the back door with an eery creak, confirming the passing of Auntie's presence.

Jahtara bent to Auntie, the spell broken, but Heddha held her back by saying, "Something feels strange here. Neither of us fought in combat with a sword, yet I have helped with farm butchering. The power needed to make such a stroke would prove difficult even for a trained cniht."

Nodding in agreement, Jahtara said, "I have trained with a sword on stout wood, and it seems incredible one could hack through her arm twice and completely across her body with a carve of a sword." Jahtara sniffed the air saying, "Something burns horrible. Heddha, pull the breakfast pot away from the fire."

"Naught hangs over the fire. Look here. The wound shows burns along the sword's single stroke; no hacking blows. See how her arm bends, and a knife lays a short distance from her hand. She raised her arm to defend, and her attacker felled her with a single stroke. The sword cut through her wrist, upper arm, chest, belly, and backbones, taking leave through the hip. I have never seen a cut so powerful and clean."

Jahtara half-listened as spots filled her vision and the room tilted. She felt something hit her back and slid down the cabinet to the floor, tilting uncontrollably to her side. Jahtara lay there with unfocused eyes, gazing into the fixed stare of Auntie's face. A couple of days ago, Auntie sat by the fire, complaining of her pains. Heddha wiped a cold cloth on Jahtara's neck, which provoked a return of her senses, but anger brought her to a sitting position.

"Jahtara, my pardon. We both have a fondness for Auntie. Why someone would cut her down where she stood is..."

"No, not standing. The intruder broke her jaw. Her face lays towards me, and I could see the misshapen line of her jaw when down on the stones. A powerful blow knocked her to the floor. A furrow cuts the stone along the sword's course. The powerful slash occurred while she lay on the stone floor."

"What steel could do this?"

"Indeed! Hand me your knife."

Jahtara placed the knife's tip into the furrow at its beginning, a hand's width from the severed wrist. The trough filled with blood, aiding in marking the cut's depth. "See how the mark moves up the blade, sounding closer to the body."

Heddha, nodding, took the blade from her and wiped it clean with the wet cloth she used on Jahtara. She went to the other end and dipped the knife into the track, moving closer to the body each time. "A swing of an arm made this cut: shallow at the edges and deeper at the center."

"Look here at the cut edges of the stone. Do you see the fine powder?

Heddha leaned close, touching the powder with her fingertip looking at it closely, rubbing it between her finger and thumb. "Stone turned to powder. Someone felled her with a heavy blow, perhaps insensible. Who would do this to Auntie? What could do this?"

"Heddha, I have something to tell. At the teacher's lodge I..." The sound of a large object hitting the wooden floor above stopped Jahtara.

Clutching her knife, Heddha exclaimed, "Our room," and bolted for the stairs.

Does the womon ever consider before running into danger, Jahtara thought, starting after her. Arriving at the room, Jahtara discovered Heddha climbing onto the windowsill, preparing to jump out. Jahtara rushed forward, grabbing Heddha by the back of the shirt.

"Consider please, Heddha. You have only a knife. You could not endure what killed Auntie. Did you see anyone?"

"No, nothing." Regarding the room, Heddha said, "Like an old womon's money sock on rent dei, turned inside out."

Jahtara made for the opposite sill, lifting a loose stone to reveal a cavity containing something wrapped in cloth. Unwrapping the fabric, she produced the ornate knife taken from her betrothed.

Jahtara's eyes filled with tears, "Heddha, please tell me Auntie's death did not happen because I took the knife."

"The fates cannot be fathomed, nor the moment of death known."

"Do not recite such nonsense to me," Jahtara said before breaking down completely, her shoulders shaking with the sobs of her torment.

Heddha crossed to her friend and held her allowing Jahtara to cry out her anguish.

The district sheriff grew skeptical of their story; indeed, the part about how they came to Concupia led him to question the whole of it. The sheriff sat on a cane chair, his corpulent belly resting on his thighs. After each response to his questioning, the sheriff would raise one great brow and let out a harrumph that echoed around his abdomen. At the end of his examination, he let out a long sigh, deflating himself of the falsity. "I would appreciate you both continuing your presence in the district until the story of this butchery becomes known." The chair creaked as the Sheriff, his duty done, stood and lumbered to the kitchen.

Once out of hearing, Heddha urged, "We must take our leave without delay."

They learned from Pug that a hooded man ran through the stable and slipped out an opening at the back. Peeking through the slots between the wallboards, Pug saw the slayer jump the wall of the adjoining abode, disappearing among the honeycomb of houses. Other than a hood, Pug identified a small pouch at his waist. Heddha sent Pug to fetch the authorities while Jahtara consoled Auntie's daughters. Heddha roused the other guests, most of whom quickly fled the boarding house, which Heddha suggested they also do.

"Jahtara! We must move. We continue in peril here. Wake from your stupor. We must leave."

"Aye, I suppose. Heddha, I need to talk to you desperately."

"We can speak while riding. Shall we travel Solauraward or inland? We reside closer to the inland road, yet perhaps they would not expect us to move Solauraward. Consider it. I will ready the mounts." Heddha moved to the kitchen door, then checked herself and went out the front to the stable.

Jahtara removed the splendid knife from her jerkin pocket, holding it in both hands. Here lies the cause of auntie's passing either in a material sense, or it came to Jahtara unintended, and Auntie got in their way: possibly both. Jahtara spent the noite with the person who showed up at the boarding house to recover it, stumbling into Auntie on his way. Did she tell him of it last noite, mention where she lodged, spoke of Heddha, or did he know this beforehand? Her memory remained a dim, obscure dream. It could have been Heddha sliced through the bone, lying in a pool of blood, if Auntie hadn't delayed him. How could she persist so naive and helpless in the world? What have her actions wrought since leaving the keyndom of her father? She must talk to Heddha now; tell her all.

"Su grandeza?" questioned a voice.

Turning to look at the speaker, the surprise caused Jahtara to stand.

"Prinus, my child, I am astonished to find you here. You have grown so, matured into a womon. It is you, is it not?"

The Thane Adron Esryn Kirrydon stood inside the front door, the smile she remembered adorning their countenance. Besides the beaming smile, they wore deep purple pantaloons with white knee-length stockings, a white blouse trimmed in lace, a thin blue cape with epaulets covered with tiny stars, and a collar adorned with fur. In their hand, they held a black walking stick topped with a gold otter, the symbol of Concupia.

"'Tis me, Thane Kirrydon." Jahtara curtsied, saying, "I am astonished you recognize me, especially in this attire. I have grown, although, at this moment, I do not feel mature."

Bowing deeply, they answered, "Your hair, Prinus; even as they described it, I thought of you. I usually do not acquaint myself with such cases. The sheriff sent a messenger when he learned of the situation here, thinking to inform the district administrator, especially with certain peculiarities present in this case. When I heard you described, I knew I must come, especially since I was presented with news of you just a dei ago."

From the front door, Heddha queried, "News from where?"

Jahtara quickly cut in, "Thane Kirrydon, may I present my companion Heddha Jlussi once of the refined household of Keyn Nyssa of the High Mountain dominions.

With a somewhat puzzled look, the thane nodded to Heddha while Jahtara, out of their line of sight, gestured to Heddha to curtsy.

Heddha bowed instead.

The thane considered all the possibilities. Then said to Jahtara, "That you have a retainer and do not travel alone comforts me."

Before Jahtara could respond, Heddha said, "I am a free womon, thane, in no one's retinue."

The thane's smile returned, bowing slightly deeper, they said, "Well met Heddha Jlussi of the High Mountain Keyndom. The news includes mention of you as well."

Jahtara responded, "Thane, I beg you, relay the news. This morgn's tragedy strains us, yet I hope we will not sustain further harm."

"By the fates, prinus, harm may continue, yet I cannot judge the extent. I received a rider from my liege Laud Keyn Tergon, carrying news of lineage Davuda. Your brother, Prinus Baeddan, crowned himself keyn. The fate of your parents remains unknown. You and your companion," the thane nodded to Heddha, "are sought on the charge of treason."

Heddha and Jahtara stood in silence until, unable to carry the weight of the dei, Jahtara sank into a chair.

Couple of Rungs

We evolve in the consummate universe, perhaps because codependent origination attunes the totality. This harmonized, complicated orchestration endures, never missing a beat that would cause the ensemble to stop playing.

Reducing the cosmos to its fundamental elements seems wondrous. Does the intellect create these reductive explanations searching for self-fulfilling cerebrations, or do we search for something else? Diminution provides no answers, only information. Whereas witnessed acts of understanding and kindness ripple through consciousness, shaking the rational with profound joy, instantly realizing the eloquence of our interbeing.

Convention would predict the converse when attempting to harm, where the superficial prospers with concepts like sin, wickedness, transgression, illicitness, depravity, greed, and evil. Yet witnessing a harmful act highlights and deepens the wisdom revealed: the illusion of self-gain tethers one to suffering. We gain insight into how volition turns the wheel of life by loosening these bonds of vested interests. A slip of a couple of rungs on our climb to wisdom can happen to any of us. Been there, done that, got the bumper sticker, tee-shirt, shot glass, selfie, and the karma that rules them all.

We share the ability to start anew in every moment, and compassion begins with understanding suffering, and love follows.

This tale continues to evolve, but what intent moves us forward?

The new dei found Jahtara sitting on the loggia outside a second-floor room on Thane Kirrydon's estate. Shadow engulfed the balcony, and a cool breeze swept up from the Setting Sea. Jahtara sat wrapped in a beautifully intricate quilt, watching the shadow from the surrounding hills recede up the bay as the Solaura climbed into the sky. In truth, Inlanda's spinning like a top in its orbit around a star creates the illusion of the Solaura climbing in Inlanda's sky. And the star, part of a great arm of stars and gas, orbits a massive black hole at the center of a spiral galaxy. Simultaneously, the galaxy interacts within a web of innumerable galaxies in an expanding universe. Jahtara knew none of this; she felt insignificant, her heart contracted under the weight of sorrow, staring into an unalterable past.

Yesterdei constituted a chain of circumstances manifesting out of a fog into painfully sharp focus before receding again into confusion and sadness. The thane insisted on Jahtara and Heddha moving to their estate, but Heddha refused. She wished to stay at Auntie's to help and only relented after Jahtara convinced her that staying at Auntie's might put Pug and the daughters at risk. The murderer would advance his cause unabated to obtain his goal. Atfi Dunnyn kindly stepped forward to assist the daughters in running Auntie's Boarding House.

Dinner at the thane's felt a tedious task leaving Jahtara without the taste for food, especially amid a headache reaching a crescendo. Her only respite came when she excused herself to a dark room. She wanted to speak to Heddha throughout the dei, but the opportunity never presented itself by fate or choice. Jahtara resolved to talk to Heddha at the first opportunity this morgn. Jahtara's feelings concerning Heddha were shrouded in sadness and shame. How could she hope to alter the course of her life? What arrogance to think this possible. Her lineage and realm were in disarray. Her longing for purpose and intimacy turned to shame because she acted on a whim. Taking Alyeska's knife ultimately resulted in Auntie's loss of life. Jahtara's whirling feelings pulled Heddha into a vortex spinning out of control. Jahtara needed to stop this; no going back, but she could halt the spinning and regain the path.

Jahtara knew it must start with Heddha, and the steadfast passion in her heart would guide her forward.

Heddha lay on a too-soft bed in one of the thane's rooms, observing her surroundings. She once heard a word to describe this room, but it hid from her. The room spoke of sumptuousness, overly so, to the point she could but gawk... the word floated to the top - gaudy. The room secreted gaudiness. Plush red and purple velvet covered every-thing: chairs, settee, comforters, canopied bed, curtains, and pillows of the same fabric with gold tassels. The gray tile floor with lush red rugs recalled auntie's blood on the stone floor. Heddha turned her eyes away and gazed out the large window where the sky started to lighten. A black-bodied spider with long multi-jointed legs sat on its orbed web in the upper corner of the window, patiently rotating the morgn's catch, expressing silk to entomb its prey.

Heddha struggled to sit in the engulfing bed but slumped back, a base sigh escaping her center, jaded by the effort. Heddha couldn't become trapped here, smothered under layers of plush comfort entombing her. Her life had been harsh, hard, and often harrowing, yet this sort of comfort did not entice her. Since adjoining to Jahtara, her life took on an adventurous mutuality. Most appealing, Heddha didn't need to guard herself with Jahtara. The preceding morgn, upon seeing Jahtara standing in the open door at Auntie's, Heddha bound down the stairs with openness and enthusiasm not experienced in a long time, if ever.

Heddha threw back the bed coverings with the renewed intention of not losing those feelings todei. She would find Jahtara to share this growing excitement, yet when her feet touched the blood-red rug, urgent knocking interrupted Heddha's intent.

"Heddha, I am Laud Renesmee. We did not receive a proper introduction with all the dreadful goings-on," she greeted, sweeping into the room.

Heddha, having just removed herself from bed in only a noite shirt, started to object when the laud of the house continued. "This room must appear like gilding on a barn stall to you, my dear." Upon seeing Heddha's look of consternation, she hurriedly added, "An affliction of my spouse, a reaction to growing up on a farm. I offer no offense to you, dear one. The house must be suffocating to you, whereas my mate likes the cushioning to remind how far they have risen, and you can see they enjoy the facade from their dress. These surroundings occupy a far ride from your upbringing, I am sure, and yet the endless cold of the Long Noites in the keeps of the High Mountain Keyndom with those hanging tapestries can grow oppressive. I have observed this myself." She took a quick breath looking about the room. "I do not let this solace extend to the public rooms, you understand, without some moderation." Her eyes met Heddha's, slowly ending with, "You and I need to talk, my sweet."

Heddha watched Laud Renesmee remove cushions from the settee, looking for a place to put them and, finding none dumped them on the floor. She looked a petite womon with small hands, slender fingers, graceful feet, and delicate facial features dominated by incisive eyes as if her missing mass converted into energy constantly twinkling in her ever-moving eyes. She turned those eyes on Heddha, taking her by the hand to sit on the sofa.

Heddha, a bit taken aback, opened her mouth to speak but closed it, unsure what to say. She wasn't confident of the laud's meaning since entering the room.

Laud Renesmee patted Heddha on the knee. "Not to worry, dear, I will clarify in short order. You see, child, I located to the High

Mountain Keyndom quite some time ago. Well, I accompanied Thane Adron in truth. Come to consider, they were not a thane back then. Where was I? Aye, the High Keyndom. I understand you have some familiarity with the realm. The thane, a counselor at the time, accompanied a Middle Keyndom emissary, and we became acquainted with the refined household and ministrants. One ministrant had just introduced his youngling, Absan, a well-mannered lad, to the refined." Laud Renesmee looked straight into Heddha's eyes, fathoming those depths to find the hidden ambition behind Heddha's vertical pupils. "You see, I am on the point of it, child. Absan, grown into the form of a broad-shouldered man, presented at Keyn Tergon's privy council on Keyn's Dei this jahr. Paying his respects to the thane and me, he remains quite well-mannered yet infused with naivety. He travels Solauraward with several other cnihts, joined by four more from the Middle Keyndom at Keyn Tergon's behest. Strange tidings from this region justified an inquiry. And here the point sharpens, child, Sir Absan bears a quest of his own; he searches for a geyrle, once a retainer in the household of the High Mountain Keyndom."

Time, so the tale goes, doesn't flow backward, yet Heddha suddenly slipped and slid down the slick retrograde slope of time into a confused superimposed state of feelings. Her heart aching with young love, her back carrying the burden of shame, lash by lash. Standing on cold stones, her spirit bared under the disapproving eyes of the privy council judicature, Heddha's feelings for Absan the only thing restraining her anger. In the strange focus of the mind's eye, Absan grew close, tears rolling down his cheeks until he wiped them away, altering her awareness, making Heddha conscious of the gulf between them. Yet, she bore the accusations each lash of fate laid on her back: womon, bondserf, whore, outcast, undeserving, shame. Heddha clothed her naked spirit in layers of anger with a thin undergarment of reminiscence hidden under the wrath. Laud Renesmee laid bare this remembrance. Heddha's eyes filled with tears, and she quickly blinked them away. She would not expose those feelings to the cold winds of time. Heddha quashed the tears; looking aside from Laud Renesmee's penetrating eyes, she found the spider's web. The prey secured, the rent from the struggle repaired, now the spider enlarged the web with strands of her own making.

Heddha stood, struggling against the urge to move, to run!

The laud rose, sensing Heddha's panic. Looking around the room, she pulled a leg warmer off the foot of the bed and placed it over Heddha's shoulders, suggesting, "Let us move outside, child. This room seems confining," guiding Heddha to the door.

The brightening dei warmed the balcony, though the cold stones drew the heat from Heddha's bare feet. Heddha sat cross-legged next to her laudship on a cushioned wicker settee. The view near the crest of the hill backing Concupia included the town, outlet, and farms beyond the bay. Heddha, calmed by the expanse, took a deep breath, pulling the coverlet tight around herself.

"Dear one, I fear I have misjudged you. My mission todei meant to uncover why you travel with the prinus and the extent of your dealings with Absan. I considered your intentions mayhap unworthy of their positions. My prying meant to protect Prinus Jahtara, yet I suspect you have protected her and mayhap Absan. You carry a deep pain from your relations with the High Mountain council. My fondness for the prinus ruled my head, yet now my heart comes to feel its truth. I fear I irritate an old wound, child."

"The wound seems my fate. One I cannot accept. It will not leave me alone cause I cannot leave it alone. I constantly pick at the scab, so it will not heal." Heddha chanced a glanced at Laud Renesmee before explaining, "Jahtara's mount, Trusted Companion, was groomed to accept only royal riders, yet I know it matters naught to the mount which it carries. The steed and I befriended one another, spanning the divide. Perhaps the gulf proves deeper than I can bridge with people, and I should let it scar over. It matters not what truth the heart feels, begging your pardon for my directness su laudship."

Laud Renesmee watched the gulf widen with the honorific but

knew its convention. "Laudship?" She looked to the farms on the other side of the bay. "Aye, my father trained me to be a laud. He held a small amount of land, contriving to use my youth and beauty to advance himself. The estate's laud became widowed, and with fifteen comings of the Warming, I became betrothed, married, and a laud of the land. I did my duty and grew into it. Having seen many more harvests than myself, my laud became frail in body and feeble of mind; therefore, I administered the estates and manor through him. I, in effect, became my father's laud. It tickles me still." Her smile faded, saying, "And then his laudship passed. In accordance, I became incapable of doing what I had been doing all along. Instead, I became a dependent of the keyn, who, to control the land, married me to Thane Kirrydon. Well, they would become the thane with time.

"Of course, no one cared for my thoughts. Yet our relationship grew comfortable for us; we have become great friends and share a love for our daughters. I should not be surprised at the lovely parent Thane Adron became. I manage the estates and the thane's private affairs. Occasionally I assist with diplomatic missions," her smile returned, "like this one.

"Fate takes many paths, child. The High Mountain Keyndom holds no deltas, I know. However, the Naloon Delta lies to the Solauraward, where the river fans out. Like a delta, we can follow the ever-changing stronger flow or choose a different course; some channels with sand or gravel bars make passage quite trying. The delta grows anew moment to moment and can move in any direction, choose wisely the course you take, yet take the heading from your heart, dear. Choosing may be difficult, but the act can bring boundless joy."

"Those eyes do not miss much. I see why the thane relies on you, milaud. When I awoke, my intention seemed clear." Heddha paused then asked, "And if I chose the wrong course?"

"We do not always have perfect choices. We can only do our best, child." With a knowing smile, the Laud added, "And amend along the way."

"My past thins, yet it brought me here. Now I must follow my heart: in this, I have no choice."

Laud Renesmee smiled, patted Heddha's hand, and standing, they embraced. "Well met, Heddha well met. Now to your toilet child, join us to break our noite's fast, and following, the thane wishes to see you both."

Heddha liked the food choices better than her garish room. She bypassed the sauces, heavy creams, dressings, and condiments, fixing a plate of black beans covered with moist shredded pork and a poached egg, all scooped up with warm flatbread. At one point, needing more bread, she went to the sideboard for more and felt a warm hand slip into hers. She turned to find Jahtara and her heart bounded. Even Jahtara's serious face couldn't stop the joy filling Heddha's heart.

Jahtara squeezed Heddha's hand, leaning to whisper, "I need to tell… that is, explain myself urgently."

A strand of lilac-scented copper hair brushed Heddha's cheek, and Jahtara's breath on her ear made Heddha giddy. Heddha nodded, but just then, a tender approached, asking if she could assist, so they separated. Heddha returned to the table, and Jahtara found food to her liking. Between the thane, Laud Renesmee and their three talkative daughters, Jahtara and Heddha, couldn't converse in private. So, they found themselves entering the thane's study hand in hand, unable to confide further.

Laud Renesmee accompanied them into the book-lined study, and the three of them sat in tall backed chairs in front of an ornate desk, and the thane slipped into the chair behind. The door opened as they settled, and an attendant announced the sheriff.

"I asked the sheriff to inform us of any advances into his inquires of the gruesome circumstances of the prior dei. If you please, sheriff."

"At your pleasure, laudship. Due to the tale told by the prinus and her companion," indicating Heddha, "I inquired at the seeker's compound, speaking to several there, including this teacher fellow, who though appearing decrepit, seems quite vital. The assistant has gone missing."

Jahtara stared at her folded hands, avoiding Heddha's attempt to make eye contact.

"No one claims much knowledge of this fellow: where he came from, who he is. He just showed up one dei offering to help. Gave the name of… got it in my head somewhere, aye, Enan Tiomer. I gave a look through his quarters. Found some peculiar things." Reaching into a satchel, he brought forth, "A strangely made flattened glass flask with a mystifying stopper one turns on and off with the hand. To be thorough, I just tasted the liquid left inside. Initially, it samples like honey yet grows bitter when swallowed, with an odd effect on the pallet. Not untogether all pheasant…. I, ahh, beg the thane's pardon! I meant to say not altogether unpleasant." the sheriff corrected while attempting to slip the container into his pocket.

Thane Kirrydon cleared their throat, and the constable reluctantly handed over the flask. The thane examined the bottle, exclaiming, "I have not seen such adeptness in glassware even from Murano," and, setting it on the desk, noticed Jahtara's ashen appearance. "My dear, you look distressed?" Unable to speak, she shook her head to the contrary. Keeping their gaze on her bowed head, they asked the sheriff, "Continue if you will."

"Aye, I discovered his blue hooded robe discarded in a corner. Then under his bunk," he said, producing, "a long grey hairpiece, I think, and old tattered rags of clothes." He said with a sniff and harrumph.

Jahtara covered her face on recognizing the articles.

Heddha, puzzled and concerned, asked, "What causes this distress?"

Unable to look at Heddha, she said to Laud Renesmee, "I stumbled into an old man in the street three deis ago or four. He wore like garments and his hair… What transpires here? This happened before I even knew of the compound and the teacher. The man groped me.

Scratched my arm. I... I thought he searched for money or proved a lecher. Oh, laud, this cannot be, please, no!"

Heddha looked confused; Jahtara desperate; Laud Renesmee could fathom neither, so she came to stand between them, holding Jahtara's hand.

"I would wager he stumbled into you for a purpose and assuredly represents the man from the compound and the one seen running from the stable by the youngling, Pug. No doubt. Your story of this man and how you know of him smells foul," the constable added with a raised brow.

"I am sure I have no need to remind you, sheriff. This laud remains a prinus of lineage Davuda," said the thane.

Heddha, still trying to accept this new tangent, asked, "I do not understand. He knew who you were before we went to Quest Alley. Yet I was the one he spoke to at the compound."

"Well," began the sheriff eyeing the thane, "it seems the old sage fellow talked to the prinus on the morgn of the killing as she snuck out of the assistant's quarters, shortly after the assistant left."

Time stopped or made a good approximation of stopping. Tiny dust particles floated slowly in the Solaura's rays streaming through the windows. The sheriff's belly quivered, Thane Kirrydon and Laud Renesmee stared in disbelief, and Heddha, dear Heddha, tried hard to work through the implications. Jahtara, floating through the immensity of space, clung to a speck of consequence on the underbelly of eternity, and though she wished it, could not change yesterdei, for the past took flight on the wings of time.

Heddha's chair struck a bookcase with a crash sending books filled with ancient knowledge tumbling to the floor, bringing Jahtara to the stark present.

"With him," her words a dagger. "With Auntie's murderer!" She struck deeper. "The one instrumental in your betrothal, a keyn's death, and how many more killings!" Slash, slice, and rend. "He usurps, sucking people's power; he assumes any pleasing shape, any desire you wish, twisting it to his purpose. He leaves life in ruin," Heddha screamed the death blow with spittle flying, some striking Laud Renesmee, shielding Jahtara.

Jahtara offered no defense; form and function liquified, spiraling into the black hole of shame; Jahtara slipped out of her chair, slumping to the floor. The miasm of remorse mingled with self-loathing bore her down, and regret streamed down her cheeks, life ebbing out of her.

Fearing for Laud Renesmee, the sheriff started unsteadily forward, admonishing, "See here, you have no call to threaten…" Heddha abruptly lowered her shoulder into his midriff, catching the man with such surprise and force he lost his balance, breath, and wits. He lay wallowing on the floor, Heddha standing over him, surprised at her strength.

Heddha turned, neck red with rising anger, leaning over Jahtara, fists clenched, back burning with the shame of exposing herself again. She stormed to the oversized door yanking it open with such force it slammed into the wall, splintering. Heddha pushed her way through the startled attendants and disappeared.

The Solaura's solstice came and passed, the deis turning hot, humid, and hazy. The thane entertained envoys, commerce continued, ships and teamsters came and went, and Jahtara's melancholy deepened. The Solaura's appearance each morgn couldn't warm her heart. She cared naught for food; it didn't nourish. Sleep would not refresh. Her only feeling: utter emptiness. Withered.

Laud Renesmee tried old remedies and some new ones to no avail. She couldn't entice Jahtara to relate the events leading up to the dei in the thane's study, what happened between her and her brother, or how she ended up in Concupia. The laud tried to interest Jahtara in quilting; Jahtara would start her stab stitches in a daze, then stop.

Laud Renesmee would find her staring at the frame, lost in the warp, weft, and incomplete tessellations.

At the wake after Auntie's sea burial, Laud Renesmee saw Heddha, but she wouldn't converse. The companion, Pug, said she worked on the ships with him and helped the geyrles at the boarding house. Laud Renesmee tried speaking to her at one of the vessels, but Heddha politely told her laudship she wanted no part of her schemes as she called them. Jahtara needed to work it out for herself.

Hope appeared one dei, unbidden, while Jahtara and Laud Remesmee sat under shade trees in the side garden. The Laud's daughters played on the lawn, enjoying the outside before the heat of the dei. They chased each other and the barking dogs, screeching and teasing as younglings often do, except for Arita, the middle one, sitting aloof and bored, head in hand. Raga, the youngest, and the sandy-haired hound chased Tanhā, who tried to look the dignified eldest. Jahtara sat with defocused eyes, unperturbed by the laughing, shouting Raga. The two geyrles ran from the vivid light on the lawn to the notional aspect under the pergola, turning their forms into dancing sparkles of indiscernible light and dark racing down the length of the arbor. Upon bursting into the bright Solaura again, Tanhā braced to a stop, turned, and held her hand up to halt Raga in her tracks. Her passion barely contained, Raga danced up and down, whining about continuing the pursuit with the dog panting its assent at her side.

Tanhā remained immovable in her stance, stating, "I wish to stop! I crave food and a cool drink, tangy and oh so sweet."

"Don't eat, please! Rest later, when we can no longer run, and then we will collapse on the blanket and tickle our noses with blades of grass, please!" Raga pleaded, dancing harlequin-like under the dappled light of the tented grapevines.

Squinting against the late morgn Solaura, Tanhā, in her best adult voice, said, "I want what I want when I want it, and I want it now," and abruptly strode to the terrace in search of refreshments.

Raga looked from the listless Arita to the withdrawn Prinus

Jahtara, leaned against her mother, and with slumped shoulders, watched her crochet.

Jahtara registered none of this: the geyrles' words vague noises, pursued and pursuer abstract flashes against a backdrop of greens and greys, desire and passion lost in a pool so deep only blackness knew the bottom. If breathing were not the natural state, she would have suffocated long ago, so fathomless was her melancholy. Yet the deep still contained sulky currents assembling the flashes, filling in gaps with wordless emotion of color and timbre, deciphering the code, and integrating the puzzle until her mind awakened with clarity. Jahtara came to her feet with conviction, pointing, like a compass, to what she found in her heart.

Laud Renesmee, unsure what to say or do at Jahtara's suddenness, blurted out, "Where do you go? Wait, let me summon an escort."

Jahtara simply stated, "I will take care, with no wish for hindrance." Then over her shoulder to Raga, she said, "Arouse Arita with your passion. She will thank you for it."

The hill's slant carried Jahtara forward until the road flattened at the waterfront, and there she didn't know where to turn. She paced one direction on the quay, then the other, stopping at each pier, a hand shading the Solaura from her eyes, to spy down its length until finally, she saw Pug empty a pail of water from a cabin window. Jahtara, not wanting a commotion dockside, sat on a crate and waited. The Solaura gained in the sky, and still, she waited. She thought she saw Heddha on deck once, and even so, she waited. Then Pug walked towards her, his head down until he stopped in front of her, still unable to look her in the eye.

"Good dei, Pug."

"She not want to see you, su alteza."

Jahtara searched the ship halfway down the pier for any sign of Heddha. Seeing none, she turned to Pug, imploring, "Please, Pug, call me Jahtara."

"Things be as they be, me being common folk. The high bearin' got choices, yet the low gets the dregs of fate. It hard seein' the refined without covetin' and begrudgin'. It not up to Pug to change the way things be."

"Yet amazingly, you change how I perceive you every dei, Pug!" She paused, then, with still no sign of Heddha, continued, "I hurt our friend severely. I only want... I miss her. I..." She stopped, not knowing what to say, what would bring Heddha here. She did not wish unmet desires to overwhelm her with melancholy again. In the garden todei, with her laudship's children playing, she awoke to understand relationships as gifts. Not a gift filled with concepts to pick and choose from, but rather an endowment to be filled with effort, experience, and shared meaning. Jahtara needed a way to fill their love with shared intentions. At the moment, the only access to Heddha existed through their mutual friend, Pug. Here she would start. "How do you and the geyrles get on, Pug?"

"We hurtin'. Master Dunnyn be a good man and sends boarders to the house. Heddha works hard helpin', too hard, methinks. Pug hear her, a noite cryin'." Pug looked up at her, then quickly down again, saying, "I never known a prinus afore."

Jahtara smiled and, lifting his chin, said, "Not sure I am a prinus anymore, Pug. I just want to be a friend. Please, Pug, tell Heddha I wish to talk."

She watched Pug head back to the ship and, for the first time, noticed the name of the vessel in raised gold letters under the windows of the great cabin - Auspicious Ambiguities.

Heddha stood at the foot of the gangplank when Pug arrived at the ship. Jahtara stood watching them converse. Finally, Heddha looked up the pier at Jahtara and, without looking away, patted Pug's shoulder and strode up the dock with determined purpose.

Jahtara waited under the hot Solaura, its glare reflecting off the bay, causing her pupil slits to close except for small diamond-shaped openings, leaving Heddha the only object in focus advancing dream-like towards her. Heddha halted in front of her. Jahtara, desperate to share everything in her heart, could only get out, "Heddha, I am so regretful and sorrow-filled."

Heddha swallowed hard, barely able to croak out, "Not here."

Heddha pivoted downriver onto the quay, not watching if she followed. Jahtara followed, knowing she must tell Heddha without delay, without fear, without shame, what she felt, to reveal the superficiality filling her life up to this point. Even with her long legs, she lengthened her stride to keep up. Watching Heddha comb the short dark hair off her face, Jahtara ached to be with her again. She followed how Heddha held her shoulders, the swing of her hips, the turning of one foot inward, and her stride, always with urgency and purpose, all renewing Jahtara's longing.

Heddha twisted back towards Jahtara at the end of the quay, saying, "All of Concupia knows of the prinus, Auntie, and the teacher's assistant. We need not broaden their gossip with a middei convergence on the quay."

"Not my intention."

"Aye, and where lies your intention," but ahead of Jahtara's answer, Heddha held up her hand, stifling any response, and headed towards a path off the end of the quay leading to the spit separating the bay from the sea.

As they reached the crest, the smell of the city's effluent caused Heddha to turn up a trail leading to the hill backing Concupia and running to the sea. Heddha found an overgrown animal run along the hill's face to follow, finally stopping where a creek crossed the path. They radiated heat from the brisk hike in the growing heat and welcomed this isolated respite. Heddha removed her over-shirt, revealing her bound breast. She quickly unwound the binding cloth and dipped it several times in the freshwater, using the dripping cloth to wipe her face, neck, and breasts. She submerged it again, wrung it out, then dunked again, offering the wet cloth to Jahtara. Jahtara, drinking from cupped hands, raised her gaze to the cloth, continuing up to Heddha's face, then nodding, took the offering bringing it to her face letting it absorb the heat and emotion, and moved it to her perspiring neck and chest, soaking her top in the process.

Heddha laid her shirt on a log and leaned her back against it, sitting on the moss-covered ground across the humble creek from Jahtara. She raised a brow, asking, now they were alone, "And your intention?"

Jahtara, removing her shoes, nodded to Heddha's query. She pulled up her skirt and placed her feet in the cool water. The foliage attenuated the heat, and a slight breeze swayed the limbs, causing areas of light and shade to play across them. While Heddha waited for Jahtara's answer, Jahtara drank her in - her dark brows with a small scar intersecting the one, her full lips, defined muscle extending from her shoulders to the outer edge of each breast, and dark nipples erect from the cold water. Heddha's natural sensuality brought the heat back to Jahtara's face and engulfed her. She could hold it back no longer and let it rush out. "I love you." Simple words for complicated feelings.

Heddha's focus changed; the world shifted, colors brightened, and the meaning of words altered. She woke to an unbelievable dream coming true. Heddha underwent a metamorphosis, her leaden heart transmuting to gold. A key turned, opening the door; what Heddha kept imprisoned in her heart sprang forth at Jahtara's utterance. The muted shifting light under the trees unbalanced Heddha making it hard to hold an image. She closed her eyes to regain stability. Did Jahtara mean what Heddha felt? It must!

Jahtara had said it, rushing out of her to pour into the world; she released her feelings to flow into Heddha, her love! And Heddha didn't move, hadn't blinked; the outside world remained unchanged, whereas a storm raged in Jahtara. The world still looked beautiful, the play of light dreamlike, the flowing water sensuous, but Heddha was unmoved. And now she closed her eyes - shutting her out? Heddha couldn't release her anger, the hurt too deep, the past set in stone.

"Heddha, my feelings grow intense and true. I regret deeply to have hurt you so."

"Shush!" Heddha's eyes opened wide. "Say it again."

Heddha wanted it confirmed! Had a transformation taken hold of her? Jahtara echoed her feelings, although more deliberate. "I love you."

The following silence regained familiarity yet transposed, like a favored article of lost clothing, found, repaired, and washed, smelling of the Solaura and warm breezes, comfortable, soft, and fitting intimately; so, you never wanted to take it off. They hesitated, not moving, unsure how to react, not wanting to change the moment with superficiality. A light sea breeze wafted Jahtara's hair. The cooling water coursing over her feet pulled the heat from her head into her chest, reddening the skin over her beating heart.

Heddha sat upright, emotion infusing a radiant smile; she gestured to their nest-like respite from worldly concern, "I have this very moment discovered, unknown to the rest of Inlanda, a new creature. A lovely songbird with an irresistible call. A love song so beautiful the forest quiets, my head turns to reveal, my heart thrills, and my legs quiver. Copper crowned, green-eyed, red-breasted, such a pleasingly tailed creature of the air. I am lost in the deep emerald pools of your eyes, captivated forever singing my song, serenading you with love."

Jahtara gaped, jaw slack until her heart resumed rhythm, and she could utter, "You amaze once more. Heddha, my touchstone, my solid base on which Inlanda sits, an airy poet inhabits you! I thought you lost forever with my foolishness, my naïveté. I possess much and wanted more to please my selfishness. Craved intimacy yet knew not how to give it nor who deserves it." She reached out, running her thumb across the scar on Heddha's brow. "I hurt you to the quick and thought not to see you again."

"Anger overtook me, the depth still shocks me, yet the anger brought up a truth." At Jahtara's puzzled look, Heddha explained, "Fury blinded me, yet the Sheriff carries some bulk and I a mite smaller. Though it came to me later, it seemed I felled him with ease. Then I membered the recollection on your face when he brought forth the assistant's flask; you saw it previously, I would stake my heart on it. You drank of it, or he foxed you into drinking it, more likely. When I met that craven man at the compound, I wanted to spit and wash my ears of him, so potent my disgust. A disgust I have clung to and even let it spread to you until this dei when I saw the truth of it. A growing feeling revealed he slipped you a good measure of the foul liquid. Seeing what a small quaff of the elixir did to the sheriff, you exerted great strength to walk about the next morgn."

"Oh, Heddha, could I be taken in so readily?" Chagrin replaced shame, "I blamed myself after waking that morgn. He did slip a nostrum into the tea he offered. I remembered nothing except the shame afterward." Her vexation would not yet make the short vault to anger. "I am too trusting and naive."

"Aye, I adore this aspect of you– leading with your heart. The fault lies not with you. It lies with this seducer who used you to his own ends. He planned in preparation to meet you, attested by the beggar who groped you in search of the knife. At least to my way of seeing." Reaching out to hold Jahtara's hand, Heddha continued, "Yet I am just a thief who stole your heart."

"I give my heart freely!" Tears of joy welled up. Jahtara leaned forward to kiss Heddha lightly on her muscled shoulder, neck, cheek, and Heddha turned towards her, their lips meeting. Both tasting the salt of their mingled tears and the pleasure of their reflected love.

The dei lavished its heat by the foresetting, and the light muted to a lavender hue in their hideaway. Heddha lay with her head against the log and her arm around Jahtara. Jahtara traced a path along the edge of Heddha's rib cage to her protruding pelvic bone, then through her mons' soft sinuous hair and up again to her ribs, ending by caressing Heddha's breast.

Heddha laid her hand on Jahtara's, pressing her palm against the nipple, and brushed open lips against Jahtara's. "I love you touching me,"

"I have never known a pleasure shared so deeply."

A drift of tiny insects wove an intricate pattern in a shaft of light, worrying the fading beam. Heddha and Jahtara glowed in the passion of this intermezzo; however, their ardor touched off a similar question, expressed reluctantly and concurrently, "Now what?"

They giggled and pinched one another at the synchronicity of the thoughts. This distraction all too conveniently covered the uncomfortable question.

In the receding laughter, circumstances intervened. They heard a rustling coming along the path. Jahtara lowering her pitch, challenged, "Man or beast, beware who enters here!" Followed by a giggle from Heddha.

"Prinus? Heddha?"

"Pug? Did I not ask you to surveil on the quay? And pray come no further if you value your sight!" Heddha, still quelling her laughter, handed Jahtara her skirt. "And how long you been sneaking about?"

"Pug got eyes and ears and knows when to be usin' them, and I be usin' them at the end of the Quay keeping watch for you. I be here at the bidding of Master Dunnyn, ma'ams. Were no sneakin' involved."

Jahtara pushed her way through the tangle of growth, garnishing a fair amount of detritus, then used the debris to excuse her brushing and straightening her clothes and hair before bowing to Pug. "I have no doubt you represent the best of gents, Pug, with more discretion than most. Now convey your message, sir."

"It for you boths," he said, crossing his arms, waiting for Heddha to appear.

"Seems you have become less deferential to a prinus since we last talked, Pug."

"Don't be knowin' such word, yet you say you not one no more."

"Quite right, and with such a keen edge."

Heddha stooped under the tangle overhanging the animal trail to stand beside Jahtara on the narrow path. "I thank you for your steadfastness, Pug. Now, can we hear the message?"

Pug cleared his throat to make the telling official, "Master Dunnyn say there be two strangers at the thane's, lookin' for you boths!"

When they reached the Quay, the setting Solaura painted the high clouds with broad pink, red, and salmon strokes. These colors reflected crimson off the inlet's undulating waters in the gathering dusk, imbuing the crests with feigned dancing flames threatening the ships at anchor. Heddha and Jahtara strode side by side, hand in hand. The climb across the borough made no demands on the lovers; they held onto their love, looking ahead to the end of this resplendent dei. However, others enjoying the Solaura's setting beheld a different sight supported by tradition. Some felt uncomfortable watching the lovers, turning from the display or covering their faces, others tsked or spat off their porches, the youngers giggled, and some men cursed. With knowing smiles, others minded naught, and all would surely fill the market in the morgn with bushel baskets of gossip about a prinus and a dock worker walking hand in hand through town.

The meanings assigned to words can rule perception, and Heddha and Jahtara's understanding broadened, changing the meaning of customs and traditions. Such transformations can sever the chains that bind consciousness. Approaching the domicile of the lauds of Concupia, this unfettering would serve them well over the next deis.

Their pace slowed when they drew near the house and saw a light in the thane's study. "Once again, I am caught unaware, Heddha. I fear the past still abides in the future. What awaits us within; the two missing from the Cold Waste or Kasumi and Jorma, perhaps my brother's constables here to return us to the realm or some other unknown agency mayhap emissaries of the thane's liege laud who wish to question us?"

"Bad tidings will not diminish the happiness of this dei. We will face whatever presents itself side by side," Heddha said.

They were met at the door by Tanhā, who curtsied to Prinus Jahtara and kissed Heddha on both cheeks, exclaiming, "Please invite your strange friends to dinner, please!"

Jahtara looked to Heddha and repeated, "Friends?"

But before Tanhā could answer, Thane Kirrydon came from the study saying, "Ah, good to see you together and well. You gave the laud a fright when you rushed off. The attendants and guards searched most of the dei until Atfi Dunnyn suggested the urchin Pug could find you. Here you are, at last, and have visitors waiting! Quite interesting travelers, I must say, with curious tales from afar. Please use my study and invite them to dinner and, if they wish, to spend the noite. I would so enjoy listening to their discourses till late."

Entering the study, their 'friends' stood, and friend or foe, they recognized Jorma and Kasumi. Jorma's broad smile at seeing them broke Heddha's protective stance, and she moved forward to embrace Kasumi momentarily and gave a smiling nod to Jorma.

Jahtara hung back, remembering the twosome's possible involvement in her recent past. "I hold in abeyance any pleasure at seeing you due to fear of the tidings you bear. I require knowledge of your involvement in our circumstances. Including the killing of a fine womon, Auntie, and the orphaning of her children. And Heddha's death avoided by the narrowest of margins." Plunged into a recall of past events and Heddha's revelations, anger and frustration erupted. "And the violation of my person, my body, in the vilest way! A thief of the dark noite, accosting my spirit with the privileged thought it belonged to him. What colleagues would condone such a thing!" Screaming this last utterance tore at her throat. Jahtara sat, legs shaking with aftershocks of fury.

Heddha, indicating the door to Kasumi, went to Jahtara wrapping her arms around her shoulders, whispering to her, allowing this wave of emotion to crest. Jahtara's wrath waned into staccato inhalations followed by long sobbing exhalations. Heddha stroked her hair, whispering assurances of the worth of allowing these feelings to rise to the surface.

As the sobs diminished, a light knock came from the door, and with Heddha's consent, Kasumi opened the thane's repaired study door. An attendant stood there, holding a tray.

"Not wishing to disturb, ma'am. Su laudship thought the prinus might need some tea."

"Indeed, we could all use some," Kasumi said, noticing four mugs, and stepped back to allow her to enter.

After laying the tray on the desk, the attendant asked if they wished her to pour.

Heddha responded, "No," and seeing the attendant take a quick look at Jahtara, added, "Thank you for your kindness," knowing from personal experience that tenders often must remain invisible, especially in stressful situations.

Jahtara sat with her hands wrapped around the stout mug remembering the noite at Way's Respite when she first met these strangers, realizing her life had grown more complicated since that noite. She looked up at the two, slowly and steadily saying, "In the past, I, in my naivety or ignorance, grew fond of our acquaintance, though lacking in openness. Over time the situation turned menacing, and I will not condone further obscurations. Reveal the totality now, or I must believe you have a part in these transgressions."

Jorma spoke. "We come for exactly such a purpose, prinus."

"Do not address me such. Have you not heard I am a traitor and Heddha, a provocateur?"

"True, your brother proclaimed himself keyn and you a traitor, yet your refined status may still serve a purpose. The fate of your parents remains unknown. Alyeska ascends to the throne, his father, though in advanced age, dead under unusual occurrences. Certain of your father's cnihts and ministrants give their allegiance to your brother. Resistance exists, and the state of affairs confuses."

"And your missing compatriots?"

"Dead. Assassinated."

"By whom?"

Kasumi answered this, "By our colleague. From the manner of their wounds, it could only have been him. The single man we were looking for, still look for, alluded us even though we have the means to track him. These men carried certain artifacts, also missing."

Heddha asked, "What manner of wounds? And what sort of artifacts?" Then standing, she continued, "By what means can you track this man over such great expanses?"

With a faint smile, Kasumi answered, "You have some depth to you, Heddha. We wish to satisfy you; however, the answers would be incomprehensible."

"Just another way of saying you refuse to answer if I gather your meaning." This from Jahtara.

Heddha took a step closer to the two, demanding, "Could it be the wounds appeared seared or burnt by a blade with immense strength? And one of the missing artifacts happens to be the knife given to Prinus Alyeska or keyn - whatever he became?"

Jorma tried this time. "We came here because this man, who calls himself by the sinister name of Enan Tiomer, acted legally and morally to the detriment of both our peoples and you personally, Jahtara. We entertained suspicions when last we met; now, we possess facts, at least some of them. Also, rules and laws meant to protect you restrained us.

"This man, Enan, could not proceed without assistance from some of our people. This predicament puts Kasumi and me in a precarious position. We do not know who we can turn to for help. Keyn Alyeska possesses one of these advanced tools of our people. A similar weapon killed our two colleagues and, after hearing the thane's account, killed the womon of whom you spoke, Jahtara."

Kasumi knelt next to Jahtara's chair, taking her hand. "You said Enan assaulted you?"

"He gave her some potion and took her by force!" Stated Heddha.

"I am so sorry for what this man did to you, Jahtara. The thane showed us some substance from a flask. Jorma believes the potion tastes of a powerful medicine used by our people to weaken the mind and paralyze the body. We cannot fathom Enan's purpose, or even more perplexing, how he can continue these crimes. Our principles expressly forbid any interference in your lives.

"Explaining will be hard, impossible, so I will just say it. You undoubtedly saw some artifacts at our ears when we last met." Jahtara and Heddha both nodded assent. "Well," she continued after a glance at Jorma, "We talk over long distances and track our location with these devices. Our people can follow our movements, which is why we do not wear them now. We have no wish to endanger your lives to any greater extent or cause them to suspect us. We found you along the trail by tracking the knife you took from Alyeska. I know I rush through this, and it must sound absurd." Kasumi finished almost pleadingly.

There followed a long silence. Jahtara removed her hand from Kasumi's, looking to Heddha for any understanding. Finally, she said, "I am not sure who or what to believe at this moment since I have failed so miserably recently. Surely what you say sounds fantastic, yet it would explain much."

Heddha asked Jorma, "Why do this man's eyes look like ours?"

"Aye, he wears a covering, like a mask, he can place over his eyes, making them appear like yours, and he can see through them."

Jahtara's hand covered her mouth, "I saw him in the morgn doing some ritual with his eyes."

"Aye, these coverings can irritate the eyes and must occasionally be cleaned and put back in place."

Heddha asked Kasumi if she could examine her clothes, and she consented. Heddha found it unusual for clothes extensively traveled in to be clean with no sign of wear. They felt unnatural, unlike any cloth Heddha had handled before. Heddha noticed something else, no stitching in the whole garment! Heddha picked up a mug of cooled tea and spilled some on Kasumi's pants, but instead of soaking them, the tea ran right off, not even beading up. Kasumi's boots, too, appeared unnatural, with thick soles and no stitching anywhere. The strange closures on the footwear seemed to adjust on their own.

Heddha backed away, thinking deeply before asking, "Why do you not wear these eye coverings?"

Kasumi smiled, admitting, "We reasoned people would believe we came from a different land."

Jahtara cleared her throat, uneasily asking, "And your land's whereabouts?"

A disquieting awkwardness filled the study distancing everyone with a fear of saying the unsayable.

The Truth of Magic

Historical turning points enable society's shrouded secrets to surface, manifesting to a changing world in memetic shifts. Those clinging to the past can lose buoyancy during such times, grasping for insubstantial familiarity to keep afloat in the roaring rapids and phantom falls of change.

Experiencing such transitions inspires a kind of Copernicus effect, shifting the cosmological balance. The keystone no longer supports the arch of existence; instead, it becomes a mere cog unable to sustain reality's myths, causing the seemingly fixed arch to collapse onto the rubble of fables.

How to know what to hold onto and what to let slip into the past, a lesson learned? Which societal constructs perish, and what endures authentically? People above things, life over death, love transcends hate, compassion trumps greed, ability replaces power, responsiveness sets aside responsibility.

These fluxes of catalytic reframing impel consciousness through a metamorphic chrysalis that, upon emergence, recognizes the universe as possibilities, limitless and full. Such awareness constitutes a lens examining every direction! Consciousness creates new narratives through the magic of philosophical alchemy.

This illusionary chronicle utilizes such memes to reallocate to a richer truth.

The warm unmoving air of the early morgn foreshadowed the torrid heat of the coming dei. Nothing moved on the inlet's placid surface, and insects stirring in the slack air would vacate with the approaching swelter. A slender slip of smoke rose unmolested over the railing of the loggia where Heddha and Jahtara sat, the sweet smell summoning the memory of a first encounter. Jahtara rose and, peering over the balustrade, spied Jorma sitting cross-legged on the ground below, contemplating the wisp of smoke ascending lazily upwards from the bowl of his pipe.

"What occupies your mind this sultry morgn, sir?" Jahtara asked. Heddha joined her to wave a greeting.

Standing, he answered, "Time and place, Jahtara, time and place."

Cocking her head to one side, Heddha inquired, "Past or future then?"

"I have naught in the past, so I contemplate what lies ahead and where. For Kasumi, she harbors constraints from a past time and place, which concern her greatly."

"Deep thoughts prior to breaking our fast."

"Aye, yet the vapors from my pipe bring me to these profound musings. I hope our predicament grows clearer this dei."

"Are you both so deeply involved in these crimes? Find the offender, and it will end."

"I hoped such a solution would appear, Heddha. However, I fear this spreads beyond the personal horror that befalls us alone to involve realms and Inlanda herself. My people's involvement troubles me gravely, considering my colleagues' fate. My actions could leave me stranded here on Inlanda, unable to leave and, in the extreme, place my life at risk."

Heddha pulled Jahtara away from the balustrade and, glancing to confirm Jorma could not see, said in a serious tone, "Recall when first we met, I spied you riding in a vast plain, arms outstretched, tears pouring down your face, and I considered you a mad woman. I take any such charge back. Just affirm Jorma's madness. He believes he exists in the guise of a god or traveling magician!"

"Oh, Heddha, it all sounds so fantastic. Magic or the stuff of gods, I cannot say, yet you examined Auntie's death blow, saw the knife, inspected their clothes, and I saw this man doing something with his eyes."

After a moment of silence, Heddha replied, "Mayhap mind sickness possesses us all. I hope we can all come to our senses before long. If not, stay in close approximation; I prefer our madness to theirs."

Stepping back to the railing, Heddha and Jahtara smiled and waved to Jorma, suggesting they all break their fast before making rash decisions!

"May I summarize the situation? First, I wish to state my confusion, for clarity escapes me after listening to the two principal parties involved. I am in twilight, expecting the Solaura to dawn and shed illumination on a subject no one wishes to reach the light of dei," said Thane Adron Esryn Kirrydon. They sank exasperated into their ornate chair, continuing, "I have negotiated with mad keyns containing more significance than this council after a long morgn. We liken to a collection of anglers trying to catch fish by setting our hooks in each other's drinking firkins, beset the dei long starving for substance yet intoxicated, and hooked on each other's barbs."

The thane looked at the reluctant participants ending on Laud Renesmee's weak smile, asking her, "Do you have a way forward, my dear?"

"I propose removing the lynchpin from the first gate, and the next will open with greater ease until we see a clear way through. Please excuse my mudding the waters of your adroit simile, dear. Kasumi, pardon if I assume too much, yet I perceive you obstruct the discussion here."

"Obstruct?" Kasumi looked to Jorma, admitting, "Perhaps, aye." Twisting her bracelet around her wrist, she continued, "I have someone I wish to return to with the utmost desire, and Jorma restrains his words on my account. I enjoy my work here; however, I do not want to sacrifice my life for a job. Yet, the situation grows desperate, three, possibly four murders, and something much deeper transpires, persisting just out of our grasp. We, my people, were meant to be overlooked or mayhap blend in is a better way to state it, yet one of us wormed himself deeply into your lives."

The thane asked, "You mean this man from the Blue Grotto?"

Kasumi nodded, "and possibly others. By 'your lives,' I mean Inlanda. Something secretive transpires in Prinus Jahtara's realm and the Cold Waste. Jorma and I have little news, yet it seems Solaura-ward something considerable occurs also. However, the deeper we probe, the darker the explanations grow."

Laud Renesmee cleared her throat and said, "I fear the lynchpin slips free. Where do you wish to return to; where do you desire to rejoin your life?"

'If I may, su laudship," this from Jorma, "One of our major principles states that we shall not reveal ourselves or meddle in your lives. We maintain this uppermost to protect your society and its development. Also, we do not want to give one group an advantage over another. To do so might introduce an unstable element, possi-bly destroying your culture or, at the least, changing it drastically. What we call unintended consequences. Kasumi and I have struggled with these uncertainties legally and morally. Someone, either on their own or at the direction of superiors, decided to meddle in your," Jorma shrugged, finally saying, "world." After being uttered, the word sounded so foreign Jorma stopped, unsure how to explain further.

The thane about to laugh thought better of it. Laud Renesmee sat looking thoughtfully at Kasumi. Heddha, remembering her reac-tion last time she misunderstood a situation in this study, kept her thoughts to herself.

And Prinus Jahtara of lineage Davuda quietly said, "Of course."

"Herein lies a circumstance requiring the learning of a new lan-guage to describe and thus is unbelievable by present means," started

Jorma. "If I may explain in the following way – I assume you accept primitive peoples live beyond the known keyndoms in this region. Some have traveled to these dominions and brought back depictions of what we would call hunter-gatherer peoples."

"I have heard such reports," affirmed the thane. "Occasionally, a captain will inform us of contact with natural peoples across the Setting Sea. I expect you imply we contain a kinship to these peoples in your eyes."

"Not at all su laudship. The measures of societies differ widely, some simpler than yours, yet a few more advanced. We have witnessed worlds without life in our travels and others more sophisticated by some measures than our own. Some physical attributes of a culture may appear rather primitive, yet other aspects, say philosophy, emerge more advanced. No, I point out the difficulties of language in describing your culture to naïve clans in their native tongue. It is arduous to explain things such as the wheel, trebuchets, metal smelting, sailing ships, or even farming when the words do not exist"

Jahtara leaned forward, interjecting thoughtfully, "It would appear things happened by magic. Like swords cutting through stone or locating the whereabouts of an artifact or person over long distances or sending messages over the same distances."

"Precisely, these things appear quite common to us yet look like magic to you."

"Or the acts of Gods," suggested the thane.

"Adron Esryn Kirrydon, since when do you believe in gods?" Admonished the laud of the house.

"I am entertaining the idea more deeply with every addition to this tale, my dear. This home, or dare I say world you claim to come from, revolves around Inlanda much like the Luna, Solaura, and other bodies do?"

With a smile at Jorma, Kasumi said, "Here we go. In truth, your laudship, Inlanda, and the other observed noitetime bodies except for the Luna orbit the Solaura.

"In the noite sky, what you call stars, many are Solauras with worlds orbiting them, and we come from one such star called Sol with its scheme of orbiting worlds." Kasumi made a motion with a finger revolving around her fist.

Now the thane did laugh out loud, saying, "I have seen to educate myself in several subjects, and what you say appears blatantly false. Authorities see the Luna as a disk circling Inlanda, keeping only its one side visible to us. Everyone can see this. We can also ascertain Inlanda's form similarly by its shadow on the Luna. If Inlanda circled the Solaura, dei would last forever, and noite would not exist. Therefore, the Solaura must circle, orbit was the word you used, Inlanda with the resultant dei and noite." He finished with a flurry thinking the argument won.

"Unless Inlanda, which takes the shape of a globe, turns like a child's spinning top with dei and noite progressing around your world. With your permission, allow me to demonstrate, thane." Kasumi started clearing the thane's desk of papers and books. She took fruit from a large bowl on the side table, placing a big yellow globe-shaped one in the center of the developing orbital plane. A smaller, green-colored fruit orbited the central melon with a smaller nut representing the Luna. Kasumi then demonstrated the rotation of Inlanda, causing the Solaura to appear at the Rising and disappear at the Setting. The thane and Kasumi, intent on their discussion, decided to take their middei meal in the study, discussing lunar phases, change of saisons due to Inlanda's tilt, and the significance of a complete orbit around the Solaura.

The womyn with Jorma recessed to the veranda's shade for their meal. Jorma chose to roam the grounds while the womyn sat silently, observing light and shadow move across the terrace, contemplating changed perceptions of their world.

Jahtara, excited by these ideas, could not hold her thoughts, "Such wondrous advancements seem like magic when first encountered yet could lead to a more equitable world."

Heddha countered, "These advanced visitors to Inlanda seem as backward as the rest of us if we consider recent actions."

Laud Renesmee added thoughtfully, "Evil does not belong to any one time, place, social standing, stranger or friend."

Heddha replied, "I would agree somewhat with Jahtara if sharing these advances occurred equally. However, when evil feeds on poverty, fear, ignorance, or greed, the climb upwards gets eased for some, while the slope hinders every step for others with loose soil, pulling one to the basest levels. Yet, the vista gained, when shared, can fill the heart with hope."

Jahtara, more subdued, mused, "Perhaps, I enjoy the thought of an unbound spirit, yet these strangers seem bound to ignorance like us. Still, might we join with these foreigners? They too seem mystified by these circumstances; mayhap together we can gain this new vista."

Upon returning, they found Kasumi and Thane Kirrydon absorbed in discussion over the fruit-filled desk. A few pieces of fruit broke open, making the desk sticky. The thane suggested moving to the sitting room while he and Kasumi washed their hands.

When back together, Jahtara brought the knife from a pouch and asked how it worked. Jorma said, "Two things you need to know. This knife possesses many uses, including an advanced weapon. The knife can sense who holds it, so we need to introduce it to you specifically."

"Similar to Travelling Companion allowing specific riders.

"Aye. Second, the weapon always remains, how should I say... ready, yet the blade does not activate and explains how we tracked you. To pair it to you sends a message alerting our superiors. We delay activating it due to the dangerous position it would put us in. And thirdly, the weapon is risky to wield; you need instruction in its use. I am not certain how Alyeska obtained it. Did he come by it intentionally as a bribe or by accident? Perhaps someone intended the knife to come to you?"

"Jorma and I wish to return to our ship to report our findings without revealing our suspicions of this man Enan. Also, we will determine if we have allies among the ship's crew. Possibly we can pair you with the knife when we return."

Heddha, eyebrows raised, asked, "You have a ship on the Setting Sea?"

Jorma laughed. "Not on the Setting Sea," he said, pointing up. The Inlandani looked to the ceiling, painted sky blue with idyllic clouds at the periphery.

Kasumi, smiling broadly, said to Jorma, "I explained planets. Their next questions are yours."

The four Inlandani, with new perspectives on the meaning of the word, watched Kasumi and Jorma ride down the hill from the thane's estate. In the still heat of the foresetting, they felt like they spent the dei leaning into a daunting wind: numb, eyes wide, blown in every direction. The entire experience produced imbalance and jumbled thoughts.

The thane cleared their throat and spoke first, "I am distressed I did not record the events of the dei; for now, I am not sure I trust my recall. I must consult with the astronomers. Do you credit they have a ship up there?" He made a gesture indicating the sky.

Heddha rubbing her temples said. "Ship seems inadequate for such a vessel. How would it hang in the sky; if I throw a rock or bring a bird down with an arrow, they return to the ground! It may seem wondrous, yet unbelievable."

"And yet the Luna and clouds do not fall, mayhap this vessel consists of clouds," the thane wondered.

"And when it rains from this cloud-ship, does it disperse?"

Jahtara smiled at Laud Renesmee's remark. "Truly spoken. We may learn more if they return with their superordinate. The superior's title sounded strange. Plant...," Jahtara turned to Heddha, unable to find the name.

"Planet"

"Aye, Planet Protection Officer, thank you, Heddha. I have no grasp of the meaning of the office."

"To my understanding," Heddha said, "it represents a constable."

Laud Renesmee interjected, "Their position turns dangerous. Similarly, the danger concerning the two of you grows, I fear. They know not who to trust in their inquiry. Imagine returning to your realm, Prinus Jahtara. Who could you trust not to inform your brother? Kasumi seems torn; she wishes desperately to return to her spouse yet feels something unseemly takes place here. Jorma knows his direction yet does not wish his actions to harm Kasumi."

The thane agreed, "Your assessment sounds right, my dear. I must see the keyn to receive his counsel, and I think it best if Prinus Jahtara and Heddha accompany me."

Jahtara and Heddha shook their heads in unison. Jahtara spoke first, saying, "With all due respect, thane, we do not know the situation at the Middle keyndom's palatial seat. What if we are detained and held for my brother, now regent of lineage Davuda? Who would believe us if we shared this tale? Heddha and I will remain at the estate if you agree, Laud Renesmee."

From Heddha, "The prinus wishes to dwell here, milaud. However, I must decline." Then to Jahtara, "I agree with Laud Renesmee. We remain in danger, and I prefer we leave Concupia. Yet, waiting for Kasumi and Jorma to return sounds fair. I will return to Auntie's Boarding House and work on the ships. It seems safer for Jahtara to stay here. And I agree that we need not spread this account. Who can say where it will end up, and I am not sure I accept it myself!"

Thane Kirrydon responded, "Then I will remain till we know more and not set off to see Keyn Tergon, yet I must fulfill my duty eventually."

In the gathering dusk, Jahtara stood on the balcony of her room, feeling the dei cool: an emotional, confusing, astounding dei. A glimmering of stars appeared in the noite sky, joined by flickering lamps emerging along the bayfront. The interacting gravitational masses of Inlanda and the Luna resulted in a rising tide around Concupia.

Jahtara gazed with unseeing eyes at the full Luna's reflection along the length of the bay. Jahtara's mind lay unfocused, suspended in bardo, knowing naught.

Does knowing you orbit a fusional mass of hydrogen change you? Does the caterpillar know what it will become? Jahtara, just this moment, came to accept she shared her body with another. Knowing, she instinctively rebalanced herself around her newfound center of gravity. Inlanda seemed unchanged. Yet, it altered substantially from one instant to the next, even as the fetus within her changed moment to moment. The form moved again. Everything changed! Closing her eyes, she moved her consciousness to orbit the life at her center. She knew. Even if she didn't explicitly know her biology, she implicitly trusted it, confidence flowing from her experience as a womyn in the river of life, making her wise. She knew and loved what grew inside, experience merging with knowing. At this moment, her universe became love.

This rising tide of love washed over her, sweeping up and engulfing her, except for the one obstacle where in hesitation, it flowed around. Heddha, what would her reaction be? Jahtara wished for Heddha's participation in their family; she trusted Heddha would not be ripped away by the undercurrents of her experiences as a youngling. Jahtara gave no consideration, at this moment, about the why of it all; her anger arose at the act, not the result. The release of emotion last noite allowed her to recognize and accept these changes in her body. Jahtara opened her eyes, seeing the veracity of what lay before her. She lifted her sight from the wondrous reflection on the bay to the bright Luna and finally to the sky studded with the light of uncountable distant galaxies and stars. She felt certain, one dei, this child would look up at a noite sky, stand upright in the gravity of truth and know love.

Heddha climbed the rigging to the foretop and sat contemplating the morgn with her back to the foremast, sipping water from her flask. Pug returned to Auntie's (the inn's official name now), and Heddha finished up a couple of chores and then decided to see what the world looked like from midway up the mast. Her perch certainly gave her a bird's eye view of the goings and comings on a ship preparing to leave on the evening's tide. She could feel the ship's swaying motion to a greater extent up here and couldn't imagine what it must be like to be up the mast in rough seas. She thought she heard, among the harbor din, a bird call high and shrill, answered by another. A two-note call she did not know, though it sounded familiar. She looked to the tops but saw nothing but Gulls. Cupping a hand to her ear, she realized the call sounded her name – eed haaa, eed haaa! Looking to the deck, she spied Tanhā and an attendant calling to the bird high in the rigging.

The strangers returned, and the geyrles came to fetch her. Tanhā's pride shone at being given the very adult errand of getting Heddha and even more to stand aboard a seagoing vessel. On their way back, as they passed the public fountain, Jahtara called out, "I came looking for you, yet Tanhā completed my task. Please tell them we will arrive shortly. I need to speak with Heddha in confidence."

Jahtara found a secluded and shaded bench near the fountain, where Heddha joined her after rinsing her face and hands. To Jahtara's intent regard, Heddha, with one of her wry smiles, challenged, "You cannot divine my thoughts, sweet one, now out with this news filling you to bursting."

"Quite right. Well then... I am with child; that is, we will be parents!"

Time did not stop or slow, yet its passage assumed a meticulous quality, more acute. The distinct splashing of the fountain, a lyrical laugh heard among a murmur of voices, the small hook at the end of Heddha's brow scar just now noticed, and Jahtara's rising heartbeat, the parts summing a precise whole.

Heddha lifted her head slowly, tears to the brim. She took Jahtara's hand in hers and said in a voice from deep at her core, "Difficulty fills my life, and my youngling time strained my longing for family. Childhood did not provide me with the depth of love to overcome what I bore, nor am I sure I have an acquaintance with nurturing a youngling. I sense a seed of hope in my heart, yet I do not wish to afflict a hapless child with my misreckoning of life."

"Oh, Heddha, I do not intend to replicate my memories of distance and discontent either. Your heart overflows with love. I see the care you provide animals, the compassion expressed to Auntie's family, and the understanding and love you have afforded me. I know our love will do much to support any youngling."

Heddha lifted Jahtara's hand, pressing it to her cheek, saying, "You have opened shutters I closed to the light. Perhaps, I could attempt this with you; in truth, I feel my heart swelling at the prospect. Can you feel it?" Heddha laid Jahtara's hand over her chest, and then, putting her hand over Jahtara's heart, she declared, "You once proclaimed by your honor to share our journey. I now openly state my desire to share these efforts and joys with you!"

"Aye, and right after my proclamation, my brother appeared. Let us hope our future fares better this dei."

"Mayhap our future awaits us even now with the thane. What assured you of this expectancy?

"I do not remember beginning my estrum. Not sure what to expect, this being my first, yet my belly feels swollen, and the child quickened."

"Movement, truly!" Heddha exclaimed.

"Aye, the first last evening!"

"In the thane's study, you expressed great anger towards this man's aggress. Surely this emotion lies deep. How can our feelings not affect this child?"

"Aye, I attempted to work those tangles out, an illegitimate child born to a prinus of the lineage Davuda. Yet, I am no longer a prinus, and perhaps you and I can make a family."

"Aye. Yet, I speak of deep hurt. You cannot cleanse it with cursory washing. A bitter seed may grow into a vine wrapping itself around your innards, perhaps choking your feelings towards this child."

"I shall not allow it. Wonderment fills me to the brim since discovering my condition. Let us not spoil the moment."

Heddha nodded. Smiling, she asked, "Have you told any others?"

"I have told no others, Heddha. Let us see how this dei proceeds, yet I thought not to tell anyone else just now."

Arriving at the laudship's study, Tanhā waited, hardly containing herself with news. An intriguing third stranger appeared todei, and Tanhā seemed quite upset when the thane shooed her out and closed the study doors.

Another womon did accompany Jorma and Kasumi. She wore her hair severely combed back in a tight bun. Her attire consisted of a long dress of offworlder material, a collar high on her neck, long sleeves, and bulky layers of petticoats. Kasumi introduced Cora Krupin, Planetary Protection Officer on the Corporate ship Nadasagrado.

"Well," she began, "It seems I have overdressed for the saison, and I did not know womyn here wore britches." Nodding at Laud Renesmee, she continued, "At least most of them. I wonder if you would mind if I disrobed? I am sweltering in this dress. Do not worry. I have my officer's uniform on beneath." She looked at the three Inlanda womyn staring back with blank gazes, then looking at Kasumi and Jorma, she asked, "Am I speaking too fast?"

Kasumi and this womon talked for a few moments in their language, then Kasumi spoke on her behalf, "This is Cora's, if I may be informal, first outing to Inlanda, and she misjudged her dress. She feels uncomfortable due to this lapse and begs your indulgence. Cora wears an officer's uniform under her costume; however, our dress appears more revealing than your fashion permits. Also, I have asked her to speak slower."

Laud Renesmee cleared her throat to say, "The thane and I have traveled widely, encountering many different customs and dress. We wish your superordinate's comfort. She can put herself at ease if the prinus does not mind."

Jahtara added, "Please, she does not need to accommodate herself to our manner. I do wish for a fuller understanding of her office and its duties. I consider it much like a constable, correct? I am surprised she is not more involved in light of what happens here."

"I prefer if you would call me Cora," the PPO started slower this time. "And if I could just make myself comfortable, I will attempt to give an accounting of myself."

"Of course," Jahtara intoned.

With Kasumi's help unlacing the ties on the back of the dress, Cora quickly stepped out of the gown, kneeled at the thane's desk, and removed cosmetic lenses from her eyes. She dislodged the constraints from her hair and let it fall forward with a shake of her head. When Cora stood, the Inlandani could appreciate the ostentatious display of her uniform. Heddha and her laudship, having grown up on farms, were familiar with naked bodies and the rawness of life around animals. Jahtara had lived a sheltered life with refined dress occasionally exposing a full measure of cleavage while emphasizing small waists, but skirts were monstrosities, obscuring a womon's form. Jahtara thought Cora's uniform consisted of paint hiding blemishes similar to face paint. Parts of the garment were skintight and followed every protrusion, crease, mound, and curve. Although it could hardly be called blousy, the blouse's glossy blue material looked like small scales pasted onto her skin. The pants were a mat blue with red stripes running around her waist and down the sides of her legs: the ensemble left nothing to the imagination. No collar existed at the neck, and black epaulets squared the shoulders. The epilates and left cuff exhibited red striped insignia, two thicker with a thinner one in-between. On Inlanda, the custom was for womyn to wear their blouses longer over their striders. Instead, this uniform fit like zest on spice.

The Thane admired a culture able to condone the sheer audacity, and Laud Renesmee delighted in the look of the fabric yet appeared uncomfortable with its form. Jahtara stared open-mouthed, and Heddha simply smiled at everyone's reaction. Comfortable with their cultural norms, Kasumi and Jorma looked chagrined for the Inlandani.

Cora, oblivious to it all, sat, crossed her legs, and let out a long breath exclaiming, "Oh, by the gods of the multiple worlds, this feels better!

"Now, Jorma and Kasumi have told me of their investigation... perhaps, inquiry sounds preferable, into our colleagues' disappearance and apparent deaths. They have some quite troubling suspicions. My role as Planetary Protection Officer obligates me to follow up on this line of inquiry because these two men died while on Inlanda. At first, I assumed they died at the hands of Inlandani. Now I have some concerning questions. Am I making myself clear, not speaking too fast?"

"For the most part, aye. If I understand correctly, you only concern yourself with what happens here, on Inlanda?" questioned Jahtara.

"Aye, prinus, I have no direct authority on board ship; the vessel constitutes corporate property, with the captain an executive officer for the Nadasagrado corporation. I have jurisdiction over orbiting masses in the system due to my officer's commission from the Commonwealth, not directly from the corporation. If this sounds straightforward, I can assure you many ambiguities exist in this type of hierarchal affiliation, and the regulations were drafted specifically with equivocation in mind."

Thane Kirrydon raised his walking stick and, when noticed by the PPO, thoughtfully asked, "Here and in most keyndoms, to my knowledge, the monarchy regulates or owns most enterprises, in some cases with the aristocracy. Still, everyone must do the bidding of our sovereign."

"Aye, the pendulum of time swings in wide arcs through the spiral of history. In our small patch of space, the pendulum swings in the direction of corporations circuitously owning the Commonwealth, meaning I, an officer of the Commonwealth, am indirectly an employee of the corporations. All this complicates my authority. If the corporation does not directly involve itself in the situation on Inlanda, the captain will likely back my position. If the corporation's direct involvement exists, my position will have to coincide with theirs, or I will place myself in the same menace facing Kasumi and Jorma. The degree of compulsion the corporation applies depends on the time and money they have devoted to this venture. Oh, and how much they and their investors stand to gain! My pardon, this must sound difficult due to your unfamiliarity with our society."

Looking at the others, Jahtara ventured, "Aye, yet I feel I have the marrow of the situation. I also judge Inlandani account for some involvement, not in the demise of your colleagues, yet Keyn Alyeska's artifact came from these men."

Misunderstanding, Cora went on a tangent, "An important aspect of my duties comprises the prevention of contamination of your world with illnesses, ideas, and products that could change the course of life here until sufficiently advanced to absorb those changes without danger to your development."

"How parental of you. You wish to keep us backward and go through the same mistakes and hardships you have experienced."

Cora smiled at Jahtara's retort, "Or you may suffer different mistakes and hardships, swinging your society in unknowable directions from ours." She shrugged, continuing, "This represents our society's current philosophy. Significantly, my charge todei; the protection of resources here from theft and exploitation. In other words, from interstellar piracy.

"I agree. Keyn Alyeska and probably your brother involved themselves. Assuredly, the corporation initiated whatever goes on here and Solauraward. Most importantly, all this revolves around you, Prinus Jahtara."

"Of course, through an arranged marriage to shore up a treaty. I thwarted this scheme when I fled, correct? So except for my possession of the knife obtained from Alyeska, how am I involved?"

"With my deepest regret, I must inform you of the profound extent of su grandeza's involvement. I have failed in the duties of Planetary Protection Officer by allowing myself to be deceived." Cora didn't look directly at Jahtara while saying this.

Jahtara said, "The depth of your regret concerns me. I am at a loss. Why so disturbed at my involvement?"

Cora looked to Jorma, who said, "You must tell her."

Without further delay, Cora said, "Certainly, you know or suspect you await a child."

The thane stood in shock; laud Renesmee appeared staggered, covering her gaping mouth; Heddha held Jahtara's hand. Jahtara said directly, "I came to know of this only last evening when the child moved most distinctly, and I told Heddha a few moments ago. You came to know how?"

Jorma spoke first, "This will take some explaining, prinus."

"I think I have revoked any claim to the title, prinus of the realm. It would please me if everyone stopped addressing me so."

"I fear circumstances may suggest other intrigues, yet if you wish. Cora and I searched this man's background, Enan Tiomer, not his real name. We found he brought specialized tools aboard our vessel. He can use these tools for... well, Heddha knows growing up on a farm, you can breed for certain characteristics in sheep for, say, bigger ewes or longer coats, and by choosing for these traits, you can eventually produce larger ewes with longer coats. Farmers make the same selections with plants producing larger fruits or grains that separate from the chaff easier during thrashing. Each animal or plant contains unique instructions to pass these traits to its offspring. Instructions akin to a book with individual letters making words combined into sentences joined to make up passages until you have complete directions. An instruction manual copied, or we would say replicated during reproduction. This man specializes in the advanced understanding of this process and can use machines to manipulate the letters and words to match or make new instructions or traits, what we call genes. He then can introduce these changes into a conceiving."

Jorma took a deep breath to continue, "We found evidence in the records of the initial exploratory visit to Inlanda many jahrs ago, and it told of samples taken from individuals here. These samples represent the instruction book on how to replicate everyone examined. One of those samples came from your great-grandmother, Jahtara. She stood out since she held a copy of a trait or gene different from other samples. This trait controlled the making of substances affecting activity in the brain," he said, pointing to his head. "Unfortunately, her samples and the sequencing of the gene were lost. The records we found suffered from removed or missing details yet remarked on the potential for great advantage.

"The study of manipulating instructions and their controls advanced significantly since the first journey here and our return. Enan, can increase the control and effectiveness of these traits and even make extra copies to strengthen the effects."

Jahtara, with wide-eyed concern, asked, "I understand breeding can enhance traits in animals. However, I could not completely understand the rest. You say this Enan manipulated something in this child or me?"

"We believe his intentions did not involve the typical motivations for rape, although he certainly assaulted you. He wanted to implant an egg into your womb or place something like a seed, fertilizing your egg."

Jahtara released Heddha's hand and sat upright in her chair, asking again, "What did he do to this child or me!"

Kasumi said, "He assembled this conceiving, manipulating the traits. We do not think this will affect you, yet the child will certainly be impacted. We do not understand why he did this or devised to do it this way. He could have made these changes independent of you and implanted the egg into a womon of our kind."

"Will the child turn out a monster?"

Cora continued, "We feel not. Evidence supports he planned this to avoid these types of problems. Besides the biological reason for impregnating you, Enan may have legal reasons; in fact, the legal reasons may be of paramount importance. After reviewing all the evidence, I feel he took extraordinary measures to ensure the compatibility of you and this child. By this, I mean, you can carry this pregnancy to completion, and the child will be a mixture or, more properly, a hybrid of our two peoples with possible enhancement of some traits."

Kasumi sighed, saying, "Oh Jahtara, we do not know enough at this point. The company backed all this, or mayhap the Nadasagrado Corporation instigated the whole endeavor, all highly unethical and illegal. No one of us knows how this will conclude. This seems madness!"

Jahtara's hands were shaking. She took a deep trembling breath, letting it escape in a long exhale. She placed her still hands over her abdomen, remembering the experience of last noite. Jahtara didn't think things happened for a reason. Instead, she created the reasoning for what happened in her life and determined her response; she was not responsible, not a victim. She looked to Heddha and, finding her eyes saw deep concern there. Leaving one hand on her belly, she took Heddha's hand, asking, "Have your feelings changed?"

"What is, is. What comes concerns me. I do not understand much of what Jorma said; however, I heard Cora say this man's intent meant to gain a lawful advantage. Can you explain this, Kasumi?"

"Perhaps Cora could answer this better. Her duties include knowing the legalities involved in such situations, although this seems unprecedented."

Cora started with, "I said these laws and connected rules exist intentionally vague and open to interpretations. They make inhabited worlds appear protected from exploitation while containing many loopholes. I beg your pardon. Mayhap you might comprehend the word opportunities better; many options for corporations to render the law to their advantage. Jahtara, I regret speaking of this child in such an unnatural way.

"Of disputes involving children, unless determined otherwise, the issue or offspring live equally under the guardianship of both parents. The law considers corporate entities people. Suppose the corporation proved it originated a significant portion of an issue. In that case, the corporation constitutes an owner or parent. If that holds, a corporation could attempt to claim the child, stipulating the child a product, and the company could patent the child or a sizable portion thereof." At the quizzical looks from the Inlandani, she added, "I beg your pardon, patent signifies a legally binding instrument showing ownership of a process or product. The patent holder would not own the child but the information it carried. And here it gets horrible – If one of the parents or genetic donors dies, the remaining parent could legally assume full ownership and total control of all patents.

"Once they show they have full control and the product originated on Inlanda, they might claim other resources of Inlanda. Suppose the corporation claims certain substances necessary to the child's well-being exist principally on Inlanda. They may also claim heredity rights, control of land, realms, and even sovereignty over people. If Jahtara dies without the company's involvement, say in battle, all the better for their case. Especially if they can show that Jahtara stole, introduced, used, and usurped offworld knowledge or products. Jahtara obtaining the knife may not comprise part of their original plan, yet they can use it. Such a scenario plays into the corporation's plan if they, for instance, intervene to prevent extensive bloodshed. I know many 'what-ifs,' yet remember we dwell far from our home - and the company controls all information. Much that has happened could fit into such a scheme, assuming their employees back their story, including me. Patenting plants or their constituents in healing and agriculture happens commonly. Even making living organisms with unique genomes occurs. But nothing like this. Making a self-aware chimeric being extends to the unconscionable. For the first time, this suggests a willingness for a corporation to assert claims concerning living organisms within the," Cora switched to Galactic Standard, "taxonomic subtribe Homininae." Then back to Inlandani, "Which includes both our peoples."

The thane raised his otter-headed cane again, "This discussion alarms me. While I do not follow all of it, the earlier portion applies more to my understanding, considering my office. Your society's merchants seem to be in authority. Could this assumption be correct?"

"Aye. From your perspective, I am sure this seems unusual, yet not so different from Inlanda, where a monarch comprises the authority. The keyn controls the land, including the creatures inhabiting this land. Law and justice do not exist equally, yet those who command the law sway justice. Am I correct su laudship?"

"Now you have me spun around. The very nature of your existence keeps me spinning this dei. I will need to ponder this matter; however, mere merchants rising to these heights seems inconceivable."

Jorma addressed Jahtara, "We have discovered much, yet more conjecture than proof, su alt… Jahtara. I think you can understand that danger surrounds you. I feel they will not act till the child's birth. Still, they may attempt to steal you away."

Heddha stood with urgency, pacing, "This was my feeling all along. We must leave at once. Everything told todei only enforces this feeling, does it not?"

"I concur, Heddha." Then Jorma continued to Jahtara, "I can instruct you in the use…."

"I feel faint at this dei's news," interrupted Jahtara. "Before I swoon, could we take a repose?"

Laud Remesmee stood and, with a knowing nod to Jahtara, indicated the study door, "I am feeling lightheaded myself with all this talk. I will have the servants set out refreshments in the garden."

Jahtara held Heddha back. Heddha, now even more concerned, asked, "Does the child make you tired? Do you wish to lay down? I will help you to your room?"

Placing her hands on Heddha's shoulders, Jahtara admonished, "Heddha, do not speak such nonsense. We have important matters to discuss. Come to my room." She turned to leave then, looking back over her shoulder, said to the bewildered Heddha, "Get a wiggle on!"

Before closing the door to her bedroom, Jahtara rechecked the hallway. "Tell me, Heddha, have your feelings changed in light of what this dei reveals?"

"I persist steadfastly. I pledged to join you in this family. A promise of love, and no matter the circumstances, love remains."

"Aye, my feelings in this have grown stronger. This child needs protectors along a dangerous path, and we do not know who to trust. Therefore, we must keep our own counsel in this matter. Agreed?"

"Aye, confiding in others could endanger them and ourselves."

"I recognize other grounds for concern. The knife, the meeting at the Ways Respite, and the suggestion we take the coast road seem planned. How about the intrigues involving potential danger to themselves? Are they trustworthy? How could Enan plan this by himself? He knew what, where and when things were going to happen. Too many unknowns, for instance, what if my brother's revolt fails, does the corporation lose?"

"Perhaps not. If you prevail, you become queyn of the Davuda realm and this child your heir. If you die by whatever means, the corporation becomes regent to the heir. They win either way, at least in their eyes. It seems we find ourselves alone once again. In this, no one must know our plans."

"Aye, only us then," they hugged, holding their embrace until Jahtara said, "It seems we need a plan?"

"I would consider continuing Solauraward. Perhaps we could find something to show the realms how these usurpers abuse them. It also confuses any pursuit!" Heddha added, "Did you know Absan traveled Solauraward with a delegation of cnihts some time ago?"

"What? How do you know of this?"

"Laud Remesmee spoke with him at the Middle Keyndom celebration of Keyn's Dei. Both realms sent cnihts to inquire into unusual tidings along the Solauraward bearing."

"So both keyndoms know something strange occurs there, yet I hold no hope such knowledge will change my brother's or Alyeska's course."

Before Heddha could respond, a light knock sounded. She moved quickly to open the door a fraction, then wider for Jorma to slip through.

"Pardon my intrusion. I told the others I would check on you. I suspected you wished some discretion, and I wanted to share a way to activate the knife while deactivating the ability to follow its whereabouts."

Heddha interrupted, "And you can do this now?"

"I am able. This knife can harm, and although it holds safeguards, it can also cause great injury. I want to offer my services to instruct Jahtara in its use."

"Do you."

"Aye," then cocking his head to the side, said, "I understand your hesitancy. You do not know who to trust. I would remain here alone only to instruct you."

"Without Kasumi, that seems unusual."

"Kasumi's concerns conflict with my thinking of late."

With narrowed eyes, Heddha asked, "Do you suspect her?"

Jorma shook his head, "Although technically we work with the Commonwealth, the corporation hires us. We tend to keep separate from the corporation crew. Kasumi worked for the company for quite some time and has a strong relationship binding her. Would you put such a relationship at risk?"

Jahtara placed her hand on Heddha's arm, saying, "No," then to Jorma, "Still, we are wary. However, I see no harm and some benefit from your offer. I accept and thank you. How will you remain without Kasumi?"

"She feels torn by what occurs here yet would not protest remaining aboard ship, especially if the ship's Planetary Protection Officer asked her to return with her."

"And they will leave this dei?"

"Aye."

"Good, we will return to the garden directly and start my instruction on the new dei. I thank you for your sincerity, Jorma."

With Jorma gone, Heddha said, "Recall Jorma's telling of encounters with wildlings? This story brought to mind large rodents I saw once that built complicated dams and island homes with underwater entrances. They manipulate the lands around them to enhance their survival, yet we consider them simple animals and hunt them for their desirable fur. I believe this is how these offworlders view us; they mean to manipulate us with a sense of superiority. You will not keep this arrangement with Jorma, am I correct?"

"Quite so. While I sense no harm in Jorma, these strangers are just that, outsiders, and their purpose proves difficult to fathom. Heddha, can we leave this noite?"

"We can always ride to the valley then Solauraward following Absan's path. However, the thane stables our mounts; we cannot leave without them finding out."

"By ship, then? If Absan's troop left some time ago, might we take the faster route, join them, and learn what information they obtained?" Jahtara took Heddha's hand, asking, "What are your feelings on this?"

Heddha sighed, "I still bear the scars, yet let us see what comes to pass. The ship Pug and I just prepared leaves this noite after dusk. A small private room remained available. Ah, this leads to a difficulty purchasing the space without Dunnyn discovering it and informing the thane."

"Instruct Pug to acquire the berths. If asked, he can say a merchant boarding at Aunties directed him to obtain them."

"Excellent. I will leave now if you can make my excuses."

Jahtara took Heddha in her arms. "Heddha, I cannot imagine you lived this way for so many jahrs, always taking flight."

"Aye, yet with a companion, it seems easier."

"Go now and prepare. We will meet dockside at dusk."

"You will not bring the knife?"

"No, I will leave it with the thane."

"Probably for the best if they can use it to find us. Till dusk then."

"Wait! The name of the ship?"

"Aye, on the Morgn Star's seaward dock, the Insanely Lucid."

Jahtara slipped unseen through a defect in the estate's wall onto the gathering shadows along the road. In the dwindling deilight, she followed the descent from the thane's estate through the varied edifices populating the town. Initially, she could see the bay and ship's masts over the rooftops, but now Concupia closed in, funneling her to the bayfront and obscuring her view. Jahtara hoped to sail by the time the thane's household settled in for dinner. Kasumi had left with Cora walking down the same hill Jahtara now stole along. Kasumi seemed sincere when taking her leave, even giving Jahtara an embrace. Whatever Jorma's intentions, they would be foiled by Jahtara stealing away. She left behind a letter for the thane and the knife for safekeeping.

Jahtara harbored some uneasiness taking a sea voyage, not knowing the effects of the rolling ship while pregnant, though could it be worse than a long journey mounted. Traveling by ship occupied her mind nearing the quay. A wainwright shop stood by the side of the road, including a small yard harboring various wagons needing repair. A damaged cart lay on its side in the ditch, missing the wheels on its downward flank, and a brazier burned near the corner, filled with the dei's unusable scraps. She didn't see the cniht leading his mount turn from the quay into her path from the opposite direction, and Jahtara clipped his shoulder, knocking herself to the ground. The cniht kindly helped Jahtara to her feet, and she saw the crest of the High Mountain Keyndom on his breastplate. Jahtara raised her face to his concerned look.

"I beg your pardon. Matters occupied my attention, and I did not see you approach," the cniht stammered, starting to brush the dust from Jahtara's garments, then thought better of touching any part of her anatomy.

"You come from the High Keyndom?"

"Very astute, ma'am. I mean to say… Most would not know the High Mountain Keyndom crest here in Concupia."

Jahtara noticed the dented armor and worn, dusty clothes. With a hitch in her voice, Jahtara hesitatingly asked, "You journeyed far, sir?"

"Aye and have a way further to end my travels. I come directly from the Middle Keyndom palatial seat, and beforehand, I traveled Solauraward on a warrant from my keyn." The cniht looked away, continuing, "Alas, I am the only one to return. I traveled here with a messenger conveying important developments to Thane Kirrydon. We separated on the outskirts of town. I currently look for someone at an establishment named, I believe, Auntie's."

Jahtara took a step back, asking, "If you please, sir, your name?"

The cniht's head came up quickly, answering, "Sir Absan Nusri, son to Ministrant Nusri, counselor to Su Alteza Keyn Nessa. To whom do I speak?"

Jahtara could speak another name, be on her way, and Absan would never find Heddha. None would know except her. She lifted her chin to pronounce, "Jahtara, kind sir."

Sir Absan dropped to a knee, head bowed, uttering, "Su majeste!"

"Sir, I am no longer a prinus of the realm."

"Quite right, you became queyn, yet how did you know, su majeste?"

"My brother became the regent, not I. Sir Absan, please stand."

With his head still bowed and in a confused voice, he stated, "You have sovereignty over the Middle Keyndom, not lineage Davuda."

Jahtara glanced about, confirming her world had not tilted. Out to sea, a gradient of light hung above the horizon, shrinking Jahtara's existence to this insignificant corner, lit by a brazier illuminating a dusty street cluttered with a graveyard of broken carriages. Before her knelt a cniht, Heddha's past lover, naming her queyn; her life turned surreal.

She knelt, explaining, "Sir Absan, Keyn Tergon remains the sovereign. You are confused by your journey and hardships."

"Alas not, su grace, the keyn died. This comprises the urgent message for Thane Kirrydon."

"Still, I am not in line to be regent of the Middle Keyndom."

"I am told the keyn sired only one child, an heir who died after seven Warmings. No other relative lives except you and your brother. I am certain su alteza recalls, the sister of the then keyn of the Middle Keyndom wed your great grandfather."

"Yet," she persisted, "my father or brother occupy their place in the line of descent, surely."

"I beg your pardon. No one knows if your father lives. Keyn Tergon named you on his death bed, not Prinus Baeddan. A rumor circulating suggests your brother raises an army against the Middle Realm. You are queyn, su majeste!"

Deep in thought, Jahtara walked to the carriage lying on its side, clutching one of the broken wheels until finally, she gave it a light spin. When it stopped creaking, she turned to Sir Absan, asking, "You look for Heddha?"

"Aye. I learned she abides in Concupia. It seems a lifetime passed for us, yet I wish to see Heddha again. We were unknowing younglings, and I now comprehend the price of life... I care to see her again, a womon, to know her course since her banishment.

"You shall find her a fine womon. Absan, I must ask you. What did you discover on your travels, Solauraward?"

"Tortured people within a tortured world. I find it hard to describe even now, yet I must. My charge includes reporting to the sovereign of the Middle Keyndom on my way home.

"People go there with promises of work and recompense. Those in charge cheat and degrade, working folks to death. The over-lauds pay the workers, deducting for food and lodgings, overcharging for supplies, and underpaying for labor. The miners dig great rents in Inlanda, producing unbreathable, choking dust. The womyn befit only cooks and comfort womyn. People die, and yet more come. Shanghaiers travel about with full purses to fool others into coming. It goes on dei after dei. And always they extract, for what I know naught. Mayhap some new metal. At first, we demanded explanations in the name of our keyns. They laughed. We persisted, and the first of us died. Some tried to appear like serfs, dressing similarly, to discover what went on there. We never saw them again. Those remaining decided to leave to warn our sovereigns, and they road us down. They have strange weapons, like fire sticks, melting through us like a hot knife at lard; weapons and armor offered little resistance. I escaped the slaughter yet, not the fear."

Jahtara noticed movement across the street. A shape stepped from the shadows of an alleyway. Even in the light of the fire, the figure retained a shadow-like presence, ominous and indistinct. A noitemare swept over Jahtara, transitioning to harsh reality, yet its dark somnolent feeling lingered. The saturnine Enan strode forth, stopping a short distance from her. He appeared different yet the same: shorter hair, rounded pupils, but with the brooding appearance Jahtara remembered from the noite she halted him at the bottom of the stairs.

With a mocking smile, Enan said, "I did not dare wish to catch you both this noite. So nice to hear the wonderful report from Sir Absan. Is it not Jahtara?"

"What business do you have with Queyn Jahtara?" Absan said, stepping between Jahtara and Enan.

Jahtara questioned, "How do you know of Sir Absan?"

Enan smiled, but it didn't brighten his features, "Do you not love it when a plan comes together? I will answer Sir Absan first with your permission, su majeste, although he will not make sense of most of it."

Absan replied, "I have heard of the queyn's plight within lineage Davuda. Surely this subversion lies in the past. She stands as queyn of the Middle Realm."

Enan chuckled, "Oh, you have not heard the whole tale. Even the queyn does not possess the complete narrative, Sir Absan. Queyn Jahtara murdered two foreign men in the Cold Waste, with the discarded suiter, Keyn Alyeska, issuing a warrant. The would-be monarch stole a valuable knife from one of the murdered men, bringing it to Concupia. In fact, she murdered a womon here with the weapon. I believe everyone called the unfortunate womon Auntie. Left behind daughters, if I am not mistaken."

Jahtara lunged at the braggart, but Absan held her back with a straightened arm.

"Witnesses saw Jahtara leaving the Blue Robes compound and entering the boarding house prior to discovery of the body. Jorma and Kasumi will testify to seeing Jahtara with the knife on several occasions. And one of the murdered men fathered her unborn child."

Jahtara stopped struggling and stood still. Quietly she said, "You lie, Jorma, and Kasumi will not speak your falsehood. You killed those men and Auntie. You stupefied and assaulted me at the sanctuary. When you return to your home, they will expose your treachery."

"Are you sure you know us this well," he mocked. "Kasumi will not jeopardize her future, and Jorma, with his unsavory past, will find himself far from home if he does not cooperate. When I arrive back home - all this will have occurred in the past and very far away – bribes will be made, influenced applied, and people will not care. The whole business will appear to embrace the ideal of the law. We manipulate the view of denizens by the truth we tell. Ultimately, they believe the Nadasagrado Corporation provides valuable services at economical prices. And no one will care about anything else."

Jahtara tasted bilious anger rising, "I care, and you will not succeed in this assault on Inlanda or me." Saying this, Jahtara felt a mounting benevolence for her home world.

"Jahtara, such simpleton beliefs. You think you have a say on the matter? This world belongs to those with the knowledge, means, and power to exploit it. Your world's resources are turned into products by the corporation, on the cheap, who then market them for whatever they demand. All of it, the information the child carries, the minerals of this planet, anything we choose to exploit, including food or water, are ours to take."

Enan slowed his breathing, "You have annoyed me once again. Yet, the last time you foiled my aims by running away from your betrothed, it simplified the plan. My failed attempt to steal back the knife at the boarding house turned out fortunate, and the plan advanced. Evidence will show you murdered Absan and Heddha with the fire sword you process." Absan stepped forward, drawing his sword, but Enan held up a hand, halting him in place. "If you could wait a trifle, Sir Absan." Then to Jahtara, "Mayhap Heddha can wait until after the birthing, removing you together, unless she becomes troublesome in the meantime."

Absan started forward, Jahtara grabbing his shoulder to restrain him, but he eluded her to pull free. She never saw one of these knives in action but knew its effect on Auntie and sought to stop the inevitable result. "Absan, please, you know the terrible outcome of these fire sticks. Ride away while I divert him; he will not harm me."

"You can do naught here, queynie. Absan's death will prejudice the High Keyndom to join your brother in the fight against the Middle Realm. The demise of a ministrant's son and cniht of the realm seems sufficient cause to go to war, especially when the queyn of the Middle Realm brings about his end. You have helped me immensely, Jahtara." Turning to Absan, Enan baited, "Your journey to the High Mountain Keyndom with your knowledge will end here. If you please, Sir Absan." Enan bowed and, straightening, drew a knife similar to Jahtara's.

Sir Absan circled away from Jahtara, placing the firelight behind him, looking for any advantage. Enan advanced on Absan, who lifted his heavy sword overhead using both hands, bringing it down with strength to cleave Enan with a mighty blow. Enan, without haste, switched the knife to his left hand. A flame leaped from the blade's tip, and, holding it high, Enan let Absan's sword come to meet it. The sword passed through the fiery shaft, cleaving it in two, the freed blade clattering to the street. Absan's momentum carried his swing to the ground, still holding the haft. He backed away, throwing the useless hilt down. Without hope, he drew a long knife from his side. The wheel from the damaged wagon hit the back of his thighs, halting his retreat. Enan arrogantly strode forward until he held the plasma tip close to Absan's chest plate.

Absan dropped the knife, declaring defiantly, "I understood little of your accusations against Queyn Jahtara. Yet, I understand you to be an unwholesome being who reaps sorrow in multitude. I am relieved to join my valiant companions."

Saying nothing, Enan straightened his arm, plunging the blazing thin tip through Absan's armor, piercing his chest and, easy as slicing freshly churned butter, inscribed a neat circle around his heart. He extinguished the fiery shaft and watched the blood gush from Absan's chest. The body sagged backward onto the unbalanced wheel, slowly swinging back and forth until it tilted fully to one side, dumping the limp body to the ground. Sir Absan excarnated, and the creaking wheel turned.

The smell of burnt flesh sickened Jahtara, and the act's cold, calculated cruelty stunned her innocence.

Enan turned to Jahtara, speaking as if conversing over a fine after-dinner wine, "I enjoyed this immensely, having anticipated the act since he fled. Your presence made it noteworthy. I await the closing act of this drama when you complete your womanly duty, and I collect my property, having no further use for you."

Jahtara swallowed upwelling bile. With a hand on her belly and self-reverence, she said, "I do not exist for your use, nor do I anticipate cruelty. I look forward to the birth of this child and sharing the loving experience with Heddha. I fear not death at your hands. If you use force to alter who I am, I die by increments that I will not do."

"What you will find…." An arrow creased Enan's hip from out of nowhere, leaving a rent in his pants and an oozing wound. Jahtara squatted low, a second arrow arching overhead, striking the knife in Enan's hand. It did minor damage yet caused him to switch on the fire sword. A third flew over Jahtara, and in readiness, he stepped aside, cutting the missile in half. He turned, running up the darkened alley, the blade extinguished.

Heddha, a fourth shaft notched, ran up, watching the shadows for further danger. "Are you harmed?" she checked.

"I have no wounds to my body. Yet, I grieve, Absan lies dead with his heart exscinded."

"Absan? Yet, how…?" Heddha knelt at his side, trying to understand what she saw. He seemed more substantial. Maybe the High Keyndom armor increased his significance. She gently brushed a curl off his forehead. Out of a dream, she said, "Some noites I agonized for sleep on the cold stone floor beneath my mistress' bed. My dry, cracked nose burned with every inspiration, chilling me to my cold heart, each frigid breath torture to endure, to the point I wished for my last. Thoughts of Absan warmed my heart, and I took my next breath for him. A good spirit."

"He came to see you, see the womon, and know you are well. He seemed too kind to deserve this."

"And what does Enan deserve for the evil killing of Absan?" Heddha countered through clenched teeth.

"Deserve? He deserves what we all deserve, a path out of ignorance to stop our suffering."

"And what of Absan's suffering?"

"His suffers no longer in this life." Jahtara stood, laying her hand on Heddha's shoulder, adding, "Do not dwell long. Others come. I have more tidings to tell at the ship."

Bardo

Transitions offer an opportunity to move from the confusion of igno-rance to clarity. Through such renewal, the marvel of consciousness manifests: opening the door to a new dei upon wakening, reflecting on impermanence at death, welcoming the opportunity for a first breath at birth or even the next breath in the present.

Such passages remind us of our interdependence. We exist together, not during pursuits that keep us distracted and separate, but in the emptiness between thoughts, the pause between sentences, and the space between exhale and inhale: a mindful awareness amid thoughts, words, and deeds; a bardo connecting intervals of separation.

This tale arose from emptiness and fades with impermanence.

Jahtara approached the docking berth of the Insanely Lucid, spotting Pug standing next to Heddha's belongings. "Pug, good to see you here. Heddha suffered a shock. Her friend lies dead, murdered, by the man that killed Auntie." Pug moved towards the quay; Jahtara stopped him with, "The killer fled, and Heddha comes, presently. Pug, can you accompany Heddha on this voyage? There exists some danger."

"Aye," he held up a parcel of his belongings, "sep she says I cannot come. You not comin'?"

"Complications have arisen. I must stay."

"Stay?" Heddha questioned, coming up to Jahtara.

"Aye, you must leave at once, with Pug to go with you."

"And you? What changed our plans? Come on, out with the story."

"This seems too incredible to be untrue." Jahtara admitted running a hand through her hair, "Remember once you were astonished a prinus would attend to removing your shoes, well... now you have a queyn for a lover!" Pug turned away in mortification. Giving Pug a push on the shoulder, Jahtara admonished, "Pug, if you wish to join us in this enterprise, you must know the truth of your fellow questers." Then to Heddha, "Absan advised me I rule the Middle Keyndom. Keyn Tergon died, leaving no close kin, and we share a distant family tie. On his death bed, he named me to succeed him!" Hearing this, Pug dropped to a knee. "Why do people keep doing this? Pug, please stand. I doubt you ever gave a wit about the keyn." Pug stood with a wink to Heddha and a hesitant shove to the shoulder of the reluctant queyn.

Putting her hand on Pug's shoulder, Jahtara continued, "Enan threatened Heddha's life, so there exists plenty of danger on this journey." Then to Heddha, she pleaded, "I feel you must leave with Pug this instant." Jahtara knew objections were coming and cut Heddha off with, "He will not attempt to harm me till after the birthing. He said this. I will go into hiding; I have a place in mind and will let Laud Renesmee know the way. I must keep him from this child at all expense and thus keep myself sound. I will name Thane Kirrydon my regent, and hopefully, he can use his skills to keep the realm together until we figure out our course."

Heddha interjected in a neutral voice, "You certainly sound like a queyn."

"I regret my tone Heddha. I am in shock and scared. The way Enan killed Absan, I have never witnessed such cruelty. The reasons for proceeding Solauraward still stand, it may confuse pursuit, and we must find evidence to gather others to our cause."

"We partake in a campaign now?"

"Heddha, I will miss your wry wit. I love you so," and she gathered Heddha in her arms. They clung to their love, feeling the other's heartbeat against their own. "I am afraid for you. I want you far away from Enan. Absan said Solauraward they mine some metal, a difficult to find mineral mayhap. We need witnesses or other confirmation of what they do. I will protect this child and thereby myself. You must go, Heddha."

Heddha looked to Pug, who nodded his assent. With a long exhale, Heddha agreed, saying, "Aye, we will go to this place, although I am not persuaded we will find less peril there."

Dockworkers came, preparing to remove the mooring lines from the bollards. Pug picked up his belongings and Heddha's saddlebag and started up the planking to the main deck.

"Heddha, you should look and behave like common laborers or farmers. Absan and his companions drew attention, announcing they were there on a warrant from their Sovereigns. For this, the offworlders annihilated them." Jahtara blinked away tears, continuing, "Enan killed Absan to compel Keyn Nyssa to join my brother against the Middle Keyndom. Once again, someone close to us died, and I do not wish it to happen again. Please, Heddha, take care." Jahtara paused, looking back up the quay, "Absan seemed honorable and kindhearted."

"Aye, and where does he abide now? Only in my lasting memories. His curled lock of hair, his smile, his loving thoughts. All gone in time." With glistening eyes, Heddha hugged and kissed Jahtara, wishing, "Fare well, Queyn Jahtara."

"And uncomplicated travels to you. Return to me by the Long Noite's Solstice."

"I spy the thane and Jorma upon the quay where Absan lies. I carry you deep in my heart," turning Heddha ascended the ship's plank.

Jahtara waved to Pug, yelling, "Stay with her. I will inform Auntie's daughters of your leaving," she turned, heading up the wharf.

Reaching the quay, she looked back to see the lines let loose and the plank withdrawn onto the vessel. Even now, the departure from her love made her heartache. The ship slipped away, guided by the Luna's reflection on the bay.

Jahtara and Jorma rode the coastal road out of Concupia, the Luna hanging a hands width above the Setting Sea. The Maiden rose, pouring her stars across the noite sky. Jorma attempted to point out the corporation ship, a bright spot among the stars towards the Cold Waste, but to Jahtara, they all appeared much the same.

Jahtara had changed since riding this road into Concupia, from a self-demarcating individual to an entity that included Heddha, a child, a queyndom, and extended into the consciousness of Inlanda. Could this awareness expand further to encompass a universal sentiency? The noite sky turned overhead, an immensity of stars whose newfound meanings transformed Jahtara.

Jahtara spent most of the noite in conference with Thane Kirrydon. Although disagreeing initially, they concurred in sending an emissary to the High Keyndom explaining Sir Absan's death. Jahtara found little hope for diplomacy, feeling Enan held influence there. The High Mountain Keyndom couldn't raise an army and transverse the mountain passes sooner than the following Warming. This delay gives the thane time to gather allegiances to the new queyn while sending spies to the lowlands of lineage Davuda to seek out any loyal to Queyn Jahtara or those who disliked her brother more. Thane Kirrydon would notify the Morgn Star Carriers to look out for Heddha and Pug's return. For Jahtara, the plan gave her time to nest in a safe place until she birthed this child and devised a way to keep them all safe.

Jahtara decided to allow Jorma to accompany her to the shore where the road turned inland, giving her time to learn the basics of the fire sword. Her change of heart came out of Absan's death. Jahtara accepted there was little hope of defeating Enan without a similar weapon. Jorma showed her the knob that, when set to the sinistral, pressed down, and rotated to the dextral, deactivated the location function. They also attuned the knife to her cellular ligands, allowing Jahtara to control the weapon. He shared that the knife retained a record of its use, and examination would show the time of the blade's activation.

The road rose as the hills once again intruded into the sea, and at the crest, Jorma looked back to see a rider moving fast up the road. "A rider comes with speed. If someone follows, we should pull off the path."

"Aye, although the rider seems inexperienced and out of rhythm with their mount."

Jahtara found thick undergrowth to conceal themselves, awaiting the hurried rider. However, when the hoof beats drew near, the rider appeared young, and within a few strides, Jahtara recognized Tanhā! Jahtara called her name, and Tanha, with some difficulty, halted her mount. Pulling alongside and seeing Tahnā's flushed cheeks, disheveled hair, and wide eyes, Jahtara urgently asked, "Are there new tidings from your father?

"No," smoothing her hair, she said, "I am coming with you as your retainer. I carry a letter from my mother, Jahtara... Pardon, su majeste, a petition to serve in your entourage!" Tahnā produced a crumpled letter from the waist of her dress, handing it to Jahtara.

Reading only the first sentence, Jahtara looked sternly up at Tahnā, saying, "This petitions to serve at the household, not in the keyn's forest!"

"Queyn's, su majeste."

"What?"

"Queyn's forest now."

Jahtara could only stare at Tahnā's young, sincere face. She looked to Jorma, who shrugged, then back to Tanhā. "You ran away from your parents!"

"Last noite, we thought you would take your place at the palatial seat. I left mother a note and followed the instructions in her letter when I saw you leave. Besides, it appears improper for you to travel without a duenna. And I overheard you ran away from…."

"Enough!" Jahtara cut her off. She sat silent before asking Jorma, "Should we turn back to Concupia?"

"I think not. The town awakens, and many may see us."

Tahnā changed her smile to a grim countenance under Jahtara's stare. Jahtara took in the landscape surrounding them. Finally, after blowing her breath out through puffed cheeks, she said, "I am the queyn of these lands… almost. I will not send you back on your own. I hope you crave adventure because it hunts me out. Tell me you have something other than a dress for riding." Saying this, Jahtara thought of Heddha. "And where did you learn to ride?"

"I appreciate your kindness and hope to serve you well, milaud. I spend too much time traveling by carriage. However, I am a quick learner. And aye, I have britches, having fled with some of my father's clothes from the laundry," she patted the saddlebag. Looking around, she asked, "Where are your attendants and cook?"

The journey took on a rhythm yet not a monotony, the meager group often rising with the Solaura and obtaining the road before the ocean mists cleared. Jahtara and Jorma spent much time conversing about his travels. He spoke of cultures and worlds challenging to imagine. He admitted her world appeared strange to him, having never ridden an animal, bathed in a cold stream, or relieved himself in a forest. Especially concerning for him was food grown in dirt. However, it seemed easier for him to recognize familiar elements here than for her to get to his future. Tanhā assumed the role of go-between for the two, quickly learning to adapt to her new surroundings while grasping, even craving, the new concepts explained by Jorma. And Jahtara taught both to ride.

In the evenings, Jorma drilled Jahtara in the fundamentals of the fire sword, which he called a plasma weapon. He tried to explain plasma, a common state of matter in the universe, by relating it to lightning or the Solaura, the most obvious examples. Using the weapon deily, it became familiar in her hand, and she lost her awe of its magic. She learned its many uses other than a sword. What Jahtara called the blade could adopt a longer or shorter length. She used it short to heat water or start the evening fire. She could cut wood without lighting the downed branches if she was quick. The fire sword did something akin to aiming an arrow by looking down the blade. Like an arrow, a flame leaped from the knife to a target. She cracked many rocks practicing this feature and could only imagine what this would do to a person or animal. Another aspect Jorma showed her involved the plasma blade switching off if it crossed a part of her body. Scary, but she grew accustomed to this feature after long periods of practice, although she set her blouse afire once.

One evening, after a particularly strenuous session with the plasma weapon, Jahtara sat pensively. Jorma interrupted her musings, "Jahtara, does something trouble you?"

"A philosophical unease and I argue both sides."

"Does the weapon's power concern you?"

"Is my face so expressive, or do you dowse my thoughts?" Jahtara said, breaking her contemplation. "Quite right, though. Any weapon can kill and maim. This weapon escalates the magnitude of violence and decreases the ability to defend against such a threat. I would naturally fend for myself if attacked, yet we have no way to oppose such a weapon.

"Enan murders to obtain his filthy ends. How can we impose justice for such crimes? I can see no way to shame him, especially in his world, where it would have its greatest effect. More drastic measures allow him no opportunity to understand the futility of the suffering he causes. Having someone comprehend the horror of their actions seems a deeper restorative justice than killing them. Making Enan an outcast only moves the problem down the road. Enabling someone to become aware of the suffering they cause seems possible, yet most do not have the diligence to change. Has your world solved this justly?"

"Perhaps more just, yet still difficult."

"Mayhap, throw him in a dungeon, hurl away the key, and let him work out the details of his next life."

"Seems a possibility if certain and without bias. Rare in my estimation. A governing ruler or state, judge, or culture always have prejudices and should not have the power of death."

"After witnessing Absan's death, Enan certainly committed an offense."

"Did you not say Absan drew his sword and attacked?"

"He did yet…even if he just stood there, Enan would have killed him!"

"Who now reads minds? We can kill people with devices like a plasma weapon from a world away. It seems barbaric sitting here around this noite's fire, yet we justify it rationally, calling it self-defense even though the people we assail have little defense against such attacks."

Jahtara responded, "The plasma sword seems much like a wizard's wand. Yet, I know it is a terrible weapon, especially with my memory of Enan's cruelty. I will defend if he comes for me or the child once birthed."

"As you should. However, the plasma sword's value exists in how you use it; make sure it does not use you."

When Jahtara awoke to the grey Rising the next dei, she felt the heavy burden of her position. Tanhā, true to her word, appeared to be a quick learner with an agile mind. Tanhā craved to please and had already made a fire. She attended to the break fast, and upon seeing Jahtara awake, she greeted her, "I am glad to see su astrum sleep late this morgn. With your permission, I saw some fruiting fungi not far into su altezza's forest, hoping a cooked meal will suffice to still your appetite."

Jahtara didn't wish to dampen her enthusiasm but couldn't take the flippant addition to her burdens. "I should not have slept late. We usually gain the road early with a cold breaking of our fast. I do not consider the land, my forest, nor my shrooms. Please leave them be. Also, do not address me with the honorifics 'su astrum or alteza,' for our safety!" Turning, she strode into the forest, emotion lengthening her strides until far from their encampment. Jahtara halted in a dank depression bordered by a fallen log blanketed with lichen and bracket fungi and surrounded by tall, straight trunks topped by an obscuring canopy. She sank back against the log, covering her face with both hands, and let the tears flow. How did she acquire so much responsibility? The refined household of her youth mired her in its drudgery and silliness. Yet now, the burdening thoughts of obligation weighed on her. Hadn't she run from responsibility? She labored under the blame she placed on herself for Auntie and Absan's deaths, involving Heddha and sending her away, endangering the thane, dragging her laudship's daughter on a hazardous journey, the worry for this child, and a coming war. How could she embody a queyn!

She let her tears flow, spending the emotion, wiping the remnants away with the back of her hand. The Solaura cleared the top of the coastal range peeking through the canopy with bright, slanted shafts animating the lush forest, drawing Jahtara out of herself, enabling her to take in the immensity of her surroundings. She seemed to float out of her body, gazing down from above, seeing a young woman who ran into the forest without slipping on her boots and now stood squishing her toes in black mud. Jahtara laughed, lifting her heart; she didn't have to take responsibility for what happened. She would respond with the good intentions of her heart, and others could make their choice. Jahtara would let this aspiration guide her.

The morgn chill dissipated in the presence of a warm breeze coming off the sea. The small party broke from the trees to ride along the firm sand of a vast shore stretching ahead. Jahtara turned to gaze back at Tanhā, who returned her smile. Tanhā sat straight in her saddle, moving easily with the mount, and Jahtara could see she grew daily in confidence. When Jahtara returned from her retreat into the forest, Tanhā had begun packing for their dei's ride. Jahtara thanked her for her efforts, suggesting they sauté the mushrooms with the remaining garlic, onions, and spinach leaves, enjoying them with hot tea to fortify their ride.

Jahtara made a clicking noise with her cheek, and Trusted Companion quickened its pace to catch up to Jorma. He looked content smoking his pipe, riding in a cloistered manner; Jahtara felt reluctant to disturb him. She remained silent until he turned his head, raising a brow in acquiescence.

"Kasumi, yourself, and even Enan have hinted at the lack of ties binding you to any one place. I, too, fled bonds, although I have bound myself to new circumstances. I wonder what predicament would make you consider leaving your world for another. That seems stronger than I intended. Forgive me. I meant not to judge."

"You have no wish to reach out to other stars, other worlds, cultures, and peoples?"

"I have just found such things exist, and here I am discussing them like I know them with certainty." Rubbing her belly, she continued, "I am in a tangle, bound by cords of numerous uncertainties. I cannot run only to face similar suffering repeatedly. I must challenge my fears until I no longer dread them. This way, my nature will expand instead of growing stagnant or contracting."

Jorma took a long draw and put the pipe in its pouch. Gesturing toward the shoreline, tree-covered hills, and rocky outcroppings, he said, "You would not see a sight like this on my world: such splendors no longer exist." Looking sideways at Jahtara, he continued, "I do not wish to be glib or evasive. I obtained the status of a scholar, not in a specific area, yet versed in many subjects: the past, societies, and cultures, how the mind works, how our bodies work, the advancement of machines, and art. Some would call me a forecaster of trends. I know you cannot understand and think much of this silly, yet I built my whole life on the premise of using machines to predict the future. In the process, my present slipped into an unattainable past, and tomorrow became a void filled with fantasy.

"I gave a type of machine instructions on making predictions about people, trends, and the future. In my world, change came at a furious pace." Jorma drifted into having a conversation with his past. "These machines could learn from the outcomes of their forecasting. We manipulated people with tens of thousands of bits of their information. Most of the information they did not know we gathered: the timbre and cadence of voices, number of times people cleaned their teeth, who spoke to whom, travel, or what people bought, watched, liked, or disliked; in essence, everything about them. People were both the product and consumer, like a dog chasing its tail. These machines did well at what we instructed them to do. Unfortunately, I made some professional miscalculations; the instructions contained small biases that the machines magnified. I clung to these blunders with undo ferocity. Not until the direction of society and governance were affected did I realize the damage done. When I awoke from the noitemare, I discovered my daughter had grown into a young womon, not knowing her father. My spouse had been non-aligned mentally for jahrs, then moved on physically. I had highjacked my own life, a life that existed mostly in my head. I accepted this position with the corporation to escape. A lot of good that did."

Jorma rode silently, watching the panorama pass, finally reflecting, "If I could choose, at this moment, I would dwell like a noble tree sitting in meditation for millennia watching time work, for cognition seems overrated."

Jahtara, who knew the suffering of living an unwanted life, said, "Not hugely ambitious, a tree contemplating the eons. Careful what you aspire towards."

"I judge it tremendously aspirational, awakening from the endurance of surviving to a peace in loving."

"Perhaps. Recently, I have gained through the challenges of life, coming to a deeper understanding."

"In myself, confrontation brings out imperfections. I thank you for this chance to ventilate, Jahtara. It increased the fire like a bellows and annealed my decision to remain on Inlanda. I was ambivalent about giving up my world, yet perhaps I stand to gain more here. May I make supplication to act as your liaison to off-world contacts?" Jorma made a slight bow in his saddle.

Jahtara said, "You will serve a ministrant of, I hope to say this properly, Non-Inlanda System Affairs," they laughed.

"So now you have a regent, a ministrant, and a laud in waiting," and they laughed again. Turning to Tanhā, Jorma asked, "And what think you of this, lass?"

With a fair amount of seriousness, Tanhā responded, "If you do not return to your world, may I have the thingy you put in your ear?" And all laughed.

Jorma returned to his world or ship when the coastal byway turned inland. They thought this course prudent to keep informed of any developments. When Jahtara and Tanhā waved their goodbyes to Jorma, Jahtara reflected on the detail she still had not told him - to where she traveled. Jorma would ride Solauraward for a couple of deis, then call for a ride to the ship. Jahtara, accompanied by Tanhā, took the road through the coastal range towards the village she and Heddha had left seemingly ages ago.

Heddha clung to the leeward rail of the ship as another wall of sea-water crashed over the windward side, cascading across the deck. She soon stood thigh-deep in the sloshing torrent against the bulwark, yet she preferred the weather deck to a dark pitching cabin even in this inundation. When they came aboard, Pug, without hesitation, climbed into the standing rigging, swinging on the stays and even ascending to the crosstrees. When the storm approached, he joined the able seamen to haul in the buntlines, put the course sails in their gear, and clambered out on the topsail yards to free the sheets before furling, and now he quaffed grog below deck; just the thought of grog made Heddha dry heave over the rail one more time.

The voyage started idyllic enough. However, mentioning Atfi Dunnyn's name didn't allow Pug and Heddha to share a berth. Pug knew a couple of the crew, and the captain allowed him to bunk with them while Heddha bunked alone in a small cabin with only a port-hole for light. The captain would not allow Heddha to share meals at his table, considering her a laborer, and permitted her to use only the cabin or open deck. Custom shunned womyn from other portions of the vessel. She enjoyed the blue-grey expanse of water filled with fantastic creatures. Heddha saw fast swimmers riding the bow wave, immense beasts the size of ships blowing spouts in the air, flying fish, and glowing noite creatures in the ship's wake.

At first, Heddha felt apprehensive out of sight of land until she learned from the commandare some basics of navigation using the stars. A star the commandare called Steadfast intrigued Heddha. The captain addressed the star by its proper name, the Dhruva Tāra, because of its resoluteness in the noite sky. Heddha hadn't realized the helpful natural signs at sea: the direction of waves, wind, and clouds, the position of the Luna, Solaura, and stars. Heddha always followed the first road leading away from trouble, and at this moment, she sorely wished her feet were on solid ground, taking her away from this storm.

The dawn broke with a much-becalmed sea, a downy blanket of grey clouds overhead, and the good news they would make their intended port by the foresetting. Pug, looking somewhat peaked, wel-comed this news. These tidings lifted Heddha's spirit likewise. She sent Pug amidships for much-needed sleep, and she set to consider their way forward once in port. The commandare's sister and mate ran a livery where they might find mounts to travel inland. He warned them to stay clear of bounty-motivated recruiters, often seizing folks to work the mines.

Once ashore, they found the livery. The operator would allow them to sleep in the loft and leave early the next dei. Feeling confident, they sought a tavern to quell their hunger and thirst without a pitching deck under their feet.

They had given a server their requests and enjoyed a pint when approached by a large, bearded man, asking if they were local folk or just passing through.

Heddha, wishing to keep the conversation short, said, "We labor on a ship presently in port and will sail with the tide." Pug and Heddha then resumed their conversation, ignoring the man.

But he picked up Pug's beer, draining it in one tilt, wiped his mouth along his arm, then set the tankard down hard on the table. "The lad looks like he needs work," he said over their heads.

Heddha shook her head slightly at Pug. But unable to let it go, she asked, "And no work for the likes of me?"

The bear of a man tipped his head back, laughing. "The youngling be a mite willowy yet could complete a dei's work if pressed. You best sit there quietly, little lass, or I will find you a suited purpose."

"You expect my spirit to be diminutive because I am slight, and wish me meek to make yourself seem larger. These attributes I do not excel at."

The lout stared down at Heddha with an uncomprehending expression. He lifted Heddha's pint, draining it in a breath, and, in a violent motion, slammed the mug down, shattering it and denting the tabletop. Leaning forward and placing his hands on the end of the table, he blubbered, beer dribbling out of his mouth, "You best not be speaking such to me, or you will find yourself earning the keep of a comfort womon, much to my pleasure."

"Since I am a womon, you expect I should oblige by serving only your pleasure?

"It be God's purpose to create you with this curse."

"My purpose may be to create, yet you seem the one cursed."

"How be I cursed?"

"Your God made you a man!"

The enraged goon came at Heddha leading with his head, so Heddha fulfilled her purpose by smashing Pug's empty mug across the bridge of his nose, sending him staggering back with blood gushing down his face. Inertia carried the fool backward until interrupted by a stool, and he crashed to the floor, unresponsive, at the table of his origin. Four likewise loutish goons stared at him in amazement, then lifted their collective gaze to glare at Heddha.

Heddha expected to wake in the morgn with the smell of straw and animal dung in her nose, and she certainly detected the odor of the latter, but she couldn't fathom what her head kept hitting. She attempted opening her eyes, managing to get one open a trifle, and yes, a boot covered in drying neddy muffins stood a hand's width from her face. Her head bounced on the floor of a wagon traveling over a rough road, and it appeared light out, but she couldn't open her topmost eye, making it hard to tell. In between bounces, she managed to turn her head to the other side and caught a glimpse of Pug sitting on the wagon floor. Heddha struggled to roll over, but something substantial weighed on her legs. Pug, seeing her toil, kicked a large bag off her legs. Having the weight off didn't make much difference. Finally, she managed to roll over with Pug's help and slowly push herself into a sitting position. After recovering from her exertion, she explored her face with the one hand that wasn't swollen and covered with abrasions. What she found wasn't encouraging: a puffy eye, dried blood on her nose and chin. Her top lip was so swollen on one side she couldn't find her bottom lip. Heddha's jerkin looked torn and covered with blood; she hoped not all hers. Her sides and thighs felt bruised. Squinting at Pug through a pounding headache, he looked like her twin with a swollen eye, a large knot on his forehead, and bloodied face. Pug gave Heddha a thumbs up, saying, "Them folks in the pub lookin' more nasty than Pug and Heddha!"

From Pug's story, she understood the two fearlessly struggled against crushing odds and gave worse than they got. Weighing Pug's tenacity against his self-aggrandizement, Heddha figured they gave a good account of themselves. After being overcome, the recruiters dragged them to a waiting wagon containing several men in more or less the same condition. Pug, whose hands were tied, got in with assistance. They threw Heddha unceremoniously onto the floor of the buckboard, where the ill-kept road continued to box her head against the wagon's deck until she awoke in the morgn.

They traveled for five deis over rough and little-used byways. They were untied after the first dei, and a mounted rider with a whip brought down a man attempting to run. They ate stew made of fish scraps, but by the fourth dei, it turned foul, and everyone except Heddha got horribly sick, with one poor man dying. Heddha hadn't eaten the stew due to her lip and cut tongue. She consumed only silty water and mashed berries. Heddha tended to Pug and the others through a long dei of the men retching and soiling themselves. She gathered a concoction of wild ginger and basil leaves, forcing them to drink copious amounts of water. The man in charge gave the cook several lashes for the loss of profit due to the dead man and treated Heddha slightly better after the other's recovery.

On the sixth dei, the wagon entered a desolate valley absent of vegetation and covered with fine grey dust. Everyone donned a moist cloth to protect themselves from the unbreathable dust. A small river flowed with the motion of a thickened slurry, its brown sludge banking and drying in the Solaura into great pillows of cracked clay. Even stranger, the area lacked animal life: no small animals or more substantial game, and most distressing, no insects! After half a dei of riding through this forlorn devastation, they climbed a hill through multiple switchbacks to gain an immense plateau. Here existed extensive life and activity but with the color and vitality drawn out of it.

Far-reaching camps of tents, lean-tos, and shacks made from mea-ger trunks spread before the group. Endless lines of men, carts, and animals moved in perpetual ovate swarms between vast excavations and massive constructions. Shrouds of dust obscured and settled on everything in sight, sapping all color from the scene except the flicker-ing orange light of campfires in the fading deilight. This atonal, ashen landscape seemed a monstrous assault on the land.

The whip-bearing rider directed the wagon down a lesser-used path to a shoddy building at the edge of the encampment, going inside while they waited. After a brief time, he emerged with a slight, balding, stoop-shouldered man and called Heddha down from the wagon.

Heddha gave Pug's hand a squeeze assuring him, "I will find you," then jumped to the ground next to the balding man.

He stood at a height scarcely equal to Heddha and smelled of peppermint. He looked Heddha over and said, "The man says you healed his charges. Is this true?"

"I have a knowledge of herbs and the care of animals."

"Hmmm, can you sew?"

"Aye."

"You will do." He turned abruptly and disappeared into the build-ing.

The physician, named Benedus, came from the Middle Realms, where he worked in an arldom until the laud's spouse died of a diar-rheal affliction. Benedus claimed the womon appeared poisoned — a mistake. The arl bought in a new healer who, after an exchange of coins, declared Benedus a charlatan, and the arl ran him out of town.

After observing the healer in the overcrowded sick house, Heddha believed the healer's account. He proved to be a compassionate and excellent healer under very trying circumstances. He worked tirelessly, and Heddha often ran to keep up with him.

She learned the sewing acquired at her mother's knee and repair-ing her mistress's clothing was not the sewing Benedus meant her to carry out. After several deis observing, she found herself doing simple skin closures. Heddha enjoyed learning these skills but worried about Pug, afraid he might get injured or be found out by asking questions. One dei, changing the Manuka honey dressing on a foot laceration, the youngling asked for her name. With her response, he recounted how Pug helped him after a sharp-edged rock cut his foot and whispered her name, giving him a message: Pug visited many stalls at a market but couldn't enter the larger stalls. Heddha took this to mean Pug explored the larger structures but couldn't enter. While finishing the dressing, she asked the boy if he knew about Pug's work. After some thought between grimaces, he guessed Pug might be a runner among the overseers. Heddha thanked the youngling, smiling to herself; once again, Pug proved very resourceful.

A few deis later, a rider from the pit came to the sick house, asking Benedus for assistance with a laborer partially buried in a landslide. Currently setting a broken arm, Benedus refused to go and told the rider to take Heddha on his mount. Arriving at the landfall, she discovered fellow workers digging him out, but in such pain that the pit boss slit his throat. Heddha thought the killing mercy since the man looked severely mashed up.

Heddha looked about for Pug but, not finding him started to walk back to the sick house. Halfway out of the pit, Pug ran up behind her, slowing to a walk. His clothes, hair, and skin were all a uniform dust color, but his smile shone like the Solaura leaking into a darkened room.

"Pug, I am relieved you are well," Heddha said, padding his shoulder and raising a cloud of dust. "I got your message and took it to mean you have access to some places here yet not the large stronghold."

"Aye." Then bringing a finger to his lips, he shushed Heddha speaking low, "There be an overseer to the fore. Keep your eyes down. Speak naught."

After passing the man, pug continued, "I be runnin' messages and tellin' the teamsters where the boss needs them wagons. Nobody queries me."

"Please, Pug, be heedful. A danger lingers here. Have you encountered any strangeness? Men or womyn with round eyes?"

"I sense much strangeness here. I see two, mayhap three such men. There be more, yet out of sight. Methinks they not want to be seen."

"I agree. Those men do not want it known what they do here. They make it look like we mine and ill-treat our world."

Pug questioned, "Who be these men?"

"Pardon Pug, I will acquaint you with this long tale later. For now, believe they use us for their gain."

"Aye, from what Pug be seein' me reckon this true." He stopped and pulled Heddha to the side of the road, continuing, "These men kill Auntie. And Jahtara says they want to kill you."

"One man, aye. Worse still, Jahtara carries a child, and once she gives birth, they want her dead. Mayhap some of these round-eyed strangers could be our friends, yet I fear most will turn all Inlanda into what we see here."

Pug scratched his head and then nodded saying. "I likes you cause of how you treat me, Jahtara too. Bein' on the bottom not mean the likes of me cannot help." Pug spat to clear the dust from his mouth. "At noite, everyone must leave the pit. Pug peek and see somethin' big like the ship we come on cept it moves on land. I hear loud booms like thunder, and in the morgn, the rock be crushed. We take the rock to the large stronghold with guarded doors. Nobody Pug asks go inside. They say at noite, crates be loaded onto wagons and moved around the pit to the other side. Then everyone must leave."

"Has anyone seen what fills these crates?"

"No. When Pug asks those loadin' the wagons, they say they be heavy with strange writin'."

"Pug, asking these questions is dangerous! You must stop. I am not sure what more we can do."

Pug suddenly turned and started to walk away, surprising Heddha. Then a man rode up, shouting, "Healer, you cannot leave the man lying in the pit. He will affect the work of others. Move him before he starts to stink!"

Pug turning back and keeping his eyes down, said, "She tell me to fetch a wagon to move the man."

The rider looked to Heddha and then back to Pug, "Do not be wasting a wagon. Get a pack animal and be quick about it!"

Pug ran up the road. The man spit at Heddha's feet, saying, "Get out of the pit, womon," then turned, riding down into the chasm.

Several days passed with Heddha unsure how to proceed. Pug's safety arose uppermost in her mind, and the longer they stayed here, the more likely Pug could suffer an accident or, worse, be found out, meeting the fate of the cnihts accompanying Absan. She saw no way past the guards at the citadel-like building, unsure if they could obtain more evidence. It seemed to Heddha that the offworlders made something from the ore and somehow took it to their ship, but how? Certainly, they wouldn't take the raw stone to their vessel. Too much remains concealed. She needed to get into the large building. Thus far, the evidence seemed weak and unverified: this place did exist, and offworlders seemed in control, yet what is the purpose of mining? Maybe she and Pug best leave with the knowledge already acquired. Hadn't Jahtara sent them away to be safe? In the morgn, Heddha would find Pug and withdraw while they still could.

The next morgn, Benedus sent Heddha to the market to obtain fortified wine and dried medicinal herbs for making tinctures but gave her no money to purchase them, telling her to be creative. She accepted the assignment gladly, thinking it gave her an excuse to look for Pug.

A market spread between the road from the seaport and the inland road. Some buyers attended from the camps, but also merchants from larger towns. It wasn't the most bountiful of markets, but some wares were unusual. She saw vials like the one the sheriff took from Enan, strange metal containers, and other goods brightly colored and made of some unknown material.

While Benedus gave her no money, she did have articles left behind at the infirmary by departed or dead workers: a copper ring, a pair of boots, some belts, and a seaman's coin earring. Heddha obtained the dried herbs and fortified wine by bartering these articles and the goodwill engendered by Benedus.

Heddha passed a black smith's stall and, seeing an assortment of knives, stopped to peruse them. The smith came over to point out the attributes of each blade. When Heddha described Jahtara's dagger, the large one-eyed man became quiet while looking around suspiciously, and his eye widened looking up the street behind Heddha. Heddha returned a knife to its place, discreetly glancing up the road, recognizing the man with the whip. He didn't focus on Heddha, just gazed down the street. She slowly returned to the smith. Heddha's expression must look grim, for he nodded slightly and called out, "Ananeurin." When the geyrle appeared, he continued, "When I say, take this womon out back and give her some water." Then under his breath, looking up the street, "You know this man?"

Heddha nodded once.

"You expected him to be here?"

This time she shook her head slightly.

"Would he be looking for you?"

"It's possible, yes."

The grimy-looking smith quickly looked along the street and said, "Go now with the geyrle and wait."

Heddha followed Ananeurin through the soiled curtain, down a dark passageway, and out into an open space blocked at the back by a colorfully painted rambler's wagon. The geyrle put a cushion on a stool and indicated Heddha sit.

"Tea or water, ma'am?"

"Water will do it, my thanks."

After giving Heddha water, Ananeurin dunked a cloth in hot

water from the firepot and hung it with a dry towel over wooden pegs.

Presently the smith came through from the front, telling the geyrle, "Watch the front for me now, Ananeurin."

He used the wet cloth to wipe his face and hands before drying with the other.

Heddha couldn't help but stare at his dark skin covered with burn scars over the side of his chest, shoulder, and extending to his head, including the patched eye.

Watching Heddha scrutinize his wounds, he asked, "You will want to know how I came by them? They were a lesson for me and a warning to your likes. Especially a distinctive woman, asking about unusual knives, only the round eye strangers have." He smiled, extending his arm, greeting Heddha with, "I am Jit, general smithy, over-inquisitive alchemist, loving father, and friend to the unjustly hunted."

She grabbed Jit's muscular forearm, and they shook once. Heddha introduced herself with a smile, "Heddha. Incessant womon of distinction, on a quest of inquiry and always searching for friends. Your inquisitiveness led to these disfigurements?"

"Well met Heddha, you make me think of Ananeurin's mother, a womon of bold speech now and again. And aye, my curiosity bestowed this defacement on me, yet turned out to be a life tutelage: some men wish to keep others dense as stone."

"You learned this lesson at the guarded stronghold that receives the rock from the pit? You worked inside?"

Jit gazed long at Heddha before stating, "The telling of this dangerous knowledge could cost my life and why I sent Ananeurin out front. I wish to keep her safe."

Heddha stared firmly at Jit, considering her options before saying, "We all face hard times, yet this knowledge, in the possession of the right person, could hinder even more challenging times ahead for all of Inlanda, including you and your daughter. I sense you already feel this.

"I received a warrant to collect evidence of hideous deeds, where people have died, here and elsewhere on Inlanda. The queyn of the Middle Realms sent me to provide evidence of certain rumors and misdeeds. I have seen some things with my eyes, yet the cause behind these events eludes me. If you have information that could assist Queyn Jahtara in her deliberations, then I beseech you, please be forthcoming for all our sakes." Heddha thought she overstated the situation after hearing her words, even knowing the whole truth proved far worse and more inconceivable.

"Keyn Tergon remains the monarch of the Middle Realms, does he not?" questioned Jit, and rightly so.

Heddha shook her head, saying, "The keyn died not long ago, before the Rose Luna, and on his death bed named Prinus Jahtara heir. The queyn has not received investiture yet; however, su grandeza assumed the office and duties. If you or your daughter need help, seek out Queyn Jahtara, and she will honor you for helping us." By the fates, Heddha spoke of her lover like this? By what pretense could Heddha, a mere farm geyrle, ask this of a father and daughter? Yet she could ask it in the name of Queyn Jahtara and, more importantly, Inlanda. "You know what takes place in this enormous fortress?"

Jit leaned forward, placing his elbows on his knees and rounding his back. He started, "I came here with my wife and brother having a promise of work. We three grew up together in a small village where my father labored. On occasion, he did metalwork for a monastery and, in return, arranged for me to receive instruction in alchemy and the elements. Arriving here, my brother soon found livelihood doing manual labor and moved up to a calling more befitting his skill, telling others what to do."

He glanced at Heddha, then down, admitting, "Aye, I worked at those refinement works, processing ore. We all did very well for a time. My wife with child, and us happy, or I thought so. After the birthing of Ananeurin, my wife fell into a deep melancholy and finally passed due to mental anguish, breasts engorged, unable to nourish her daughter due to this despair. My brother, Tho, and I argued, and he left our camp shortly thereafter. Tho and I have not spoken since. Ananeurin and I survive alone."

After a moment in silence, Heddha added softly, "This man with the whip is your brother." Jit could only nod, so Heddha continued carefully, "And Ananeurin, his daughter."

Jit shrugged then in a shaky voice, "Aye, more than likely. I have never spoken aloud such thoughts." He blinked away the emotion, then continued, "We build fences around ourselves with beliefs that cannot stand in a steady wind, for what? Pride? And who do we hurt?"

Heddha waited, letting the emotion and internal dialog wash over him, knowing he buried this deep. She knew love and loss; she also knew pride and what persisted unsaid.

She found the connection, "Aye, pride. Mine frequently led to anger, and often, the anger harmed me. Hearing your fervor, I recognize the depth of my pride and how anger repeatedly distanced me from others. I also understand the longing for family. And importantly, it matters not from where family comes. Help me, and perhaps we can both regain a sense of belonging."

Jit grabbed the cloth he used to dry his face and wiped his nose. Fixing on Heddha's face, he nodded, "A foreignness pervades much here, difficult to comprehend, at least for me. I once thought of it like magic, yet now I am unsure. People watch what I do in awe of my ability to make, form, and shape metal, yet the work feels quite common to me. What passes here appears magical; however, through observation, I understood it represents a process, not magic. I credit my monk teachers for showing me the power of observation. The monk's ideas of metallurgy and alchemy did not achieve the desired practical result; however, they tried to turn one metal into another by transmutation, which would be truly magical."

"The monks were trying to alter the elements of creation. This seems profane?"

"Not at all. The monks of this canon adhere to a belief that questions creation and demands them to examine and solve its riddles. In this way, will they find God in their quest.

"The roundeyes do not find a god in what they do here, yet they find treasure, to be sure, in the form of metal. The process separates and concentrates ore. A smithy smelts in a bloomery furnace then hammers and reshapes. The ore from the pit gets broken up and dissolved by adding water and corrosive liquid. My disfigurement attests to its caustic ability. The mash passes through what they call spider webs, huge pots taller than trees where these webs magically extract the different metals. It seemed simpler than what I do to extract iron from ore and, at the same time, inconceivably more complicated.

"This results in several powders the round eyes call rare metals yet not like any metal I have seen. Waste, what I would call slag, gets dumped off the plateau's edge. Perhaps you saw the valley this waste slowly flows through."

"Aye, nothing seems alive there, no animals, plants, or even insects."

"You can see what this unwanted spoilage did to me."

"What do they do with the metal reaped from the ore?"

"Here, it gets even stranger. When I began working there, I befriended one of the roundeyes. He could not speak our speech well, yet I taught him our words and queried him about everything I could over many months. They were friendlier in the beginning before many began to die in the pits, and they needed more and more workers. Though I know he kept much from me, the story I learned from him withered in its believability and grew in its strangeness. I know this sounds raving, yet I puzzled about these round eyes coming from somewhere other than…"

"Other than Inlanda!" Heddha cut in. "I have associated with roundeyes, and now I sound deranged; however, they admit to coming from some home among the stars, traveling on ships of a sort." Heddha described Kasumi, Jorma, Cora, and Enan to Jit in hopes he noticed any of them here.

Jit seemed pleased with Heddha's revelation, "What you have con-firmed for me makes this tale fall together much like when a boy, I realized frogs came from tadpoles." Jit laughed loudly, but Heddha sensed an uneasiness creep into his laugh. "No, these you describe have not been here."

"The first three said they were not here, and the last can change his appearance. Please continue. What were you able to glean from this man's story?"

"I would rather hear your tale; it grows more savory with every morsel you dish out." When Heddha didn't elaborate, Jit shrugged and continued, "Well, you have my mouth watering for more. Com-bining what you said and the tale from this man, these metals concen-trate on Inlanda in a way they do not on other... I am not sure what word to use for other places like Inlanda or their home?"

"They use the word 'planet' or world to mean all such places. I heard no name for their home, although they may come from many worlds."

"Worlds," Jit said slowly, then grew quiet for a moment before continuing, "makes me feel small. It all sounds more sensible now if you can call it sense. Mountains surround this plateau, and the rains wash them down over many eons, along with the runoff from many hot springs, filling a basin to create this plateau. Clay soils were washed down over time to create what he called a placer deposit and concentrated the mined minerals. The higher metal concentration here makes it easier to mine and extract. He said elsewhere that many of the easiest places were depleted by mining. I now realize the other places were somewhere other than on Inlanda. These people seem more... how would you say – elevated or progressed."

"In some ways, it seems so, yet not gods. I ask again, did this man say what they used these metals for?"

"Oh aye, lost my direction with all this talk. Have you seen the objects they wear in the ear?"

"Yes, and the knives at their waist."

"Not decorative, nor knives. The one I spoke to did not carry what you call a knife yet did have the ear decoration and used it somehow to speak with others. Some carried something like small saucers, constantly poking them. They also have small tables tipped at an angle with glowing symbols, which they spoke to or touched. This man said they have many such things where they came from, and all use these metals. Inside these large buildings, they use an uncommonly bright light, not torches, dazzling like the Solaura yet extinguished by touching one of the saucers they carried. Mayhap by magic."

Heddha smiled, saying, "I thought it madness, then magic, and now it seems believable if not common, yet we do not understand the full measure. Perhaps I am in a dream or deranged, a madness or...... mayhap, stolen away to a mysterious world."

"Well, lass, then I am there with you." Jit ran his hand up his scared but muscled arm, continuing, "Soon after Ananeurin birthed and her mother passed, I found it hard to spend time around Ananeurin and instead occupied my deis working. Things turned hard between the roundeyes and us, with most Inlandani moved to work the pits. I heard of a new overlaud, a nasty sort wanting work to proceed at a faster pace. One dei I strained to push a large vessel of the corrosive waste, and with no warning, he approached, lighting what you called a knife yet looks like a flame. I caught just a flicker of it scorch my back, and without thought or command, my backside arched with such force that I lost my grip. I grappled with catching the far edge, slipping into the thick slurry. Pulling myself upright, I turned, glaring at the brute, who laughed, saying, 'he will die by the morrow's Setting.' His meaning dawned on me as pain became my existence, and I wished to escape from this life. I blacked out and woke five deis later with Benedus. I knew naught of how I came there, and the healer would not say. I outlived Overseer Tiomer's prediction and have not left Ananeurin's side since."

"The same man Enan Tiomer I mentioned earlier. He slew others, one most cruelly." Heddha stood, "I must be wary, for he vowed to dispatch me for my meddling. I commend you for this tale, a hard account to tell." She turned to go but pivoted back to Jit, asking, "Would the folks here rise against the roundeyes to shut down this place?"

"I heard some talk, a fair amount of grumbling, and there exist many more of us, yet versus these fire weapons, few will oppose."

Heddha smiled, encouraging, "There may be a way to obtain some of these fire sticks, yet I sense what we need most is a leader." She nodded to Jit and left, swallowed up by the curtain.

Miracles

Where do you end, and the rest of the world begin? Here a paradox arises emblematic of conscious experience - the world starts and ends with you. Not in a narcissistic sense, but quite the opposite, especially if you understand perception acts like a mirror echoing your beliefs. Depicting the world through the looking glass of perceptual experience, the world and you merge, with intentions reflecting the karmic constructs of your mind. The world arises at your inception; it resides in you; it dies with you. To change the world, remodel your mind.

Another paradox of space and time - distances stretch infinitely, yet we only experience the now. Each of us exists in the guise of a miracle in this exacting moment. A marvel the universe conspired to create: a lily of the field, a deep breath of fresh air, the hope of sun on a cold morgn, the warming of hearts cuddling under the covers. Each miracle exists as an equal and codependent part of the whole, like a murmuration of starlings creating astounding transitions in flight. You belong in this moment; rejoice and be mindful of the overwhelming truth in the power of now.

Each of us ordains the world, interacting through a murmuration of sentiency, generating the present whole we call life, rippling through time. Living constitutes a miracle, yet it feels so natural and conditioned that being alive seems ordinary.

This story materializes conventionally, yet upon reflection, embodies the miraculous.

⸎

Jahtara waded barefoot upstream through the ankle-deep cold water using a wooden staff for balance. Her feet, which tingled at the start, were now numb. She placed her feet carefully to avoid rocks and shelled creepers until a waist-high cascading fall of water obstructed, querying her confidence to proceed further owing to her altered center of gravity. Giving a slight bow to the barrier, Jahtara sat on a dry sill, extending from the side of the fall, pulling her insensible feet from the water, intending to rub some warmth back into the icy skin.

Jahtara and Tanhā rode through the coastal range in the reverse order she and Heddha had traveled the road until recognizing the moss-covered River Rock Inn, set in a beautiful glen. Heddha and Jahtara steered clear of the inn, but it suited Jahtara's purpose to spend her gravidity and confinement here. Travelers would be sparse through these passes during the coming Long Noites, making it a tranquil hideaway.

Jahtara's foot massage succeeded only in making her hands cold. She sat back, giving space to her expanded belly. Later in the Long Noite saison, Heddha would return, the child born, then the Warming reappear, and if all went well, its warmth would embrace their family. Jahtara smiled at such thoughts. At least these ponderings rose in a positive vein; she started this outdoor excursion in hopes of bringing an end to the incessant anxiety overtaking her. It seemed that the tranquility of the place could not quell her inner concerns.

Jahtara needed a release from her self-imposed immurement or perhaps space away from Tanhā. The cold foot bath dissipated Jahtara's headache and her vexations about Heddha. But the problem did not lie with Tanhā nor Heddha, although Jahtara truly ached for

Heddha's return. Instead, the ill embodied a strange vagueness lurking all around her.

She caught a glimpse of something, not among the coastal mountain fauna; instead, she found it in the shadows of her mind. An insight cascaded through her, imbibed from the surrounding forest, a learning formed from the patterns in nature. She gained continuity by letting go, for coherency surrounded her. The water cared not of its course; the forest and everything in it cared not of its disposition. They all followed their nature, the nature of place, and time. If a tree fell, it created space, light, and fodder for new life. The landscape adapted to the saison, drought, or fire, not by pushing against the winds of change with fear and anxiety but with adaptation. Jahtara often resisted her refined life, using defiance to gain sanctuary from outside control. Yet, her confidence eroded in torrents when forced to engage outside her privilege. Could these lingering notions pose an opportunity to adapt, to develop resiliency?

Instead of making this a time of fretful waiting, she would embrace it. With the chill water flowing around her ankles again, Jahtara strode across the stream, taking a new path back to the inn. She would inquire if the proprietor knew of any midwives to attend her birthing. A good start, although she sensed something else unfathomed, a ridge of emotion overtaking her sanctuary and pulling it apart piece by piece. She needed help, and Heddha resided elsewhere. Oh, why did she send her away?

Striding across the yard, Jahtara came upon a robust womon who, amid mounting her steed, got a foot tangled in her cloak. Jahtara immediately realized the womon's dilemma, caught between the inability to throw her leg over the mount and helpless to dismount with her foot entangled in the cloak. She quickly went to the womon's aid, disentangling her foot and holding the wrap back while she dismounted.

"Blessed be, my thanks, sweet child, the endurance of my stirrup leg lessened by the moment and truly so." Seeing Jahtara's expanded belly, she added, "Oh and look at you, you swung the dory around on me; you carrying and all, I should help you haul out. You work for the mistress, aye?"

"I must look begrimed with no shoes and muddied, yet I am a guest for the saison and likely, will give birth here or haul out, I think you said."

The womon, tall and large-boned with kind, empathetic eyes, smiled warmly, introducing herself as, "Babaor, more a title than a name, yet what I am called in these parts. And blessed be, I am hoping you shall call me Babaor soon. Come, let us retire inside and speak near the hearth."

Once through the entrance, Babaor removed her boots while Jahtara stood to the side, unsure if she should enter with muddy feet. Kalama, the proprietor, rushed up, handing her baby to her eldest daughter and sending the next youngest for Tanhā.

"And get a bucket of warm water for the laud," she yelled after the youngling, then back to Jahtara, "Please come by the fire, and Tanhā can clean your feet, milaud. I sent my husband to find you, hoping you could meet my Babaor. She gets through so rarely in this saison. The truth be told, we hardly see any during the Long Noites, and since you said you might abide here for some time, I thought it a blessing the fates brought Babaor here."

Babaor accounted for fate's presence by explaining, "I attended to another family for several deis and thought to stop here to check on the wee one. I am anxious to be off home to see my family, being away for so long and truly so."

Tanhā entered the great room with a large bowl and towels, followed by the youngling carrying a pail of warm water. She gave a slight curtsy to Jahtara, which the youngling mimicked. Jahtara had to keep from rolling her eyes at Tanhā, fixing her with a stern stare instead.

Babaor then asked, "Your husband travels with you?"

Jahtara fell back on the old tale, "No, we live on a farm towards the Great Grassland. My husband left some time ago, and we came Solauraward searching for him. The fates abandoned us in our search; thus, we return home yet, not wishing to get caught in the mountain passes, decided to spend the saison here in this beautiful inn. At least until the birthing of this child." Jahtara finished by giving Babaor a thin smile.

Tanhā, holding both feet above the dirtied water bowl, chose this moment to say, "I have finished, su alte...." Jahtara dropped her feet into the basin, causing Tanhā to jump back.

Kalama's partner Talou at the front door added to the commotion, bellowing, "Babaor, your mare wanders the paddock. Oh, begging your pardon, gentlewomyn."

"I meet with trouble mounting when helped so kindly by... Pardon, I know not what to call you?"

"Jahtara would do best," pointedly looking at Tanhā, "Thank you, Tanhā, I will not need you for now."

Babaor sat back in her chair, looking deeply at Jahtara. Kalama tread with caution into this silence, "I beg your pardon, milaud, I forget myself. Babaor, my midwife, just returns from attending a birth. She stopped to check on our little one, and I hope I am not presuming too much to suggest her assistance for you."

"On my walk, it occurred to me I am in need of a midwife, and here you are," to her host, she continued, "The timing proved perfect, and I thank you for it."

"Well, we will leave you to it then. Babaor, thank you for the kindness of stopping by. Geyrles, with me. Talou, do not track your muddy boots through my great room." She left Babaor and Jahtara to themselves next to the hearth.

"Jahtara, is it? Your position seems more elevated than my notion in the yard and truly so."

"It matters not. I wish for assistance during my confinement with this child. I am hoping you will provide such."

"Blessed be woman, you show with child, you do not come down

with a plague and will not need confinement. Your first, I gather?"
Jahtara nodded assent, so Babaor continued, "I come from three deis
at a wonderful birthing of a first, yet it can be a tiring travail even
when all goes well. I have a long stretch of attending births, bringing comfort when needed." Babaor paused, then, coming to a decision, continued, "I sense a hidden tale here; you carry a heavy basket
weighed down with vexations." When Jahtara said nothing, just gazed
into her lap, Babaor said, "You appear a womon of high bearing,
milaud, or should I say, su alteza?" Jahtara's head came up quickly to
search Babaor's face.

"I will not share my suspicions with others. However, birthing
requires bringing feelings out into the open, and truly so. Keeping
fear locked within only retards our passages, young laud." Babaor
paused and, taking Jahtara's hand, continued, "I would like you to
feel safe, Jahtara." Again, Jahtara only gazed at her lap.

"Twice, you said this child, not my child." Jahtara looked up,
tears forming, and nodded but could not speak. With nothing forthcoming, Babaor continued, "Blessed be, no child born of a womon
is misbegotten. Children naturally prevail complete, whole, nothing
less. We all come endowed with breath equally and truly so."

Now the tears flowed; Jahtara could not hold them back. All the
doubt and fear creeping into Jahtara about her life as a womon, lover,
queyn, and mother poured out with her tears. Babaor held her hand
until the well pinged dry. After a time, the fire burned to glowing
coals, and the middei Solaura streamed through the windows. Jahtara
looked around the great room in the new light. Babaor dozed in the
chair next to her, which midwives were known to do during their
labors. Without hesitation, Jahtara woke her, telling Babaor of herself,
her unborn child, her lover, and the coming trials. Ending with, "I
find naught yet love for my child. I know this sounds strange; nonetheless, I asked my child in the end. I found love and a sense they will
make the best of the choices life presents them!"

Babaor stated, "I accept your wish that I attend your birth with joy and deep honor, su alteza … and per your wish, I will henceforth call you Jahtara." She patted Jahtara on her knee. "Blessed be, the fates have gifted you a heavy burden, yet we caryatids can share this heavy load and need not get crushed by the weight of Inlanda we carry. Mayhap we shall join, like the creatrix Nu Kua, to repair the pillars holding up the sky, rebalancing Inlanda, so we no longer reside strangers in a strange land," she ended with a lilting voice.

For several deis, a growing worry gnawed at Heddha. She searched without success for Pug, and her concern for him matured to desperation. Yesterdei, she descended into the pit, and the dei before wandered the camps, both times in vain. This foresetting her dread grew more incautious, to the point she walked the road around the lip of the pit. She heard a plodding animal halfway around and hid behind a tree when a rider appeared cantering towards her. The trot grew closer without a change in cadence until, in anticipation of the rider moving past her, Heddha eased her breathe, then the rhythm stopped. She heard the rider's tack creaking in the silence as his weight shifted.

"Back out to the track with ya now." When Heddha didn't move, she heard a deep sigh. "Ya do not want me to come over there to drag ya out." Heddha reluctantly stepped from behind the tree, dusting debris from her clothes.

"You!" The rider exclaimed, recognizing Heddha. "Get over here, womon."

"Heddha."

"I know your name. Move now!"

"Tho?" Heddha saw his eyes widen and slits narrow. "Or should I call you brother or mayhap father?" Heddha's desperation had emboldened her or made her reckless.

"You spoke to my brother, then?" He slipped the knot fastening his whip to the saddle, passing his hand through the wrist loop, gripped the handle, and let the thong drop.

Heddha dropped her gaze. "Ananeurin grows beautiful and kind."

Again, the creaking of leather. Tho lifted the whip up and down, watching it coil and uncoil on the ground. Finally, "She takes after her mother."

"Perhaps… Yet, I have seen kindness in you."

"Sympathy gets you naught. See where leniency got me with you."

"Kindness could reunite your family."

"And what of Ananeurin? Her mother died unable to choose." Tho turned his head away to gaze into the darkening pit. "Kindness seeped into her from my brother."

"Perhaps she could nurture your kindness."

He looked sideways at Heddha. "She knows naught of my existence."

"Love brought your daughter into existence. Perhaps her love can bridge the space separating brothers. Unification forms your brother's intent. Make it yours, and the intent can build the foundation of a bonding. At the least, you can have a part in Ananeurin's life in remembrance of her mother, whom you both loved."

Tho looked to the sky, blinking away the pain, "Too much time has passed."

Heddha raised her head to look at Tho, "I thought my life set by fate, many times in truth. The last just now, trying to disappear behind yonder tree, yet we now discuss your daughter, therein lies the potency of the present."

Tho sat silently for a few moments, then slowly wound the whip into loops and knotted it to the saddle, "You confound me, womon. And I will probably rue asking you, yet an itch needs scratching, Heddha, what do you do here?"

"I have not seen my friend, Pug, in deis and am worried for his safety. I fear he traveled down this road in his boldness."

"Then his boldness harmed him, and you cannot help him. I

hold no confidence in the roundeyes, and I fear my brother told you his tale of what they did to him. He remains unaware that I brought him to Benedus' infirmary after they wounded him and arranged for a womon to look after Ananeurin until he recovered." Tho sat quietly, then said, "Still, I must do the only thing I know, getting men to do what they do not wish to do.

"Here, I make certain no watchful eyes tarry along this road. I will return leading wagons to the clearing and leave crates to be picked up. I do this every other dei. If your friend strayed anywhere here, you would not find him. You must leave now. Check the camps. Go now, Heddha, for I wish no harm come to you. Do not be seen here; leave the roadway not to be discovered." Tho road off towards the camps, not looking back.

Heddha stood, watching him until he vanished into the trees towards the Setting, never looking back for her. She cocked her head with a wry smile forming. The smile stemmed from an unfamiliar source. She never experienced interactions with men like this, Jit and Tho both. Did her fears diminish, replaced by confidence, an understanding imparting peace? And he never looked back to see if she followed, curious.

The pit darkened, and the sky toward the Setting glowed through the leafless branches, dusk gathering. Heddha turned away from the Setting. She needed to know what happened to Pug. He followed her on this journey; maybe his nature led him along this road. She would do all she could to find him.

She walked, darkness engulfing the road, until coming to a gateway set across the track but a gate unlike any she knew. The thick, stiff netting offering no foot or hand purchase and a fence of the same material continued to the pit's edge and far into the dark on the opposite side. The posts were twice her height and made of a hard-smooth substance, not wood or metal, with the netting buried in the ground. A rail lay sunk even with the road below the gate. Heddha could find no way to open the gate. Now what? Tho would soon return with the wagons. What did he say? Had he instructed her to leave the road?

Heddha lay hidden in some low growth until she heard a rider whoa their mount. Looking through the undergrowth, she saw a bright glow illuminate the rider's face, he spoke, and the gate slid sideways, opening on its own. He waited until the first wagon appeared, leading it through the gate. Heddha counted fifteen more wagons pass the gate, followed by Tho, who stopped inside the entrance.

When the last wagon moved out of sight, Heddha crept along the fence and slipped through the gate to stand beside Tho's steed.

He did not turn to look at her but said quietly, "You are a fool, Heddha, yet prove an unfailing friend to Pug. When we leave, the gate will close and not open for two deis. A large, I can only call it an airship, will come and take the crates. When this airship drops, the roundeyes have a way of seeing anyone in the compound. I know this because a teamster hid inside once. I never saw this man again. Remain next to the fence until the ship arrives. Then, you may inspect the compound. Take care near the clearing.

"I must go with the wagons now. Good hunting, Heddha. I hope to see you again." Tho disappeared into the darkness, with only the steed's fading hoof falls heard until Heddha stood alone in the silent dark.

After the wagons and Tho headed to the camp, the lone rider closed the gate from outside. Heddha waited until she heard a strange high-pitched whine. The wavering sound grew in intensity until it stopped abruptly, followed by hissing.

Then she heard voices, too far away to understand but shouts with laughter. Heddha moved, staying off the road and shifting from tree to bush until she saw light and movement. She slowly crept closer, finally seeing faces with round pupils and hearing distinct words in their language. Men and womyn, in blue loose one-piece clothing, pushed strange carts under the crates that lifted and pulled them up the ramp into the ship. Bright light washed the area, coming from just above a wide ramp.

Offworlders worked fast to load the crates onto the ship. They divided into three groups of two workers, and one supervisor directed their activity. Another observing from the ramp wore a tight-fitting suit like Cora wore.

Heddha moved into the deep shadow at the ship's side, wanting a closer look. The enormous vessel appeared made of rigid material colored a lustrous burgundy with a design in gold along the side. A shrill noise sounded four times with a pause, then four times again. Heddha walked hunched over to the ship's rear to see what the noise signified. Peering over the ramp, she saw the crates gone, with everyone except the overseer running up the ramp. With the workers inside, the remaining woman raised her hands, showing six fingers, shouting something to the man at the top of the ramp, who responded by waving the woman up the incline.

The sequence of noises repeated, the ramp started to lift, and the light dimmed. Heddha realized they were leaving and looked for somewhere to run when suddenly an animal ran down the closing ramp and jumped off the ship, followed by the blue-clothed crew yelling and chasing the animal. A single loud blast of noise sounded and repeated. One crew member turned and drew a finger across his neck, and the noise stopped. Heddha popped her head over the ramp to look inside, seeing only the officer turn, going deeper into the ship.

If Heddha stopped to think about what she did, she couldn't have articulated a reason except to find Pug. The ramp appeared empty, the large door stood open, and the light dimmed, presenting an opportunity to look inside, and Heddha gave no thought to how she would get out. Her heart pounding, she leaped onto the ramp and, with four racing steps, disappeared in the shadow beside the door, moving further inside the ship. Then her knees gave way, and she sank to the floor, her rush extinguished. She concentrated on slowing her breath while watching two workers finish securing crates to the deck of the hold with containment covers.

Catching her breath, Heddha heard offworlders returning up the ramp. Crew members cheered their return except the officer standing inside the ramp, who shouted before walking over to a womon holding the animal and petting its head. The ramp closed. Everyone headed up ladders and stairs to the main deck except the man in the officer's uniform who checked the crates, then he too went to the upper compartment, and the hold dimmed.

Heddha cautiously moved out into the hold but saw no one. She went to the ramp but could find no latches to open it. Next, she explored the officer's domain and still couldn't find a way to open the ramp. In the dim light, she saw her reflection in a black mirror set at an angle just above waist height. She reached out and let her finger brush her image, and the mirror glowed to light. The surface filled with geometric shapes and symbols Heddha could not fathom, so she backed away. In the glowing light, she did see a blue suit hanging clasped to the sidewall. She unfastened the garment to examine when the panel extinguished, and a chime sounded three times, startling her. Now what?

Her answer came with a reoccurrence of the whining noise, only louder in the ship. When it reached an apex, the craft wobbled like a ship at sea, and a force slammed Heddha against the rear wall of the cargo space, taking her breath away. She tried pushing away from the wall, hardly moving until the effect gradually lessened. Heddha rolled onto her knees against the ramp door, then stood, and suddenly floated into the hold, somersaulting backward towards the ceiling while wind-milling her arms. This motion left her nauseous, much like during the storm on the ship.

Heddha clung to something protruding from the rear wall with the ceiling just above her, although she seemed unsure if above was the proper word. The ship gave no clue it moved. Heddha's immediate task involved getting down from the rear wall and crossing the hold to the stairs and the deck above. Maybe she could find Kasumi, Jorma, or even Cora.

The waves of the Setting Sea came to mind, each wave pushing her to and fro. She would dive under a wave and shove off the sandy bottom to reach the surface again. Heddha wondered if such a maneuver could propel her to the stairs from her present position. She pushed off and sensed immediately she thrust too hard, missing a first handhold and slipping off the second. By her third try, she held fast, but her body rotated around this axis, and she let go, fearful of crashing into the stairs. Heddha managed to grab the stair railing with two hands and, by tucking her legs in and using the strength in her arms, made a semisoft coordinated landing. She pulled herself over the railing and, using her hands, 'walked' up the remaining steps until she could see onto the main deck, which looked smaller than expected.

She saw rows of high-backed chairs split by a central aisle with the crew seated in this area. The officer sat at a side wall in front of glowing panels like the one on the cargo deck. Forward were stairs to an even smaller room where three officers sat at tilted panels with something like a bubble overhead. Through the bubble appeared what looked like another vessel, getting bigger by the moment.

Heddha suddenly realized they journeyed to a large ship on a smaller transport ship, something like a barge, and she would not find the ones she knew on this ship. Heddha's heart sank, realizing her dilemma.

The officer barked something, and everyone tightened a sash over their shoulders. The other ship loomed massive above the upper deck. Something touched Heddha's shoulder, causing her to jerk, and she saw the blue one-piece garment drifting up the stairs. Heddha quickly grabbed it with a free hand. Shortly, a slight tug pulled Heddha towards the stairs, growing more robust, so she flipped over the railing and tucked into a dark space where steps joined the ceiling. Her weight gradually returned.

A hissing sounded again, followed by the ship rocking and bumping noises. The crew filed into the hold, opened the rear door, and unloaded the cargo. The area quieted, and Heddha considered climbing out when three officers clambered down the stairs and off the ship. One carried the small animal in a netted cylinder enclosure.

Now what? Her impulsiveness landed her in the poacher's pouch with no way out. When sounds outside the ship grew sparse, Heddha carefully climbed down from her perch and crept to the ramp door. Just when she thought it might be safe to look around, most of the light disappeared with a snap, except in a few areas with what looked like candlelight. Heddha stepped onto the ramp, then jumped off the edge to the main floor and moved into the darkness under the ramp. Over the next while, she became bolder, moving around the hold. The further Heddha explored, the more overwhelmed she became by the size: three barge-sized ships rested here, six vessels each the size of a small barn, and scattered around the hold stood numerous craft similar to a wagon with bubbles covering a seating for two to four.

She came across personal items and found a pair of boots fitting her. They snuggled down tight on their own when she put them on. Creepy. Heddha slipped on the one-piece garment from the cargo hold but grappled with closing the front until she held the closure together at the top, and the seam closed on its own. Spooky. Heddha also found a strange hat with what looked like a faceplate on a cniht's helmet, but when she tried to lower it over her face, the back lifted off her head, so she pulled the hat low on her forehead to hide her eyes. She hid her sandals and went looking for a way out.

She found a couple of candidates for doors but found no way to open them. The only handle-looking thing comprised a bright red lever with a webbed cord looped through it. She could see moving the bar would break the material and refrained from this route, but closer inspection identified a small panel next to the door that brightened when she touched it. The symbols on its face held no meaning to her. Heddha touched a couple of them, and the panel started flashing red. Characters in the lower part began changing, and the flashing got faster and faster. Then the door popped open and swung outward, causing Heddha to jump. Someone in similar clothing stepped through the door, surprised to see her. Keeping her head down, Heddha could only think to wave a greeting. The man slapped her palm and kept right on going. Having turned green when the door opened, the panel turned yellow, emitting a quiet chirp. Heddha, thanking the fates, quickly turned sideways to slip through the closing door.

A brighter, warmer passageway on the other side of the door gave no clue which direction to take. Hearing footsteps coming from one direction propelled her the opposite way. She walked until she heard or saw someone, then took another route. Smelling something like food, she followed her nose and, peeking through a doorway, spied Cora sitting at a table with two others. Cora glanced at her, turned back to the others for an instant, then cocked her head at Heddha, knitting her brows, mouth dropping open, and stood all in one motion. She sputtered something to her table mates and made for Heddha.

She waved Heddha back as she came through the door, pulling her along the hallway, muttering something repeatedly. Cora stopped at a set of doors with no handles and touched a panel, looking both ways along the hall while still repeating the word. The doors slid open from the center, and they entered a small empty room, and the doors slid closed. Cora turned to face the doors and spoke a different word once to no one, and Heddha became heavier, then lighter. Cora stuck her head out when the doors opened and, seeing no one, pulled Heddha down the passageway, which had changed color. Stopping in front of another door, Cora spoke, it opened, and she pushed Heddha into the room. Cora shouted, "How in the name of hooved fornicating animals do you come stupefyingly strolling here?"

Cora paced an elliptical path around her room. Every couple of orbits, she would stop, look at Heddha, and shake her head. She talked to her handheld panel once and told Heddha they would wait, seemingly too upset to say anything else coherent. The small, sparse room appeared colorful and clean. A portrait of an older womon and another of two younglings stood on a shelf. The paintings looked strange, like you could stick your finger into the portraits. Heddha wanted a closer inspection but thought it better she didn't get in Cora's way.

A chime sounded, and Jorma stepped into the room when the door opened. The first word he said sounded like the phrase Cora repeated upon seeing Heddha. He and Cora engaged in a heated exchange, Heddha not understanding anything. At first, she politely asked them to speak to her. When this produced no response, she stood between them, demanding they talk to her.

With a sigh, Jorma asked, "Heddha, what...no, how...I mean, why are you here? Did anyone see you? And how did you find Cora?"

"Well, last to first: I followed my nose; yes; I sought Pug; I foxed my way onto the first ship when no one looked. I know you think me foolhardy, yet I thought I would find my friend on the airship, not knowing many ships existed. I am here and unable to reverse my actions," Heddha shrugged, "The milk soured, yet much can still be done with clabbered milk."

Cora did not seem amused, and Heddha thought she would ask about clabbered milk, but in mid utterance switched to another concern, "Wait, wait, did you say someone saw you?"

"Yes and no, they greeted me, opening the door to where the ship was, then I slipped out the door after them. Mayhap they thought I belonged here."

"Without one of these," Cora produced her handheld and pointed to her wrist, "you should have set off the alarm going through that door!"

Heddha grimaced, saying, "I tried to open the door using the shiny thing. It started changing red on and off, and perhaps it did not work properly."

Jorma ventured, "The panel may have reset after the other person opened the door – very lucky indeed!"

"What do we do now? Heddha cannot stay in my room!"

"She will have to until we can figure some way to get her back down."

"What about Kasumi?"

"No, it's too risky; she shares a room."

"What about my risk?"

"Planet Protection Officer, sound familiar and this," gesturing to Heddha. "I mean, Heddha originates from the planet. For Heddha and the crew's sake, you should start by thoroughly cleaning her inside and out and give her the appropriate," he switched to Galactic Standard (GS), "microbiota fecal transplant."

Heddha, confused, stared at them.

The deep green foliage faded to yellow among the riparian trees with the shorter deis and cool noites. Further up the slope, the tall conifer spires swayed in a wind that did not touch the meadow. A doe and fawn, feeding on the still plentiful grasses, kept a watchful eye on Jahtara. Even though she took pleasure in the snug inn, endowed with its meadow, stream, and forests, Jahtara grew bored.

She tried to engage Talou in conversation. He appeared at a loss for words outside of farming, animal husbandry, or hunting. Kalama found it even harder to converse about anything beyond the inn's upkeep or her children. Just this morgn watching Kalama work and manage the younglings, Jahtara expressed fears concerning how her life would change with a child. The innkeeper, with an expression of incomprehension, moved strands of loose hair behind her ear, adjusted the youngest in the sling across her chest, added a plate to the stack of dishes on her arm, grabbed the hand of her next oldest, who pulled at her skirt, and mumbled, "Not sure I would know, do not have a moment to consider it."

And Tanhā endured, well, Tanhā: always wanting after something she did not have or not wanting what she did not like and suffering through it all.

Jahtara wrapped her shawl tighter around her shoulders and quickened her steps on the path toward the road leading through the mountains. Since arriving at the glen, she hadn't come this way for fear of a passerby seeing her, but todei, she longed to see anyone. She leaned into the lane, looking in each direction, seeing no one, just more damp forest. She turned towards the small bridge spanning the stream, recalling the day she and Heddha crossed this bridge, a brighter day with the Solaura's rays streaming through the trees and Heddha pointing out the edible and medicinal herbs of the under-growth.

And a feeling came welling up, unbidden; Jahtara realized she wasn't as adept at being alone as she had believed. She missed Heddha and what they were together, yearning for their closeness.

Early morgn gray drained the color from the forest as time slipped into the saison of lengthening noites. Still, she felt no chill when stepping off the path into the shallow water, floating over the muted multicolored pebbles strewn across the creek bottom. She headed upstream in the steadily deepening water with a mist swirling along the steepening bank. Rising water eddied around her chest, and long hair-like moss made for unreliable footing. She caught movement along the bank ahead. She struggled to keep upright, pulling herself along using tenuous branches that often broke or slipped through her hands in the strengthening current. A silhouette climbed onto a large boulder balanced further up the bank, and when the figure turned, she recognized Pug waving her forward. Her footing erred, plunging her under the water. Searching for traction and finding none, she kicked for the distant surface, floundering towards an annulus of light sporadically swept by churned froth. Muted sounds reached her as she struggled to attain the interface.

Heddha woke to Cora shushing and wiping a cold cloth over her face. Heddha pushed her away, tearing the facecloth off, gasping for breath. In Galactic Standard (GS), "By the fates, woman, are you trying to drown me!"

"Certainly not! I brought you some breakfast, but you gasped and thrashed about, so I thought I should wake you with a cold cloth. You dreamt again?"

"Gone now in a whiff of smoke. I left the path. I chose without thinking. Now I have no choice."

"Yes, well, my method involves waiting for the available choices to eliminate themselves until only one option remains, then choosing that one. Very limiting; however, it takes advantage of blaming the fates for any poor outcome. But you have a friend to consider and chose him."

"Yes, and lost Jahtara along the way." Heddha used the cool cloth to wipe her face and neck.

"No one has discovered you're here, and Jorma works on returning you to Inlanda. It may work out."

"I haven't left this room. Time stands still, and on Inlanda, time flies!"

"It's not a total waste. You've done well learning Galactic Standard with the VR techcap and...." The chime sounded, and Jorma slipped through the door, checking behind himself before it closed. Cora said, "Speaking of the rascal."

Jorma smirked, "Well, according to the crew textchat, I'm your lover, and we're taking romantic meals in your love shack!"

The PPO's cheeks reddened. "Please don't tell me that. Even the captain called me aside to ask if I engaged in a relationship with a crew member."

"See, Cora, your love life improved dramatically, or at least the perception of a love life."

"Tell us you have a plan. My nerves will not take this much longer!"

"I have a plan though it will take some time." Cora rolled her eyes. "It's also tricky, but Heddha learning Galactic will help. We received a new crew member, part of the geology team, at the start of this mission. His previous assignment was on a planet with an emerging intelligent species, and he became infested with a parasite through fecal/oral transmission before transferring to Chaz's Beagle. These single-cell animals form colonies in the gut wall, gaining control over the enteric nervous system's transmitters. These neurotransmitters changed the infected host's response to food substances, especially certain amino acids, which are parasite growth factors.

"Anyway, this crew member got through quarantine and onto Chaz's Beagle due to the parasite's long latency period. On ship day thirty, security discovered him hoarding certain foods and the lysine/arginine amino acid inks from the 3D food printer. Three days later, the captain confined him to the brig after he made sexually explicit suggestions toward a crew member, and during questioning, he propositioned one of the investigators. A thorough medical exam found protozoa infecting the GI tract, but in his case, it proliferated to the retina of his eyes, unlike in its natural host. From there, it spread to the visual cortex affecting the perception of visual stimuli through nerve tracts to reward and sexual centers of the brain. A cofactor in the pathology of this organism happens through the ingestion of copious amounts of the amino acid arginine, which augments the blood supply to the GI tract and the genital organs through the production of nitric oxide. Leading to increased tumescence of the penis."

Cora stopped him by making an X sign with her forearms, saying, "How does this relate to getting Heddha out of my quarters, off this ship, and back to her planet?"

"I'm getting there. I just thought to relate an interesting medical anecdote of the phylogenic comparative approach to codependency in astrobiology."

With a baffled look, Cora silently shook her head while Heddha said, "Can we hear the plan, please?"

"Where was I? Oh yes, making a long story shorter. After the cause and lack of treatment on the ship were explained, the infected crew member agreed to cryometabolic suspension for the duration. In return for dropping all charges, he'll receive free treatment upon debarkation, allow the study of the protozoa's pathology, and give patent rights to the corporation." At this point, Heddha rolled her eyes. Jorma quickly continued, "The whole incident, including the medical files, were deleted from the computer and stored in a password-protected file in the Captain's log. Here's the beauty of the plan, the crew member's original check-in onboard and the issuance of embedded seed identity with passcodes, ship, and planet transit rights still exist in force. So we'll have Heddha assume his identity!"

With an incredulous look, Cora said, "Jorma, the crew member is male...." She couldn't finish; instead, she gestured toward Heddha. "What if someone checks her new identity seed? The photo won't match, or worse, what if one of the crew members he sexually harassed recognizes the name? And every time she goes through a door lock or onto the transport ship, the sensors will alarm!"

"I think I've got most of that worked out. Heddha can wear the baggy crew overalls, and outside breastfeeding, Inlandani breasts aren't large; she could pass for male. What do you say, Heddha?"

"If it gets me off this ship, I'll do it," she said.

He continued, "I can alter a photo to blend Heddha, and Achebe, the crew member. They have similar skin tones, so if someone looks him up, they'll see some similarities to Heddha, enough to confuse them, hopefully. We'll stay away from areas of the ship where the harassed crew members work and live. I checked neither of them travels planetside.

"I can enter Heddha's cellular ligand signature, his crew ID number, and personal info onto a seed chip we'll inject under her skin. Then, substitute Heddha's info for Achebe's in the computer for the RFID readers. I checked; no face recognition or retinal checks needed to board the transport ship. Lastly, I'll have pupil masks made for her eyes, and with her proficiency in Galactic Standard, it could work." Jorma ended with a broad grin.

"I find it hard to believe you can hack the ship's computer systems." Questioned Cora.

"I have advanced degrees in political science, psychology, history, computer engineering, and programming. During the Corporate Wars in the Fornax Cluster, I hacked for the SinoCorp. I know, a long time ago, but you just need the right hacking program like fuzzer or Galleon these days. Although an AI could do the hack faster, I don't trust the AI not to report me."

"What do you think, Heddha?" Cora asked.

"My use of Galactic improves impressively; the VR techcap makes learning effortless. I've reviewed medical sciences for the last few weeks. I wanted to know what happened to the baby. So, I understood some of what you were saying about this crew member. Although I agree with Cora, it drifted off point. I can even see a connection between DNA providing instructions and these computer machines using… Is it programming? Jorma can change the instruction about this Achebe guy and replace it with my instructions. Right?"

"Close, I change the information the computer uses to plug into its instructions. Does using the VR techcap or your time on the ship make any of it seem less magical?"

"Maybe a little, but it's just facts with no connection to the past or how you got to this…" Heddha gestured to the ship around her. "To me, you live like termites in this nest. It's missing the natural world with nothing alive: stale air, insipid water, and constant vibration. Your food tastes strange and lacks vitality. Everything looks the same, turning uniqueness into mundane abundance. And very peculiar to me – you live and bathe in the same room with the toilet. It gives me shivers just thinking about it."

Cora impatiently said, "Ok, enough of the cross-cultural criticisms. The plan seems improbable to me, but we must get Heddha off this ship. Can you do this, Heddha?"

In a measured voice, Heddha said, "I know you don't want me here; you feel I have complicated your life, Cora. Well, I wish I wasn't here. I don't want you complicating my life and Inlanda. Most of all, I wish to be with Jahtara. But wishing doesn't make it so. I must try this plan of Jorma's."

Jahtara exhaled into the cold morgn stillness, forming a thin condensate that slowly dissipated until her next exhalation. These metronome breaths were the only external measure of time. Internally Jahtara drank in the riotous colors adorning the hillside opposite, more festive than the banners and dress on Keyn's Day. She sat on a saddle blanket, laid atop the low stone wall bordering the meadow, protected from the chill by a wool pullover hat, a shawl across her shoulders, and a full skirt.

Sheltered from the world beyond this sanctuary, Jahtara longed to return to greater Inlanda. Still, todei, she enjoyed the beauty and tranquility as the Solaura's warming rays edged towards her across the meadow. She heard the hoofbeats of a traveler turning off the coastal road onto the inn's path. Soon the rider came into view atop a fine old war steed. Jahtara would have let him pass, but his inquisitive, searching posture caused her to call out to the youth, "Whoa, squire, what do you so keenly search for?"

He reined in his mount, saying, "Begging your pardon, ma'am, yet I may not say."

"Yet how will you know your quest ends on this coddiwomple journey?"

"At the start of my journey, the way seemed clear, yet grew less so the further I traveled."

He sat in the saddle silently, then asked, "Would you mind if I dismounted and spoke with you in more proximity?" Jahtara smiled, nodding assent. He slipped the steed and leapt the rail fence in a

fluid motion, then, after tying the reins to the rail, walked the stone
wall to within a respectful distance and, indicating the wall asked,
"May I, ma'am?" Again, Jahtara nodded. He sat, staring out across
the meadow.

"You seem at a loss."

"Aye, ma'am. I search for a person yet may not say who, and
I know this person only by the description given to me. I am in a
quandary."

"I see."

"I am troubled; I may fail in my mission, dishonoring my father
in whose name I undertook this task."

"This war mount belongs to your father?"

The young man looked at the animal, smiling. "Aye, the old steed
was his favorite. I rode it to honor him, although found myself wishing for a swifter mount as the journey progressed."

"Often, we must find our own way when we fly the nest. My
pardon, did you say was?"

"Aye, he died in service to Keyn Tergon, Solauraward, in the company of other cnihts, with only one returning. I undertook this trek
to honor them and for my queyn."

"You speak of Sir Absan?"

"You knew him, ma'am?"

"Only a brief moment before his death," Jahtara said, removing
her head covering.

The squire stared out at the bouquet of colors celebrating the cycle
of change until the significance of Jahtara's words drained through the
colander of his thoughts and feelings. He turned to look at the cop-
per-haired womon as it dawned on him: he sat in the presence of his
queyn. He dropped to his knees and bowed, saying, "Su majeste, I
pledge you my sword."

Jahtara stared at the kneeling squire, only slightly shocked, for she
knew the tradition and grew up at its periphery. This stranger, full
of honor and vigor, pledged himself to her, a womon only slightly

older than himself. She also knew he depended on her to continue his father's holdings. Jahtara sighed, imploring quietly, "Please, rise and sit next to me."

He lifted his head, looking confused, "Su grandeza?"

"I try to conceal my identity for my unborn child's safety. Although I am not entirely successful." Jahtara looked to the inn's yard to see Talou crossing to the barn. He slowed when he spied the war steed and gazed into the meadow with the kneeling squire. The confused squire seemed determined to grow roots where he was. "Your queyn commands you to rise and sit your honor and sword on this wall." He followed her command. Jahtara was taken aback at hearing her father's voice in her dictate.

Tears flowed at the thought of her mother and father and their fate; no matter their station or Jahtara's rejection of her role, she loved them. Jahtara turned away, again realizing the past's bearing on the moment. "I regret your father and Absan's death. I know of their honor from speaking to Absan and personally experienced the shock of his death." Turning to him, she requested, "Your father's name?"

"The second arl of Twisting River Township, Laud Abiola, su alteza."

"We will dispense with the honorifics. Call me, Jahtara."

"As you please, su laudship," he said with a bow from the waist.

"And no bowing or taking a knee. Jahtara only. And what shall I call you?"

"Sefu, my given name."

"Ah, and you wish to serve as the queyn's sword?"

"A sword of the queyn's, aye."

Jahtara sat straighter and turned to gaze again at the flourish of color. The warmth of the new dei's Solaura reached Jahtara accompanied by a breeze, swaying branches, and dropping leaves that fell in twisting dances joining the detritus from saisons past on the forest floor. Speaking not to Sefu but into the crisp air of the meadow, she told of the change she knew came, "'Tis the saison of remembrance, of what we have lost… and gained. A time to consolidate what we reap from earlier sowing, examine our learnings, and strengthen our intentions for the coming Warming. Change our only constant." She turned to Sefu smiling, "Journeying here proved an obscure twisting road, and in your service to me, you may face unfamiliar circumstances where you need your sword and heart. All done with honor. You wish to pledge yourself to this quest?"

"You have turned the intention of my journey down a different path. A sword tempered by the heart will increase the justice in its strength. I pledge my heart and sword to your cause… Jahtara."

"I accept your allegiance on behalf of Inlanda. Have you messages or news for me from my regent or Laud Renesmee?"

"Aye… Jahtara," still not feeling comfortable with this new way of addressing a monarch, yet willing to attempt this dropping of the old traditions. With growing confidence, he said, "Official documents from both and a personal letter from Laud Renesmee to her daughter."

Seeing Tanhā and Kalama approaching along the fence, she smiled, knowing curiosity brought them forth. A way to explain Sefu's presence sprang to mind. "Hold my correspondence for now and present Tahnā with hers. She approaches." Sefu stood when the two womyn arrived, and Jahtara patted the stone wall indicating Tahnā should sit. Taking Tahnā's hand, she said, "I have good news in a letter from your father and mother, conveyed here by Sefu. They approve your betrothal to Sefu, with the joining proposed for three jahrs hence." Jahtara gave Tahnā a pointed wink and her hand a squeeze as Kalama's gaze shifted to Sefu. Tahnā's mouth dropped open and closed again with the dawn of a knowing.

Tahnā leaped into the startled Sefu's arms, squealing with delight, knocking him back a couple of paces. Looking to the proprietor, Jahtara said, "The young Sefu will need a room. Perhaps tomorrow, a celebration dinner?"

"Such good news, I am sure we will have a fine celebration. If we can pry Tanhā away, I will show her betrothed to his room. He will need a bath after his journey, and you all can carry on the festivity at the break fast."

Tanhā watched Sefu move away while Jahtara questioned, "You understand this is a ruse?"

"With certainly, I wish only to serve you with my best measure in this," she ended with a giggle.

Heddha gazed dejectedly at the bland room she shared with Cora. Nothing changed: the tasteless gruel daily, the sour air breath after breath, the acrid smell of metal, the closed-in volume without movement, and the fearful chaperon. The only thing that gave her joy was the VR techcap, learning astrobiology, among other subjects. She loved the maze-like journey with the techcap, each new twist or turn prompting further questions leading to deeper minutia, building an ever-finer map of understanding. Without the VR techcap, she would have long ago pulled her hair out, gagged Cora, and found a way to escape the ship on her own.

The chime sounded, and Cora entered, bringing food and informing Heddha Jorma was on his way. When the door chimed again, Cora stepped into the passageway for a secret conference with Jorma. Heddha frowned; she would not let Cora and her insecurities prevent her from getting back to Jahtara and Inlanda.

The door slid aside, and Jorma, with Cora following, entered. They both looked solemn, and Cora's face flushed. Jorma spoke in GS. "I came here with good news, I thought, but Cora has concerns she wishes us to discuss first. Your use the VR techcap. She feels you could use the knowledge gained to change Inlandan culture."

Heddha answered forcefully, "Cora's corporate sponsor changed Inlanda by stealing our genetic information, implanting a transgenic recombinant DNA embryo into Jahtara, saying nothing of killing

Inlandani and offworlders on Inlanda."

Cora turned to Jorma, responding, "See, I told you she knows too much. Why did I ever allow this? We must contain this now."

"What do you suggest we do, Cora, space her? How about a lobotomy?" Jorma paused to slow his breathing, continuing, "I think our history shows an advanced society does more damage through detribalizing, disease, and genocide than the use of advanced technology by a less advanced society. Technological advances wreak havoc on our own culture through unforeseen consequences." Jorma turned to Heddha, asking, "What do you want, Heddha?"

"I don't want the outcomes you suggested, nor do I think Cora wishes those either," Heddha said, looking directly at Cora.

"Of course not."

"I know you want me gone. Didn't Jorma say we were close to fulfilling his plan?"

"What if it doesn't work? What then?." Cora quickly glanced at the photos on her shelf, continuing, "I have disappointed in every aspect of my position here. The corporation could charge me with an offense against the Planetary Protection Act. Cora fought to hold back tears.

Heddha wrapped her arm around Cora's waist, pulling her over to the bed so they could sit. She handed Cora several pieces of soft paper to dry her eyes and rubbed her back. Heddha spoke softly but firmly, saying, "You were chosen to fail, chosen for your inexperience and desire to please in your new position. They don't want an official of the commonwealth to speak the truth. They expect you to go along as a corporate employee, but you can stand up to them as a commonwealth official. You know what they have done. Only you occupy a strong enough position to do this. Their scheme will unravel. The Planetary Protection Officer performed her duties."

Jorma knelt next to Cora, asking. "Cora, the girls in the photo, your daughters?"

Sniffling, Cora nodded, then sighed, explaining, "I failed them with weakness when I should have been strong." Drying her eyes, she said, "If I am weak again, I will lose them forever. I will help in any way I can."

Jorma stepped out into the corridor, followed by Heddha, cautiously exiting Cora's quarters, and Heddha jumped when the door suddenly slid closed.

Jorma put a hand on her shoulder and spoke in GS. "Act like you belong. If anyone checks, the morphed pic of you looks surprisingly good. I know the eye masks feel uncomfortable, but you will get used to them.

"Come on. I want to show you a special place. I'm sure you'll appreciate it after being cooped up for so long. We can talk there." They walked far, passing other crew members, and making several turns. Jorma reminded Heddha to keep her head up since she tended to look at the floor if she saw anyone else. Jorma stopped in front of one of those doors opening in the middle. Entering the elevator, he whispered to Heddha, nodding encouragement.

"Deck 15," Heddha said in GS, feeling strange talking to an empty room. The elevator moved and opened onto a different hallway. Two crew waiting moved back slightly to let them off. Heddha looked at them, saying, "Thanks," and stepped by them.

Jorma brought them to a wide door, pressed his left wrist to a small panel, turning it green, then tapped it, which opened the door. Heddha stepped into a short hallway with cushioned walls and floor. The door slid shut, cutting off the light, and coming to the end of the hall, Heddha stopped in her tracks at seeing the large room with one wall and ceiling opening to the firmament outside. She grabbed for a strap on the wall, hanging on for life.

Jorma walked out into the room and turned towards her, grinning. "My apologies. I should have warned you. It's a window, made of thick clear plastisteal, like a diamond – if you've ever seen one of those?"

"I have seen gems of many forms, not like this, though. It won't cleave like gemstone?"

"No, it's a strong transparent metal. Come, I want to show you the beauty of space and Inlanda."

Heddha stepped tentatively into the room, stopping to stand with her hands out to her sides, feeling a little more confident when suddenly a vessel shot out from somewhere beneath them in a curving arc. Heddha tipped back on her heels, lost her balance, and ended up on her back, looking up at the vastness of space filled with an enormity of stars.

Jorma squatted next to her, explaining, "Sometimes when those shuttles leave, it's hard to tell who's doing the moving, throwing off your balance. You okay?"

"Yes, but maybe it's best to just lie here for now."

"You'll adjust to it. You were cooped up in a small space for too long. Try crawling over to the window. It's quite strong."

Heddha gave him a dubious look but rolled over and crawled to the window, placing her hand on the hard, cold surface. "You're right. It does feel..." Heddha's eyes drifted to the scene below and, with a sharp breath, said, "That... I mean, is that..."

"Inlanda, yes, your beautiful world."

After a long silence, Heddha asked, "Where do I look for the Middle Realm? I can't make anything out."

"That large brown patch is the Great Grassland coming out of the darkness. Down this way," he said, making a line on the window, "are the rolling hills where Kasumi and I met you. I can barely make out the river flowing by the inn. Then across these mountains to the Setting Sea, where I parted from Jahtara and Tanhā. Jahtara would call the lengthy line of white the Rising Mounts with the High Mountain Realm beyond."

"Inlanda looks so different from up here, much larger yet smaller. It seems I could go from the inn to the Setting Sea in a single step, and the lands I traveled for lunas only a small part of the whole."

Heddha pressed her face to the window, the heat of her breath causing condensation to form, but she couldn't make out the trail towards the Setting Sea. She sat back with a sigh, "She didn't reveal where she went. Did she seem well when you last saw her and Tanhā traveled with her?"

"She started to show, and the child moved more often. She got better at acknowledging her position. Even accepted my offer to become a minister to the offworlders and made Tanhā her attendant." He turned to look at Heddha, "She didn't tell me where she went."

Heddha turned away from Inlanda to regard the innumerable lights above her. "Your home orbits one of those stars?"

"Many of those lights constitute galaxies filled with many stars." Jorma pondered, "Out of those multitudes of stars, I have decided to make Inlanda my home." He paused, then to himself, "One must eventually decide whether to play the game or seek a way to escape it."

Heddha turned back to Inlanda with a tender smile, "I often wished to be somewhere else, but now I long to go back." She looked up at Jorma, "When can we leave?"

"Only you can leave by the method I have devised. I do not have authorization to take a shuttle down to the pit, and I suspect I would set off alarms if I tried. You must do this alone."

"Yet, Cora wants to stop me?"

"She does want you to go. A battle rages in her head, a conflict between going along to get along and what she feels is the right thing to do. She does not like where she landed in life." He paused again, shrugging, "We all occasionally discover ourselves in some inexplicable place and time, amazed or shocked at the circumstance, wondering how we got there." Jorma turned to look at Heddha, remembering her presence, "Cora finds herself at such a place. She has concerns about what you learn and its effect on you and Inlanda. I am concerned for a different reason. Using the VR techcap can have effects from long-term use."

"Effects, how could it affect me?"

"You have gorged on a lot of information, and each session can cause euphoria… like bliss or rapture. However, it can cause dysphoria when not using it. A disconnected feeling and strange dream-like experiences."

Heddha, eyes widening, asked, "Will it affect me permanently?"

"No, no, I would suggest moderating your use in the time remaining."

"I am going to feel the loss of it. I thank you for encouraging me to learn. I have acquired much and still do not understand how Jahtara's baby came into existence. I want our child to feel… I am not sure of the word happy, wanted, or loved." She turned to look down at Inlanda, "Maybe family gives voice to what I wish. My ache for family and home grows stronger every day, and I have hidden in Cora's room longer than Jahtara and I traveled together. A piece of my heart is missing." Heddha flopped back, staring up at the bespeckled darkness.

"We will get you back to Inlanda soon, to family and home. To your other concern. I'm not an expert, but this type of genetic engineering has existed for quite some time. Limited not so much by laws or morality but by adverse effects, sometimes called unintended consequences, and, more importantly, by the genome's long-term diversity, crucial for responding to change.

"The placental trophoblastic tissue would have genetic alterations to limit Jahtara's immune response. I suspect most genetic material remains Inlandani to reduce adverse effects, but I cannot say what portion he manipulated. I'm certain genes from Jahtara's grandmother were amplified or added. They spent an enormous amount of time and money to do this, and the child should be healthy, but there could be future unforeseen results."

Heddha said, "I've also been thinking about the astrobiology aspect of two worlds so far apart, yet we look similar."

"Externally, yes, you must remember the laws of physics, and the propensity for atoms and molecules to act in specific ways stays the same throughout the universe under similar circumstances. Nature is efficient, efficacious, and elegant but happens fortuitously. There occur few alternatives to the DNA building blocks. Few replicating information systems are as elegant as DNA until you get into quantum scale techniques. Hence, the similarities given comparable physical conditions. No, it's the fortuitous part that proves remarkable. Our evolution contained several extinction episodes where most of life disappeared forever. Due to their diversity and adaptability, the remaining organisms could fan out again to fill many niches. Limited ways exist to obtain energy, separate from the surrounding milieu, move, or perceive one's environment given similar conditions. Fortunately, we can see, hear, and communicate with each other. At the same time, our proteins have different structures or sequences of amino acids internally. Then there's always the possibility an ancient culture seeded the universe with biology making us similar.

"Strangely, I defend the company's or Enan's competence. They've been working on this for some time. They wouldn't have gone to the expense unless the corporation figured out a strategy ahead of time, at least in theory, although the legalities remain fragile. I think we missed something justifying the enormous expense and risk."

"You don't believe we stand a chance?"

Jorma smiled, "I think you do; otherwise, I wouldn't be helping. We must increase the corporation's risk, both here and in my system until the expenses grow more than they want to pay. They have a fiduciary duty to their shareholders and will back out when the risks become too high. Unfortunately, I don't think that option exists for Enan since he assaulted and killed people, and he would most likely be a scapegoat."

'Scapegoat?"

"Like a whipping boy who takes the punishment for others, although Enan's guilt looks undeniable.

"Then let us get on with it."

"Ever the practical, Heddha."

"Where I grew up, practicality prevails if you want to eat."

"I brought you to this room for another impractical reason," Jorma smiled, stabbing at his handheld. Floating off the floor slightly, he pushed off with his feet, slowly somersaulting to the opposite wall.

Synchronous Continuity

It's a law of physics – give up control, and you gain continuity. Ok, so it's not physics, maybe more of a mental attitude. Nonetheless, this principle proves essential to understanding life, perhaps a subdivision of a rule: section A, subheading 1, category b, paragraph 8 – [How you set about something affects how it appears]. We attempt to control an unknown future out of fear, anticipating disorder and loss of control. Opting for going against the flow makes you an obstacle, impacted by all the shit coursing downstream, an interaction requiring dualism that involves a manipulator and victim. We drift out of order by not acknowledging the natural course and end up at crosscurrents. Yet, we can come to appreciate the beauty of this probabilistic flow in time. To know symmetry, turn around in the current, in resonance with the flow, without fear or resistance. Accept and respond.

We collect or reject attributes through life, trying to control who we are, affixing them to ourselves like stickum notes, separating self from nonself. Dispel these notions of separateness like rain on water.

Synchronicity arises from pure headwaters, allowing obscuring thoughts to recede, revealing clear skies, unmasking the penetrating depths of a crystalline lake, and on the shore stand sublime snowy peaks, the air crisp with whispering sounds of equanimity. Entangled with this whole rests a noble cessation, having opened the grasping hand to become ubiquitous; no conditioned point of view enabling a reflection to form, a space out of time.

Letting go of the conventional begins the entry point into the dharmic stream of happiness, the power of now, clear sight, and wisdom. These words contain ineffable meanings, half-truths, approximations, and conjectures attempting to explain the inexplicable. Yet once reached, the absolute truth at the labyrinth's center supersedes convention: not to escape into a blissful nothingness but to bring this eloquent suchness to the present.

Not quite there yet. However, the well of consciousness begins to realize it profoundly connects to everything. If we turn around, entering the flow of our journey, the mists of confusion and ignorance will thin, leaving us with a growing sense of synchronous continuity.

Well, so much for sheltering incognito, although the pretense proved doomed from the start. Heddha originally saw through to the truth, and any remaining veneer cracked and peeled away in time, with the arrival of Jahtara's midwife Babaor, followed by Sefu stumbling upon Jahtara, searching for a queyn. Then yesterdei, the charade withered again. A diminutive, disheveled creature covered in fur with several bone piercings arrived during the first snowfall, proclaiming his clan sent him Solauraward searching for the essence of an ancient prophecy.

Jahtara first heard of the traveler the following morgn while gazing out the great-room window studying the meadow covered in a layer of new snow. Kalama, stoking the fire, told of the traveler, saying she let him stay in the feed shed and would have her husband move him on his way shortly.

Jahtara absently asked, "Did he tell of the vatic?"

The innkeeper straightened her back, still holding a piece of wood, thinking, "Let me see… Some nonsense about a wobble in the ground, a new star above the cold wastes and the coming of fire emeralds, whatever that intends, I know naught." Then throwing the wood on the fire, she continued, "Although peoples from beyond the Cold Waste likely hope for fire ceaselessly."

Jahtara turned from the scene outside, saying, "Not sure they have the wood for ceaseless fires, yet they occasionally have ribbons of green fire in the noite sky. Yet why travel Solauraward? Would you prepare food and hot tea for him? I wish to speak with this traveler of his quest." Then seeing Tanhā descending the stair, she said, "Tanhā, fetch our cloaks and boots. We will venture out on this chilly morgn to inquire of long-ago divinations."

Wrapped in their cloaks, they trod carefully across the yard, Jahtara stepping high while Tanhā shuffled her feet, giggling when she occasionally slipped trying to catch snowflakes on her tongue. Upon reaching the shed, Jahtara rapped on the loosely hung door and entered the musty-smelling outbuilding. Her eyes adjusting, she saw a figure standing among the haystacks, clothed in beautiful furs with symmetrical patterns of grey, white and brown pelts trimmed with intricate embroidery at the cuffs, hem, and frontal opening. The coat presently hung open but fastened with bone or ivory closures. He wore pants similar to the jacket's pelts. Under the overcoat, he wore a quilted garment, and over the shoulders draped an embroidered purple tippet trimmed at both ends with alternating black and white round feathers. A sinew band hung from the neck, strung with massive claws.

Jahtara heard Tanhā gasp when the figure pushed back the fur hood to reveal carved ivory piercings. Seeing the round flat face with exceedingly kind eyes, Jahtara realized this was a womon, barely the height of Tanhā.

Although her face appeared grimy and hair wild from travel, she bore a sense of asseveration. The womon focused on Jahtara, her eyes widening, and a satisfied smile animated her face. She promptly withdrew a painted wooden rattle from a pouch and shook it nine times at Jahtara while repeating an opaque utterance. Tanhā took a step back. Finishing, tears of joy flooded her eyes, and she nodded her head to Jahtara, saying in a raspy voice filled with emotion, "Fire hair, emerald eye."

While keeping eye contact with the womon, Jahtara spoke to Tanhā quietly, "Go to the kitchen to fetch food and tea and ask Kalama to prepare a room and hot bath. I will pay."

Tanhā stood staring at the peculiar womon, finally asking, "Are you sure?"

"More than! Scoot now," and Tanhā backed out of the shed. Jahtara spoke supportively to the sojourner, "Your travels have taken you far into strange lands. I would venture a difficult journey. Would you kindly break fast with me?"

"Our soul satiates to witness our vision manifest. Aye, our way endures long and at times arduous, yet this proves so for us all. You delight us with your invitation and even more with the offer of a bath." She ended with a wink.

"I am solely a common sight, a womon with child, on her journey and not what you seek. Yet, you intrigue me."

The womon smiled at a knowing only she knew, nodding her head, saying, "Perhaps yours is the correct view, and you wish no part in our people's vision, yet it is you standing here, you that intrigues us, and you, we deem not common. Aside from, we do not quest after you, for the vision does not concern you." She advanced; their eyes locked until she gently laid her hands on the child of both their visions.

Jahtara carried a tray with two large mugs of tea into the great room and set one next to the wayfarer. After a bath, her braided black hair, ruddy cheeks, cream-colored piercings, and unabashed smile harmonized with her confident, relaxed cantilena, one leg dangling off the edge of the hearth, drinking her tea. She looked equally at home here as in the dank hay-strewn shed.

Jahtara inquired, "You have journeyed far; you must yearn for home?"

"There is here, here is there," she said with a grin and shrug. "We felt a hand on our back and a whisper in our ear compelling us forward. One step flows from the previous and leads to the next, a walking meditation on impermanence." She let her other leg drop to the floor and leaned forward, sipping the tea. "At our changing, we quested for our spirit in a vintro fox. The white bear found us first and gave their life in a lesson of perseverance, a tough teaching for mother bear and us; in this struggle, a new element grew within us," she said, fingering the claw-strung necklace. Then quietly, "in me,"

"You obtained the scars during the encounter?"

She nodded, her hand drifting to her flank, where Jahtara saw the worst of her wounds while bringing hot water to the bathing room. "You have a similar lesson? We see disquiet upon your face."

"I have a dear friend who carries such wounds on her back, though not as deep; she carries the deeper shame inside from the wounding."

"We each have our share of wounds, concealing vulnerabilities."

Jahtara caressed her belly, deflecting, "What can I call you?"

"Atiqtalik and you."

"Jahtara. Well come Atiqtalik."

"Well met Jahtara."

"Pardon my inquisitiveness. Could I ask about the markings on your body?" When Jahtara saw Atiqtalik's scars, she noticed black patterns covering parts of her body. Angular figures extended from Atiqtalik's shoulders, down her flat breasts to her prominent dark nipples. Seeing Atiqtalik nod, she asked, "On your breasts, those markings symbolize fish with open mouths and large teeth preparing to bite or suckle?"

"We wear our skins like greatcoats with markings to tell our traveling story. Those on our breasts do not symbolize fish, yet breathe air, hunt, and bear their young like us. These brave, fast, and cunning swimmers occasionally assist us by driving prey into the shallows, helping the hunt. While they seem a danger, we know them to grieve. We learn from and value one another. They and we suckle our young, so in respect, we honor our sisters with this tatau."

Jahtara sat silently, then said, "Atiqtalik, I honor your tales and admire your traditions. However, of your vision, I cannot abide by your semblance of who my daughter will become; the time ahead remains unset. Fate does not rush towards us from the future; fate chases us from the past, arising out of our choices, the path the wheel has tread. Our present exists at the juncture of past and future, where we change fate through intention, shaping the contours of an unknown future. I desire a more responsive vision for my child. Our past choices have set the path taken, yet the wheel's direction presently remains under the direction of our intentions."

Atiqtalik, silent, drinking her tea, finally conceded, "What you say contains truths. We do not wish them any impediment. We would offer that remembering and imagining resemble aspects of time. In remembering our past, we alter those memories, and those echoed memories influence our choices in the present. We also create a future memory by imagining, a creative conceiving. We cannot make choices we do not know we have. Hence, we learn from our remembered choices and our imagined intentions. Our people's vision comes out of Dreamtime, a portending mash of past and future in the present."

Again, a smile touched Atiqtalik's lips at an inward, knowing, "If truth be told, we used this vision to account for leaving our lands. When we were a youngling, our father acquired the position of the seer to a refined swayer, imagining the future. Our experiences presented us... me," she paused, expecting admonishment, "with a varied panorama of life. Returning home, we could not endure our place there. We find difficulty speaking of ourselves separate from family, village, or place. If I may combine our thoughts, I grew responsive to my fate and conceived a changed future. We recall wise words: if you do not like what happens, change what you do. So here... I be."

Jahtara smiled, remembering Jorma. "I am acquainted with someone whose work involved predicting the future, much like your father. That did not work out well, although he advanced to be my ministrant."

"And what would a common woman need with a ministrant?"

"I believe this tea possesses loquacious properties, does it not?"

"Most definitely!" They clinked their cups, laughing in agreement.

With Jorma at her side, Heddha stood in the corridor leading to the ship's hangar. She shifted her weight from leg to leg, eyes burning from the cosmetic lenses and heart-pounding, anticipating her return to Inlanda, yet dreading the journey. They lingered in the passageway because Jorma wanted to shorten the time spent with the crew.

Heddha thwarted the desire to rub her eyes by running her hand over her short-cropped hair, saying in GS, "Talk to me, distract me from this expectancy."

"I have something for you," he began in GS, producing a plasma sword like Jahtara's. "I removed it from the evidence locker of the second one murdered in the Cold Waste. We discovered it at the site. I disabled the locator. You activate the weapon by turning…."

"The knob here, I know, and then what… push and turn while holding my thumb in this indentation to pair it to me, correct?" In response to Jorma's arched brows, Heddha answered, "I looked up its operation on the VR Techcap. I didn't think it could hurt to know such things. I hoped to 'borrow' one once back on Inlanda. You have saved me the task." Heddha paused, feeling the heft of the technology in her hand, continuing, "No, it does not harm to know, but the intent can harm."

"You have revenge in mind, Heddha? For, I believe there lies an empty, desolate path. A path where the heart turns grey and shrivels with each step along the way, I speak from experience."

"I know life involves suffering and often lacks justice. I want to think my intention takes a different path, decreasing suffering and growing justice, but it's not always been so. The downward course appears easier to travel, especially with convention dragging us downward. Jahtara expresses a unique way, more difficult to my eye, but she led a sheltered existence, and I have not. However, I see a long-term truth in her view, but it does not satisfy the short term. Sorry, I am rambling, anxious to set out on my way. I intend to use this weapon for protection: Inlanda's, Jahtara's, and mine. I appreciate your trust in giving it to me."

"It's a long upward passage to trust my judgment again. I no longer forecast the future, choosing an outcome. I believe I've come to know you in your time spent here and have placed my trust well. Have you learned much?"

"I would have liked to discover how these ships move or float and what they consist of," she said, patting the ship's wall.

"I'm not a physicist or engineer, but quickly while we wait, I will attempt to distract you with what I don't know." He smiled, continuing, "On Inlanda, ships move by wind and sail, rowing or pushing with poles. Water wheels power mills, and draft animals pull wagons. A machine called an Escher Space Drive powers this ship - it shouldn't work, yet it does; one must change their perception of reality to understand the physics involved. On the observation deck: changing the dimensions of space by manipulating a field's interaction with mass affects acceleration through that space. Graphene-reinforced metal nanocomposite polymers make up the walls and hull..."

The pressure door opposite opened, and a crew member, dressed similarly to Heddha, checked the passageway asking, "You the geological engineer?"

Heddha cleared her throat and said, "Yes, we ready to go?"

"Just waiting on you."

Taking the plasma sword from Heddha, Jorma said, "Let me stow this in your pack." Patting the pack, he said, "Good luck, planetside, Achebe. See you back in a couple of days." Turning to go, he took a few steps, then backtracked to the crew member, asking, "Crew chief, Achebe is uncomfortable asking, but he experiences space vertigo. Could he transit down on the cargo deck?"

"Sure, not a problem. Don't like those wide-open spaces through the pilot windows, huh? I'll clear it with the shuttle captain."

Sounding relieved, Heddha said, "Thanks, chief," and started her way back to Inlanda.

The ship wobbled slightly, settling with a thump, and Heddha took a deep breath, releasing it slowly, relieved to have landed back on Inlanda. She liberated herself from the restraints upon hearing the chief clatter down the stairs, followed by the deck crew. The chief touched the portal entry screen to start the cargo door egress procedure. Looking over his shoulder, he asked if Achebe felt alright.

Realizing he meant her, Heddha answered in the affirmative, shouldered her pack, and stood in front of the cargo door, anxious to leave. It occurred to her she didn't know how to open the gate to exit the landing site, the one thing Jorma missed, probably because he'd never visited the site. As the door started to open, Heddha contemplated hiding in the compound until the next cargo delivery when the chief tapped her shoulder.

Gesturing to the screen, he said in GS, "Need to have you sign off the ship and acknowledge the regress procedures," Heddha touched her wrist to the screen's seed reader twice: once to sign out and again, pledging she wouldn't bring any Inlanda material back aboard the ship. This made her smile considering where she'd been for the last few lunas. Heddha said, "I suppose this doesn't cover the cargo crates waiting to be loaded?"

The chief smiled back, acknowledging, "That's the purview of the Special Operations Officer and above our pay grade. Ok, you're good to go. You'll get a Standard text on your handheld from mining operations to assist you exiting the compound, and they left someone at the gate to give you a ride to refining."

"Much obliged, chief." The door tipped down, becoming a ramp, and the chill of the noite air hit her. The saison turned, reminding Heddha of the urgent need to rejoin Jahtara before her birthing.

She stepped onto the ramp, and the chief called, "Heard a rumor we'll leave soon. Would the geological engineer visiting mining operations confirm the rumor?"

"If I have anything to do with it, chief, you will depart soon." Heddha stepped onto Inlanda and headed towards the gate.

A couple of turns in the path and darkness enveloped Heddha revealing an immense dome of stars. Her vision adjusting, she expanded into it, home again. Although her breath showed with every exhale, she didn't feel chilled, realizing her offworlder clothes kept her warm. As she neared the gate, Heddha's handheld vibrated. She fished the handheld out of her overall pocket, its screen blinking yellow, begging for attention. She touched the blinking screen, and the gate opened. Magical!

Moving through the gate, Heddha remembered her disbelief on first learning of the offworlders and how her awe dissipated with the prolonged stay on their ship. The thought brought her up short. Her unique position offered an opportunity to affect the course of events on Inlanda. But how and when to act. Heddha strove to push her rashness down; she needed boldness yet in the wisdom of the whole. An inkling of a way arose, but it required further thought and help to put into action. Lost in this plot, she came upon a teamster's wagon on the path. Heddha heard a voice from behind speaking in Inlandani, "You the one needing a ride to the pit."

Heddha turned to the voice to confirm Tho, although it was hard to distinguish features with his dark coloring in the Luna-shine. She realized they probably wouldn't have sent anyone else, and after all this time, she felt joy at seeing another Inlandani.

With no answer from the shadow on the road, Tho continued, "Figures they would send some idiot I cannot talk to." He gestured to the wagon, "Come on, get up there, and I will get you to your people."

"Tho, I am Heddha."

He took a step back, eyes blinking, thinking he saw an apparition, saying only one word, questioning its truth, "No."

"Aye, 'tis me. I expect you astounded to see me and I, you. I have altered my appearance some, yet Heddha stands before you."

"Not some roundeye trick... magic mayhap? I wish to see your eyes."

Heddha showed the handheld on her face and, switching it on, said, "Steady now."

Tho took another step back, asking, "How can this be?"

"A type of mask covers my eyes. I can remove them. Tho, I wish to discuss much with you. I have a plan; however, I need your help."

"By the fates womon, you confound me. I just discovered you live, and you wish to entangle me in your schemes. Besides, much has happened here, and I have much to tell. Firstly, Pug lives..." Heddha dropped to her knees, the news sapping her strength but lifting her spirit. "Aye, figured you would want that bit first." Tho bent down on one knee continuing, "We found him in a ravine with a nasty head wound, and I delivered him to Benedus. He does not remember how he came to be in the gully. In light of other happenings, he recovers with my brother, learns some smithing, and seems well."

Heddha reached out to hold Tho's hand before he was able to snatch it away, saying, "Thank you again for all you have done."

Tho stood, unable to hold her gaze, stating, "I have more to tell. Jit knows when he was injured, I helped him and arranged for a womon to stay with Ananeurin. We sense the rest; nevertheless, we have not talked of it.

"I spend time with Ananeurin, though it tears at my heart, I see her mother in her and a bit of me; my brother comes out in her nature. I am baffled how out of such pain joy can come."

"The talk will come, and bonds strengthen perhaps when you and your brother can share the pain you both cling to."

Tho continued, "Some men, who the roundeyes consider troublemakers, disappear, whether killed or imprisoned, I know naught. I feel things will end here soon and have a foreboding for all those remaining when that happens."

"Aye. Enan will not want what happens here known. We have an opportunity; however, we must act this noite, for once they find me out, we will lose the means of surprise and deception. We need your brother in this also."

Tho nodded once, offering his hand to help Heddha stand. Together they walked to the wagon. Heddha lifted her pack over the sideboard, letting it drop in, then climbed the spokes to the top of the wheel and sat next to Tho on the hardboard. Tho asked, "Where do we go?"

"I have not asked this before. Perhaps now we can speak of it. A dear friend, a cniht from the High Keyndom, traveled here with others on a warrant." Heddha felt shaky and interlocked her fingers to steady her hands, "Someone killed them with fire swords, except my friend. The roundeye named Enan killed him later in Concupia." Heddha turned directly to him, "Tho did you attack them?"

Tho dropped the reins, sitting up straighter to answer Heddha, "I have not treated others well, ridden men hard to ensure work gets done. If I appear other than strong in my position, others will see me as weak. I stuff my feelings into sturdy boxes, burying them in deep anguish. I saw the cause of my father's inattention in Jit and Talulah's death in Ananeurin.

"I did not attack these cnihts. Even the hardened man I became could not ford that river. I came across a cniht, wounded without a mount, giving him mine, then sent the roundeyes looking for him in another direction. I felt this represented weakness at the time. This cniht did wear High Mountain armor. I am relieved I can say it was not me that killed these men."

"We know naught of the burdens others carry, yet I recognized some of my past self in you. I felt kindness when you delivered me to Benedus and saw strength in that act. Tho, I deeply appreciate your assistance to Absan."

Tho released the rest to Heddha, saying, "Does it not seem strange I highjacked you to do the work of a comfort womon and now follow you in a scheme to overthrow the roundeyes?"

"No, this has been my intention all along, and it does not end there. What think you of a homefolk militia?"

"Pug talks of you varyingly as occupying a queyn's consort, counselor, or warrior. I have come to consider you all three. Aye, I will help. I have conditions, though."

"Good, all things occur conditioned." Heddha pointed down the road, saying, "That way."

Tho made a clucking noise with his tongue, letting loose the brake, and they started forward.

Jahtara removed the pillow between her legs and rolled onto her back, quickly pulling the layers of covers up around her neck, letting in the smallest measure of cold possible. She exhaled warm breath into the cold room, a whale spouting in preparation for the deep.

A knock at the door, or in her dream? Jahtara opened her eyes to the early light seeping through the window, intricate fern-like ice crystals on the panes. The snow swirled outside. No one lit the fire; still early. Then again, a knock, definite this time. Jahtara turned in answer to her child's aroused kick, moving off her back. Pulling the covers over her head, she grumbled, "Come."

The door opened, and Atiqtalik, peering over an armload of firewood, entered, "Hiding will do you no good, Jahtara. We will get the fire lit, then you must sit up, and we will bring you tea. Break fast for you, and your daughter consists of sautéed onions and dried mushrooms baked in an egg pie."

A groan came from the bed, then Jahtara asked, "Tanhā should get me food and set the fire!"

"We told her to stay in her room. A traveler arrived."

Jahtara pushed herself to a sitting position, asking, "A stranger? I must get dressed!"

"Stay." Atiqtalik urged while bringing Jahtara a shawl. "His mount walks lamely; he may not tarry. Talou reshods the animal, and the cniht eats in the common room. He does not convey much, except he goes towards Concupia, traveling with two pack animals, laden with armor, mail, and supplies."

"Did you see a blazon?"

"Perhaps, yet we could not decipher its meaning. We align ourselves into clans, often using names of the land we live on or animals we revere."

Jahtara stood, lifting her gown, and squatted over the chamber pot. "Can you give an account of any part of it?"

Atiqtalik tried to recall, adding wood to the fire. "He took off his tabard, and Kalama laid it over a chair in front of the fire, so we could only see the bottom."

"Aye, so you could not see the blazon. Did you see a shield, plants, animals, or colors?"

"Mostly maroon. Mayhap plants on the shield and on the side a stag or just the antlers."

Jahtara moved to the washstand, filling the bowl with water after breaking the thin ice on the pitcher's surface. Before washing her face and hands, she prompted, "Do you recall what type of plants."

"We have not recognized much plant growth for the last three lunas of our travels, much less know anything of their names. We hunt mostly, occasionally gather tubers, berries, grasses, and kelp."

Jahtara washed with the biting icy water, recalling the discussion about explaining one's culture to others from a different time or place. Thoughtfully Jahtara asked, "The name of your clan?"

"A name meaning The People, and then we add words before or after to be more descriptive: people of the snow, wet snow, or grey skies."

"Let us see if we can find some descriptive words from this blazon. Can you depict the plants on the shield in more detail?"

Atiqtalik shrugged, thinking, "Stocks with seeds at the top (a grass, I suppose). A flower, red, with tight peddles in the center and opening more toward the outside," She stopped, seeing acorns lined up on a shelf above the fireplace, "There, something like those too."

"Aye, mighty oaks, wheat, a stag with maroon pennants and roses for the Douxess' family. We must attempt to talk with this cniht. Have you any weapons?"

"Weapons? We barely stand to your breast. What weapon could we wield having any effect on this bear of a man?"

"Did you not once kill a bear?" Then it occurred to Jahtara that she did possess a mighty cruel weapon, an unthinkable weapon. Could she use such an instrument? Her baby moved, a stretch to try its confines. "If you would, make sure this cniht does not leave. Tell him someone wishes to speak with him, no more. I will dress and come down shortly." Atiqtalik turned to leave, but Jahtara stopped her, "Thank you for your foresight in this matter."

Jahtara stood at the top of the stairs observing the large man seated at a table in the common room, his grey hair curling and long, falling down his back. He tipped a pint of stout draining it. Wiping his mouth, he set the schooner down and released such an eructation Jahtara heard it rattled the windows. She observed him until he pushed back from the table to stand. "Doux Buccleuch, how unexpected to meet here, yet a pleasure, I am sure."

"Ah, unexpected indeed, yet these are unexpected times. And a pleasure, for I will not have to ride further in this damnable cold in search of you, lass."

Jahtara stood motionless, saying nothing from the top of the stairs.

The moment stretched to an uncomfortable silence until the doux cleared his throat, saying, "My pardon, Prinus Lass or perhaps Queyn Lass now."

Jahtara let a slight smile grace her lips, "And what takes you from your vales and dales?"

"Your nefarious brother, daughter of lineage Davuda. Speaking would be easier if you joined me before the fire."

Jahtara hesitated for only an instant brushing her hand against the plasma sword in a hidden pocket at her waist, then descended the stairs in her accustomed wide stance.

"I see evidence of the hearsay," the doux said, offering Jahtara his hand upon her reaching the bottom step.

"Do you wish to provoke me, Doux?"

"If I did, you would have no need to ask."

"You have come all this way to confirm the mutterings of rumor mongers?"

"I have a distaste for the refined goings-on, as you well know; I sent my eldest son to represent my interests with your brother. And my base-born son I sent to the Middle Realm while I searched for the lost Prinus Davuda. A farmer must vary crops to ensure a full larder. The reports from all directions are confusing and scandalous. I now have ears along most routes."

"Ever the cautious man, doux."

"The douxy remains a freehold by tenure after many generations, and I will see it continue."

"And your daughter, Heatha?"

"She performs the most important part in all this. The douxess' infirmity progresses; therefore, Heatha cares for the landhold in my absence. She will oversee gathering and organizing the cotters pledged by the douxy for their part in the coming battle. She also gathers the supplies and food a militia needs for such an endeavor."

"What do you consider my part in all this, Doux Buccleuch?"

"This remains to see, su alteza. I do not trust your brother, and the High Mountain Keyndom shows signs of manipulation by my way of thinking. As queyn of the Middle Realms, all centers around you. You characterize the most trustworthy from what I have gathered, yet much remains unexplained. Why did you flee the realm, and what came of the Cold Waste keyn and your parents? I hear wisps of a report about a delegation lost Solauraward?"

"I can explain to some extent; however, I cannot warrant your understanding will increase. This telling will take some time, and I need nourishment," Jahtara said, patting her belly. "Could you fetch Atiqtalik?"

"Your consort who, stories tell, disabled four cnihts of the realm?"

"You do have ears in many places, doux. No, Atiqtalik, a quite interesting acquaintance that appeared recently. Heddha, whom I miss more each day, fulfills a warrant on my behalf. She inquires into those rumors from Solauraward."

"Atiqtalik did well at distracting me while steering attention away from you," Doux Buccleuch said, heading for the kitchen.

The doux sat in a large stuffed armchair, facing the hearth with an empty pint in his hand. For many moments after Jahtara finished her tale, he remained this way, contemplating the fire transmute its fuel to heat and ash.

Jahtara, fearing he fell asleep, finally asked, "What think you of this tale, Uncle?"

"'Tis a strange odyssey, yet I have no reason to doubt you. I heard nonsense about your brother wielding a firebrand in his left hand after your consort winged him and reports he aligns with a wizard. Your account brings some sense to a confusing plot and an urgency to end it. However, I do not pretend to understand how you begot this child. Do you trust these... I know not what to name them."

"Offworlders would describe them, and I trust in varying degrees," Jahtara paused, then pressed on with what concerned her the most, "Uncle, can I place my trust in you? You dwell on the furthest boundaries of the realm, the douxs of Buccleuch have changed allegiance to suit their continuance, and you seem to have placed your wagers to cover all concerns in this affair."

"Aye, I have. Yet of my sister-in-law's issue, you are my favorite, and this affair reaches further than the continuance of my douxy. I traveled here to confirm the veracity of your claims. While your story aligns with some of what I know or suspect, I find you hiding in a cozy inn with one retainer and an affable yet strange womon from the far side of the Cold Waste. Possessing no peerage, no army, and even lacking personal guards."

Jahtara replied, "I am sorry my aunt does not feel well, uncle. I know my mother was close to her sister. You speak the truth yet let me make things clearer. My person remains safe until I birth my child, very few know my whereabouts, and I am in communication with my regent, who raises an army in my stead." Jahtara stopped to add three pieces of wood to the dying fire, then, turning to her uncle, said, "And finally…." She drew the plasma sword from her skirt, turned to the hearth, and activating the blade, ignited the wood in a blaze of sparks. Turning to him, she asked again, "Can I rely on you?"

The scene appeared strange. Flanked by Tahnā and the small pierced womon, Queyn Jahtara stood in the inn's gathering room, hidden in a snowy vale along the coast road. The inn's proprietors stood to one side with their children, unsure of what took place. In front of Jahtara knelt her uncle wearing the tabard with his blazon. Jahtara, in a refined formal voice, proclaimed, "Doux Buccleuch, Cniht of lineage Davuda, Twelfth Laud of the Douxy Buccleuch, what say ye."

"In this place and before these assembled, I pay homage and pledge my allegiance to Prinus Jahtara, the rightful heir of lineage Davuda and Queyn Jahtara, sovereign of the Middle Queyndom. I will defend such realms and Inlanda against all usurpers."

The innkeepers, mouths gaping, stood staring at Jahtara until Kalama poked her husband in the ribs, and they both knelt. In answer to the doux's pledge, Jahtara stated, "Rise, uncle, to the mutual trust of this pledge: you serve as a cniht of both realms, and I name you to the Great Office of Captain of the Queyn's Guard, held hereditarily in gross."

The doux stood, and Tanhā muttered, "Finally," then louder, "Can we eat now?"

The fire blazing in the hearth behind him, the doux replied, "I will drink to that, lass."

⚬⚬⚬

Pug threw wood on the fire, releasing a spray of sparks. Ananeurin tapped him on the ear, then danced around to his other side, pulling away giggling when Pug made an exaggerated grab for her. Jit stumbled out of the caravan, standing on the top step gazing at Heddha, then said, "We thought you lying dead at the bottom of some ravine much like Pug; instead, you have joined the roundeyes."

Heddha smiled. "Only to escape them and with your help to deceive them, yet we must act this noite before they discover my true person."

"Tho and I have felt something like this coming. Did you not tell Heddha, Tho? They stopped preparing rock for refining. Only one of the great contrivances abides in the pit. A ship came to remove the machines. Rock prepared for processing will last maybe a luna. Men have always died in the pit, yet men have now vanished, the troublesome ones. I spoke to others, and we feel it unlikely any of us will leave this place."

Heddha paced in front of the fire, telling them, "Aye, those at the head of this scheme need to keep all that happens here secreted. Another perilous sign comes with the Wolf Luna, Queyn Jahtara gives birth then, and the child weighs heavy in their plans. All those knowing the truth of this child stand in peril. Offworlders helping me suggested increasing the toll on those responsible for this intrigue. We must strike now; help folks escape and pressure the offworlders to leave. We must use our advantage this noite."

Jit and Tho regarded the other in silence for a few moments until Tho spoke, "Ever seen a badger, Heddha?"

"I have heard of such in the mountains bordering where I am from, aye."

He smiled at Jit in unspoken agreement before proclaiming, "We will call this militia the Badgers; a smart, sturdy and annoying vexation, never giving up."

"Heddha's Badgers," this from Jit.

And from Pug, "Aye, I saw she never back down even when facin' many."

Heddha's wry grin crept into place, adding, "We will get a banner made, yet the noite slips away. Pug, take Ananeurin to the healer's place and stay with her till we come to get you." When he started to protest, he cautioned, "You received a grave injury. Please watch over Ananeurin and help Benedus get ready to leave.

"Tho, you mentioned a condition for your help?"

He nodded, indicating Jit, "Aye," then, with a sideways glance at Ananeurin, said, "We will speak of it later."

Jit interjected, "We have only knives against these firebrands the roundeyes wield."

"We have surprise, deception, and something more," she said, opening her pack and removing, "A flame sword. Hopefully, we can obtain more this noite." Placing her fingers on the failsafe, she activated the plasma sword, and their shadows leaped onto the side of the caravan.

Ananeurin gasped and hid behind Tho. Pug, mouth agape, said solemnly, "This what did my auntie in?"

"Aye and caused Jit's wounds. Killed my friend."

Pug's gaze left the sword and found Heddha's eyes, "I will have one."

Switching off the sword, Heddha nodded once, saying, "Aye. Now be quick, off with you two. We have much to do."

Pug looked awkward hugging Heddha; however, she held him tight, bushing hair over the scars on his head. He pulled away but reached out to run his hand over the fuzz left of Heddha's hair, then mounted a steed. Ananeurin hugged Tho tightly, then ran, jumping into Jit's arms, who lifted her in front of Pug. They were off with a wave, disappearing into the noite.

Heddha tied her pack behind the saddle and mounted up, watching Jit and Tho do the same. She thanked Jit for "taking care of Pug. Tell me of this condition you do not want Ananeurin to hear."

Jit began, "You proclaimed you were the queyn's agent, and if we assist the queyn, we would be in her graces."

"Aye, I am, and you will be."

Tho asked, "And how will you be returning to Queyn Jahtara?"

"By the way we came, hopefully not by the same means." Although she wasn't sure, Tho understood her meaning.

Tho continued, "We will travel the land route to the Middle Realm, hopefully, with a large party of people and wagons."

Heddha sighed loudly, "This sounds like a tooth puller extracting teeth one at a time until finding the bad one. How many conditions must we list to arrive at the one giving the result."

Jit cleared his throat to say, "Will you take Ananeurin and make her a ward of the queyn until we prevail in our commission?"

"She just joined her unbroken family, and you wish me to take her away?"

"Our journey will take a long, dangerous route, of men and camp followers. We will travel through the Long Noites hunger times to reach the palatial seat by early Warming. You and Pug, who she grows close to, will have speedier travels."

Tho continued the onrush, "Hardships will arise on this journey, and my brother and I have much to reconcile and bring into accord."

Heddha yielded, "I hope you fight equal to how you have planned this campaign. I will take the geyrle on one, no two conditions. First, you aim to meet us by the early Warming. And next, attempt reconciliation on all accounts with your brother. On all accounts, do you wish it any plainer?"

Tho halted, resisting in a whisper even though Jit remained within easy earshot, "Tell her who her father be? Not sure I can speak of this or if she should know at all."

"When Ananeurin discovers the truth, and she will, she should not have to question you or your brother's love for her or doubt her worth. You both loved her mother. Do you know for certain which one fathered her? Father or uncle, what difference can exist in love? Her mother died torn, not knowing who to love. This calamity must not happen to Ananeurin." Heddha prodded her animal, spurring it ahead.

Heddha stood in the stirrups, trying to see the citadel-like building. They stopped at the last bend in the road before it straightened its course to the refinement structure. Heddha understood the building's design meant to look like it belonged in this period on Inlanda, and it would look much like the ship inside. Even with cosmetic contacts obscuring her vision, she could discern the light of a flickering fire illuminating an area around a door and one or two figures moving against the wall from this distance.

Heddha tipped forward in the stirrups, attempting to see better through the darkness. She suspected unseen security measures existed other than those at the door. She would rely on Jorma's identity deceptions and her ability to speak Galactic Standard to get inside. Heddha turned to Jit, saying, "Stay out of sight here. They can penetrate the dark and will know you should not ride here. Tho will summon you when safe to proceed." Tho and Heddha cantered down the track with a snort from her mount.

They dismounted, walking the short path to where two offlanders waited backlit by the fire. One spoke to Heddha in GS, "Took you a while to get here, Achebe." He looked at his handheld, then at Heddha, and back down at the handheld, probably confirming Achebe's presence.

Heddha dragged her feet slightly and kept her lower spine stable, speaking with concern, "Ya well, I got turned around, and this local set me straight."

He gave Tho a stern look, saying, "Tell the cat-eye to be on his way. Quanshay will check you in."

Heddha stepped to the seed reader, intending to check herself in, when Quanshay flipped the cover open and placed her wrist on the lit pad. It blinked green. Heddha turned to the other offworlder and said in GS, "I left my kit on the steed. I'll tell him to get it for me."

"No, tell him to move out now. I'll get it," he answered in GS, grabbing Tho by the arm and turning him.

Heddha switched back to Inlandani, "Tho, this offworlder wishes you to leave, oblige him."

They headed back to the mounts, and Heddha heard the door click open. Turning back to the woman, she swiftly drew the plasma sword from a pocket, placing the tip under her sternum while activating it but leaving the blade off. When she felt the hum of the mechanism vibrating against her abdomen, the woman's eyes widened. Heddha prodded her with the metal tip, asking in GS, "Calm now, and no harm will come to you. Who remains beyond the door?"

"No one," she answered in GS with a shaky voice. "I watched the sensors and stepped out when I saw your approach. Everyone else sleeps. What's happening?"

"Hush now," Heddha commanded, taking Quanshay's handheld, and pushing her toward the door. Out on the path, she heard the thump of the other offworlder hitting the ground.

Heddha followed the woman in, peaking around her for anyone else present at the entrance; the room appeared empty. The large anteroom seemed excessively bright from the offworlder lights. There were no windows, but the wall held an array of monitors next to the door. She could see herself and Quanshay on one, disorienting her, and causing her to stumble, so she looked away. The rest of the monitors were of dimed rooms, hallways, or large working areas, Heddha guessed. Several showed areas outside the building. Heddha pulled a chair to the middle of the room and sat Quanshay on it.

Tho came through the door dragging the male roundeye, letting him slump to the floor next to the woman. When Quanshay noticed the blood on his head, she pleaded in GS, "Is he alive? Please help him."

Heddha looked from the woman to Tho, who shrugged, not knowing what was said. Looking at the man on the floor, Heddha saw he bled from the back of his head; however, it appeared scant, and his chest rose and fell. Trying to soothe the womon, Heddha said to the offworlder in GS, "He's breathing. We'll let your people check him out once we get you all rounded up."

"My people? Who are you?"

Heddha ignored her question and scanned the room. Two doors exited the space, plus the one they came in: one just an opening, the other a door with a faceplate next to it, so probably secured. The other end of the room held storage shelves, but a quick look revealed nothing recognizable. She pointed and asked Tho to "Check over there for anything to bind their wrists." On the monitors, she noticed Jit dismounting and running to the door. When she let him in, he shaded his eyes from the lights.

Heddha returned to the screens and caught movement on one showing a passageway with a bright opening at the end. She whispered in Jit's ear and pointed to the open doorway. Keeping her eyes on the display, she waved to Jit, and he crossed in front of the opening. Heddha saw the bright space darken on the monitor. She hissed at Tho, pointing to the offworlder woman while pinching her lips. Heddha went silently to the opposite side of the door from Jit, signaling him to wait. Checking on Tho, she saw him behind the offworlder, a hand over her mouth and a knife at her neck.

Heddha slowed her breathing, feeling the plasma sword in her pocket, when suddenly a grey-haired head peeked past the edge of the doorway. Instinctively her hand snapped out to grab the curly hair, and she leaned back, pulling the sneak into the room while Jit wrapped him up.

"What's happening? Was the alarm raised?" The man asked in GS, his eyes sliding to Tho with the knife at Quanshay's neck, and his knees gave way. Heddha tipped her head toward the darkened passageway, and Jit disappeared down it. The newcomer, dressed in overalls with a knapsack slipping off his shoulder, lay in a puddle, mumbling, "Not now, not now." He stopped when he realized he wasn't being restrained. Looking up at Heddha, he asked, "What's going on here? Has the evacuation started?" Then indicating Tho, continued, "or a rebellion?" Heddha furrowed her brows now; that last part sounded hopeful. She picked up the knapsack and discovered the man's handheld, food, and a plasma sword. Jit returned, confirming an empty passageway. Attempting to regain his feet, the man asked in broken Inlandani, "Jit? It you? Others said me, you die."

Pulling him up by the shoulder, Jit explained, "Would have if not for my brother. Your use of our language has improved, Obdalti. What passes here?"

Looking at the other round eyes, he pleaded, "We talk private," then, indicating Heddha, asked, "Who this?"

Heddha prodded him, "It matters naught, speak now or join your accomplices."

"I not return ship with others. I steal away this noite," turning to Jit, suggesting, "Join you, now you live. I no like what they do you and I not have family for return. This world different, alive."

Heddha seeing an opportunity, spoke to take advantage, "Join us, help us then, atone for what offworlders do here, earn a place on Inlanda."

Obdalti looked to Jit, who nodded. The offworlder said, "Agree, not harm friends."

"We have no intention of harming them if they do not attack us," Heddha agreed, indicating Tho should release Quanshay. Tho returned to the storage shelves, and Obdalti shook Jit's wrist, relieved he still lived. Tho returned carrying short, rigid pieces of cord, "I found this to bind the offworlders, yet they seem too stiff to tie."

"No, they work," Obdalti said, taking one and showing them how to pass the tapered end through a small buckle-like device at the other end, making a loop. "These restrain men here. Pull hard, must cut," he said, making a scissor motion with his fingers.

Tho grabbed his arm, questioning him, "These men remain alive, and you can lead us to them?"

Obdalti nodded, showing them one of the monitors - a hallway with a series of doors, "enter by offworlder with…" he indicated his wrist.

Tho looked to Heddha, who explained, "Obdalti or I can open these doors." She scanned the monitors for any movement or guards, noting, "We can free the prisoners first, and they can help round up the offworlders." Heddha froze, seeing motion again on one of the outside displays. She waved Tho over to the outer door. Someone approached the entrance, clinging to the wall and out of the firelight. Heddha joined Tho, and when they heard someone push on the door, Tho pulled it ajar with force, causing the intruder to fall into the room. The newcomer quickly rolled over, arms raised in a protective posture.

"Pug!" Heddha exclaimed, stopping Tho from pummeling him. "Did I not say to watch over Ananeurin!"

"Meaning no disrespect, yet you not the overseer of me. She safe with Benedus. Jahtara says…" Pug stood taller, "Queyn Jahtara, say to stay by you." He crossed his arms and stood his ground.

Heddha nodded, "Aye, here you be. Have Tho show you how to truss the offworlders and bind them tightly." Then to Jit and Tho, "Have Obdalti guide you to the imprisoned men. Release them and bring them here, then we can fetch the offworlders.

Next to Obdalti, "Where do the offworlders stay?"

"Sleep chambers, two or four each. No lock door."

"Pug and I will remain here. If Pug approves," she said, smiling at him. "Take them quietly one or two chambers at a time and see they come to no harm unless they aggress." Then in GS asked, "Obdalti, do you know what lies behind this other door?"

"Valuable tools and plasma weapons."

"I thought so. If you could open it, I will deactivate the tracking software on the weapons. When you return, I need to discuss a means of contacting someone aboard the ship."

Finally, in Inlandani to Jit and Tho, "Off with you, take caution, and work quietly."

Heddha, alone in the secure storeroom, removed her no longer needed eye masks, then started filling knapsacks with plasma swords, leaving three weapons on the table for Pug, Tho, and Jit. Obdalti entered to inform her in Inlandani, "Everyone in the control room. Not what I expected." He walked to the table and twirled one of the knives in a circle with a single finger.

Heddha grabbed the moving knife and, meeting Obdalti gaze, said in GS, "What did you expect? To steal away on a strange world by yourself?"

"Jit say you go to ship. That seems strange." He shrugged, starting again in GS, "I have grown disenchanted in my role here, especially after receiving an entangled message. My partner took her life. I didn't comprehend the depth of her despair and feel responsible. Our son died five years ago. He was a company medic on an exploratory mission to a Class P4Rsp planet. While he attended to locals, members of a religious society killed him, claiming he practiced demonic magic." He took a shuttering breath before continuing, "I have no reason to return. There is good land here. I wish to farm. My ancestors farmed."

"I'm sorry for your loss, having lost someone close to me, murdered by an offworlder. For now, we can't return a plasma weapon to you. In fact, except for these three, I will not give out the rest until we make certain someone can't steal the weapons." With a genuine smile, Heddha said, "You may find working the land as a serf difficult."

Obdalti nodded, continuing in GS, "There is another way, with the plasma swords, I mean. You can link a group of them to one control weapon. I can show you how and once done, only the operator of the control weapon can release the restraint." He then addressed her other concerns. "I understand your mistrust, but I can't continue in my world any longer and will adjust to the ways of this world."

A disturbance in the anteroom pulled them to the door, where an offworlder, hands bound at his back, stood chest to chest with Jit, yelling and pushing. Behind Jit, Tho and Pug restrained several Inlandani moving forward to join the clash.

Heddha strode across the room to face the men who wanted to avenge jahrs of suffering from the roundeyes. She kept the men at bay with a clenched jaw and her plasma sword swinging slowly from side to side. Heddha breathed unevenly, hissing in Inlandani, "I know you wish to hurt the folks who hurt you. They have wounded and murdered my friends. Yet, I wish to place something greater in front of you. Revenge does not serve us. How we plow and sow this field determines what sustenance we reap. Harming these offworlders could injure a greater purpose in play." She paused, scanning their faces. "Truly, I know the difficulty of letting this fall to the wayside, yet I beg you to stay your hand."

"You will all pay for this, including this traitor to his people." In Inlandani, from the offworlder yelling earlier.

Heddha turned on the offworlder, holding the plasma blade at his chest, she let her anger rise as she addressed him in Inlandani, "I am no traitor to my people, nor am I a man. Much like what your people did, I assumed a guise. I learned much while aboard your ship, although I gained little understanding. I know you would steal our world, attempt to thieve our very lives, have us toil for your benefit, and in the end, concoct a lie to make it right in the eyes of your people. Your mistake lies in thinking us backward, divided, and unable to understand your purpose. Now, sit down."

"This is absurd. I demand…"

"You are no longer in charge here!" Heddha swung the sword just above the man's head, singeing his hair, dropping him to the floor. She let her motion carry her around to face the Inlandani men; all took a step back. Heddha let out a long breath, turning off the plasma weapon. Seeing Tho, she winked at him, saying, "Badgers, huh?"

Heddha did not sign in with her data seed to enter the building or any of the rooms, for she knew once she did, those on board the ship might grow aware of what happened here. That could put Jorma in jeopardy. Once those aboard worked backward from Achebe's presence on Inlanda, they could connect him with Jorma due to the chief's testimony. She had to warn him, let him know he should get off the ship. However, the bigger problem was what to do with the prisoners. How to get them off Inlanda? Obdalti had aided with information; perhaps he knew of a way to remove them from the planet.

She called Tho and Obdalti into the storeroom. Heddha spoke to Obdalti in GS, "We must somehow get your people off Inlanda. I understand you wish them no harm; any way to make that happen? Could we get a ship to come to remove them? And something else, any defense against the plasma weapons?" Heddha held her hand up when Obdalti started to answer, "Finally, I need to communicate with someone on Chaz's Beagle without anyone else knowing."

Obdalti answered in GS, "The last request seems easiest. The other two will require some thought. We can get a ship to come down, but a large group in the landing area would make the pilots suspicious. I will need access to a terminal to communicate with the main ship."

"Use the one here. And thank you. I suspect you must have confused feelings about your loyalties. Truly, I am appreciative of your help."

"Right follows right; it does not change for whom or where.

Heddha watched him sign in with his data seed. She translated for Tho, explaining they would probably need the wagons to transport the offworlders to the landing site.

Obdalti made a clicking noise with his tongue, continuing in GS, "This appears fortunate. The refining supervisor forwarded mail stating that corporate wants to increase refining of any remaining heavy and light RE ores and transport them to the ship. The order authorizes expedited shipping daily if necessary. I could set up a pickup for tonight, but how to get them to take on the remaining crew, then leave?"

"Why wouldn't they want to leave."

"They don't want to abandon the refining equipment and other technology, much less the REs. It's evidence proving what happened here."

Heddha paced back and forth behind Obdalti, again translating for Tho. Tho suggested putting the offworlders in the transport crates.

"Not work. Bang on box in ship. Still want machines," Obdalti said in Inlandani.

Heddha continued in GS. "Destroy the equipment, building, and machine in the pit. They will have nothing to come back for."

"Maybe, but we'll have to wait until after they land to destroy it, or they won't land. These offworlders may want to fight. The ships have weapons for defensive use, but that's semantics; they can use them offensively."

They stood quietly; the only sound, Obdalti's finger tapping the tabletop, suddenly he exclaimed, staying with GS, "Trojan horse with a twist! Yes, I was thinking, what could we put in the crates to make them heavy enough for the crew to believe they were full of REs because we don't want to give them the real stuff. We have powdered magnesium. Magnesium burns! You show the loudmouth supervisor we've made a bomb. We don't use it; we just make them believe we will if they don't leave." When he saw Heddha's questioning look, he explained, "Magnesium, a metal, will burn when ignited with a plasma weapon. We'll need to drill holes in the crates and add water containers that produce hydrogen and oxygen with burning magnesium, keeping up the deception. We won't ignite it, but they won't know that. Put a plasma weapon in a crate, then show the supervisor that you have bound all the weapons to your plasma sword. You tell him you've rigged all the boxes like this, and you'll set off the bombs if they don't lift off immediately.

"If they don't lift off or when they do take off, we blow up the mining machine in the pit and the refining building! No, wait, we don't even have to destroy the building. We start fires around it or on the roof, and they'll believe it's destroyed. We'll still have the refining technology and the REs left here. Brilliant!" He ended, breathing heavily.

Heddha feeling a little wind burnt from the force of the explanation, said in GS, "If you say so. Not sure I got all that or what a Trojan horse is, but maybe we can have a small demonstration." She gave Tho a brief explanation of what little she understood in Inlandani, ending with, "We will need the teamsters, draft animals and wagons, also men to guard the prisoners, all for after dark this dei. Have the men put the prisoners in the rooms with the locks, and I will have Obdalti change the locks. Then everyone should sleep till middei, and we will start our preparations for after dark."

Tho turned to go; she stopped him saying, "And ask Jit to come here. We will set up a demonstration of this...." Heddha gestured to Obdalti.

"Magnesium."

"We will see magic when I touch the fire sword to this metal." Then to Obdalti in GS, "Now, to send some messages."

Heddha stood at the loading docks at the back of the refinery building. The teamsters lined up wagons two abreast, two crates in each with holes in their tops and sides. The magnesium and water jugs were loaded but with tops not yet affixed. After Heddha showed the supervisor the setup, they would attach the lids. Four carts remained empty for prisoners. Heddha assigned plasma weapons to Tho, Jit, and Pug, and they spent much of the dei acquainting themselves with their use. The four of them, with additional escorts, would watch over the offworlders.

Tho and Pug stood with her as Obdalti and Jit approached, carrying two small containers. They dumped out a grey powder from one of the boxes on a flat rock away from the wagons and directed everyone to stand back. Obdalti whispered instructions to Heddha. She nodded and lit the plasma weapon to the length of two hands, touching it to the powder. The magnesium sputtered and sparked, then ignited with a white light causing everyone to shield their eyes. Obdalti threw water from the second vessel on the fire from a well-advised distance, causing the white flame to intensify explosively, and they all took another three steps back.

Tho declared, "That should do it." But upon seeing Obdalti's look, he corrected, "meaning they leave and not come back." Jit and Tho then left to fetch the supervisor.

Obdalti pulled Heddha aside, confirming in GS, "Our intention continues unchanged?"

"We want them to leave and not return. I'll remove the plasma weapons from the crates before we close them. However, we will sacrifice one weapon to ignite a fire in the mining machine."

He nodded, giving her a slight bow of the head. "I go to prepare the machine in the pit now." Then turning back, he said, "I almost forgot. Jorma answered your message. He said, 'Glad the trip down occurred uneventfully, but I expected nothing less. Will be safe and meet you at fate's abode. Make sense?"

She smiled, answering, "Yes, thanks. Off with you."

Presently Jit and Tho returned, the supervisor between them with Pug following, carrying several plasma weapons, which he placed on the back of one of the wagons. Tho cut the supervisor's ties, and Heddha instructed him in GS to "Inspect the crates in the wagons."

After going halfway down the line of wagons, he turned to Heddha, demanding in GS, "What do you attempt here?"

"As I'm sure you're aware, the crates contain magnesium with water in the containers."

"This won't work," he chuckled.

Heddha went to the plasma weapons, picked one separated from the rest, and handed it to the supervisor. "You'll find you can't arm that weapon," she held up her plasma weapon, continuing, "But I have bound your blade to mine. After our demonstration, we will place it along with these other blades into the crates and transfer them to your ship. Watch your leg." She activated her blade, and instantly the supervisor's blade sprang forth, setting the grass on fire at his feet. He reflexly threw it away from himself. Heddha switched both weapons off.

"You're crazy! You will inundate the ship with smoke and fire. We will die. It's diabolical."

"Interesting Galactic Standard word. I'm not entirely sure of the meaning, but if I were to guess, I'd say it would describe most offworlders fairly well. Pug's" Heddha indicated Pug, "aunt and a friend were murdered with one of these." She picked up the discarded weapon. "Another dear friend assaulted, and her parents are missing, probably dead, and a king murdered. An offworlder killed two of your colleagues, and we don't want to leave out the cruel deaths here in the pit. Does any of this fit the definition of diabolical?"

Heddha advanced on him, and Tho stopped the man from backing up. "You and I will reach an understanding. Leave here and never return, and we will not have to become diabolical."

Heddha shifted in the saddle, gazing up at the points of light in the sky, thinking of Jorma and hoping he made it safely away from the main ship since, in a few moments, everyone onboard the ship would know circumstances had changed on Inlanda. Heddha's thought brought to mind the dei she caught the trout on the way to the Setting Sea. She slipped off a rock, falling headfirst into a pool of water. Heddha broke the interface between mediums, opening her eyes to a different world. The water's tumultuous surface sparkled with the Solaura's spectral reflections. Jahtara sat on the bank, hugging her knees, head back, laughing with her in a spontaneous carefree moment. The world changed for Heddha in that untroubled consequence.

Heddha, with the mining supervisor standing next to her, watched the transport crew load the last crates onto the ship. Heddha turned in the saddle to alert those waiting thirty paces back. The large party had lingered at the gate while the wagons delivered the crates to the landing site. Once the wagons returned and the ship landed, they crept forward to watch its loading.

As the last crate loaded, Heddha nudged the offworlder with her foot. When he looked up at her, she reminded him in GS of his task, "You will have the count of thirty to inform the chief of the contents of the crates, convince them to leave immediately and not return. I activate my plasma weapon if they don't leave immediately or the ship doesn't head to orbit. After you lift off, we destroy the refinery and other equipment to ensure you do not return."

"Destroy it all? That wasn't part of the deal!"

"No deal. A non-negotiable understanding, and I just amended it." Four warning blasts sounded. She pushed the supervisor harder with her foot, ordering, "Run now, they take off!"

She watched him run awkwardly, leaning forward, tripping, struggling to regain his feet, and finally collapsing on the loading ramp. The officer and chief ran down the incline to help him up. Heddha turned around, signaling the others forward, and as they passed by her, she ordered them in GS to, "Run! Run for your lives!" Tho cracked his whip over-head, and in moments they were in a headlong, confused dash for the ship, and Heddha's Badgers rode for the gate, making full use of the disarray.

Once at the gate, Heddha dismounted, already hearing the whine of the ship's engines behind her. She jogged to the lip of the pit, and with the whine reaching a peak, she activated her plasma weapon. A small light appeared far down in the darkness, flaring and growing in spurts until a bright flame lit the entire pit with intense white light. A loud boom sent flares and debris arching out in all directions, the blast reverberating around the chasm. Looking across the opening, Heddha saw several orange blazes illuminating the refinery. The dark shape of the ship lifted into the sky, blocking stars in an ever-higher arc. Heddha remounted, and the Inlandani rode hard to catch up with the wagons.

The rising Solaura found billowing smoke still escaping the pit and revealed people swarming over the refinery like maggots on a cadaverous beast. Random jumbles of stone blocked the entrance doors, and masonry scattered around the building, making it look ruined. Smoke rose from areas on the roof and around the loading docks. Obdalti blackened sections of the eaves and placed other debris to add to the havoc. The wooden awning over the loading dock hung partially down, leaning against the shuttered doors and burned platform. Overall, it made the building look destroyed and abandoned.

Heddha and Pug stood with three mounts, one smaller than the others, watching a weary Obdalti walk towards them. He bowed slightly, congratulating them in GS with, "A splendid day's work, masterly carried out."

"Due to your tremendous ideas and help," Heddha responded in GS.

"Quite a performance. You should join a traveling troop."

"I already have," she jested, patting Pug on the back. "Is there much more to do?"

"No, not much. I've shut down the refinery's communication gear. The arrays from the roof lay dismantled and strewn about." He changed the subject, "I think a defense exists against the plasma weapons, but it's cumbersome, making it awkward to use. A strong magnet can disrupt the blade. One of the metals mined here makes an excellent magnet. We can make shields out of this Neodymium, but those carrying them could not be near others with such a shield, nor could they have any other metals on their person. I don't consider such a shield practical."

"Too bad; hopefully, we'll have more weapons than they do." They clasped wrists, and Pug did the same, then Obdalti shuffled back up the path, passing Tho and Jit, who brought Ananeurin down the track.

Heddha greeted them in Inlandani, hugging Ananeurin, then addressed Jit, "When will you start on your way."

"Some of the wagons depart now. Those riding with mounts leave later, catching up to the wagons."

Tho continued, "Two hundred agree to join with a promise of land to farm. We remain short of mounts yet may get more on the way with the promissory notes you provided. Benedus will do our healing, and we provided him with the use of three wagons. One of the woman joining the Badgers will make us a standard. My gratitude for all you have done."

"I will send a message to Thane Kirrydon, the queyn's regent; they will expect you."

Tho quickly grasped her wrist and turned away.

Jit also took her wrist, saying, "Truly, very grateful for what you did for us."

"It may seem like what happened relied on me, yet it took a joining of us all to produce this outcome. Your monks attempted to change one metal to another; we have transformed our circumstances."

"So, Heddha changed us to gold?"

"I am a single gem in a multi-jeweled parure in which we all sparkle." They both grinned.

"The fates be with you, Heddha."

"The fates be where they may, naught I can do except respond when they arrive." Heddha waved and turned to mount up.

Jit and Tho hugged Ananeurin, making their farewells, then lifted her on the pony. As they walked away, Ananeurin called, "Daddy," they turned in unison. She waved and said, "I love you both."

Pug reached to take the reins from Ananeurin; holding her hand, he said, "You lucky to have such a family."

Ananeurin squeezed his hand, telling him, "You are family."

"Aye. I take the rein to lead till you learn the filly." He mounted up, clearing his eyes with his free hand.

Once astride, Heddha led out, saying, "Back to Concupia and family."

By fate, luck, or synchronicity, their party of three rode into port simultaneous with Captain Ikbar preparing to sail up the coast. Director Dunnyn had notified the captain to look out for the pair, and he was relieved to see them. He agreed to convey them to Concupia along with the youngling.

They sailed against a cold headwind, tacking most of the way until the wind came around late yesterdei, speeding their passage to Concupia on choppy seas. Once on the Quay, Pug headed to Aunties. Heddha continued to Thane Kirrydon's estate, following Jorma's instruction to meet at Fate's abode, knowing her mount remained stabled there.

Heddha and Ananeurin were shown into the library, where a new-laid fire sputtered and popped to life. A pair of legs, propped on a stool, extended from a high-backed chair, and Jorma's head peered around the armchair's edge. He lay down his book, standing to greet Heddha with a warm, welcoming hug, saying, "Come, stand by the fire. You must have traveled by ship, for I arrived less than a luna ago."

"Ahhh, this fire will help ring the cold saltwater from soggy bones!" Heddha said, showing her hands to the fire.

"And who might this be?"

"Ananeurin, Jit and Tho's daughter. They asked for her to become a ward of Queyn Jahtara. Ananeurin, meet Jorma, a ministrant to the queyn."

Jorma welcomed Ananeurin with, "So very happy to meet a laud to the queyn, Ananeurin." He took her hand, kissing the back of it lightly. "I look forward to hearing all about your travels. First, let me see if I can find you two some hot vittles and drink."

Sitting by the library fire, Jorma and Heddha spoke into the noite.

When Heddha finished her tale, Jorma exhaled the smoke of his pipe, contemplating her story, finally saying, "Well, not what I expected, yet all in all, I think it works to our advantage. That you killed no one proves important, and you came through with your colors flying literally. Heddha's Badgers, you say, and they will arrive at the start of the Warming. Certainly good to see you back on Inlanda, Heddha."

Heddha asked, "And you, you cut ties to your past? I have done it, not by choice, yet I would not change the fact. Well, not most of it."

"At this moment, I miss none of my past and look forward to our present undertaking, followed by a peaceful future. Bringing us to what comes next?"

"I am desperate to find and meet up with Jahtara. I think it optimal not to linger here, for surely, we are sought."

"Agreed, I understand a letter awaits you from Laud Renesmee."

"Then it must contain Jahtara's whereabouts, and we shall start our travels soon."

"I hope it does. I have pieced together information tying together much of Enan's intrigue. However, the only Inlandan with the knowledge to comprehend it is you. A complicated tale that will wait for the road and help pass the journey."

Laud Renesmee's letter did contain a cryptic mention of a herb used in birthing and found in coast range meadows. An herb Heddha had discussed with Jahtara on their long-ago trek to the Setting Sea. They would leave the next dei!

Replication

How would you go about creating a universe? Take your time. Not making an attempt at omnipotence, even though we all do kinda construct our own worlds. How did it come about that you perceive these words at this moment?

One conceivable way is through cosmological natural selection, leading to the semi-stable iteration we find ourselves in now. This progression alters entropy's rate by improbable and increasingly complex organization, making local adaptions more likely. For instance, giant stars' triple-alpha reaction producing carbon, the foundation of known life. These adaptive evolutionary processes generate the building blocks of life and consciousness: mentality and matter influencing each other through natural selection, creating a representation of the cosmos, a map. Each map joining a multiverse of consciousness.

Consciousness replicates through DNA over a relatively brief time after epochs of evolution. Rather than originating from a single evolutionary tree, it encompasses an evolutionary forest beginning with the expansion of space, energy consolidation into mass, and in time self-replicating molecules. Ultimately, complex catalysts and information structures like intron-rich split genes emerge bound by membranes, followed by sexual reproduction, multi-cellular/organs/systems, including self-aware consciousness, planetary ecosystems, and societies. We are not technologists; we are the technology! An entangled, replicating, deeply feeling universal consciousness awakening to an inherited presence.

This tale evolves. Though we must remember stories, maps, or math are not the experience.

❧

Jahtara looked out the great room's multi-paned window at the glacial world outside: the meadow, stone walls, and tree-covered hillsides lay veiled in-depth with snow. The conifer branches bent low, the dark green boughs appearing like shadows beneath the mounded snowfall. The flowing stream seemed suspended by a covering of ice. Nothing moved; the window appeared as a painted frozen scene.

Jahtara felt veiled in time among the deepening snow surrounding the inn. With a sigh, she started another circuit of the great room. She got up because her back ached, but waddling around the room, her hips felt loose. Jahtara had started her gravidity full of energy, yet now she grew overheated, short of breath with feet big as tubers, and she spent too much time going to the privy!

Surely, the rest of Inlanda didn't exist under this veil: what happened out there, did her allies prevail, was it all passing Jahtara by, and what of Heddha? Jahtara sighed, filling her lungs to appease her air hunger. Then, she chuckled, remembering her forced engagement almost a jahr ago. Did that prinus still exist or the fleeing prinus unhindered on the vast plain, or was she the queyn with child wanting to rejoin the world?

The inn's door burst open with a swirl of snow, and in thumped Atiqtalik covered in furs resembling a small bear roaring with joy. Looking up to find Jahtara, she smiled broadly, throwing her a snowball, proclaiming, "I thrive on this gloriously frigid dei!"

Catching the cold orb, Jahtara took a bite, breaking off a chunk to rub on her face and neck, feeling glorious!

❧

The company of four took their leave while a light frost still clung to the sedges along the shore road leading from Concupia. The party shared a common destination, yet the four suffered separately: Jorma knew not whether he ran from or to a perplexity but sensed it mattered; Pug started with an appreciation of a larger purpose wrapped in his fondness for Heddha, now narrowing to revenge for Auntie's death; Ananeurin longed for her uncle and father even though the meaning of those words existed in a state of superposition. With the distance to Jahtara dwindling, Heddha's insecurities grew regarding Jahtara's elevated station and the brevity of their passion. The day turned colder, each traveler wrapped in their cocoons of warmth and thought.

The next dei arose worse with freezing rain falling on the party, forcing them to stop early, adding to Heddha's disquiet, fearing she must miss the birthing. However, she resigned to the delay by helping Pug construct a makeshift shelter. Jorma laid a blazing fire at its entrance, and Ananeurin made a warming tea while roasting potatoes and onions on rocks at the fire's edge.

When they were warm and full, Jorma sat next to Heddha in the gathering darkness listening to the clinking of frozen rain striking the rocks. Jorma and Heddha began the discussion using Galactic Standard; it contained the nouns and in-depth concepts needed to explain what Jorma discovered. However, though not fully known, the implications could be understood in any language. Heddha acquired much knowledge through the VR techcap, but she still needed to interrupt Jorma on many occasions. Over several deis, Heddha came to understand most of his findings.

Jorma quickly hit a dead-end with his investigation aboard Chaz's Beagle. Through Cora, he sent an entangled message request to a colleague with access to a library collating research and findings from stellar explorations. Whereas the data from the exploratory undertaking to Inlanda was heavily redacted or removed from corporate files, this colleague found a complete scientific summary from the original mission presented at an off-planet Conference on Biofields and Consciousness.

The summary opened with a report on the biological role of rare elements, concluding that Inlanda's geological and climate history led to some intriguing inclusion of these metals in the biology and evolution of Inlanda. Nadasagrado Corporation mined these metals not to use in electronics but for their unique biological applications. Plants took up RE metals, concentrating them for biochemical processes such as seed sprouting, increasing growth rates, extracting energy from light, and directing growth in weak magnetic fields.

Planet ecologists surmised this led to plants with higher concentrations of these metals through a cycle of sequestering RE locally. Animals consumed these plants incorporating RE metals into their biochemistry, affecting growth, influencing hormones, and healing, especially in the brain, protecting it from trauma. In limited studies of Inlandani, the research showed a type of large molecules incorporating these rare metals. The molecules' role remained unknown until they discovered the duplicated genes in Jahtara's ancestor that produced a class of cryptochromes. RE cryptochromes combine, like iron-containing heme, with certain RE metals to form complex biomolecules in the brain.

On the second dei of Jorma's explanation, riding through light snow, Heddha stopped him to ask, "How did they obtain this information from Jahtara's ancestor?"

After a long silence, he asked, "Did Jahtara ever say how her great grandmother died?"

"I do not like this question, not at all."

Jorma switched to Galactic, "The summary referred to the research subject by a number. The information I discovered on the ship referred to Jahtara's relative by position and name. I found a corporate reference number, but another intermediate document must exist connecting the two numbers. However, the demographic data on both papers were similar.

"Machines and techniques exist to obtain this kind of biological data in vivo, but they were unavailable on the type of vessel journeying here many years ago. Perhaps they took Jahtara's great-grandmother off-planet for these types of analysis, and she died later. Then upon her death, they studied her brain and other organs. In any case, such behavior represents criminal research and kidnapping."

Not until the next dei could Heddha bring herself to ask Jorma to continue his account.

The research found cryptochrome molecules in the subject's eyes, a light receptor stimulated by the blue to ultraviolet spectrum. It's also possible the detection and tracking of magnetic and biofield emissions existed with these molecules. The investigators found a series of complexes in the brain incorporating magnetized Neodymium with iron heme-like molecules. On three-dimensional imaging, they appeared in a concave-shaped structure with a focal point near the Inlandani's more substantial pineal-like gland. From there, efferent and afferent tracts relayed information and stored data in the relevant neuronal microtubules as quantum coherences.

The end of the summery was speculative. The researchers postulated this arrangement acted like an antenna in which the complexes could change shape due to feedback from other brain areas, focusing signals from electromagnetic inputs; in effect, all this data combines to visualize electromagnetic biofields. Add the infrared sensors in the Inlandani eye, and it creates a kind of heads-up display of an external object. Such a system can collate data to create a complex picture, including heart and respiratory rate, brain wave activity, vulnerable body organs, stress, and even emotional states. Some animals use these types of magnetic sensitive molecules to determine the position and distance to other animals.

If reversed, this system could convey signals from the pineal area to a focal point outside the sender's body. This involves the Inlandan eye slit focusing ability. When the pupillary slit closes, the small diamond-shaped openings could determine the biofield source's optimal distance. The entire system receives information from multiple inputs, focuses it, correlates the data, sends it to the brain's relevant areas, provides an interpretation, stores the particulars, tracks, and focuses on the source, then possibly sends a signal to communicate or somehow affect the source.

As Jorma's explanation concluded on the seventh dei of their travels, Heddha pulled Fate's Choice up, forcing the rest of the party to stop. She stood in the stirrups, stretching her back, then realizing everyone halted, she waved them on and cantered up beside Jorma.

Coming out of deep thought, Heddha finally asked in Inlandani, "I think I understand your explanation of what they found in Jahtara's grandmother, yet what does it mean? How does this new way of seeing serve?"

"At best, it implies a different means of perceiving the world and communicating with other sentiencies."

"And at worst?"

"Did Jahtara ever speak of her great grandmother?

"Jahtara was a youngling when her great-grandmother lived, and I do not think she remembers much. Would this trait pass on to Jahtara?"

Switching to Galactic, he responded, "Possibly. More likely, the inheritance involved multiple genes and epigenetic controls. Royal family trees contain a lot of inbreeding; maybe her ancestor occupied a fortuitous combination of circumstances. Have you noticed any strangeness about Jahtara, like having access to information others wouldn't have?"

She stayed with Inlandani, "Hard to say, perhaps."

"Aye, well, we will have some questions for her when next we meet."

"And the child will have these changes?"

"This appears to be Enan's purpose." Switching to GS, "They collected plants from Inlanda requiring these elements to survive, which will supply the higher nutritional concentrations needed in this system's biochemistry. They have a private supply of rare elements to feed their prodigies."

Heddha pushed the group late into the dei with a renewed will to reach Jahtara ahead of her giving birth.

The next dei arose cool with lazuline skies and no wind. The migrating troop came upon a modest estuary with extensive flats that appeared from under the receding tide. Heddha spied an elderly man working his way up a narrow path and realized she knew him, "Teacher to some, you have lost your sangha, or did it lose you?"

"You have me at a disadvantage, child, for by your ire, you seem to know me; however, I do not recollect you."

"Nor should you, a mutuality, connects us. What do you do here?"

"I oar a boat for those wishing a conveyance to a farther shore. I see you have a means of travel, yet the way to the upriver crossing grows lengthy. If any wish to break from their path, I can take one or two, and you could reconvene further up the road."

Heddha replied, "I would enjoy a different view and a break from Fate's Choice." She turned to look at Jorma.

"I will keep my feet dry."

Pug and Ananeurin shook their heads. "'Tis me alone then," stated Heddha. She handed the reins to Jorma and left the road for the bay.

Heddha leaned back against the stern transom, content to let the old man pull at the oars. Finally, she said, "How does this serve you?"

"How does your anger serve you?" he parried.

Heddha smiled and nodded, agreeing, "It does not, of course, except to show me the uselessness of what I still hold on to, yet that surpasses listening to you. Your discourses are like an ox grazing on life, regurgitating macerated insights to chew on and then filling the pasture with paddies of wisdom. I would do better feeding on the mushrooms growing on these droppings to gain insight."

Now the sage threw his head back, laughing. "I regret not recalling our previous meeting, for you have some truth within you. I wish only to serve, to gain merit for my next life."

"Striving for merit does not serve if I am not reborn. I wish to live a good life, not harming others, where wholesomeness comes from within, and when I finish this journey, I will return to the soil to nourish the fauna and flora that sustained me, living on only in the reflections of others. This sort of life serves me and causes no harm.

"We have not met before; however, a dear friend endured harm not by you directly, yet under your auspices." Heddha paused, "In this telling, my anger found a path to its ceasing." She continued by suggesting, "You could gain merit in my eyes by accompanying me to help thwart your prior assistant's plans."

The teacher stopped rowing, letting the boat drift. "Ah, you would be the focus of a love from behind the veil." At Heddha's raised brows, he explained, "A womon and I engaged in conversation early one morgn about intimacy and a veiled passion in her heart. I later learned I failed her by not acting on a vagueness growing in my own heart and the false pride that my assistant would change. That morgn, she discovered you the intimate of her heart."

Tears filled Heddha's eyes, thinking of events delayed that dei.

The teacher leaned forward, extending his arm, offering, "I have been called Rinpoche, yet I wish you to know me by my childhood name, Tendrel Zangpo."

Heddha took his wrist, the dory drifting, the Solaura at his back, and ripples on the bay lit up with a multitude of sparkling illuminations like light through a jewel. Heddha introduced herself, ending with, "Well met Tendrel Zangpo, and I thank you for your help crossing this expanse."

"Well met, Heddha. Our meeting in this life enriches me."

Tendrel Zangpo rowed again with renewed vigor across the estuary, pulling the boat onto the slippery flat. He helped steady Heddha to the dry path, returned to the dinghy to retrieve a walking stick and small bundle, and rejoined Heddha walking behind her. When she realized he followed her, she asked, "I am happy you join us; however, you will merely leave the vessel?"

"The dory served me well, yet the vessel started to leak, and this river does not sing of my death. I will leave the conveyance for someone to discover, repair, and serve.

Jahtara stood at the top of the stair, waiting for a light contraction to finish, her belly decompressing, releasing its grip on her daughter. She filled her lungs, let the breath out, and headed down the stairs.

Kalama moved past her on the stairs. The Innkeeper paused, turning back to Jahtara, asking, "Everything as it should be?"

"Just a tightening, and it passes."

"It comes near time we should fetch Babaor. It will take my mate a half dei to go to her, and by the time she returns, it will be a full dei. I have invited her to bring the whole clan when she comes." She kept talking while descending the stairs, "Better she be here with idle hands than wayfaring through darkness bent over in a blowing blizzard in a time of need. This forms my counsel and sets me above reproach in any refined parturiency, just saying…." The door to the kitchen cut off any understanding of what came after.

Jahtara smiled at the effect a title produced, but she supposed we all acted so, attaching such status to many constructs.

Atiqtalik, from a chair set by the hearth, said, "She grows concerned you give birth without her Babaor in attendance."

"Time remains. I wish for the attendance of Heddha, and I decree the birth postponed until such condition is met."

"You feel settled with Heddha present."

"Aye, contented in her arms. She treats me like the spirit I truly am. Well, except you, of course, and on occasion Tanhā when contrary. If only I knew where Heddha was."

"Queyn represents only an utterance; you can have it mean what you wish. Is this not so?

"I will not be sovereign!"

"Aye, yet you are placed in a vortex by circumstances, a unique position whether sovereign or not, much good could come of it. You become a mother soon; would you abrogate that?"

"Atiqtalik, you should be a seamster, stitching dissimilar pieces of cloth together into a single garment."

"I speak what I understand. The land appears frozen now, held in abeyance. Yet come the Warming, everything will change, brought forth from seed and root. This land, hill, and dale, these plants, flowers, trees, and seeds constitute your sisters, mother, father, and brothers. All represent your ancestors and the sustenance from which our future flows. All Inlandani carry this onus, yet your shoulders carry a unique duty: to persevere and bring it to fruition. A mother must protect this heritage and variety, for if someone else holds sway over this birthright, they plunder our soul."

"I agree the situation is dire, and by the authority of some circumstance, I am placed at the center, although I would not place myself at the core."

"Perhaps you have found your Ikigai, your reason for being. The finding of such often requires a deep search. Perhaps, in this instance, it found you."

"I cannot rule people. How can I get them to join in this quest?"

The doux's deep voice boomed from the back of the great room, "Consider music, my dear. Contrast, difference, contrary makes one note distinguished from the next like war sets one against the next, and the conductor shall bring these notes to heel in one movement."

"Uncle, you shall cause my child to make an early entrance, sneaking up on me. Kindly make your presence known instead of hiding away," she retorted, peeved. "Your outlook on ruling may seem a rational paradigm, yet if I may offer another view. I experience people in resonance, one to another, in harmony, interdependent one to the next. The presence of each note embodies a mirror to the prior and the following, thus making the melody."

Her uncle winked at Atiqtalik, saying to Jahtara, "This proves why I am not a keyn and why you shall make a great queyn, su sereno grandeza!"

The track in this region consists of sandy loam, and while dusty in the dry time, when wet, it drains admirably, and the group made excellent time. Tendrel found himself a small space astride the pack neddy Stolen Pleasure. The conditions remained frigid at noite yet snowed only miserly with a wind coming off the Setting Sea.

Rocky crags, covered with wind-shaped trees, jutted into the sea hemming in sandy shores overblown with swiftly moving clouds, and all flowed past with equal haste as the fivesome dispatched the road driven by Heddha's want. They traveled till late each dei, sleeping deep in their exhaustion, rising in the dark with their breath hanging in the air and eating dry bread moistened with coagulate butter, then mounted again to plunge through space and time.

Late one dei, the group achieved the turn away from the Setting Sea onto the inland track, and Heddha paused, asking Jorma, "I have a mind to stop here in the little hidden depression where Jahtara and I spent a wonderful dei on our trek. What think you?"

"I know the reminiscence would warm your heart. However, I wish to eat without the sting of blowing sand. I think a storm comes, and I would, by darkness, like to rest behind the lee of the ridge. I tire of this exposure."

Heddha replied, "During time aboard your ship, I felt confined, and I dreamt of being out in the open."

"I thank good fortune for living during an era of indoor privies, ummm… hot and cold running water," continuing in GS, "central heating, and cooling."

"So, you long to return to your comforts then?"

"A return with too many unwanted attachments. I would not give up the beauty, challenges, and friendships found here. Having said this, let us find a sheltered place to enjoy our simple fair without the abrasive sand."

Heddha took one last look at the long stretch of shore, noticing a shadowy passage along the waterline, a gather of small birds skimming low, racing their mirror images intermittently reflecting off the thin wash of receding waves.

Heddha and Jorma, their backs against a rock, sat on saddle blankets looking out on a snow-covered clearing surrounded by deep forest. Jorma toked his pipe, and they sipped steaming tea, enjoying the time off their mounts at the end of the dei.

Heddha mused, "I remember looking down from your ship to where we sit, unable to distinguish tree, road, or stream in the immensity of Inlanda. Now, sitting here, I cannot distinguish the ship among the glittering array."

Two previously unseen snowbirds sprung out of the boughs with a fluttering of wings, causing a flurry of snow to drift down. Jorma blew out a ring of smoke, reflecting, "A vast amount of life escapes us when we focus instead on the inconsequential wonderings of our mind. Such is the enormity of our existence." A white rabbit streaked under a fallen log, and an uplifting on the surface of the snow gave evidence of the rodent moving beneath.

Heddha sat silently watching the Luna rise to illuminate the snowy landscape, finally admitting, "The meaning of it all is beyond me at this moment of exhaustion and concern for Jahtara. I am content enjoying my tea in this snow-filled meadow." A raptor silently appeared, slowing its flight to hang motionless over some unseen quarry, then plunged headfirst and, at the last instant, brought its clawed feet around to land hard in the snow. Heddha thought the raptor missed its unseen prey, but it made a small hop, then another giving a strong downstroke, and leaped into the air, in its claw, a dark shape with a long thin tail.

Jahtara sat at the large table in the great room, folding pieces of cloth and assembling small bundles when the innkeeper came in from the kitchen. Upon seeing Jahtara, she observed, "You arose early this morgn and have completed my chore of laying the fire, I see."

"Aye, I awoke before the Solaura's rising and could not bring back sleep. I intended to make use of the time and straighten my room. In doing so, I came across these nappies Tanhā made up and am adding moss Atiqtalik gathered to draw the child's mess. Your kind mate obtained some leaf lard from the last slaughter, and I shall make a salve with these root herbs Atiqtalik gathered, thus having it ready if the youngling becomes psoric."

Kalama sat next to Jahtara, helping her put the moss into small bundles. She inquired with a strange smile, "You feel a surge then?" With Jahtara's nod, she continued, "Then I had good news at the foresetting yesterdei," at Jahtara's reaction, she hurried on, "'Tis not your Heddha. 'Twas Holwell passing by with his team and sleigh hauling a load of cut wood for the widow and her younglings who ran out on Willow Glen. Holwell displays such a good heart, and you know I heard him coming from behind the crest with his big minstrel voice, for he sings what news he carries, so's not to tarry on the road."

Hearing Jahtara clear her throat, Kalama rushed to finish saying, "He passed Babaor and her clan on the road middei, and she advanced the message she would spend the noite at the miller's place, arriving here this midmorgn. I reckon a good occasion; this nesting bustle promises we will see this child soon."

Heddha stood amid sleigh tracks in the road, waiting for the rest of the party to arrive. "These tracks signify a weighted sleigh and a party including younglings walking in the tracks. Both be filled in with snow somewhat, the sleigh a bit more. I venture the sleigh passed yesterdei and the party later the same dei. It troubles me a party travels in this cold and with younglings. Should we carry through or stop to rest? What think you?" she said to Jorma.

He sighed, saying, "It grows late and cold. I see a difficult choice. How about you, old man?"

"I have my robes and meditation. If the neddy can proceed, then I shall accompany it."

Heddha looked to Pug and Ananeurin, "What say you?"

Ananeurin smiled and nodded, having been adventurous since encountering the snowy forest. Pug declared, "I would brave the road for a hearth with warm stew and drink."

Jorma agreed, "We intend to continue then. I suggest we dismount and give the animals their oat bags while supping on the last bread and sweet jam. With the entire party refreshed, push on."

Heddha, with a grin, thanked them all, saying, "I appreciate your steadfastness. We may arrive near midnoite, and no matter the circumstance, able to halt with my anxiety laid to rest.

Jahtara lay on her side in bed, the fire burning low and a single candle to light the room. She tried to sleep after the intensity of the dei, a fervent dei, now seemingly spent and thwarted. The waves of constrictions started midmorgn shortly before Babaor arrived with her family, and the moments following were of general commotion and busyness.

Jahtara started her labor with a sense of excitement and assured expectation, gradually blurring into endless waves of ever-mounting discomfit. The shrouded quandaries consolidated in time, and strength, sending Jahtara to her center while drawing her mind to the brink, finally releasing, letting her slide down the far slope. Again, she grew aware of those surrounding her with reassuring caresses, loving hands, and encouraging voices acknowledging her strength to endure and transcend, allowing Jahtara to relax between the worst of the travail. During this time, Babaor and Atiqtalik walked her around the inn providing support during standing or squatting contractions. Even Tanhā helped by applying pressure on her low back.

On occasion, Jahtara realized she appeared snippy with those around her but knew she reached a low point when she pondered the cause of her current state and, not wishing to bring forth her child with blame, moved to a yearning for Heddha. She couldn't recall the rationale for impulsively sending her elsewhere. Then, before the midnoite, her robust contractions ceased, even with indications suggesting she would soon give birth.

Jahtara sighed; the birthing process had saturated her, and now she felt frustrated, wanting fulfillment. She glanced around her room: by the fire, Babaor sat on the hearth knitting, her sweet apprentice daughter, Dewi, slumbered in a chair with her feet before the low fire, and across the room on the floor, Atiqtalik braided her long black hair. Jahtara considered dismissing them to their rooms when the babe moved in a prolonged stretch, followed by a sharp contraction. She sat up, confident of her feeling. She looked to Babaor and Atiqtalik, saying, "She comes!"

"You feel you must push?" Babaor said, laying aside her knitting.

Jahtara answered, "No, however, the babe will come now Heddha approaches."

Atiqtalik stood, "I will wake the proprietors so they may stable the mounts and lay the table with hot fare."

Even though the crossing lay covered in snow, Heddha recognized the stone bridge and spurred Fate's Choice to a judicious gallop in the snowy lane turning to the inn. Coming near, a man stepped from under the portico lifting a lantern, offering to take the reins while suggesting, "There be food and drink set on the table and a warming fire."

Heddha sliding from her mount, declined, saying, "Those following will want to partake."

The main door opened, and a beautifully adorned womon appeared, beckoning Heddha forward, "We will take you to her. Your appearance happens fortuitously."

Heddha pushed into the dimly lit room, heart beating with the tempo of a hummingbird coming upon a trove of golden nectar. She extended forward to rush to a beaming Jahtara, but a hand on her arm obstructed, and Atiqtalik whispered. "Your clothes are cold and wet. Shed them by the door."

Dewi crept forward and, in a whisper, asked, "I can fetch you my noitegown for warmth if you wish?"

"I am afraid I would only get entangled in it or tie it at my waist to prevent becoming so. My lover's exertions will warm me." Heddha thanked her, rushing to Jahtara.

Jahtara, having finished a powerful contraction, sat back on her heels. Heddha let her breathe out the tension, then kissed her lightly, allowed another breath, and this time let her kiss linger. Jahtara ran her hands over Heddha's shoulders, arms pulling her close, confirming her presence. Jahtara whispered in Heddha's ear, "I have missed you like life itself and would not want to part ever again, yet womon, you smell of a long trail ride. I am going to retch." Heddha pulled back, and Jahtara purged into a small bucket provided by Dewi. Rinsing her mouth, Jahtara continued, "One of these fine womyn will fetch warm lavender water and a cloth. I engage in birthing our daughter." Then drawing in a breath, another wave broke over her. But she was able to affirm, "Aye, a daughter!"

Contractions later, Jahtara squatted on the floor, Heddha at her side supporting and Babaor seated in front of her. The tightening intensified, and Jahtara grunted with the pressure. Looking to Babaor, she admitted, "I feel my bowels will move."

"Quite common, I assure. Blessed be, if you feel you must push, your babe comes, do what she requires."

Jahtara grunted through the pressure and smiled as it lessened, entwined her hand with Heddha's, whispering, "I feared to do this without you, not the birthing yet greeting our daughter. You have moved me again with your timing, for you anchor me."

"So, how do you know we have a daughter to greet this noite?"

Feeling pressure intensifying again, Jahtara added, "Long story, yet it would seem so, and if mistaken, my pronouncement would only be flawed by half." Then an urge to push overtook her. Grabbing her ankles and letting her knees spread wide, she bore down. Five efforts later, Jahtara's shirt was soaked from her exertions. Babaor peeled off the noiteshirt, and Heddha wiped her face with a cool cloth.

Heddha attempted encouragement with, "The end comes near. A few more pushes to reward our labors."

Jahtara glanced toward Heddha out of the corner of her eye, "Aye, when you have labored all dei, you can tell me how close we are." Then in response to the hurt on Heddha's face, she continued, "And now you think I am over-sensitive in opposition to your insensitivity!" Heddha kissed the back of Jahtara's hand hesitantly. The touch of Heddha's lips broke Jahtara's peevishness, causing her to reply, "Well, perhaps I am a little sensitive. I know nothing of your troubles in getting here, and I am glad you returned this noite."

Jahtara pushed on all fours with her knees apart, and after several strong urges, Babaor quietly said, "I see a small portion of the babe's head during a push. You be close, child, and truly so."

At length, with a generous portion of the crown visible, Jahtara exclaimed, "Babaor, it burns so!"

"Aye, this be to the good. The babe stretches you. Breath during the urge and let your womb labor for you."

And she did, Heddha supporting her upper body while she squatted on her knees with Babaor behind until her midwife proclaimed, "Ahhh, sweet child, her head passes without obstruction and in the caul, blessed be."

By the hearth, Atiqtalik extolled, "A rare omen surely!"

The babe's body slipped from Jahtara, and she lifted her leg over the baby and leaned against Heddha so they could gaze upon their daughter for the first time. Through the caul, they saw her hands move and eyes open in the dim light. Babaor reached down to free the child with a gush of fluids. Her round pupils looked up at them. Her chest rose slightly, followed by a cough, a deep inhalation, and air became breath. Babaor lifted her to Jahtara's belly, and Dewi gently patted her dry.

This precious issue of the universe lay with her head tipped back, quietly looking up at the two womyn who were in rapture. Jahtara ran her hand over the babe's unraised grey freckles, and Heddha held her tiny foot. They caressed their daughter, unable to remove her from their gaze.

The middei appeared brittle through the windows overlooking the meadow. Translucent dagger sickles hung precariously off the eaves. The snowing stopped, and the heavy clouds chased away; the colors of the gaining Solaura captured a vividness, lifting the oppression and replacing it with a soaring but fragile lightness.

Heddha entered the great room where the assembled waited, speaking quietly after their late noite labors or travels. Jorma introduced Heddha to those she didn't know. The proprietors laid out a grand table, and before partaking, the doux raised his tankard, saying, "From the soil to the flesh, to the spirit." The younglings and those fully-fledged enjoyed a feast honoring the prinus's birth. Jorma and Heddha exchanged glances more than once when those gathered heard of the babe's unusual eyes. Some of those present peeked at Jorma with sidelong glances, probing him for particulars, usually not in earshot of Heddha. She realized an explanation needed devising and would speak of it to Jahtara.

Near the end of the celebration, Jahtara appeared on the landing holding the new one in her arms, tipping her up slightly so those below could see. To Jorma, she said, "She exhibits the eyes of your people." Seeing all eyes turn to Jorma, some with knowing, some with questioning expressions, Jahtara stood straighter, continuing, "I acknowledge I have appeared less than truthful; some say secretive. I sense several have guessed or surmised their truth. I beg your pardon for imposing this upon you. The evasion proved necessary for the safety of myself and our newborn daughter. Hopefully, those recently arrived will complete my understanding of the situation."

Jahtara looked at the slumbering babe, "Yet this you shall know," she changed her focus to those gathered, "Heddha and I nurture her in our loving family, without necessitating male lineage or begetting."

Heddha entered the room with a tray as Jahtara finished nursing. She set up a chair by the hearth and crossed to take their daughter.

Jahtara watched Heddha moving around the room, observing her after their time apart. Heddha's skin tone seemed changed, acquiring depth, gaining the dimensions of a deep starfield, enabling Jahtara to delve into the unexplored extent of Heddha. Her eyes also looked altered. Jahtara thought Heddha's irises were a solid brown, but todei, a new world opened to over-lapping whirls of browns and greens with occasional golds adding a sparkle. Previously, she had maintained a bent protective posture and now stood upright, eyes forward, leading with her chest, indicating confidence.

Or had Jahtara deepened and matured, seeing past the superficial into an intricate present filled with beauty?

Heddha held the new come geyrle, already knitting a bond to her heart. She ran the back of her fingers over the babe's freckles, noticing the uppermost ones began to show a reddish tint. Heddha looked to Jahtara, casting a line to catch what lay in the space of their separation, "You seem changed, grown taller perhaps. Aye, you have gained in gravity." Jahtara still displayed her sweet smile, but her eyes focused on the distance.

"Now that I have birthed, my breasts prove the only parts gained."

"You know my meaning. I hope this newfound weight does not take the place of joy?"

With a smile, "Not now that you have returned."

"I see you a part of myself, Jahtara Davuda!"

"And you add to me, and I love you all the more."

Jahtara set her tray aside and came to sit on the floor at Heddha's feet, laying her head on Heddha's thigh. Lifting her eyes to Heddha's, she asked, "Have you grieved for him?"

Heddha sat silent for a moment, then explained, "Traveling back to you, I stopped at a market to trade for potatoes from a youngling. Her mother sat on the ground, embroidering a silk thread portrait. The youngling confided her mother toiled for jahrs at this image of her lost husband, endlessly dividing the silk thread to create finer features, a work without conclusion, removing her from life. Once someone passes, their memory drifts in time. Yet, the sense of grief remains. The sorrow gathered in my tear catcher evaporated, and my mourning period ended. I witnessed much suffering and loss at this mining pit, including Pug's missed summons for death. I wish to join the living, especially you and our daughter." Yet she asked, "When you met Absan, did he appear different than I described him."

"No, mayhap older, bigger, haggard, yet still the kind naive soul you knew. Remind you of anyone?"

"Well, at least I am consistent." She reached to take hold of Jahtara's hand.

Jahtara traced Heddha's fingers with her thumb, reminiscing, "I lacked deep personal contact with anyone until I met you." She kissed the back of Heddha's hand. "I remember a time when the story appeared written for me. I knew the rules: I did not like them, yet I knew when I broke them. Now everything feels new, every moment an adventure. Harder in some ways yet very freeing." She met Heddha's gaze, "By what authority am I queyn? Am I following this path out of expectation, of being born and nurtured into it? Am I right for doing this?"

"These questions indicate you possess just intentions. You are born to it, aye, yet also a bridge; an intimate connection to the cause and its effect." Heddha kissed the babe's head.

"Heddha, you do not need to do this. Leave, be someplace far away, safe. You can escape from this world; it need not be your concern."

"It would reach me eventually; I could not escape it. I will not live with just a memory of you. Member our discourse about fate and the suffering of my life? I feel more at ease with my life's path, for past experiences frame what I am now."

Jahtara nodded, "I agree I am uniquely positioned to affect this scheme. I hope high-born and common folk alike will join this quest of opposing the appropriation of what is held by all Inlandani."

Heddha huffed, "Shared causes anticipate a share of the results. The low-born have little faith in dribble-down equivalences."

"That the scale needs balancing seems obvious. By what method appears unclear without causing the calibration to swing wildly."

"Perhaps lifting the thumb that unbalances the mechanism would be prudent." Wanting to change the discussion along a different path, Heddha said, "Speaking of symmetry. The equinox comes, and our beloved's Naming Dei with it."

"Aye, I wish to discuss my thoughts on this and hear yours."

The Snow Luna waned, and soon the Worm Luna would be waxing with returning birds hunting the meadow for sustenance. The evergreen boughs were relieved of their burdens. However, snow unevenly covered the ground, and a light rain fell, turning the bridleway leading to the inn into a boot-sucking mire and would remain so until the early Warming rains abated.

A sharp knock interrupted Jahtara's dressing, and when the door opened, her ministrant of Extra Inlandani Affairs felt unsure if he should enter.

"My pardon, Jahtara."

"No, no, please enter. I must get used to the refined levee now that I am a queyn."

"Heddha will return shortly."

"Good, I am anxious to hear what you have learned. Heddha told me little of her adventures, except the part where she smuggled herself aboard your airship and seized a mining enterprise, I believe."

"More precisely, she stowed away on a spaceship, although some smaller transport ships descend through the air."

"I have no concept of the distinction. Does not air fill space?"

"Mmmmm… Well, aye…" The door swung open, admitting Heddha to observe Jahtara straightening her clothes and Jorma looking flummoxed.

Heddha, with a wink to Jahtara, placed hands on her hips in preparation for a teasing remark when Jahtara stopped her, "Heddha, please, do not start teasing the man. Jorma may not know of the refined levee, yet you know quite well."

Jorma said, "I recognize Heddha's humor. However, I have quickly realized that explaining Enan's scheme may prove more difficult than we thought."

Candles lit the great room as the foresetting approached, although those present didn't appear any more enlightened. Doux Buccleuch leaned back in a chair, feet on a wooden stool gazing into the bottom of his empty flagon. Sensing the silence in the room, he looked up, observing, "Mayhap, if I have another flagon of ale, it will help my understanding, though I doubt it. Calling this thing you hold, with the light emanating from it, a handheld seems akin to calling my war sword a handheld yet does nothing to divulge its purpose. Using a fire sword like a magical toy to set the hearth aflame does not expose its brutal intent. And I have spent my life breeding livestock; however, what you speak of represents hideous magic!"

"Uncle! You speak of our daughter. And Heddha escaped their ship."

"Oh, that makes it all the more believable!"

"Jorma embodies one of the roundeyes."

"More like the master wizard to my way of thinking. Perhaps he can fly to my manor and teach me to breed steeds with wings" He met Jahtara's stare, finally saying regretfully, "My pardon to you and Heddha. I would keep my peace if I could get my flask filled."

"Thank you, Uncle. I am sure more ale will deepen your discernment of what passes this dei." Jahtara sighed, "I must admit I, too, comprehended little of our discussion to this point. There seems to be a wide gap in our words' ability to communicate these concepts. I know this child grows sound and unaffected; she seems to thrive. Uncle, you may examine her for wings if you wish!" She raised her goblet of goat's milk towards her uncle, who lifted his firkin in response. "As to my mother's grandmother, I have no remembrance. My mother said she calmed those in her presence.

"I have no recall of anyone speaking of her passing. In our visits to the ossuary, we never left offerings of reminiscences for her. This entails all I know of her except that I rule queyn of the Middle Realm because she happened to be the sister to Keyn Tergon's grandfather."

Jorma looked up from cleaning his pipe bowl with a penknife and asked, "And you, Jahtara, can you sense other's feelings or intent to any magnitude?"

"Perhaps I can sense some impending circumstance, yet it appears capricious and dependent on the interpretation of perceptions. Cannot anyone get such impressions just by being observant?"

"Aye, no doubt. We cannot know the true function of these structures described from the traits and anatomy of what we assume comprised your great grandmother, much less their possible duplication in… My pardon, have you and Heddha found her a name yet?"

Draining his ale and setting his cup on the table none too gently, Jahtara's uncle suggested, "FitzRoy."

"Uncle, your impudence offends me again. I am certain you have named issue born out of wedlock FitzRoy; however, Heddha and I will not do so." Her eyes found her uncle until he looked away. She stated firmly, "Her naming ceremony shall take place on the Warming equinox."

Jorma broached the silence by suggesting, "The ability to use these enhancements may need a proper maturation or learning process."

Heddha asked, "How much time before observing evidence of these traits or gifts?"

"Possibly at what I believe you call her second precession, and they may not appear how we projected."

Jahtara interjected, "So, all that happened or is projected to happen stands on conjecture? People have died, reigns ended, lives disordered, war comes, and a life created based on what? Desire, greed, power, artifice?" Jahtara could not continue and sat staring at Jorma with a hand over her mouth. She calmed her breath, then resumed, "Jorma, I have little concept of the people who could envision such a plan or a corporation with the power and treasury to pursue this venture. To what end? You appear not considerably different than us and claim to represent an advanced people. Pondering these circumstances could leave one with little hope.

"Yet I wish for positive and restorative action. I have much to lose and wish to protect those I love. Actions reflect our aspirations, and we can move beyond base desires. I feel strong in this conviction. What say you all?"

Heddha, with a slight clearing of her throat, offered, "Your conviction sounds admirable and a pensive argument as a notion, yet it falls apart quickly with two armies riding against you. I would act more pragmatic than you in protecting those I love."

Jahtara answered with forbearance, "Yet I would broaden the presence of love. People of Inlanda make up these armies, inhabitants of lands we come from, children of our ancestors? Let us not churn more dirt into already muddy water. We must clarify these swirling waters so that those carried along by the maelstrom understand worthy method yields quality results. Times have brought us together so injustice could be righted yet righted justly."

Pug stood pushing the hair off his face, pondered, "My auntie endured a horrible death, and this offworlder orphaned my cousins. My body left abandoned to die." He paused, rubbing at his sparse beard while lifting his eyes to Jahtara to say, "Deeds of revenge cloud my head durin' these long noites, yet my queyn's words strike me deep. I do not want to behave like this offworlder, yet revenge would make me such." Pug looked deferentially to Heddha, Jorma, and the doux, saying, "Meanin' no disrespect, I have not seen war or wanton death like grandfather here. I wish for good, not to find myself blood-covered, standin' in a field surrounded by mayhem and death. I will do the necessary; however, our actions will endure for lifetimes. Let us not do it in hate."

Jahtara slipped from her seat to stand with Pug, praising, "You have grown into your beard since last we parted."

She now looked toward her uncle, asking, "And you, 'grandfather,' how do you respond to Pug."

The doux sat up straighter, "Contrary to expectations, I agree with him. I do not praise war or wanton death. Existing at the boundary of two realms, I and my kin prosper in peace more than at war. Yet, we will increase our chances of success by appearing strong. Perhaps we can devise a way to weaken the alliance among those opposing us."

"We agree then," Jahtara turned to Heddha, "Perhaps we shall start pragmatically by badgering the High Mountain Keyndom with a truth to redirect their vengeful anger delivered by an uplifted revenant."

Jahtara smiled at the faces of incomprehension before her, "A naming will take place at the equinox, and then we will start on our path to the betterment of all."

The Solaura's drying rays calloused the momentum-sucking mud of the dell. Flocks of birds roamed the meadow stirring a diversity of insects into the Warming dei. Jahtara filled her deis with planning councils intertwined with Heddha's bewildering explanations. These accounts from Heddha were what Jahtara considered sitting on the stone wall dividing the meadow. How could something travel through nothing to end up in this meadow as the vector of sight and warmth? Jahtara didn't wish to curb Heddha's enthusiasm but finally asked her to stop the commentaries, which only served to baffle. She cared not for the endless reductions and elucidations: excited states, photons, chemical reactions, transducers, synaptic clefts, neural networks, all to explain her experience contemplating the beautiful meadow and Warming dei. And other people's interpretations of their daughter she did not need. Jahtara would let the being she held in her arms define herself.

In this affinity with her daughter, Jahtara didn't notice a figure approaching along the wall until he came close, and she also took note of the mount he rode.

"How be you, Sefu? I see you have chosen a swifter mount for this journey."

"Aye, ma'am, these crucial dispatches call for a prompt reply."

"We have seen nearly the same number of Warmings, have we not?"

"Aye, ma'am."

"Therefore, let us drop the ma'am. Tell me how the regent proceeds in my absence."

A smile graced his lips, "Aye, Jahtara, how dwell you this dei?"

"Good todei, Sefu. I hope you will strengthen my dei with your tidings?"

"Growing numbers appear at the palatial seat and seem willing to pledge to you as their queyn, yet they wait to do so in your presence. I suppose these tallies will gain as the byways allow more travel.

"I dwelt at my manor when a sundry troop calling themselves 'Heddha's Badgers' passed through on their way to the palatial seat, presumably under a warrant from you. Although they have an ardor to serve and rough bearing, they lack experience and desire training. They tell stories of their namesake entailing great stratagem and courage, including sneaking into a stronghold and escaping unharmed with valuable information. Their tale moved me to join the troop, and somedei meet their leader."

"Well then, you shall meet my consort presently. And while Heddha's stature is a mite less than yours, she fills a room with her energy and wit. I observed her take on four cnihts of Davuda realm with great courage, saving ourselves from a fate worse than death." A smile crept to Jahtara's face, "Come, and you shall meet her. Stay on guard, though, as I understand she ascribes to the 'Arbatel de Magia Veterum' and charms all those in her presence," then unable to withhold her mirth, she laughed out loud, causing the closer birds to take flight.

The meadow was wet with dew when Jahtara and Heddha walked hand in hand towards the brightly burning braziers next to the stream. Pug waved, working on completing the fire pit. Jahtara's uncle, Jorma, Babaor's partner, and Talou lay massive wooden planks across tree stumps, serving as tables for the break fast festivities following the naming ceremony. Tanhā and Ananeurin wove flowers into the latticework of a temporary pavilion made of branches and saplings covered with boughs and ferns. Sefu and Tendrel brought another armful of flowers to the geyrles, and Jahtara watched as Tanhā laid her hand in Sefu's as they spoke. She thought it strange that Tanhā would continue the subterfuge of their engagement until she saw Sefu's gaze upon Tahnā. Looking at Heddha, she nodded to the scene, and Heddha responded with a smiling shrug.

Babaor, as the sky lightened, came across the meadow with Kalama and her children. Atiqtalik arrived last carrying the beneficiary of the naming ceremony in a plain-woven blanket.

The Solaura rose over the hill behind the assembled, bathing this portion of the meadow in light, warming those on the stream's bank while Jahtara and Heddha stood in the cold flowing water. Atiqtalik abided to the side, holding the naked nameless child.

Tendrel Zangpo, standing to his knees in the pebble-strewn waterway, gestured to Atiqtalik, who brought the babe forward. Jahtara grasped Heddha's hand and whispered, "We now bask in our unveiled truth."

Tendrel laid his hand on the newborn, asking, "Who guides this one along her path?"

Jahtara and Heddha stepped closer, each tying a ribbon around the child's tiny wrists. Teacher bent to fill a cup from the stream, intoning, "May she find the noble truths infusing us all." He sprinkled water over the babe's crown. Filling again, he said to her parents, "May you guide her well along the noble path." He poured water on her feet. Finally, filling the cup again, he addressed the gathering, "May the noble fellowship nourish her," and decanted water from the stream over her body. "And who will name this child until they name themself?"

Jahtara and Heddha again stepped forward, saying in unison, "We do."

Placing hands on their child, Heddha offered, "Maitri Pensée."

Jahtara added, "Maitri Pensée Jlussi of lineage Tergon- Davuda."

Teacher lifted Maitri Pensée high, speaking to the gathering, "Come greet the new one!"

Jahtara held up her hand, asking everyone to assemble in the pavilion for further formalities. She asked her uncle and captain of the currently non-existent Queyn's Guard for the use of his sword. Motioning Heddha to step forward, she continued, "Please kneel, Heddha Jlussi. In gratitude for service to Inlanda and completion of the queyn's warrant, showing bravery in such service, I hereby proclaim you Cniht Commandare of Heddha's Badgers." Jahtara placed the sword astride Heddha's shoulders, then gestured for her to rise.

Heddha asked, "With your permission, I would ask Pug to be my attendant if he accepts the position?"

"What say you, Pug?"

"I wish to continue in your service, Jahtara..." adding, "My queyn."

"For the service you have shown me and your wounding in said service, I am pleased to have you continue, Squire Pug.

"One last appointment ahead of celebrating this Naming Dei and the equinox. Sefu, please come forward." Jahtara asked him to kneel, "Sefu, son of Abiola the second Arl of Twisting River Township, do you pledge fidelity in homage to your liege, Queyn Jahtara,

"I affirm and pledge my fidelity to Queyn Jahtara, Laud of the Middle Realms."

She touched him on both shoulders with the sword, saying, "Rise, Laud Sefu Abiola, third arl of Twisting River Township with all the rights and privileges thereof."

With the official ceremonies completed, Doux Buccleuch organized the distribution of cups and mugs, splashing copious quantities of potent spirits into these vessels for a round of toasts. He started by raising his tankard while loudly clearing his throat, "If you will raise your cups to Prinus Maitri Pensée Jlussi of lineage Tergon Davuda: to my kindred on her Naming Dei." General cheering erupted, a few gasps as the fiery grog hit the back of throats, and a couple of murmurs about the quality of the drink (or lack thereof).

Heddha offered a second toast to "Doux Buccleuch, captain of the Queyn's Guard."

Not to be outdone, the doux raised his cup once more, "To the queyn's consort, Heddha, invested as a Cniht Commandare." More cheering.

Heddha, now feeling the festive spirit, proffered, "A fourth toast to my traveling companion and friend, Squire Pug." Heddha and Pug clunked cups.

Tanhā raised her cup and, in a high voice, shouted from the back of the pavilion, "Laud Sefu, the third Arl of Twisting River." Any voices still offending the drink were drowned out in the spirit of the fifth toast.

Jahtara stepped to Heddha, bending to her ear, "Any more of these toasts will leave everyone senseless." She nodded towards Tanhā and Sefu, standing arm in arm, noting, "And I will surely end up on the wrong side of Laud Renesmee when we meet again."

Atiqtalik offered Maitri dressed in her Naming Dei finery to Heddha, but Jahtara reached to take her, explaining, "Both of you go and enjoy the dei and our friends. I will hold Maitri, and I have one last toast to offer. Atiqtalik if you could make sure my uncle does not fill the youngling's cups with the hard spirits, we will enjoy the dei all the more."

Jorma held Jahtara's hand as she stepped onto a flat rock, then he banged a heavy pot lid with a fire tong to get everyone's attention. Jahtara looked up from gazing at Maitri, smiling at the small collection of Inlandani, "On this Warming equinox, we lie in the balance between light and dark. I wish to thank those drawn into this vortex without warnings or cautions, for you have advanced me your service and kindness. My companions and I quest to defend Inlanda from those who wish to steal our very core. The light will grow stronger in the deis ahead and push back at the darkness. I am grateful for your help along our way. Let us celebrate this dei!"

Embodied by a satiating blue expanse, the whole disassociated, horizon separating up from down, a consolidated center formed, encountering the stillness of her being. Form arose at the margins of this moment: forward, she sensed the future, and following her, the past. She aggregated in the pervasive completeness of place and time, freely striding where she may, an amalgamation of intent and the way of the path. Each step thoroughly affirmed her presence in the now. The beauty of the whole brought forth an expanding cry of joy, a pebble thrown into a pond encompassing all of existence.

Jahtara pushed from her side to sit upright in bed. The hearth glowed from the few coals remaining. As the caul of sleep dissolved, she grew aware of Maitri's breathing next to her. Jahtara reached up to feel her cheeks wet and tasted tears. The joy of the dream rose to fill her with assurance. The same awareness as the dei she rode onto the Great Grassland, the Solaura on her face, arms outstretched, feeling an awakening, except now experience deepened the intensity of emotion.

Jahtara lay watching Maitri until she woke, then breastfed her. Their exploring eyes absorbed each other. This closeness with Maitri reminded Jahtara all the more of Heddha's absence. Only a luna quartern passed since Heddha traveled with Sefu to the palatial seat, meeting up with Heddha's Badgers on a mission of import. After their long separation, the tangibility of their relationship filled in again, only to pull apart under the onus call of circumstance. An argument late on the dei of the equinox served to widen the gap. The quarrel started with a silly misunderstanding providing a breach that quickly widened under pressure driven by their differing backgrounds and recent experiences apart.

Like a puma stalking its prey, the argument sprung up to startle them both. At first, Jahtara froze, fearing to engage, wanting to leave. She ended up defending herself when Heddha directly attacked her.

Heddha remarked on the dei's proceedings lovingly, "The resplendent meadow in the early morgn's light with the winsomely adorned pavilion during the naming ceremony brought me to tears." However, her description then turned to criticism in Jahtara's mind when she started with, "The doux, the captain of a nonexistent Queyn's Guard - pure theatrics and me, a brave cniht commandare, in truth, sneaking onto that ship typified a comedy." She grew even more satiric, continuing, "And making the boy an arl with all the rights and privileges, simply cause he was born into it, made it a farcical play."

Jahtara's justifying response. "Perhaps the hard drink of the dei speaks. Sefu's loyalty will bring others to pledge, provide stores and fighters to our cause."

"Perhaps it's the hard edge of power keeping the serfs and their levies in place and fighting for you!"

"Heddha, please, we cannot change everything at once. The benefits will come indirectly. I promise."

"Aye, cept the direct gains seem never to reach us."

"Heddha, you seem to survive well enough," Jahtara accused, instantly regretting her words.

Offended, Heddha took the bait, "Learning from the off-worlder's chronicles shows me those in authority always protect theirs and grow by bounds while those below live off misery scraps from the table. If one has nothing, one clings all the tighter to the notion of having something. This will not change!"

Although the rational sensed no pause, the abstract experienced a telescoping moment of divergence. Love opted for a course out of the emotion, neither wanting deep regret to spoil their parting. Each, in their hurt and ire, heedfully decided on reciprocity.

Jahtara spoke, "Heddha, my pardon, I am a deep canyon confined to a course of my own making. How does consciousness break free of such constraints?"

Heddha responded with chagrin, "We each have our struggles along such a course. I did not consider the loneliness, toil, and anguish you faced while I traveled Solauraward. I thought only of people's suffering in the lands of my journey. I do not wish to lose you."

They embraced, spending the evening cuddling with Maitri and their shared intention.

Early the next morgn, Jahtara found Heddha by the stream, her mount enjoying the Warming's new growth of grass. Jahtara sat on the bank close to her. With a sideways glance, Heddha casually flipped a small rust-colored pebble from the stream bed onto Jahtara's lap, saying, "So, we separate again?"

"Circumstances would make it seem so."

Heddha tossed a second lavender stone onto the lap of Jahtara's dress. "Mmmmm, divergent paths."

"For a short time only."

This time, a green agate lightly rebounded from Jahtara's chest to land in Jahtara's drinking mug. "An eternity of time, Maitri being so new."

Jahtara smiled, fishing the last stone from her cup, and washed all three in the stream, "These pebbles traveled from far and differing places, ending up in this place and time together. We make the most of this serendipity." Jahtara kissed each stone in turn, handing two to Heddha. "We intend to pursue this bond to new places in our shared future, my love. These stones will always return to one other just as they found themselves in this place."

The ripples of memory from that dei brought Jahtara back to her dream of early this morgn. Where dwells its origin, and what symbolizes its meaning? The rational collates space and time into a linear representation. The abstract inhabits the nonlinear, not confined by time or space yet filled with feelings and insight. These embroiled abstractions appear as symbolic representations, a mixture of times, places, and senses, like a collage mashup! In Jahtara's dream, consciousness provides answers devoid of the rational, providing insight floating out of the deep.

Jahtara wanted to rest her thoughts, to let significance arise naturally. When Atiqtalik entered with a food tray, she asked her to care for Maitri while she went for a walk, hoping to dissipate her ruminations.

Crossing the wildflower-filled meadow, the warmth of the dei made Jahtara anxious for movement after spending so much time in the glen. She longed to put her maturation over the past jahr to use. Striding across the meadow felt delightful, no longer sharing a body, finding a new equilibrium with the world. Jahtara tread swiftly along the path, her strides long with arms swinging effortlessly. She stepped comfortably around the debris built up during the Long Noite saison until a fallen trunk and branches blocked the way. Not to be deterred, she climbed over or through these obstacles, eventually balancing on the bank of the stream, the opposite bank blocked as well.

Jahtara stood there, considering what direction came next. The waterway was the same stream she and Heddha crossed a jahr ago, the frigid stream she followed in the saison of change, and the water-course of Maitri's Naming Dei. The water flowing by todei was not the same discovered a jahr ago, was not the chilly water helping her throbbing head, nor was it the naming waters. Different water, yet the same waterway, just as Jahtara altered yet remained the same: homonym, impermanence, change. The stream offered a new path through obstructions.

Jahtara entered the rain-scoured stream without thought, using it to avoid suffering through the dense undergrowth. With water flowing around her ankles, she followed the time-worn rectitude to what lay ahead, mindful of the surroundings, at one with her place in it. A sense of peace overtook her and drew her forward. Time intended her presence.

Two deis following, Jahtara, and her humble troop mounted, heading inland to the village where she and Jorma met at Way's Respite. Holwell graciously agreed to his wagon's hire, carrying Atiqtalik, Maitri, and Ananeurin on comfortable cushions in the box with Tendrel sitting on the hard seat. Tanhā wanted to ride mounted and rode with Jahtara's uncle behind the wagon. Jahtara and Jorma led the procession with Stolen Pleasure tied to the wagon. River Rock Inn's proprietors and children lined the track to the main road bidding them farewell with good wishes.

They looked like an insufficient troop of strange souls for the task lying ahead, yet Jahtara trusted others would join them in the culmination of this quest.

Illusions of Existence

An entangled holographic monism creates the illusion of a universe with separate finite parts. At quantum levels, it's a seething superposition of quantum probabilities smoothing out into perceived reality at larger mass scales: the notion of causality averaged over vast numbers of events. These conditions give individual fundamental phenomena freedom to depart from the mean. Each interdependent phenomena in this concoction arise and cease without an inherent separate, permanent existence.

That went too far. Didn't it? A deviation towards the edge and a step out of bounds. Must we drift back to the ontological middle way? The extremes appear improbable until they exist. Or don't. And yet, life thrives with unbelievable complexity, with consciousness the most implausible. You perceive this conceived tale, and between us, we have what? An intangible shared reflection taking 14 billion years to exist. Now, take a tangible breath and feel the slight rocking of your beating heart! Truly astounding!

Nothing ceases when we die, and at birth, nothing new arises. There continues only an intangible rearrangement following the gradient of life.

Let's see where this reflection on consciousness leads, on just 2,200 kilocalories a day, resisting the entropic slide.

Heddha blew across the pewter plate holding her stew, shifting it back and forth between hands, the rising steam carrying away the heat threatening to burn her mouth while conveying the delicious aroma that set her mouth to watering. The predicament undoubtedly called for patience while her belly grumbled in dissent.

The Badgers traveled for half a luna until a scouting party returned with news of an advance party from the High Mountain Keyndom setting up a marching camp. The speculative search of the last few deis finally bore fruit.

Tho sat down heavily on a stone next to Heddha and spooned in the hot stew, taking cool evening air through his mouth while chewing, making sibilant sounds.

"Why not wait for it to cool? You would enjoy it all the more."

"Aim on taking out a party to watch the High Keyndom camp, making sure none of their scouting parties wander this way. They travel towards the Setting, and we camp Solauraward of their main march, yet I would send out lateral riders to make safe my flanks if I were them. Hence, we will keep watch."

"How did you learn the trade of a warrior?"

"I have not the inclination for smithing, and my father did not favor me; I moved on. I wandered Solauraward for some time, eventually finding myself in the Naloon Delta region, absorbed by the Wind Riders of the dry plains.'

"Wind Riders?"

Tho smiled, "Aye. When we rode, the grasses bent before us, our hooves' sounded of thunder, and we reigned terror. These were the tales we told ourselves. We fought many brutal battles over the jahrs yet finally found defeat. I would not say I enjoyed it, yet I grew good at it. When I returned home, father had died, and the village fell into decline. Jit, an accomplished metalsmith, married Talulah. They were on the move looking for work." Tho threw food from his plate to one of the camp animals. He shrugged, saying, "The rest, you know. How do you suggest we contact the High Keyndom for a council?"

"I have considered this, waiting for my food to cool," Heddha said, taking a mouthful. She gestured with the empty spoon, swallowing the savory food before continuing, "A small party will wait on the main road to parley with whomever they bring forth. I am sure the keyn will not come until informed of what transpires, if even then. I have little hope for this council, for changing the course of a river proves difficult, especially when the channel becomes a deluge following a storm."

Heddha took another bite, chewing on some thought, finally swallowing it down to continue, "I understand Jahtara's purpose for making such an attempt, yet not why I should attempt it?"

"I could not guess the queyn's thoughts, yet in my experience, you can be rather persuasive."

Heddha grinned, "Perhaps… not certain I am the best one to deliver the message considering my previous dealing with the privy council judicature. However, you shall wait further down the track with a third of the troop, and the others will flank the High Mountain Keyndom's main body. You can protect my small party while the rest of the Badgers create a diversion if needed. I will take Pug and Jit because they can speak of their experience with the offworlders, and Obdalti… well, because he is an offworlder. Although, not sure I want to go down that road. I have Thane Kirrydon's letter explaining the results of Sir Absan's warrant Solauraward and the manner of his death. Who should lead the flanking body of the Badgers?"

"Sir Sefu, I would say. He has the training of a cniht, and though young, I believe most would welcome his leadership."

"If it comes to pass, the situation calls for a glancing ploy, not a full-on charge. Can Sefu manage this?"

"In our travels to the palatial seat, we grew acquainted. At the most Solauraward extent of the Middle Keyndom, I learned small tribes of wildings have plagued his holdings using hit and run means, and he learned well from this subterfuge. I will advise him to lead them away from us if overwhelmed."

"Aye, then he will command. I have grown to like Sefu in my travels with him. He expresses an honor in his dealings, yet he lacks experience, as do I. I am encouraged to hear of his past encounters."

Heddha awoke with a determination to fulfill Jahtara's wishes in this parley, setting aside her fears. If this plan fails, it will not happen from any neglect on her part, nor will enmity increase due to her posturing. With these thoughts, Heddha stood with her shoulders pulled back in the brightening dei facing the High Mountain Keyndom's advancing army. With Heddha stood Pug, Jit, and Obdalti, all three trying to appear non-threatening yet confident. A way up the track sat a mounted Tho holding the reins of their steeds, and on a hillock was Tho's portion of the Badgers.

A rider appeared at the head of eighty mounted troops. He stopped at a tree line observing the unexpected scene, then advanced solo at a trot towards the small group, slowing to not envelope them in an obscuring cloud of dust. Heddha and the others stood hands at their sides. None of Heddha's group wore visible swords, plasma or standard, although each carried a plasma knife hidden at their waist. The rider dismounted and stood a couple of sword lengths away, examining them, settling on Jit, demanding, "State who you be, and your purpose?"

Heddha smiled; she would enjoy this, "I am Cniht Commandare Jlussi of her majesty's mounted troop Heddha's Badgers. Who do I have the pleasure of addressing?"

The man spat a glob of murky offense, with a good measure clinging to his chin. "Here was me thinkin' this was to be a good dei. Now I have to clear this ox spray off the road," he said, drawing his sword, but before the steel slipped fully from the scabbard, a flash flared, and the blade slid back into its sheath; the defanged hilt held by the lead scout.

Heddha raised an open hand high, signifying Tho should keep his place, and stepped towards the trembling man. This negotiation started poorly, and now she had only hope to save it. "Beside cniht commandare, I am consort to Queyn Jahtara, sovereign of the Middle Queyndom and rightful heir to the throne of Lineage Davuda. Su majeste entreats me to seek council with Keyn Nyssa and his ministrants in her name. Any aggress towards me amounts to an assault on her. Understand?" With the fellow nodding vigorously, Heddha continued, "Wipe the spittle from your chin. It offends me. Now deliver the message." Heddha turned her back on the man. Still holding the hilt in his hand, it took him three tries to mount his steed.

Heddha and her three companions walked a short distance to gain the shade of a lone oak as the Solaura approached its zenith. Out of frustration, she flung a stone at a vulture landing to investigate their viability. The bird flew towards the line of trees, and she noticed movement where the road exited. A parade of servants and pack animals streamed out of the hardwood stand, quickly assembling a pretorium at the side of the road. They set a semicircle of chairs in front of a small throne platform. Heddha hadn't anticipated an elaborate setting but appreciated the shade created by the tent. Riders advanced, so Heddha's group walked to the open-sided pavilion. An adjunct offered them seats and drink while the keyn's ministrants sat opposite. Some of the ministrants looked familiar, causing sweat to trickle down Heddha's cicatrized back. Those opposite looked at her with disdain, and Heddha's determination crumbled. A conversation with Laud Renesmee drifted to mind. The laud told how she expanded into the role of a laud of nobility. Heddha could wear such a guise.

One of the keyn's ministrants rose and introduced the other three, including Sir Absan's father. He continued in a derogatory tone, "We have advised Keyn Nyssa to refrain from attending this," He waved his hand, searching, "tittle-tattle until we ascertain who you truly represent and are given the privilege of a council with us. Then and only...."

Heddha stood, interrupting him, "I carry the scars of your privilege with me constantly. You do not give me the allowance to speak. That authority comes from me." She glanced at Pug and Jit, noting the scars they too carried. She took a step back, "And our queyn." She gestured to her companions, "We have vital information and have witnessed events possibly imperiling your keyn. I ask only that you listen."

And so it went, a vague accounting of the events leading to the assault on the party of cnihts from both keyndoms and ending with Absan's death. Heddha's shadowy telling of the offworlders as strange foreign provocateurs sounded confusing even to her. The High Keyndom's ministrants countered with contradictory and contentious remarks, not recognizing the inherent dangers of this path. Finally, Heddha placed the letter from the queyn's regent, Thane Kirrydon, on a table, asking Absan's father to read the account of his son's journeys and death.

Ministrant Nusri abruptly stood, grabbing the correspondence, crushing it in his hand with such venom that Heddha leaned back in her chair. Unable to speak, face flushed, veins extended at his neck, he shook the trembling hand holding the letter at Heddha. At length, he spat out the knot of emotion he held at bay, "You dare speak of insignificant matters having no bearing on the course of why we travel to our fates todei. My beloved son's death and your usurper's role in his killing set us on this road." His voice rose to a shrill scream, "The witch pretender cut out his heart with her magic! The very magic you used this dei."

Heddha leaned into the stiff wind of his fearsome attack and found a commonality of love, self-blame, conversations lost forever, and whispers of what could have been. In a faint voice, she began, "I came just after he died and can tell you Queyn Jahtara had nothing to do with his slaughter, not directly. Your son bravely protected her with duty and honor, for he knew she was named queyn. He knew naught of Enan wishing him dead for the knowledge he carried to you and Keyn Nyssa. When I approached to see what kept Jahtara,

Absan lay slain by the foreigner. I wounded this man Enan in the hip with an arrow as he fled." Heddha expressed condolences, "I felt deep sorrow at his death and feel it still. I am truly sorry for your loss."

The ministrant's eyes filled with tears; however, he could not give up the edifice built to protect himself. He turned to leave but spun on his heel to face Heddha again, saying, "This story you tell matters not. The essence remains: my son was lured to his slaughter."

Seeing the others leaving, she fled the tent with long hurried strides, her mind filled with the nugget of truth in Ministrant Nusri's accusations.

Heddha sat before the noite's campfire when a beetle, pushing its dung ball to some unknown destination, caught her attention. She set her supper aside, unable to eat, feeling at a loss to explain her actions this dei, yet the beetle seemed a good metaphor for her dei's labor. At the council todei, Heddha urged concern arising from confusing facts, facts no one wanted to hear. Instead of finding what caused the fissure Heddha widened it by overlooking what lay at the heart of the negotiation. Jahtara misplaced her confidence. Heddha spent the dei moving dung from one insignificant place to another.

Wallowing in these thoughts, she absently used a stick to make furrows to impede the beetle's progress until she noticed a pair of boots straddling the insect. Looking up, she saw Pug giving her a sly grin. Mistaking his purpose, she asked, "Is it my supper you want?"

"If you do not want it, aye," he said, picking up the plate, then added, "A patrol, left at the road to watch for any following us, found a lone rider asking to be brought to you."

"Were they pushing a dung ball?"

"Ma'am?"

"Bring them forward, bring them forward."

Tho and Jit came into the circle of light around the fire, a hooded figure between them. The hood was part of a collar covering the upper torso. When they halted a few paces from Heddha, the rider reached up and pulled the hood back.

"Ministrant Nusri, unexpected to see you here, yet I am pleased… and inquisitive of your purpose."

The ministrant looked from Jit to Tho, so Heddha gave a questioning glance at Tho.

"We found no weapons on him," Tho answered. Heddha nodded her head to the side, and both men left them.

"We have not the comforts of a pretorium. However, the stones give more ease than standing." The ministrant seemed unsure, then moved to sit facing the fire. An extended silence followed, with only the fire's popping and crackling evidence of time's passage. Heddha searched for the dung beetle, but it moved on, along with the rewards of its labor.

Ministrant Nusri cleared his throat, "Absan changed after…" he turned to look at Heddha, starting anew, "I did not know my son. Hardly took notice of him till… well, you know." Heddha's shoulder blades involuntary moved to protect her back. He held her gaze, then turned to the fire. "Aye, it came to me where I set eyes on you last, Cniht Commandare Heddha Jlussi. After… Absan pulled away and grew into his maturity, avoiding his father. Then vanished, requesting the keyn send him with a party traveling Solauraward. I wounded him yet did not realize the extent until he returned to me mortally harmed with his heart excised." He picked up the stick Heddha used to torment the beetle, throwing it on the fire. "I forced him to witness your… insult. And todei, my shame came full circle, cniht commandare.

"In deep shame, I ask you to tell me of my son."

Heddha told him, simply and honestly. She described his kind smile, dancing eyes, the curl of hair on his forehead, making him so handsome, and the tender touches they shared. She held nothing back.

She reported what she knew of his bravery, honor, and loyalty to comrades. Leaving when he alone remained alive, so he could warn others of the threat they faced.

She characterized his ragged appearance and anguish at having deserted the dead he fought alongside and his duty to report what they saw.

She made known the loving kindness he showed in wishing to find her, to show his concern for her, to know the womon she became.

And finally, she told of the bravery he exhibited in defense of Queyn Jahtara even though he faced certain death from the leader of the offworlders who attacked them at the pit.

They sat for a time, letting the fire dry their tears. Until Absan's father turned to Heddha, saying, "Thank you for knowing and sharing Absan with me. I know you cannot forget, yet I hope you can forgive a father who sincerely regrets his actions toward you both."

Heddha could not reply; still, she sensed he understood the suffering caused by his actions towards her, Absan, and himself.

Through her muteness, he reached out again, "Life slipped through my hands while I managed the trivial. I now understand what I sacrificed, the consequences of inattention."

Ministrant Nusri stood but could not face Heddha. Instead, he spoke towards the campfire, "I am acquainted with this fellow you named Enan Tiomer though he gave a different name. He shrouds round eyes and walks with a limp stemming from an injury. The tale of Jahtara's involvement in my son's slaying and his colleagues' deaths came through him. Having heard your testimony and Thane Kirrydon's letter, I now doubt this man's narrative. Yet much of your tale seems like sorcery!

"They will miss me and must get back," he paused, then asked, "If I am permitted to leave?"

"Of course, Ministrant," Heddha called for his mount and an escort back to the road.

After mounting, he looked directly at Heddha to say, "I appreciate your decent spirit, and it strengthens my remembrance of Absan. I can promise nothing, for I have lost prominence; however, I will do what I can." Then the riders slipped into the dark of the noite.

Heddha turned to the fire to see Pug standing in its glow with an inquisitive expression. She shrugged but spoke hopefully, "Our uncertainty neither heightens nor slackens. Perhaps we should hunt for something more definite to present to our queyn."

Awkwardness surrounded Queyn Jahtara's arrival at a village of the realm; she expected a large gathering of troops and refined landholders, yet only blank stares greeted her. The lack of recognition only affected Jahtara slightly, for her covertness comforted. Jahtara remembered Jorma's words by the bridge that dei, 'you possess something of great value. You do not comprehend it fully, yet somedei, you will.' Regardless of his meaning, she had come to understand her value over the last jahr, which didn't depend on others' recognition.

The situation remained unchanged until three deis later, when an advance party entered Way's Respite, asking about the presence of Queyn Jahtara. Fortunately, the doux pondering a pint in the tavern made the queyn's residency known.

Then, of course, everything changed. Jahtara recognized the importance of tradition and ceremony, yet she didn't like it. She knew from experience standing on top of convention restricted her more than it elevated her.

On a knoll beyond the village, five deis later, under a large marquee with pennons flying, Jahtara Hakika Davuda was formally installed as queyn of the Middle Realms. Wearing the crown and holding the Swayer's Scepter, she accepted oaths of fidelity from those gathered, high and low born. The assembled included some from the Realm of lineage Davuda, who considered Jahtara the rightful heir due to Prinus Baeddan's regicide of her parents. The numbers gathered were impressive, but Jahtara knew the keyndoms allied against them were a formidable force, and loyalties proved fickle against overwhelming odds.

After the middei feasting, she assembled her privy council, naming her ministrants and counselors. She attempted diplomacy in her choices, but Laud Hattings of a remote valley hereditament towards the Rising Mounts protested two of her selection.

Laud Hattings commenced patronizingly, "You constitute my queyn and sovereign."

"I have accepted this duty, yet I will not be sovereign. Towards this end, I selected these ministrants to guide me. The realm's inheritance customs will become full cognatic primogeniture. The council will consist of princeps electors chosen from the realm at large, and I will rule by negotiation rather than decree."

"I must protest, su grace. These choices go beyond decency."

"You have sworn fidelity...."

He interrupted, "You deny sovereignty yet demand fidelity through being sovereign. I have given you my allegiance, su majesty; however, we must consider tradition."

"I do not demand fidelity, your laudship, yet acknowledged the pledge you gave. I appoint Laud Renesmee high councilor to the queyn and Heddha Jlussi cniht commandare."

"Yet su grace..."

"Aye?"

"They are womyn."

"You cannot be this thick."

"Su grace?"

"Am I not a woman? You appear denser than oak to express such thoughts to me. I realize, sir, you live in privilege and know naught else. Yet by the fates man, do you not have a mother, a wife, sisters, daughters that you would condemn them so. What if your essence was caged? Or, at the next turn of the wheel, you are incarnate as someone's daughter or mother. Now sit before I name your spouse Laud Hattings master of your lands." Many raised their cups with hoots and called for the man to sit, while others exchanged strained looks.

And so it begins, Jahtara thought, then to palliate, she addressed the assembled, "We face strange circumstances, some of you know the particulars, and the rest will learn more over the coming deis. Forces of our kin assault us. By kin, I mean those inhabiting this world we all share. We also face some from afar who would steal our home and our very essence. I have chosen my council due to their talents and knowledge of what we face. I ask for your trust in an unproven queyn. We have fought skirmishes, some lost, some won, yet now I ask we unite in the coming struggle, high born and common folk alike, men and womyn, in mutuality for the common good."

Queyn Jahtara stepped down from the dais, grabbing a mug along the way, then stood next to Laud Hattings and, placing a hand on his shoulder, spoke directly to him, "I wish to release all from the cages and bonds binding us, including those bonds we place on ourselves. Uniting for the common good." Jahtara raised her tankard in salute, "Inlanda!" All present lifted their voices to pledge, "Inlanda!"

Heddha lay concealed among the late Warming's browning grasses on a hillock overlooking a cartway and meadow. Tho lay to one side and Pug on the opposite. The rest of the troops waited behind them at the bottom of the hillock by a stream.

The morgn after the encounter with Ministrant Nusri, Heddha's Badgers cut behind the High Keyndom's line of march, traveling towards the Setting for three deis before scouts spied dust rising in the distance. The party reported a heavily laden supply train progressing in the direction of the main troop. After observing this traveling storehouse, Tho estimated they would halt for the noite in the meadow. True to his expectation, the wagons pulled into the flat grass expanse, followed by livestock. Assured this was their noite's camp,

Heddha asked Tho, "When presents the best time to relieve them of their burdens? In the confusion of setting camp, during the noite while they sleep or in the morgn when sleep still clouds their heads?"

"Morgn, early at the Rising, from two directions. They seem undisciplined by not sending scouts further down the track or reconnoitering the crest where we lay. Attacking from two directions using our advantage in numbers will send them into confusion from which we can profit."

In the midst of considering the plan, Heddha noticed a large covered wagon pull into view with pennons flying and a blazon decorating the side. Heddha inexplicably stood, saying to Pug, "Fetch our mounts and bring them around to the large wagon with the flags. Have the troop stay hidden with a lookout, watching for our signal. I have seen this family blazon recently. Come Pug, stand, and say if it brings anything to memory."

Pug stood tentatively, not wishing to expose himself, until recognition dawned on his face, and he gushed, "Aye, Doux Buccleuch's blazon or much like it!"

"Aye, and in all likelihood, the doux's daughter climbs off the wagon. Have the troop wait for a signal, and I think we shall all eat well this noite."

Heddha motioned to Tho, and they headed down the hill to greet Jahtara's cousin and inspect the pantry.

Doux Buccleuch's daughter appeared well in charge of the caravan and unsurprised to see Heddha and Tho striding through the settling camp. She dressed in utilitarian boots, a blousy shirt tucked in the front of belted leather pants with long dark hair in a single braid down her back. She stood smiling with her hands on her hips, seemly unconcerned with strangers in her camp.

Heddha stopped a few paces from her and introduced herself, "Cniht Commandare Heddha Jlussi, and my second Tho."

"Heatha, daughter to Doux Buccleuch." They grasped wrists in greeting, Heatha asking, "For whom do you command?" Then nodded to Tho, who made a slight bow.

"Well met, Laud Heatha Buccleuch. I command a troop of cavalry for su grandeza, Queyn Jahtara. May I say you seem remarkedly composed to find us in your camp."

"As you seem confident to approach without an armed escort."

"Have we both grown overconfident?"

"Perhaps not overconfident, although we spotted your advance party at middei and were waiting for you to descend yon hill, we know naught of your number or purpose. The Douxy's militia marches two deis ahead and links with my brother on the morrow. Then we all march to join the realms troops."

Heddha knew Laud Heatha indulged in a strategy to obtain information while providing little in return. Which brother and whose army did she mean? Heddha recognized that signaling for Heddha's Badgers at this point could lead to a confrontation. Pug approached with their animals, and after dismounting, Heddha introduced him to cover her uncertainty, "Laud Heatha, my attendant, Pug."

Laud Heatha acknowledged him with a nod, then turned back to Heddha, saying, "I see a second and a squire yet no troops, Dame Heddha…."

Pug giggled then, realizing his gaffe, covered his mouth, apologizing, "Beg your pardon, milaud, yet Doux Buccleuch would enjoy hearin' her called thusly… Dame Heddha!"

"You know my father, then?" She asked Pug.

Pug nervously looked to Heddha for direction, but she only shrugged and left it for him to answer. "Aye ma'am, he be captain of the Queyn's Guard. We saw him more than a luna past in the company of Queyn Jahtara."

Laud Heatha turned to look at Heddha through narrowed eyes, asking, "I heard the queyn took a womon consort. Do you embody this intimate if I may inquire cniht commandare?"

"Not sure who took whom, yet 'tis me, Laud Heatha."

"Well, if it is my cousin, Queyn Jahtara, we join, please call me Heatha; I am a country womon and do not take the airs of my brother. I may call you Heddha?" Seeing Heddha nod, she continued, "My brother, Laud Gordain, looks forward to leaving the service of Prinus Baeddan. He loathes him and his refined household."

"We should send riders to warn your militia the High Keyndom army lies to their front," suggested Heddha.

"Aye, they camp a half dei before us, and Laud Gordain has joined them. We shall ally on the morrow, and you can lead us to join our queyn. My father keeps his loyalties concealed to protect us, yet I am pleased with this outcome.

"Call your troop, I will have food prepared, and we have bread enough for this repast. We will start with some drink. You would have a goblet of grog, Pug?"

"Two would settle my innards, aye ma'am."

What Jahtara and Heddha would have traveled in five deis took an army half a luna to advance in dusty fits and starts. Doux Buccleuch selected a destination offering only two avenues of approach: one from the Great Grassland, and the other followed the route Queyn Jahtara's army presently traveled. One byway towards the Setting could flank them, but a small contingent would block it where it crossed a bridge, forcing the opposing army to backtrack to the doux's preferred location.

The captain of the Queyn's Guard chose a large meadow with several geographic advantages for the queyn's troops but not enough to discourage a superior force from engaging. They planned to encamp in the valley behind the meadow. From the intervening crest, a slope descended to the meadow. Prinus Baeddan and Keyn Nyssa's armies would make camp at the field's far edge and advance across its width against Queyn Jahtara's army, who held the higher position. A dense forest rose at the Rising's end of the meadow, slowing any flanking cavalry.

While sustaining high casualties, the opposing armies' numerical advantage could overwhelm their smaller force even with the favorable terrain. Possibly Heddha's troop with their plasma swords could cause a panicked retreat. But what if the opposing army acquired advanced weapons? And what of Doux Buccleuch's family, forces, and supplies? Jahtara sent out messengers, searching for Heddha's Badgers to learn the outcome of the High Keyndom council, though she sensed little optimism on that front.

Jahtara occupied the war camp three deis ago, and still, her forces arrived. Although it rained last noite, todei's middei heat forced Jahtara under a tree to nurse Maitri with Atiqtalik sitting at her side and Tanhā showing Ananeurin some basic embroidery. Jahtara considered leaving her daughter and Atiqtalik at Way's Respite with Laud Renesmee's daughters and a small guard. In the end, she decided that whatever future faced them, they would confront it together. With Maitri asleep in Atiqtalik's arms, Jahtara stood to stretch when a warning horn sounded in the distance. Soon after, the doux rode up to inform Jahtara, "Riders approach from across the meadow, yet the dust they raise obscures them." He rode off to investigate, promising to send a messenger back with news. The opposing armies would not arrive for a dei, yet friendly forces would not come from that direction, so Jahtara was greatly relieved when Heddha rode up with a leaping dismount.

Heddha rushed to Jahtara, saying, "I so regret our parting argument. If something happened to you with that between us, I could not bear it." She hugged her.

"Heddha, what happened to affect you so? We reconciled, or so I thought."

"I spoke with Absan's father. The gap left by Absan's death torments him."

"We shall not leave any wound open nor let a dei close in anger,

Heddha. Now tell me of this meeting and its outcome."

Heddha gave a digest of her meeting with the High Keyndom council and later discussion with Ministrant Nusri, ending with her finding Laud Heatha and Laud Gordain.

Jahtara nodded, processing the tidings, "I hoped for more, yet even one ministrant deliberating the truth makes progress. Being a mother, I have a new sense of his loss, watching my heart grow daily within Maitri.

"Absan died attempting to avenge fellow warriors and protect me, though I knew no defense existed against this weapon. Mayhap he knew this also and wished to join his lost companions." Jahtara paused before continuing, "I know naught except he seemed kind and cared for my Heddha. Now there survives only the meaning we ascribe to him, living on in us, and I am glad you were able to impart such knowledge to his father." Jahtara took Heddha's hand, kissing her palm, "You have returned to me again. The doux's militia and supply train follow you?"

"We dashed between the converging armies, not knowing where to find you. Laud Gordain and the train moving at a slower pace will arrive late this dei, hopefully before being discovered."

Jahtara, watching the rest of Heddha's Badgers ride past, delivered new tidings to Heddha, "You have just returned yet must leave once again, I fear. Your Badgers are needed to turn the conjoining armies towards this position. I will send archers with you to turn my brother's army back at a narrowing, the only ford allowing them to get at our rear. With forty plasma swords and archers, your force must cause them to abandon the bridge. Then once the enemy retreats from the bridge, leave a smaller guard at the crossing and rejoin us here."

Heddha gave Jahtara a long stare, then nodded, saying, "I know you depend on me for this, yet you have sent me from you three times. When I return, I shall not abide it a fourth. We will face what comes together," with her wry smile returning, she added, "Su majeste. Now, come to meet my friends."

For a second noite, Heddha slept while riding. They left the queyn's war camp at middei, only delaying to resupply and assemble archers. A waning gibbous Luna would rise late, so the riders stopped at dusk to sleep until the Luna rose, then rode in its glow the remainder of the noite. They were taking a chance traveling in the dark, for they could advance right into the opposing camp, but the Lunashine afforded them some protection by enhancing the scene in greyscale.

At the Rising, Tho returned to the trailing main troop to announce the vanguard's arrival at the bridge and the sending of scouts further up the road to keep watch. Once at the river, the men broke their fast with a meager meal while Heddha, Pug, Jit, and Thor reconnoitered the bridge and far roadway. Crossing the bridge, Heddha thought she remembered crossing here with Jahtara on their way Solauraward. At the time, younglings fished off the upstream side of the crossing. The fast-moving river ran deep along sheer rocky sides. On the far side, the roadway followed the river, turning away from it through a stand of trees. Back across the river, the ground rose on a rocky hill. Heddha twisted in the saddle to look back at the bridge.

Satisfied, she drew her little group together to confer, "I counsel we fell trees, placing the trunks across the road to slow the advance of riders and wagons. The archers can take up positions on the opposite hillside among the rocks. That location offers them a clear sight of the roadway, and the besiegers approaching the crossing will have scarce cover." Walking the mounts back to the bridge, she asked, "Any thoughts on defending the crossing?"

After considering the problem, Tho proposed, "I recall a roguish scheme used on a causeway over a moat." He dismounted to look over the low-walled side of the bridge. Turning back to Heddha, he laid out the plan, "If time permits, we remove the soil from the upriver side of the bridge, pilling it up against the downriver wall. I will have the men withdraw four courses of stone from the lowered side. These alterations will leave the crossing with a pronounced slope making it difficult for steeds, wagons, or men to navigate the narrow causeway and no wall to hinder their plunge into the river. We then use the removed stones to build a rampart on our side of the bridge extending wider than the roadway so any attempting to cross will remain under the defenders' sights. I think they will prefer the river to the onslaught of arrows."

Heddha said, "Roguish, aye. Let us hope they turn back the way they came. I will divide and direct the archers to prepare their positions. Pug, have half the men rest and the remainder to work parties, then at middei, they can switch."

Jit, observing the stand of trees, said, "I will lead the party felling trees. Send any jacks with experience hewing to me."

Heddha nodded in general agreement but cautioned, "If the enemy comes within sight, allow none to use the plasma swords. Inlandani have only seen me with such a weapon. If they threaten to overrun us, we will use our advantage."

Heddha's tongue adhered to the roof of her parched mouth, and dust caked her nose. Did she snore? She hoped not. Even in the shade, the heat bore one down. Opening her eyes, Heddha felt a return to her uncle's farm, but when she turned over, Tho held out a water flask for her. No, not her uncle. Still, she felt the fates offered her a beating.

Tho let her drink, rinse her face, clear her nose, then said, "The men finish. Care to take a look."

Heddha stood stretching, then sat next to Tho. On the rise running along the river, archers were setting up positions. The rampart appeared complete except for an opening in the center to let men return from across the river. It would close when all were back on this side. Examining the roadway opposite, Heddha saw staggered trunks with rocks piled against their sides, making them difficult to roll. Heddha took another mouth full of water, spitting it out. Then without looking at him, asked Tho, "Do I hear you doubt what I see?"

"Aye, I crossed over to speak with Jit and stood observing the bridge with the eyes of an attacker. I have short-lived acquaintance defending, never remaining in one place long enough. The role of aggressor suited me best. Easier to move on and not deal with tangles. Living a life of dereliction." Tho stopped, glancing at Heddha, then chuckled. "You know the most recent part of that story."

"Another time, I would hear more of your tale."

"Catch me off my guard around a campfire, yet that seems your gift."

"Tell me what an aggressor does here."

"The trees across the road will only slow steeds or the charge of massed men. Their forces will do better moving through the wooded terrain out of the archers' reach and then cross the shorter upriver flat to the bridge en masse. Arrows will rain down on our archers and those bunched up behind the wall, pinning them in place. Many of theirs will fall attaining the bridge, yet once they reach the wall, it will breach. They could even use one of the downed trees as a ram. The stones support only a single thickness except near the bottom, where a second course exists for the defenders to stand. When our arrows run low, they overwhelm us and snipe at those with fire swords, making them useless. If our foe sends a smaller force, we may hold. If both armies intend to cross here, I do not expect to stop them.

"The mounted Badgers will stay in reserve to attack; however, the other side will have many more men. It lasts only a matter of lives and time."

Heddha stood staring into the wooded land across the river. Finally, she said, "I thank you for your frankness. We must delay and plague them for as long as we can. Have Jit lay a wall of smaller trunks among trees on our side upstream of the bridge. Place archers at these bulwarks to flank and harass any attempting to cross the upriver flat. With archers on either side of the bridge, they will pay a high price. Also, gather axle grease pots from the wagons and any tallow available. If all else fails, I will attempt a tactic to divide and drive them away, using an old farming practice."

Not much later, three scouts wove through the trunks, carefully walked their mounts over the bridge, and threaded the small opening through the rampart. Men immediately started filling in the breach to complete the wall while the lookouts made their way to Jit, Tho, and Heddha. One of the men rescued from the refining building dismounted and made his way to Heddha. Jit handed him a flask that he used to rinse his mouth, then drank deeply, finally speaking, "They come."

After a pause, Heddha said, "I know you a man of few words, yet could you add more detail."

He shrugged, saying, "Many."

Jit tried next, "Numbers, man, types? Both armies? Or a scouting party?"

"Well…" He paused, scratching his beard, "Surely such a party leads, yet behind comes a bigger bunch." He shrugged. Turning to one of the men still mounted, he asked, "What say ye, Master Dugan?"

The younger Master Dugan, with a smile, answered, "A scouting party followed by a large force: armed men, pikemen, archers, and mounted cnihts. No siege engines or catapults and no supply train or camp followers. Mayhap, two, two and a half thousandfold all together."

"Aye," the first man agreed, "And we seen a grand dust cloud off to the Rising heading Solauraward, tis right Master Dugan?"

"Truly, father!"

"We three think we could save you the trouble and take them on ourselves, cept Master Dugan here says we ought to let you know what we seen."

With a laugh, Heddha thanked them, "And we promise to give you a prominent position in the fight. Now, get food and rest."

Heddha began, "Well, this seems not the best news, yet not the worst. I think they intend a diversion to draw off troops from Jahtara's main force or unopposed to assail the queyn's forces from behind while their main body attacks head-on. We must hold or defeat them and rejoin quickly. Send a rider with what we know, and we shall send another on the morrow. What say you two?"

Jit laying a hand on Tho's shoulder, said, "I am only a smithy and will assist."

From Tho, "I thought to stay at the wall. I suggest the archers center their fire on any attempting to approach the bridge and drive them back. I will have pikemen behind the wall to defend any close advance. If they send pikemen with halberds, they will use hooks to pull down our barrier, then those with fire swords will have to drive them off."

Heddha nodded, adding, "The bulk of the Badgers will remain down in the hollow to charge if they breach, and I will have my thunderbolt, yet the right conditions must exist."

Jit held up his hand, stopping Heddha, and pointed to the road exiting the woods. A detachment of riders observed the clearing and bridge from the shadows under the trees. After a moment, two rode back the way they came. The awaited terminus appeared imminent. Heddha nodded towards Tho and Jit in acknowledgment, and Jit held out his hand to Heddha. She grasped it, and Tho placed his hand on top of theirs. Jit said, "May we live to see our daughters." One shake and they dispersed to their positions.

Heddha and Pug observed the scene from their concealment on the rise. Heddha wished for the offworlders' communication devices, but she would use Pug as a runner in this situation. Soon a considerable troop, including cnihts, joined those on the road. They seemed to debate the bridge with much gesturing. Looking closely, Heddha sensed one of the cnihts appeared in charge, and Heddha's hair stood on end, thinking she recognized the cniht. Was it Sir Kodo dressed in armor with a black cape draping his shoulders? He wore no helmet but stood too far away to make out his features; however, she knew it to be him, no mistakes.

Nothing happened for a while; they must ready some plan, Heddha opined. During this intermezzo, Heddha sought a diversion from ruminations on their tactics and weaknesses. Her thoughts ran to how she arrived at this moment in her life. Arising and ceasing, cause and effect, intention and fate, one thing follows another, bringing her to this unique breath - in then out. The father she never knew; an uncaring uncle; a tortuous education with the privy council judicature; a prelude to love followed by Absan's death; Jahtara's deep love; Jit then Tho - men grown to friends as rage grew to understanding. All this flowed through Heddha in a congealing moment, an insight into the intricate web we weave.

Heddha felt a tug at her sleeve and, turning her head, saw Pug pointing across the river. She saw the worry in his manner but didn't divert her attention, asking, "Pug, do you regret being here?"

He shrugged, an edgy smile adorning his face. "I be satisfied with what is and especially travels with you," his hand moved to his head, "Well, most of it. I like my part in somethin' bigger." He indicated across the river, "They be comin' out now."

Heddha took another deep breath, in then out, before turning to where Pug pointed. Several men slow-walked their mounts out of the woods, followed by more on foot, weaving their animals around the obstructions across the road. Tho's men were crouching low behind the wall, shields at the ready, and downriver, Heddha saw Jit watching across the river with occasional glances in her direction.

Having never intentionally killed anyone, Heddha hesitated. Hit, punch, cut, stab, or remove a body part, sure, mostly in a self-defensive rage. She wasn't angry now, primarily scared. She put her hand up, a sign for ready. Men on foot streamed onto the area blocked by logs. The archers with Jit drew their bows. Heddha wondered if her uncle marched with the men coming into view. She turned to Pug, who raised his brows questioningly and dropped her hand. A dark cloud passed overhead like a murder of crows returning to roost in the trees beyond. A shout, then a scream followed by more, animals neigh, rear, men run, and fall. A riderless mount with an arrow buried in its flank runs, encounters an obstacle, rears, and gallops back up the road careening through those fleeing into the wood. A comrade supports a man with a spreading red stain on his shirt; the mount tramples both.

The archers let loose a second flight, and the sky darkens again, arrows falling like heavy rain on the clearing. The air quiets except for moaning and a single cry for help. One steed tries twice to rise, finally falling still. A man pulls himself to safety with one arm, dragging limp arm and legs; the endeavor grows weaker until he lays still. All those left in the field lie still. The clearing and trunks seemed to have miraculously sprouted a host of saplings, the feathered shafts resembling budding leaves of deadwood.

Heddha became aware of heavy breathing in the new quiet, realizing it was her laboring against the constriction of horror. She turned to look at Pug, who looked like the dread she felt.

Scanning her face, he pleaded, "Will they leave now?"

"I think not, Pug. They meant only to probe our defenses. Sir Kodo will not allow them to leave until many more perish."

Heddha could already see movement deeper in the wooded savanna behind the road. They moved men and animals closer to the crossing, unwilling to expose more to the longer obstacle-covered roadway fulfilling Tho's prediction. She sent Pug to the archers on the upriver side with a warning and advised them to save their arrows for the dash coming from the woods behind the bridge. Not knowing if Jit could see the activity in the trees, Heddha caught his attention, pointing across the river. She raised her arms, covering her head, and when Jit held a shield over his head, she knew he understood to be looking for the other side's archers. Heddha also saw the Middle Queyndom's archers repositioning to reinforce the bridge, hoping to catch any attaching the bridge in a crossfire.

Heddha, watching the scene below, was startled by an arrow's thud, its head buried in the dirt two steps downhill, the shaft still quivering. She noted its angle, taking one side step to line the shaft up to her eye. It was let loose from a great distance in the vicinity of the roadway as it left the trees. A strong-armed archer with a longbow prevailed nearly on target yet lacked the range. Someone saw her signaling to Jit. The missile might have hit her if it were let loose from the closer woods backing the bridge. Heddha considered the archer's strength and the forces acting on the arrow in its arching vector, evident in the final resting position. Her hand moved to the plasma sword in its pouch, realizing conditions may call upon her to use its unnatural magic todei. She slowly backed uphill away from the arrow into the deepening shadows obscuring herself and her intent.

They didn't have long to wait. Heddha and the returned Pug sat on the hill; the line of shadow cast from the sinking Solaura to their rear, reaching for the river. Pug again saw the movement first, archers, three columns deep, advancing through the tree line into the clearing. They fired sequentially, giving no break in the fall of missiles on those below, yet with the setting Solaura in their eyes, many went astray. A miscalculation delayed the attackers from the woods behind the crossing, and the archers withdrew early under return fire, leaving the phalanx of emerging militia without cover.

Those cnihts with little experience charged ahead, and their mounts fell before reaching the bridge. Heavy armor impeded their standing, and arrows soon found weaknesses in their shielding. Behind came those on foot, shields covering the front, side, and overhead. The front ranks maintained order until they encountered dead or dying animals and men, causing the formation to slow or break. Arrows regularly found openings to the interior and mounted cnihts driving the phalanx from the rear compounded the problem. With the Solaura in their eyes and limited sight lines due to their raised shields, some plunged over the steep bank into the river. Those able to find the bridge slowed due to the angled surface while those in the back pushed on, sending more plummeting to the fast-moving water. Again, archers found many unshielded, and soon panic overtook those receiving the brunt of the onslaught. Turning to flee, they met those pushing from behind, forcing more to the watery depths.

A terror spread through the front ranks like a strong wind blowing against a mighty river can raise waves, seemingly changing the flow's direction. Men faced with such terrors respond in peculiar ways, fear tearing through their minds. Some simply walked off the edge of the bridge, swallowed by the current. Others fell to the ground, unable to move. A few blindly charged the wall until struck down by swarms of arrows. Such actions unnerved those to the rear, weakening resolve, and soon they were in total rout back to the woods.

Heddha stood staring, entranced by the savage scene as the last light rays touched the base of the trees across the river. She became aware of a wind swaying the treetops overhead. Heddha's gaze dropped to her side of the river, where archers looked for undamaged arrows around their positions. Tho picked his way up the hillside to her. When he arrived, Heddha asked for an assessment and whether he thought they would attack again this dei.

"We have many with arrow wounds, yet only ten dead. We run low on arrows, though we can reclaim some. They will attack soon before it gets too dark, and this time archers will keep our heads low while seasoned warriors and cnihts assault the wall. They grow desperate to complete their task and reach the rear of the queyn's army."

"Will our men continue the fight?"

Tho affirmed, "Aye, they have the pride of Heddha's Badgers."

Hearing the leaves rustle louder overhead, with a few fluttering to the ground, Heddha said, "The wind strengthens from our back. Across the river, Jit laid woodpiles over grease pots and splashed tallow over the dried wood. He made these cuttings look like discarded trimmings from the felled trunks, placing them at the edge of the woods. You may know farmers or foresters clear the land under trees by setting fires. Bark protects the older trees, and new trees sprout after the fire. I intend to drive the enemy away with fire. The dry grasses under the trees will burn easily, yet much can go wrong. If burning and smoking them out does not work, we still need to foil their plans and weaken them."

Pug offered to "go with you to light the fires no matter the danger."

"Dear Pug, your bravery is not needed. I can attempt it from here. Obdalti showed me new magic of these fire swords." Earlier, Heddha followed Obdalti's instructions to make the plasma sword function like a sort of bow. She pointed the activated knife at the first pile depressing her index finger, and a small red square appeared where she aimed, hovering above the blade. When she pressed again, the reticle turned green with a Galactic Standard number 1 inside the box. Heddha then proceeded down the target line until each woodpile produced a green sequentially numbered reticle. Heddha instructed Tho, "Prepare your men and the archers. I will attempt my magic after they begin their next crucial charge."

As they spoke on the hillside, Heddha saw flashes of a blue/white light from deep in the woods with large shadows moving side to side as if someone were swinging a bright lantern. She pointed this out, saying, "I think Sir Kodo shows his displeasure at the last attempt and gives incentive to those in the next. Now we know they have at least one fire sword. Let us make ready for what comes."

She sent Tho and Pug down the hill and found a flat rock with an unobstructed view of all the targets. She removed the knife from her pocket and activated it, feeling its thrum, without extending its fire blade. Heddha then sited on each target, swinging her arm along the line, each turning yellow when she hovered over it, indicating the firing mechanism engaged. Satisfied, she stepped back into the shadows to await the next provocation.

With the Solaura setting, the charge came soon and this time well-coordinated. First, columns of men carrying Halberds formed at the edge of the wood extending back under the canopy until lost in shadow. At the sound of a horn, row upon row of archers fast stepped into position on the flats. At the second sound of a horn, the archers let their arrows loose, swarms of bees after a marauding bear. Moments later, the columns of troops snaked out from under the trees to advance on the bridge. Heddha could see these were disciplined troops who kept order and course no matter what lay in their path. They afforded no opening by calling out a cadence to synchronize their step.

When Heddha thought two score of troops had moved onto the flat, she stepped upon the rock, extended her arm, and took aim at the first wood pile to the upriver side of the advancing troops. Even though the target occurred in shadow, the reticle lit up yellow, and without hesitating, Heddha triggered the knife illumining the area around her in a bright flash. The light streaked away, hitting the target unbelievably quick, sending burning debris in an arc from the riverbank to the edge of the moving column. With the second target partially hidden on the far side of the marching men, Heddha lifted the knife slightly, firing, sending the ball of plasma arching to its destination, cutting the column in two with burning wood and grease. Heddha moved methodically down the line of targets scattering the archers back under the trees. Reaching the last mark, a growing perimeter of flame ran from the upriver bank across the flat to the downriver bank cutting the area off from the woods. The troops within the ring of fire were isolated and disrupted. Wind pushed the fire and dense smoke under the canopy, the dry grasses feeding the flames.

Heddha moved from her open position to a more concealed hide, but when she saw the archers continuing to cut down the silhouetted and isolated troops, she ran towards the river to stop the slaughter.

Heddha waited at the partially dismantled wall with Pug watching over her. She did not like abiding here, but Jit and Tho demanded she wait until the Badgers rounded up the troops across the river and scouts returned with news of Sir Kodo's whereabouts. They tasked Pug with the chore of making sure she stayed put. She paced back and forth until she could stand it no more, telling Pug, "I have waited long enough. I will hide here no longer," and headed for the bridge. As the wind blew the fire further under the trees, the bridge area grew dark, so Pug chased her with a firebrand. Once across the bridge, she saw Jit directing a group of men and asked him for any news.

Staring at her in awe, Jit said, "Even with my knowledge of the fire sword, you have done magic this dei."

Heddha looked about her, finally saying, "Our tangled purpose accomplished what? Inlandani achieving a grim death. I see no victory here." She reached for relief from the grisly scene, "No news of Sir Kodo or the remainder of his force?"

"My brother looks with the scouts. At last report, the besiegers looked on the run. The extent of their retreat is unknown."

"Inform me when they return." Heddha motioned for Pug to follow her. Numerous dead or dying lay here, and she glimpsed shadows moving among them, checking for valuables. Heddha knew the custom yet wanted no part of it. Most combatants near the trees died from arrow wounds, but some had burns. A gagging sensation filled Heddha's throat, but she couldn't turn away. She must face this. She called Pug with the firebrand, thinking she glimpsed motion. Moving closer, a soot and blood-covered hand gestured her forward. With Pug's help, she rolled a body to the side and saw the hand belonged to a man bleeding from an arm wound and a shaft protruding from his thigh. His features hid under soot and ash, but she identified an old injury on his ear, like a knife cut.

Heddha gently rolled him onto his back and, moving hair from the face, suddenly pulled back, exclaiming, "Can it be? Mahdi?"

A weak voice responded, "Mother?"

"Pug, fetch water, Benedus, and something to clean and dress his wounds. Then to Mahdi, "No, I am a friend of Jahtara."

"Queyn Jahtara?"

Interesting, not prinus or usurper but queyn, she answered, "We will see su majeste soon. Rest now. Help arrives."

"It comes to me now; you nicked my ear. Will the queyn ransom me?"

"Win or lose; you shall live free. I am certain of this. Calm yourself now."

"Keyn Baeddan holds my mother in ransom for father's fealty. I... I have dishonored myself in this fight."

"Hush now, all is well," and she stroked his head until Pug returned with help to carry him across the river.

Unbound

Volition not only projects forward, engendering karma and impelling the turning of the wheel but also backward, giving us hindsight into the causes and conditions of our incarnation at this moment. Past and future, the conventional gears of time, frame the samsaric sustaining now, convening all-time in the present.

Consequences of the climb to civilization results in separation from the natural world, a squandering of our sameness, exploitation of our differences, and the clouding of nature's mirror, so we no longer understand our connection to what gave rise to us. We capitalize on consumption, commodification, and extinguishing life, separating us from sustainability, including conserving our home world. The termites of desire slowly devour the very foundations of the temple.

We seem doomed by a lack of emotional intelligence, lost without understanding, compassion, and consensus, longing for the nonjudgmental arms of love to enfold us. Instead, we search all the wrong places, lusting after the embrace of greed and power. Look to yourself for nonjudgmental love, or perhaps find a venerable teacher by befriending a dog!

This story does not symbolize a wiser or kinder life. Instead, it acknowledges the potential for what the deep expanse of consciousness could become, unbound by convention, to roam existence freely.

At first light, Heddha sat astride Fate's Choice, set to make the return trip to the queyn's war camp. Tho rejoined the Badgers to report that Sir Kodo's disarrayed forces were limping back the way they came to join the main army. The slain from both sides lay upon a constructed pyre, and the survivors of Bulwarks Crossing set the cremation fires alight. The severely wounded were set to travel back by wagon, including Mahdi. Heddha deemed only a modest force necessary to watch and eventually rebuild the bridge, for when harvest time drew near, farmers would use the crossing to deliver goods to market. And finally, scouts were assigned to keep watch and report any advances.

Heddha obtained no pride from her actions of yesterdei, nor did she bear dishonor. She hoped her actions prevented the consumption of even more Inlandani in the funeral pyre but knew her hope was thinly concealed negation. Finding Mahdi alive seemed inadequate in the context of the intensifying inferno rising at her back, yet Heddha clung to it like a memory saved from a burning home.

Jahtara stood in the shade of a tree, staring down the road Heddha left along, now four deis past. Her desire to conjure Heddha's presence could find no justice under this linden tree. Yesterdei morgn, heavy gray clouds of smoke rose from a site in the distance, dissipating towards the Rising. A rider with news of an imminent battle arrived late yesterdei, nothing since. The opposing armies assembled on the far side of the meadow, continuing to grow in strength into todei. Yet, no clue of Heddha's fate. It was a mistake to send Heddha away. Their existence rested on love, not cniht commandare and queyn.

Jahtara saw Atiqtalik approach from across the hillside carrying Maitri and waved her away. She felt too anxious to feed her now. She sent Tanhā back earlier when she brought food. Jahtara resorted to pacing, covering the worn path while keeping her gaze on the road of Heddha's rejoin.

A horn sounded then sounded again, reverberating around the camp. Riders came over the crest, proceeding past her with the Queyn's Guard captain separating to halt beside her. The doux encouraged, "Not an alarm, I think, yet promising news of the cniht commandare's return. I will ride to meet her." He spurred his mount to catch his company. She watched the doux disappear around a bend in the road. Then realizing nothing held her to this spot, she moved down the slope to greet Heddha.

Jahtara sat across the camp table from Heddha, watching her eat. It seemed such a mundane action, yet so precious to Jahtara at this moment, remembering their friendship began a jahr ago over a meal. She summoned the echo of removing the clover blossom from Heddha's lip, such an intimate connection from a simple act. Jahtara wished to reach into Heddha's heart and remove the suffering she brought back from the fighting and bloodshed to hold the crossing.

Jahtara saw the vacant look in Heddha's eyes when she arrived with the doux. Heddha cloaked it upon seeing Jahtara, yet it lingered. Jahtara did not understand the full measure of it until Heddha retired to bathe, and Jahtara went to visit the wounded under Benedus' care. There she saw deep and festering injuries from battle. Sitting next to Mahdi, seeing the same far-away stare and hearing of his torment, she wept for his pain and Heddha's part in it.

Heddha felt Jahtara's concerned gaze on her. She took Jahtara's hand, saying, "Fear not, I shall overcome this. I cannot speak of it now; somedei, we may, after filling our hearts with kinder remembrances."

Jahtara had a recollect of hope, saying, "Come, I wish to show you a sight, a vision I feel will guide our quest to its conclusion." She pulled Heddha to the crest overlooking the meadow, stretching to the opposing armies' encampment. Saturated from core to brim, the meadowland dazzled with multitudes of blue blossoms. The flowering four-pedaled lapis lazuli color stirred in a light breeze transforming the meadow into an undulating catchment giving evidence to the nature of change.

Heddha, at first, focused on the war camps opposite, her heart sinking; her eyes could not perceive the intervening sight. Her perception gradually expanded to include the field, yet she still could not make sense of the scene. A breeze stirred the flowers, and Heddha took it for ripples on water, but she rode through this meadow just deis ago, then looking at her feet, fixed on individual blue flowers, and her mind put it together. A sense of wonderment overtook her.

Jahtara explained, "The noite before you rode across the meadow, it rained briefly then this morgn I came to view the battlefield, and this filled my vision. How can war exist in the face of such abundance? We will intend for peace in the presence of such beauty." Heddha fell into Jahtara's arms taking in the rarified meadow, her eyes filling with tears.

The sky greyed towards the Rising when the queyn and cniht commandare rose. By the time they walked to the top of the hillock, the distant mountains were in black silhouette. The Solaura, not yet risen, turned the sky behind the shadowed shapes a deep red. Last noite, after finishing a fractious war council, Jahtara intended to retire when a messenger brought an official offer to her suggesting a meeting with Keyn Nyssa the next middei and included stipulations. The invitation made no mention of her brother or Enan. She and Heddha discussed the implications, including the possibility of a delaying action or diversion to remove them from camp, allowing a raiding party to attempt the abduction of Maitri. Or possibly Keyn Nyssa learned of the crossing battle and entertained second thoughts, although this seemed unlikely. The names of those requested knew of Absan's death or mission. The request bore Keyn Nyssa's seal and Ministrant Nusri's signature.

Heddha reread the offer and said, "Intriguing? A secret door with unknown possibilities on the other side. We must enter, I believe, while taking precautions."

"Agreed. The flowering bluebells have sounded. We must answer their call."

Queyn Jahtara sent their reply, and this morgn, a marquee, grew at the heart of the meadow.

At middei, Jahtara's mounted entourage sat waiting for movement from Keyn Nyssa's camp. In addition to Queyn Jahtara, the entourage included Heddha, Pug, Doux Buccleuch, Thane Kirrydon, Laud Renesmee, Jorma, and other lauds and ministrants. Heddha's Badgers, along with mounted cnihts, rode at the ready behind the hill's crest and would advance on the marquee at any sign of treachery. More Badgers with Laud Sefu surrounded Maitri and Atiqtalik to protect them from any subterfuge or, in the event of the queyn's defeat, to affect an escape.

When Queyn Jahtara saw Keyn Nyssa's group ride towards the meadow, she launched her entourage towards the pavilion. Another group from Baeddan's camp rode hard for Keyn Nyssa, halting the other parties in place. Turning to Heddha, Jahtara said, "Seems my brother received no invitation and wishes to end the meeting or, failing that, to attend this council. Mayhap his alliance crumbles." The combined group continued across the sea of flowers, and Jahtara nudged Travelling Companion forward again.

Stopping at their end of the council tent, Jahtara dismounted. She considered Enan would attend the council; the stakes proved too high to trust her brother with the outcome. Jahtara, Heddha, and Pug carried plasma swords since her brother and Enan were sure to keep theirs. Jahtara went to enter, but her uncle stopped her from going ahead, stepped inside, and offered his hand, saying, "Su majeste, you may enter safely." She took his hand with only a slight smile, making her entrance.

The three principles sat on chairs set on small daises. This was the first time Jahtara gazed upon her brother since their confrontation on the Great Grassland. His arm hung loosely at his side, and when he sat, he used his able arm to lift the inert hand onto his lap. A butterfly of compassion fluttered in her heart. Still, she knew his desirous intent brought him to this result, and he blamed only others for his suffering. His attempt to cleave her down the middle served as the impetus for Heddha's arrow to fly. One thing leads to another; can one ever escape the turning of the wheel? Jahtara would attempt to divert this flowering meadow from the trampling armies of destruction and turn the wheel along another route.

The council tent grew heated, with accusations and justifications fueling the fires of condemnation. Keyn Nyssa's confusion increased in the face of Baeddan and Enan's obscurations and diversions. They blocked Jahtara's explanations at every turn. She saw Enan's smirk grow whenever she approached the truth, knowing that revealing the offworlder existence and schemes would brand her deranged, disqualifying her rule. People would believe the magic of witches and burning swords before accepting the truth of the roundeyes.

In the heat and confusion, Keyn Nyssa asked for a pause in deliberations and exited with his ministrants. Jahtara remained lost in thought, staring across the pavilion at her brother, surrounded by Enan, Keyn Alyeska, and Sir Kodo. When Heddha stepped onto the dais to speak to Jahtara, her brother stood, and Sir Kodo moved toward Heddha, reaching under his tunic as Heddha also moved for her plasma weapon. Kodo stopped when Enan blocked his path, whispering something in his ear. Sir Kodo grinned, then turned on his heel, leaving the tent.

Jahtara took Heddha's arm, guiding her out of the tent. Outside she distracted Heddha, asking her to get them water. With a hand shading her eyes, she watched Heddha walk away, and when a shadow moved over her, she pivoted to find Pug holding a shade. Jahtara patted his shoulder, "Ever ready, Pug. I thank you for your forethought. Why have you not joined us in the tent?"

"I feel less burdened pacin' out here. The presence of this man Enan is difficult. I know what he done, and it crushes my heart."

Jahtara smoothed, "Your aunt's killing affected us all. Come, let us not allow this man to control us further. Join Heddha beside me."

To the returning Heddha, Jahtara cautioned, "The threat to murder us persist. Yet we must hold our anger this dei or lose the High Mountain Keyndom. Pug will join us, yet I have not seen Jorma. I expect my ministrant to be present, confirming my testimony."

"He descended the slope with us, yet after our pause on the way down, I have not seen him."

Seeing Laud Renesmee near, Jahtara called her over, "Laud, if you could confirm Mahdi's father tarries inside and, without attracting attention, inform him his son lives. He wears a green and brown vest, I believe." Laud Renesmee nodded, removing herself to the pavilion.

Then to Heddha, "It does not go well for our account of what brought us here. I feel Keyn Nyssa slipping away. We have nothing to clarify Enan's muddles. Mahdi places his sister and mother in jeopardy testifying that Keyn Alyeska possessed the fire sword before I absconded with it and, therefore, could not have killed the two offworlders. And Jorma remains absent. Mayhap it was wrong to trust these offworlders?"

Before Heddha could answer, her uncle motioned for them to return to the pavilion. Once assembled, Prinus Baeddan demanded to speak. Heddha felt a gaze directed at her and saw Ministrant Nusri reward her with a smile and nod of recognition. While she tried to fathom the cause for this acknowledgment, Prinus Baeddan spoke.

Addressing Keyn Nyssa, he said, "This council serves only to delay and confuse the truth of our presence here: to remove this pretender by force." Pointing at Jahtara, "This usurper dupes us all. By deception and witchery, she installed herself queyn of the Middle Realm. The womon escaped her betrothal to Keyn Alyeska, shirked her duty to lineage Davuda, and broke our parents' hearts. Then bewitched one of the old armorers to poison the keyn and queyn. She ridicules the High Mountain Keyndom with lies and denials of excising Sir Absan's heart yet admits to her presence at...."

Standing, Keyn Nyssa proclaimed, "Enough, we have heard enough. We have ample evidence of the wrongs bringing us here. We will not abide more falsehoods from those involved." Resuming his seat, Baeddan smirked at Jahtara.

King Nyssa motioned Ministrant Nusri to proceed. He began by asking, "Enan Tiomer, you have a wound on your sinistra hip?"

Enan's eyes shot towards Heddha, then quickly back to Ministrant Nusri. He composed his face, "A riding accident. I fail to see how this concerns us."

"How would cniht commandare Heddha, consort to Queyn Jahtara, know of such a wound?"

Jahtara interjected, "I witnessed when Heddha caused this wound with a flurry of well-aimed arrows."

Enan shrugged, "I attempted discretion, sir. I bedded her during the cold Long Noites, which is how she knows of the wound." He gave a slight shrug, "The farm cur told her lover, accounting for the usurper's knowledge of it. This falsity of an arrow wound cannot be believed. How would a peasant geyrle learn to handle bow and arrow, especially on the run?"

Ministrant Nusri answered, "I doubt you possess any discretion, sir. No one stated she ran when wounding you in the hip. And my son," He paused, pursing his lips before continuing, "Sir Absan taught her archery at Keyn Nyssa's refined household."

Laud Renesmee approached Queyn Jahtara from behind, whispering to her, "Mahdi's father, thanks you for the news of his son. Doux Buccleuch wishes you to know a contingent of foot and mounted troops departed Keyn Nyssa's camp and waits at the Rising end of the meadow."

Jahtara nodded as Ministrant Nusri spoke to Enan, "Witnesses have come forward saying you were present at your colleagues' murder in the Cold Wastes. Others give testimony that Queyn Jahtara remained with her parents during this time. Still, others attest to seeing Keyn Alyeska with the knife at the refined household of lineage Davuda and again in the Great Grassland where Queyn Jahtara first came into its possession."

Jahtara observed her brother's smirk replaced by a worrisome look.

Turning to Keyn Alyeska, the ministrant asked, "Do you affirm your possession of the knife, and if so, how did you come to possess it?"

Looking for a way to flee, Keyn Alyeska withered at the question before equivocating, "I do not recall." He wiped his brow, evading, "I shall consult with my ministrants." He turned, fleeing the tent.

Nusri resumed with his case, "Finally, we have a letter from the queyn's regent, Laud Kirrydon confirming Queyn Jahtara's fire sword remained in his study when my son died. A murder conceived and executed by Enan Tiomer," pointing at the accused, "to drive a wedge between The High and Middle Realms. Queyn Jahtara and Cniht Commandare Heddha corroborate this detail."

Prinus Baeddan rose, but Enan spoke, "We see nor hear witnesses, except this usurper and those depending on her continuance for their positions. Is it Jorma denouncing us? His past is criminal, and he wishes to be rid of me."

Ministrant Nusri motioned to someone at the entrance, then turned back to Enan, "I know naught of whom you speak, yet we provide three of those presenting this evidence."

Following a short commotion, Cora and Kasumi stepped through the pavilion's entrance in traditional Inlandani dress, followed by Laud Ybarra, Mahdi's father.

Cora took a step forward, addressing those in the pavilion, "My name is Cora Hayes. In my official position as constable, I traveled here to remand Enan Tiomer on multiple charges."

Heddha grabbed Jahtara's hand in relief at this outcome. But as the accusers turned to the accused, the trio across from them realized their facade no longer served a purpose. They would stop at nothing to save themselves. Enan stepped towards Cora and Kasumi while the queyn's brother advanced on Jahtara. Igniting his plasma weapon, Sir Kodo, with a broad grin, moved to Heddha.

Heddha circled away from the black and grey-clad Kodo, almost knocking over Pug, who fumbled with his plasma sword, striving to activate it. With her free hand, she pushed Pug out of danger, averting Kodo's plasma sword as it narrowly missed her arched back.

Doux Buccleuch stepped forward to block his nephew's advance, raising his sword to strike, but Baeddan separated the blade from the hilt with his plasma sword, using his functional offhand. The doux, not deterred, stepped in close to him, bringing the hilt down hard on the back of the pretender's hand, causing him to drop the plasma sword, immediately extinguishing it. Baeddan, with an eye on his uncle, grabbed for his weapon while backing away. Jahtara held her uncle's arm, saying, "You lost your sword, Doux," then lit her plasma sword, saying, "Allow me."

Enan, intent on bearing down on the two offworld womyn, didn't see Sir Ybarra spring from the side to strike him under his raised sword arm, knocking him to one knee. Baeddan, now at Sir Ybarra's back, used his fire blade to slash his knee, hobbling him.

Prinus Baeddan pivoted back to his sister, not seeing Pug cross behind him, still puzzled about his sword not lighting. The true queyn advanced, swinging the fire sword in front of her. Her estranged brother slashed at her, pulling back quickly as Jahtara brought her fiery blade up. The keyn's motion caused his limp arm to swing forward, catching the tip of Jahtara's blade just above the elbow, and the freed forearm somersaulted away. The dangling upper arm continued oscillating, and a pulsing stream of blood traced a pattern on the earthen floor. The regicidal would-be keyn lifted his fire sword, took an unsteady swaying step, and gazed questioningly about, searching for an unknown explanation before spilling onto his face.

Heddha backed towards the tent wall, dodging. When the tent brushed her backside, Heddha feigned at Kodo's sword hand, quickly springing sideways and pointing the plasma blade down to protect against a side swipe to her legs. Kodo's sword swing missed Heddha, burning through the tent fabric instead, and he saw the opening to attack her legs. Kodo pushed against Heddha's plasma sword with his own, forcing it towards her leg. Heddha strained mightily, but this battle seemed lost, and Kodo sensed it. However, his perceived victory left an opening Heddha saw at the last instant. The design of the sword assumed they would never face a similar weapon. The handle had no guard. Heddha swept her blade up along Kodo's and across the knife lopping off his fingers and burning his inner arm. Kodo dropped the plasma sword and fell to his knees, attempting to staunch the blood, head tipped back in a silent scream.

Enan worked his way painfully to his feet and started towards Cora again, switching the fire blade to his offhand so he could splint his injured side. Enan raised the fire sword to strike the screaming Cora, frozen in place. Kasumi grabbed Cora's shoulders from behind to pull her back as Cora pivoted out of the way. Kasumi was pulled forward by Cora's pivot, and Enan swung down, slicing across Kasumi's upper torso. Her body sizzled, collapsing to the blossom-strewn soil now flooded with Kasumi's blood.

Pug, flipping the knife over in his hand, figured out the problem: in anticipation of close combat, he forgot to press his thumb and forefinger simultaneously. Pug let the knife handle settle in his hand and, looking up, saw Enan's back directly in front of him.

Enan turned to Queyn Jahtara and ran into Heddha's young attendant.

They collided. Pug's head bounced off Enan's chest as his plasma sword pressing into Enan's stomach activated. The fire sword ignited to its full length leaping up through Enan's chest, piercing his heart, and exiting the back of his neck. In that instant, notes in the melody of the sinister Enan Tiomer came to a grand pause, his ensemble stopped playing, and only an infrequent off-key resonance would ever again echo in the consciousness of Inlanda.

Augury

The natural causes and conditions rendered in our evolving existence have resulted in a conceiving and perceiving of this story. Written in the truth of one mind, read in the truth of another, completed at the reflection of this interbeing. Such mutuality arises with every interaction: a murmuration of knowing.

This tale now advances to its ceasing, yet one giving rise to new reflections.

Prinus Maitri Pensée Jlussi Davuda, daughter to Queyn Jahtara and Cniht Commandare Heddha, having completed her first six jahr precession of the Three Great Iterations of her youth, stood on the gathering ground of Keep Farway on the Warming equinox to face the Solaura and greet the start of her second precession. Upon awakening, she looked forward to exploring the keep's grounds, appreciating the new flowerings and their seraphic scents — just another dei enjoying the lengthening deilight on this equinox in the Warming of her youth. Maitri sensed the elders supplied additional meanings to this dei, yet to her, festivities were always fun. She delighted in the spirit of her childhood.

With the ceremony concluded, Maitri changed into her running clothes to seek Ananeurin. They walked hand in hand throughout the grounds observing the beautiful formal attire of all those assembled.

Even Tendrel, who some still called master, wore ceremonial robes this dei. Unlike others whose heads filled with confusion and distracting colors, she liked his quiet mindfulness.

Seeing mamma Heddha, Maitri dropped Ananeurin's hand, saying she'd come back, and skipped across the intervening space, her copper hair bouncing around her head. She plopped into Heddha's lap, who immediately hugged and smothered her with kisses. Maitri cherished burrowing into Heddha's love and showed it by laughing and squirming.

"I am proud of you, beginning your second precession," Heddha beamed.

Maitri shrugged, "Ananeurin said I will notice differences when ending my second precession. She says she does. To me, she feels like a flower about to open."

"Todei nears the end of my Cniht Commandare first precession and the start of Queyn Jahtara's second as queyn." But Maitri seemed distracted, her emerald eyes set on Jorma, who sat on the other side of Heddha. Looking from the youngling to Heddha, he suddenly excused himself, saying he would find some drink.

As he moved off, Heddha admonished the celebrant, "You know you make him uncomfortable when you do that."

"He makes me feel like storm clouds."

"Sometimes a heavy rain welcomes, washing away the old and nourishing the new."

Maitri closed her eyes, erasing the vision, "Unless the storm washes away our groundation. And our feets get stuck in the mire."

Heddha gazed down at the young one before nodding, saying, "I will speak to mamma Jahtara about this awareness. Go, find Ananeurin. I see my friend Cora coming." She lifted and sent Maitri across the lawn with a pat on the back, searching for her companion.

Heddha and Cora embraced with the sensitivity of friends separated after spending an unpleasant time together: close yet tentative. "Have you just arrived then, back to Inlanda?"

"Aye, we just slipped into…" she waved her hand around searching, then gave up using the Galactic word orbit, "last noite. I brought one of my daughters with me. She tests her language skills with Tanhā and Sefu across the way. Their youngling reminds me of my other daughter's son." Heddha saw a tall, offworlder womon talking to the young couple with their newborn. A few paces to the side stood Obdalti. Sefu had taken him in, Obdalti assuming the role of an elder considering their losses.

Surprised, Heddha asked, "You are a grandmother? You look so young, and your daughters were just younglings in those pictures on the ship."

"One of the hazards of space travel. I missed so much of their lives. Though, I am quite content now. Everything worked out well with the Commonwealth. Yet, the corporation received only a slap on the wrist for its," she inserted the GS word biopiracy. "You understand the meaning of a slap on the wrist?"

"Aye."

"Corporations may have rights similar to a person under the law yet do not suffer the same consequences under those laws. A trade delegation also arrived with the ship. Inlanda received a judgment of a fair number of credits, yet I would consider the credits a trap. Be heedful; the corporations never give up. They would finance a revolt, then sell armaments to all sides. They lurk to take back the advantage, and these credits will serve to draw Inlanda back into their web. Not to mention exploiting your culture while replacing it with their own. My pardon, not the dei to dwell on such unpleasantries.

"We remain heedful."

With a wave of her hand, Cora continued, "Still, you may wish for something like the," saying VR techcap in GS. "Although I suspect you have one already. I could not locate mine after you left the ship."

Trying to hide her blossoming smile, Heddha said, "Aye, Maitri loves learning."

"Only Maitri? I venture Jorma supplied you with a fire sword also." When Heddha nodded, Cora said, "I thought he did."

"He said it belonged to the other offworlder murdered in the Cold Waste. What do you suggest?"

Cora shrugged, saying, "Well, locals having Commonwealth advancements would have strengthened the corporation's position, especially if the weapon belonged to a murdered crew member who died on Inlanda." She paused, deciding whether to proceed or not, then, "After Kasumi's cremation." She stopped and cleared her throat, starting again, "She saved my life and gave her own. I... I wanted to return her ashes to her partner. They, of course, wanted to know how... After I explained, they told me about receiving a forwarded message from her, which included an account of a disagreement with colleagues."

"Leagues or league?"

Cora shrugged again, "Not sure. Kasumi once told me she did not understand why Jorma sent Jahtara along the Setting Sea route to Concupia, leading directly to Enan Tiomer."

"Jorma assured Jahtara that Kasumi advocated the coastal path."

"No, I am certain she said they argued about it later."

"I was membering Kasumi this very dei. We encountered some difficulty meeting at Way's Respite, mayhap from being so much alike, yet I came to have an affinity for her. Strange Kasumi never visited me on the ship?"

"Jorma told me she should not be involved to protect her."

"Another question, did Jorma ever send a message through you to obtain reports from a conclave about Jahtara's grandmother?"

"No, never. Information from the inquest shows Jahtara's grand-mother died on Inlanda, her body transported offworld where the Nadasagrado corporation performed a necropsy and other investi-gations. They never did completely understand how it all worked. It consisted of wishful thinking, supposition, and an ideology of greed." Cora continued in GS, "They appeared totally in the dark about the epigenetic controls, gene expression, or the meaning of the anatomy."

"He lied? All of it a lie. To what end?"

Cora shrugged, "Mayhap Jorma used you to locate Jahtara and discover more about Jahtara and Maitri's abilities. Even stranger, Inlanda received credit payments for the metals taken by Nadasagrado, after which the metals disappeared from the Commonwealth warehouse. I do not know what that portends?"

"And then Jorma's peculiar disappearance during the confrontation in the meadow. Perhaps he worked for the corporation and Enan!"

"I believe Jorma thinks foremost of himself. He may have been conflicted and worked both sides. The information and access he obtained could only come from Enan through Nadasagrado."

"Aye." Heddha followed the small trickles of suspicion gathering, deepening, and finally cascading into a torrent of certainty. "Cora, thank you for this conversation. I will act on this added information. Give me a moment; I would love to meet your daughter."

Heddha searched for Tho or Jit and spied them together, speaking with Laud Heatha. She asked Heatha, "Could I deprive you of these fine men's company for a short period?" Heatha gave a polite nod to Heddha, backing away. But not before, Heddha keenly noticed, she graced Tho with a loving smile. While crossing the yard, Heddha relayed her conclusions to the smithy and his often-traveling brother (and Heddha now thought she knew where he traveled).

Leaving the brothers a short distance away, she sat on the ground next to Jorma. He said, not looking at Heddha, "I see Cora arrived."

"Aye, she seems quite content with her life."

Jorma swallowed heavily, "She should. She earned it."

"And you, what do you deserve?" When he didn't answer, Heddha asked, "Can there be a love that does not make demands on its object?"

Still not meeting her gaze, he said, "I do not follow."

"Ultimately, Kasumi did not let love make demands on her."

"Still not with you," finally turning to look at her.

"Despite a deep love for her partner, she did right. She made a hard choice. I do not think she intended to die, yet death proved an outcome of her willingness to testify against Enan."

Jorma nodded but said nothing, again staring at the ground.

"Jahtara remarked you once entertained a life of contemplating the absolute?"

"I often begin with good intentions and yet fall prey to the spell of false rewards."

"It matters not if the chains binding us are gold or iron; we remain bound. I think now represents a suitable time to fulfill your desire for a prolonged retreat in search of wisdom. I recommend a monastery where the monks will welcome you with loving grace. Jit and Tho will arrange your journey there."

Jorma rose to leave but stood with his back to Heddha, saying, "Be careful, Heddha, the truth lies hidden amongst the wreckage of deceit. This truth is an alluring fruit, offering sweet success, sacrificing itself only for its seed to consume those that partake of it." Tho took his arm, leading him away.

Heddha walked straight for Jahtara, who at the moment turned in a tight circle on the lawn, arms outstretched. When Heddha reached her, Jahtara wrapped those arms around her continuing to turn in a dizzying dance.

Heddha inquired, "Like what you see?"

"Aye, all of it! Come sit with me." They sat on the lawn, taking in all those gathered around them. Jahtara entwined her hand with Heddha's. "I wish Pug could get leave to visit with us this dei."

"Aye, I miss him also. He completes his midship apprenticing and will advance to lieutenant. I suspect some dei he will replace Atfi Dunnyn assuming leadership of Morgn Star Carriers."

"Aye, no doubt. I imagine spending time around these people remains difficult for Pug. He views Enan's death as something between intention and accident; both actions difficult to endure. I see Jorma takes his leave to join Kodo and my brother at the monastery of the Magnanimous Awakening Heart."

"Aye, fulfilling a wish for a long retreat."

"Plenty of time to contemplate and gain insight into his menace."

"Cora related Enan's scheme turned out only greedy speculation. Yet, before taking his leave, Jorma said the offworlders still deceive us. I took him to mean the Nadasagrado corporation, yet perhaps others." Heddha paused, chewing on a thought, and with a shrug, said. "Earlier, Maitri perceived dark thoughts emanating from Jorma, and she may have influenced him to move away from us. I am not certain. How can we accept anything Jorma says? Or Cora? It felt strange in any event. Perhaps they do keep the truth from us."

Jahtara agreed, "I often consider if others experience the world as I do. Or do I view my surroundings with some special sense? The dei we left Ways Respite, Jorma said I possessed something of immense value yet did not comprehend it. Is there a possibility he knew of the plot to make me the mother of Maitri back then? We should pay closer attention to Maitri's gift."

Heddha nodded deep in thought and, seeing Atiqtalik by the pond, stood saying, "I have a question for Atiqtalik. Go track down our daughter, and I will join you both where I find you."

Heddha approached the curious womon from beyond the Cold Waste. She sat on the moss-covered bank, her feet dangling in the water of the tree-lined pond. Drooping branches dipped to the water, heavy with the first flowers showing a pale purple. Atiqtalik opined, "I do not think I shall ever get used to this warmth and display of colors."

"Aye, most places contained a special beauty, although I have not always appreciated it." Heddha flung a flat stone low across the pond, watching it disrupt the stillness skipping to the farther bank.

"I wonder what new places we shall discover in the coming times." Atiqtalik smiled, then let it fade, fixing her gaze on Heddha. "I sense your task todei occupies probing the unknown. You harbor a question for me, then?"

"Aye, recent tidings concerning Maitri came to me, and I realized I have not asked of the vision brought from your people concerning her."

"Ah, we suspected this seeking would eventually come from you." With her knowing eyes sparkling, she said, "We shall tell you then…

Acknowledgments

In life, there are many teachers. Some that inspired me are Alan Watts, who parted the curtain; *Stranger in a Strange Land* by Robert A. Heinlein, a first read that placed an intention in the pool; Joy Chant, an inspiring painter with words; Radclyffe Hall, just cause.

For those that understand what must be done: the firefighters at Chornobyl nuclear power plant; Hazel M. Johnson, environmentalist; Greta Thunberg, climate change activist; and many more.

Attributions - Caelica 83: You that seek what life is in death by Baron Brooke Fulke Greville. I reversed the line to be *when air becomes breath*. The Zen Teaching of Huangbo by Seon Master Subul for the phrase *A bird in flight leaves no trace*. My apologies if anything else written here sounds familiar; take no offense, as time confuses the echo's origin.

First among inspiration, understanding, and attributes: Joan I., partner, teacher, and love.